Praise for
Hate Crime

"Another good read, full of courtroom fireworks, double crosses, and even a bit of romance."
—*Publishers Weekly*

"There is no end to the drama. . . . A superb thriller."
—*Romantic Times*

"It's a read with good courtroom drama, interesting characters, and a few surprises."
—*The Oklahoman*

"What a wild and terrifying thriller of a story. . . . I can't stop raving about *Hate Crime* and neither will you."
—*I Love a Mystery*

"By far Bernhardt's most ambitious effort to date, and his best. With *Hate Crime*, Bernhardt should earn a spot on many mystery fans' 'must read' list, if he's not there already."
—*The Book Reporter*

By William Bernhardt

The Ben Kincaid Novels
PRIMARY JUSTICE
BLIND JUSTICE
DEADLY JUSTICE
PERFECT JUSTICE
CRUEL JUSTICE
NAKED JUSTICE
EXTREME JUSTICE
DARK JUSTICE
SILENT JUSTICE
MURDER ONE
CRIMINAL INTENT
DEATH ROW
HATE CRIME

Other Books by William Bernhardt
THE CODE OF BUDDYHOOD
DOUBLE JEOPARDY
LEGAL BRIEFS
THE MIDNIGHT BEFORE CHRISTMAS
NATURAL SUSPECT
FINAL ROUND
DARK EYE

HATE CRIME

A NOVEL

WILLIAM BERNHARDT

BALLANTINE BOOKS • NEW YORK

Hate Crime is a work of fiction. Names, characters, places, and incidents are the products of the author's imagination or are used fictitiously. Any resemblance to actual events, locales, or persons, living or dead, is entirely coincidental.

2005 Ballantine Books Mass Market Edition

Copyright © 2004 by William Bernhardt
Excerpt from *Dark Eye* copyright © 2005 by William Bernhardt

Published in the United States by Ballantine Books, an imprint of The Random House Publishing Group, a division of Random House, Inc., New York.

Ballantine and colophon are registered trademarks of Random House, Inc.

This book contains an excerpt from the forthcoming hardcover edition of *Dark Eye*. This excerpt has been set for this edition only and may not reflect the final content of the forthcoming novel.

Originally published in hardcover in the United States by Ballantine Books, an imprint of The Random House Publishing Group, a division of Random House, Inc., in 2004.

ISBN 0-345-45148-1

Printed in the United States of America

Ballantine Books website address: www.ballantinebooks.com

OPM   9 8 7 6 5 4 3 2 1

For Theta Juan,
my mother, who taught her children
that all hate was a crime

In tragic life, God wot,
No villain need be! Passions spin the plot:
We are betrayed by what is false within.

—GEORGE MEREDITH, *Modern Love*

Prologue

SIX MONTHS EARLIER

**Broken Arrow, Oklahoma,
in the Tulsa suburbs**

CHAPTER

1

I SHOULD FEEL something more, Mike thought, as he squeezed one eye closed and pressed the other against the scope. Some twinge of reluctance, or regret. A tightening in my gut, a chill at the base of my spine. A tingling beneath the short hairs on the back of my neck. But . . .

All he felt was the strong and unmitigated desire to complete his mission, to do what he had come to do.

If the man would just come a little closer to the window, I could blow his head off, he mused. And would. With pleasure.

Major Mike Morelli of the Tulsa PD Homicide Division pulled his eye away from the reticle and wiped his brow. The world was a different place, viewed through a sniperscope. After three hours of micro-scrutinizing the apartment walls, the windows, the shadowy figures that passed just out of range, he saw everything from a new perspective. It was all deceptively larger, closer, and, as a result, it conveyed an urgency that Mike was having difficulty subduing. He wanted those bastards so badly. If he could rip out their jugulars with his teeth, he would.

The cloud cover barely allowed the sun passage. Here on the street, behind the barricade, there was a distinct coolness in the air, one Mike felt in the marrow of his bones. He had not expected this sort of weather and had not dressed for it. Even his trademark trench coat, a carryover from his younger days when he thought it gave him the stature and credibility his youthful face did not, was insufficient to warm him. It was a gloomy Oklahoma day, the perfect mirror for what he was feeling inside.

With something between a grunt and a sigh, Mike returned his eye to the scope and prayed for a clear shot. C'mon, Mr. Kidnapper, give me a chance. Come to the window for a breath of fresh air, just a tiny bit closer. I'll give you a view you'll never forget.

"Move back!" a man shouted from the darkness of the apartment, his electronically amplified voice sounding more desperate with each word. "Move back or I kill the kid!"

He'd been shouting like that off and on since the siege began, always frenzied, always violent, and always just out of range.

"I mean it! If you're not on the other side of the street in one minute, I'll ventilate him!"

Mike heard the personal radios surrounding him crackle to life, and a few moments later they were all moving back. Again. Hour twelve of the Sequoyah Heights siege. Progress made: zero.

Mike's finger rested ever so gingerly on the trigger guard, never past the safety. But if he thought he had a shot, he'd pull that trigger so fast the SOT team and their professional sharpshooters wouldn't know what happened. He knew he could do it. He could sense the electricity surging through the stock into his shoulder. He could feel the cold steel and smell the leather strap. He had the power of life and death in his hands. But the only part that interested him at the moment was death. He wanted to pull that trigger so badly. Just give me half a chance, he murmured to himself. Just half a chance.

"Are you checked out for that weapon, Major?"

Mike eased away from the rifle, laying it on its side. Party's over.

"Yes, Special Agent Swift, I am. As a matter of fact,

I'm checked out for about every kind of weapon there is. But I was only using the scope to surveil the apartment."

And if you believe that . . .

"Just making sure. Don't want any screwups on my watch."

Her watch? When the hell did this become her watch? That was the problem with Feebies—one of several. They couldn't cross the street without trying to take charge.

"Our first priority is getting that little boy out alive," Mike reminded her.

"I'm well aware of that," Agent Swift replied. She was a petite but strong woman, Mike observed, not for the first time. Dark hair, an almost perfect match to her turtleneck. Gun holstered by shoulder strap, visible when her jacket pulled back. She managed to bring off that no-nonsense, don't-mess-with-me look without suggesting that she had an ax to grind. "But if one of my men gets a shot at one of the kidnappers, I can damn well guarantee we're going to take it."

"Good to know. Of course I wouldn't dream of interfering."

She gave him a long look. "I've always prided myself on my ability to work cooperatively with local law enforcement." Mike had to grin, both because he knew that was a crock, and because for a moment he was certain she was going to say, "I've always depended upon the kindness of strangers." Swift had come from the Chicago office of the Bureau, but she was originally from the Deep South—an Alabama girl, if he recalled correctly. Mike loved the accent—a pleasant change from the unenunciated drawl you got in Oklahoma the closer you moved to the Texas border. "That's why you're here. I wanted to keep the locals involved, but I can't have you endangering the success of my operation with any hotdog stunts."

Mike peered at her credulously. "Where would you ever get the idea I might try some hotdog stunts?"

"From everyone who knows you. Including Chief of Police Blackwell."

Damn him, anyway. Whose side was he on?

"I also know you're not so crazy about working with FBI agents. I heard what happened during the Lombardi case, so I guess you've got your reasons, but I still—"

"You still won't let me endanger the success of your operation. I got that, Special Agent. I'll keep my nose clean."

"Until we catch the kidnappers. Afterward . . ." She cocked her head to one side. "You can try anything you want."

Now what was that supposed to mean? he wondered, as he watched her move down the line and start in on one of the snipers. Was this FBI agent flirting with him? That would be a gross impropriety. And darned flattering.

He stood and buttoned his rumpled coat around his forty-four-inch chest. All of a sudden he was glad he'd dropped that postsmoking weight. Those trips to the gym might've been worth it, too.

But he didn't need any distractions at the moment, or anything confusing his feelings. Eyes on the prize, he told himself. First we take down the pond scum in that apartment. He surveyed the phalanx of men surrounding him on the street, as well as the similar lineup on the rooftop of the office building just behind. Even if he didn't particularly care to acknowledge it, Swift had done a first-rate job organizing this detail. She had everyone in place and ready to roll. There was no way those child-abusing monsters were going to escape this net. It was just a matter of time, a thought which filled him with a strange warmth. If only there was some way to accelerate the process.

Off to the left, he spotted two familiar faces moving in his direction.

"Stand at attention, Special Agent," he said, raising his voice so she could hear. "The parents."

Two well-dressed adults arrived at about the same time she did. The man was wearing a tailored suit and a starched white shirt. The woman wore a dark dress and clutched a DK handbag. At first blush, Mike read the man as angry, which meant guilt-ridden, and read the woman as angry, which meant terrified. But he supposed he could be wrong. He had been wrong before. Once.

"I'm Harrison Metzger. Which one of you is in charge?"

"I am," they both answered, Swift, because she was, and Mike, because he had the irresistible urge to give her ego a tweak. They exchanged a pointed look.

"I'm a homicide detective for Tulsa PD," Mike explained. "I'm in charge of the homicide case. This is Special Agent Swift with the FBI's Child Abduction Task Force. She's in charge of the kidnapping case."

Metzger turned to Agent Swift. They always went to the Fed, Mike noted. The Oklahoma inferiority complex. Anyone from out of town had to be smarter than a local. "I want to know what's being done to save my son. Looks to me like you're all just sitting around on your asses."

To her credit, Swift remained unruffled but not unsympathetic. "Mr. Metzger—"

"Dr. Metzger."

"Doctor," she corrected. "I've had my public relations liaison brief you every hour. I think you know everything we do. We're waiting for an opportunity—"

"Who are these people, anyway?"

"The kidnappers? We don't know their names. We believe there are four of them, working together. The one who keeps speaking into the bullhorn is obviously male. The others, we're not sure."

"I don't understand why this is taking so long. You know where my boy is. Go in and get him!"

"Sir, I can assure you that—"

"Before, your excuse was that you didn't know where they were. Now you've got them surrounded, and you're still not doing anything!"

Mrs. Metzger stayed a safe distance behind her husband. Mike had the sense that she was embarrassed by her husband's tirade, but she knew better than to interfere.

"We don't think it would be prudent to storm the apartment. We know they're armed—"

"Aren't your people armed?"

"Of course."

"So what's the problem? Show some balls, girl."

Agent Swift paused barely a beat before responding. "Sir, I can assure you that when the time is right for action, we will take it. But at the moment, our top priority is getting your son out safely, which means avoiding, if possible, an exchange of fire that might endanger—"

"This is what happens when you put a woman in charge." He shifted his gaze to Mike. "Is there something you can do, Major?"

"I'm just here to support Agent Swift, sir. Whether you realize it or not, she's playing this by the book. And doing a first-rate job of it."

"Do you people know how long my son has been their captive?" His confrontational mask cracked a fraction. "There's no telling what . . . what they might have done to him!"

"I understand your concern, Mr. Metzger—"

"Dr. Metzger."

Mike drew in his breath. The man was a Ph.D., which, to his mind, barely counted and certainly didn't justify constant correction. But this was not the time to digress. "Dr. Metzger, from the start, we have moved as quickly as possible. And that hasn't changed. But what's most important is that we get Tommy out alive. Remember, the ransom demand came in almost immediately, and you paid it according to their directions. We have no reason to believe the boy has been molested."

That, of course, was a lie, statistically speaking, anyway. As Mike knew all too well, more than 90 percent of all noncustody-related child kidnappings involved some form of molestation. But in most cases the child turned up again relatively soon, after the kidnapper had taken what he wanted. When the child was held for longer than twenty-four hours, the statistics became far more grim. Less than 50 percent of those kids ever made it home again.

Tommy Metzger had been gone for eight days.

"What about poison gas?" Metzger continued. "What about a flamethrower? I want those men laid low! I want them to pay for what they've done to my family!"

On the other side of the street, Mike saw that a mini-cam reporter had spotted them and was recording the whole scene. Probably had one of those ultrapowerful spy mikes that can pick up conversations from miles away. Odds were this argument would be rehashed on the six o'clock news.

This case had been big news from the outset, from the moment one of the kidnappers grabbed eight-year-old Tommy Metzger outside his Tulsa private school. Mike had worked many a big case since he'd started with the force, but this one was something else again. The combination of the father's prominence and wealth—in addition to teaching, he had penned a series of best-selling books—the cruelty of the snatch, captured on video by a parent coming out of a dance recital, and the photogenic qualities of the abductee, made this case an instant media sensation. All the national news agencies were carrying it; posters featuring Tommy's face had blanketed the country. Every night, the evening newscasters updated the case—and if there was nothing to update, they reviewed what had gone before, usually rescreening the amateur video footage that had propelled the crime

to the forefront. The initial snatch had been botched and
the kidnappers had ended up killing the kid's nanny,
thus turning it into a homicide and bringing it into Mike's
bailiwick. It was the ransom—1.5 million in cold, hard
cash—that had allowed the Feds to trace the kidnappers. A homing device sewn into the bag had led them
to this apartment in the Tulsa suburbs. Their first approach had been subtle. Two agents disguised as UPS
men knocked on the front door. Somehow, though, the
kidnappers made them and started firing. Swift then
moved in the troops, and ten minutes later the siege had
begun. Everyone's worst fear was that if the situation escalated, the kidnappers would become desperate and
kill the kid.

If they hadn't already.

Metzger's anger was reaching a bitter crescendo.
"Lady, you may not understand how influential I am in
this community. I know people. Lots of powerful people. And if you don't do something fast to save my boy,
you're gonna end up with your tit in a wringer!"

To Mike's amazement, Special Agent Swift smiled.
"Sir, I know you're concerned about your son. I don't
blame you. But if you don't stop interfering with my operation, I will be forced to have you removed from the
premises. For your son's safety. And yours."

Mike almost whistled in admiration as the father
stomped away, mother clinging close behind.

"Man," Mike said, "you handled that brilliantly."

Swift shrugged. "If handling kidnappers was as easy
as handling parents, this would've been over a long time
ago."

"I would've been tempted to escort Metzger to the
floor. With my fist."

"Oh, he wasn't really angry. He was riddled with guilt,
venting on me as an avoidance mechanism. He and his
wife are separated, you know. He's moved in with some

hot young number in Glenpool. Future trophy wife. Metzger hasn't seen the kid in weeks."

"Really?" In fact, Mike hadn't known that.

"The mother is only marginally more attentive. My investigators tell me the one the kid was close to was the nanny."

"And now she's gone."

"Yeah." There was a slow release of air from between her lips. "And Tommy knows it, too, since he saw a bullet enter her neck."

Mike winced.

"Metzger's concerns about Tommy's well-being are utterly reasonable, all things considered. The kidnappers intentionally chose the son—not the wife, not the girlfriend. They wanted the boy. And they've had him for more than a week." Her voice faded. "And now they must be realizing they're going to get caught—possibly killed—no matter what they do . . ."

Mike swore silently. His eyes returned to the fifth-story window and the dark shadows that flickered elusively across it. "Special Agent Swift, much as I hate to agree with Metzger, we've got to get that kid out of there. Soon."

"I also agree, Major," she said, following his gaze, "but I won't do something stupid just to be doing something."

"So what's your plan?"

"Same as before. We watch and wait. Until our opportunity comes. Then we take it."

MIKE HAD ALMOST given up hope that the situation could be resolved tonight. Darkness had fallen with no improvement, not in the hostage situation, and not in Mike's soul. Just as the gloom of the day had mirrored his inner state before, so the darkness that now enveloped them seemed altogether appropriate. Swift had ordered all illumination kept to a bare minimum; the less reflective light bouncing around, the better the chance that one of her snipers might eventually get a clear shot. The kidnappers weren't talking and weren't budging. In short, the siege was going nowhere. Mike had even reluctantly called his friend Ben Kincaid with the unhappy news that he'd have to watch tonight's *Xena* rerun alone. This standoff showed no signs of resolving itself anytime soon.

Until Agent Swift's cell phone started playing the theme from *Dragnet*.

"So what's the story?" Mike asked, after she clamped her Nokia shut.

"They're offering to release the kid."

Mike's eyebrow rose. He did not smile.

"They want safe passage. An armored truck to get them to the airport, then a flight to New York that can refuel and continue on to the Netherlands."

"The Netherlands," Mike repeated. "Child porn capital of the universe."

"They say they'll leave Tommy somewhere safe and give us his location as soon as they're out of the country."

Neither of them spoke for a long while.

"You think they've already killed him?" Mike asked, finally.

"Not yet. I talked to him, just for a moment. But it's obvious they plan to. They can't let him identify them, especially now that it's a murder case. They'll take him in the truck, slash his throat, and dump him somewhere he won't be discovered until they're safely in Amsterdam."

"What'd'you tell them?"

"That we'd do it, of course. Assistant Director Blanchard was hovering over my shoulder the whole time. My orders are to comply with their demands in every respect. To take no aggressive action."

"Which means . . ."

"Yeah. But the Bureau won't be to blame. If we marched in all Waco-style and it went bad, the press would crucify us."

Mike let everything she was saying—and everything she was not saying—sink in. "So we've got? . . ."

She was staring at her watch. "Twenty-eight minutes."

"Are you going to move in?"

"Blanchard says no."

"If we let that kid get in the truck, he's dead."

"I know that."

"Any chance your superiors would authorize a small incursion? Like maybe two people?"

"None."

They looked at each other.

"You got a plan?" he said finally.

"Damn straight."

Mike checked the magazine in his gun. Fully loaded. "Let's go."

USING THE DARKNESS to their advantage, Mike and Agent Swift crouched and ran to the apartment building, weaving a serpentine trail through the back alleys. They avoided the street lamps and stayed out of the view of the kidnappers' sole window. Through the sniperscope, Mike had noticed there was a fire escape ladder that hung down the north wall of the complex. It was the only feasible approach. The kidnappers had decommissioned the elevators and were watching the stairs.

"I don't know how we get into the room without being seen," Swift whispered, as she followed him up the ladder.

"I was thinking we'd use you as a decoy. You are wearing Kevlar, right?"

"But seriously."

Above them, Mike heard glass being shattered.

"Duck!"

All around them, shards of glass from a windowpane descended in a dangerous crystalline rainfall. But that was not the worst of their problems. A moment later, the glass was supplanted by bullets.

Mike leapt off the ladder onto the fourth-story landing and pressed up against the wall.

"Over here!" he shouted.

Another flurry of gunfire rang out. Swift rolled to the edge of the landing and took cover under the eaves. They stood shoulder to shoulder, craning their necks to see where the shots were coming from. A few moments later, the section of the fire escape stretching from the fourth to the fifth floor descended with an ear-shattering clang.

"Damnation," Mike swore. "They removed the bolts."

"So quickly?"

"Must've known we were coming. But how? It's dark. We were quiet."

"They might have night-vision specs. Maybe there are more of them than we realized." She examined the ladder, now barely stretching beyond the ceiling level of the fourth floor. "Think you can reattach it?"

"From up there? Sure. From down here? No way." Mike raised his hand and pointed. "See that window?"

She followed his finger to a point about five feet above them and to the left. "Looks like a hallway."

"Whatever. It can't be far from their room. We can crawl through the window, knock down the door, and find our kidnappers. And the boy."

"How do we get the window open?"

"Since they're onto us, I see no reason to be subtle." He whipped out his trusty Sig Sauer and fired three rounds. The window shattered. "We've got to hurry."

Swift was peering overhead. "That must be five feet, up to that window landing."

Mike nodded. "I can make it."

"And about thirty feet down."

"And your point is?"

"Don't miss."

"Thanks, I won't." He sidestepped to the edge of the landing.

She grabbed his arm. "What about the gunfire?"

"I think I should try to avoid it."

She tugged at his shirt. "No, I'll go."

"This was my crazy idea."

"I'm lighter. I'm much more likely to make it."

"There's no way I'm letting—"

"Back off, Morelli. I'm in charge here." She crouched down, ready to spring. "Give me a boost."

"But I—"

"That's an order, Major!"

There was no time to argue. Mike cupped his hands together. Swift inserted her right boot, grabbed the wall, and let him lift her up. She stepped onto his shoulders and jumped.

Mike grimaced as he saw her hands slap down on the jagged edge of the window. That had to hurt, but to her credit, she wasn't complaining. She pulled herself through, then reemerged headfirst.

"No sign of them. Push up the ladder."

Mike did as instructed. Swift hooked the edges over the top rail, and a moment later, they were both on the fifth floor. Mike raced down the hallway and kicked in the front door. "Police! Freeze!"

He crouched and swung into the room, gun extended, and did a quick sweep. He went off to the right toward the bedroom, while Swift moved into the kitchenette.

No one was there.

"All clear."

"What about in the back?"

Together, they ran through the main living room and found another door in the rear. They could hear voices.

"FBI!" Swift barked. "Hands up! Nobody move!"

She kicked in the door and led the way. She took high left; he took low right.

The voices they had heard were coming from the television. Cartoon Network, if Mike wasn't mistaken. There was no one there.

No one except Tommy Metzger.

Agent Swift ran to the boy's side. "Don't worry, son. We're the police. We're here to take you home."

For the first time, the boy looked away from the television. He was holding a soda and a half-eaten Twinkie. "Go away!"

Swift blinked. "Don't be afraid, Tommy. You're safe now. Where did the bad men go?"

"They're my friends! Leave them alone!"

Mike sighed heavily. He was disappointed, but not surprised. It had been eight days. Stockholm Syndrome was a foreseeable consequence. "I'll finish securing the apartment." It didn't take long, given the size of the place. There were lots of traces of people—empty pizza boxes, a bottle of Jack Daniel's, even a toothbrush. But no people.

When he returned to the living room, Mike saw that Agent Swift had turned off the television, sending the boy into a rage. "You can't tell me what to do! Where are my friends?"

The worst of it was Mike knew the boy's reaction increased the likelihood that he had been molested. Unlike rapists, who committed sexual crimes out of anger or sadism, pedophiles typically had genuine feelings for their victims. Rather than forcing themselves, they tried to seduce their victims with presents and favors and promises of love. A boy like Tommy, who probably felt neglected by his own parents, was an easy mark. The pedophile had easily won his love and devotion, probably awakening erotic feelings in the boy for the first time.

Tommy would be in therapy for a good long stretch, sorting out his confusion and guilt.

"Please don't make me go home! Please!"

"I covered the apartment," Mike said. "No sign of the kidnappers."

Swift pulled out her walkie-talkie. "Sierra One. Do you have the perps in sight?"

"Negative. We have nothing."

She tried all the other sniper stations. No one had seen anything.

"How can that be?" She gave the order to move in. Less than fifteen minutes later the FBI team had covered the entire building, most of which had already been evacuated. There were no traces of the criminals—or the ransom money. It was almost an hour before they located the inside door in the basement laundry room, which led to a subterranean passage from that basement to an adjacent one in the apartment complex on the opposite side of the block.

"Damn!" Swift said, banging her fist against the wall. "I can't believe I let them get away!"

"It's not your fault," Mike said.

"The worst of it is, my perimeter snipers might've seen them leave an hour ago. But before we made our move, I pulled everyone in tight so they'd be sure to be caught after we flushed them out."

"You did the best you could," Mike said, trying to console her, when in truth he was just as disappointed as she was, if not more. He didn't like to see anyone escape—but child snatchers? It made him sick to his stomach.

The parents had rushed to their boy, but Tommy didn't want to be with them, and the Feds insisted on immediately beginning the painful process of debriefing him, trying to find out what little he remembered about his abductors and learning all the grisly details about his week in captivity. So far, Tommy was saying no physical abuse had occurred, but Mike knew the kid could just be keeping it all locked up inside. It might take several days, even weeks, before they learned the truth.

"Thanks for your help, Morelli," Swift said, as she started toward her car. "Sorry it didn't work out better."

"It isn't over yet," he replied, and he meant it. He was not going to let these people roam free. Not in his town—not anywhere. He would not stop searching. He would hunt them relentlessly. He would follow every lead, every possibility. He would catch those miserable perverts no matter what it took.

CHAPTER
2

THREE MONTHS EARLIER

**Evanston, Illinois,
near the Phillips College campus
Fourteen miles north of Chicago**

"WHICH ONE DO you think is the cop?" Shelly asked.

Tony surveyed the entire bar—stools, tables, dance floor, TV monitors, pool tables. "Hard to say. What do you think?"

Shelly tilted her head. "See the guy at Table Two? I think it's him."

"Why him? I see several new faces in the bar tonight. The woman with the black leather fixation. The two nerds dancing the Batusi."

She shook her head. "Nope. Table Two."

"Because he's wearing a tie?"

"Because he has food stains on his tie. Also, check out the socks. They don't match."

"And that makes him a cop?"

"Who else would have such poor personal habits?"

"Oh, anyone single. Which would be everyone in this bar."

"People coming to a singles bar hoping to hook up with someone are going to doll themselves up. Including guys. Only someone working undercover would wear those socks. I mean, one of them is argyle, for God's sake. The other is a sweat sock. They're not even close."

Tony relented. Shelly was an astute judge of humanity; that was why he put her behind the bar. "Maybe you're right. But I've got my eyes on one of the guys next to the dance floor. Table Ten."

"Which one?"

"The blonde."

"You're saying he's the cop? Or you're just saying you have your eye on him?"

Tony smiled. "How well you know me."

Shelly was, as Tony's mother was fond of saying, cute as a bug. Barely five feet tall—she had to stand on a box to reach the glasses hanging over the bar. She had a pert, trim figure, and an effervescent personality that patrons loved. It was more than just her personal adorableness—even Tony loved to watched her work as she darted from one station to the next, working three mixed drinks simultaneously and getting them all exactly right. He loved it when she pumped the Bass Ale spigot; it made a pneumatic hissing noise that reminded him of the elevator brakes in the Sears Tower. Shelly was good, and he wasn't the only one who knew it. Some of the regulars dropped by Remote Control just to see her. One of his very first actions when he became manager was making her head bartender for the after-work shift. Drink sales rose dramatically.

Decisions like that were what put Tony where he was today. Not that managing a near-campus singles bar was going to rival Supreme Court justice as one of the country's most desirable jobs. But given where he had come from, what he'd had to overcome to get to this point, he felt pretty good about it. The bar was thriving, and he liked to think he'd played some small part in that success, since the whole place was his idea.

He'd spent the whole evening trying to keep a smile on his face, but the truth was all these rumors about undercover narcs were worrying him. Even if there was nothing to it, the gossip alone could put a serious dent in their business. And that caused him considerable concern.

He tried to shrug it off, but there was a heaviness settling in, fogging his brain, that he couldn't quite shake loose. It was nothing tangible or rational—but it was there, just the same. Like a shadow hovering over his shoulder. A pervasive uneasiness he couldn't talk himself out of, since he didn't know what was causing it. He'd had black patches before; they were always there, always lurking, the enemy within. He had tried to conquer them, without success. He thought he'd mastered the situation, but even that seemed in doubt, what with everything going on at the bar, at school. With Roger.

He knew it was foolish to take everything that happened here so personally. Mario owned the place, not him. But he was its creator. He couldn't help having some paternal feelings, weird as that was. To him, this job was one long party. And he needed that party. Needed it to remind himself that he was happy. No matter what happened. Happy, happy, happy.

Remote Control was particularly crowded tonight. All the bar stools were filled and there was a half-hour wait for a table. All for the good. The bar was more fun when it was packed, more alive. The rich dark oak fixtures gave the place an Old World feel—in direct conflict with the ambience suggested by all the high-tech gadgetry. The decor was full of contradictions, and Tony embraced them all. He loved it here.

"I've got two Coronas headed to your blond boytoy's table," Shelly said, sliding the tray toward him. "I know you executive types don't normally perform manual labor, but—"

"I'll take it."

Tony checked himself in the mirror behind the bar. Sandy blond locks, bangs dangling over one eye the way he liked them. Could you tell he'd been working out? I mean, he could tell, but could anyone else? Like the blond guy at Table Ten?

"Two Coronas for the gentlemen," Tony announced as he lowered the tray. "As ordered."

The two men, one fair, the other darker in complexion, sat at opposite ends of the table. They were both young— probably college students. Not Phillips, though—more likely Northwestern. Perhaps even University of Chicago. They were doing their best to act earthy, but it wasn't convincing. Like Bertie and Jeeves trying to do *American Pie*. Their perfectly creased chinos and perfectly unscuffed Doc Martens told the true tale. It was part of the John D. Rockefeller legacy to the University of Chicago— in addition to the pseudo-Oxfordian architecture that never quite worked. Phillips students were just townies by comparison.

"Somethin' goin' on tonight?" the darker of the two asked.

Tony flashed his brightest smile. "There's always something going on in Evanston, gentlemen. Beaches, boutiques, art galleries—just depends on what you're looking for."

The blond guy smiled. "Ain't that the truth." What teeth. What a smile. What a way with words. Tony's heart did flip-flops just looking at him.

"Thought I saw you lookin' around," his companion said. "You and the chick behind the bar."

"There's a rumor goin' around that an undercover cop is haunting some of the local bars. Probably a crock, but we were trying to guess who the cop might be."

"So that's all it was?"

"Yeah. Why?"

His blond friend grinned. "Brett thought you was givin' him the eye."

They both looked at him. All at once, Tony felt like an amoeba in a science experiment. Were these guys gay, too? Was that why they were asking, because they were interested? Or just the opposite? He knew better than to assume gayness just because two guys hung out together. Especially when the frats were on the prowl. But it was so hard to know, even now when he was well out of the closet. Some of his gay buddies said they could always tell if another guy was gay, like they had some kind of biological radar. Tony didn't believe it. In any case, even if that did exist somewhere, the radar fairy hadn't brought him any. He never knew, and had learned to play it cool until he was certain.

"Didn't mean to make you uncomfortable. Just trying to spot the cop."

The blond man laughed. "Well, that's good. Brett here thought maybe you were a faggot."

Tony felt his blood turn to ice. "Here's the tab. If you need anything more, just wave at one of the waitresses."

The darker man was still staring at him. Even as Tony turned and walked away, he could feel those eyes bearing down on him. He positioned himself behind the bar, not so much to help Shelly as for the sense of security it offered. Putting a big block of oak between himself and Table Ten.

"Problem?" Shelly asked.

"No. Nothing." He was suddenly aware that his hands were shaking. What a fool he was. "I'll be in my office. Tell Mario if he comes back."

"All right. I'm almost through. Phoebe's taking over." Shelly's large round eyes brightened. "Got me a date tonight."

"Have a good evening. Don't get too crazy."

"I'll try to keep my panties on."

"And Shelly?"

"Yeah?"

He winked. "You were right. Definitely the guy with the socks."

* * *

*I CAN'T BEGIN to know what the future holds for me. But
I do know that . . .*

When he was finished, Tony shook his wrists, working
out a cramp. He caught a glimpse of the clock over the
door.

Good grief! He'd been writing in his journal for more
than two hours. Mario wouldn't be happy about that—
if he found out. He'd only intended to sit down for a
minute or two, but once he started writing, the words
just flew. Something inside him was desperate to get out,
he supposed. Two hours! That was a novel, not a diary
entry. And he hadn't even mentioned his latest problem,
the one that was weighing heaviest on his mind. And his
conscience.

He pushed out of his chair and stretched. He'd never
figured himself for the diary type. Had tried to keep one
once before—and rarely wrote more than a line or two
before bed. He gave it up after a month. But since he'd
started keeping a journal on his laptop, all that had
changed. Somehow it was easier with a keyboard. Must
have something to do with the male infatuation with
gadgetry. Whatever the cause, he'd managed to keep the
journal going for more than two years now, since his
eighteenth birthday, and that was in addition to managing this bar full-time and taking classes at Phillips part-
time.

"Tony?"

He looked up. It was Phoebe, the on-duty bartender.
"Phone call for you on Line One."

"Why don't you take a message and I'll—"

"It's Shelly."

He nodded, finished what he was writing, then
reached for the phone. He adored Shelly, but he was
aware she'd been having some . . . problems of late.
He'd have to be blind not to have noticed. What he

didn't know was what it was all about. She hadn't confided in him, at least not yet, but he had a strong feeling that she wanted to. Perhaps this was the time . . .

"Hello?"

At first, he thought she was laughing at him, but it didn't take long to realize how wrong he was. That wasn't laughter. Just the opposite. She was trying to speak, but her words were broken and convulsed by tears.

LESS THAN FIVE minutes later, Tony was outside the bar. He wrapped his coat tightly around himself. It was still cold and wet, typical Illinois spring. Not bad, but just chilly enough to require a coat. Just enough wet that he had to watch for puddles as he crossed the dark asphalt parking lot. He spotted his Volkswagen bug and began fumbling in his satchel for his keys.

"Lookit that purse. I told you he was a queer."

Tony froze.

"Nice purse, faggot. Got a lipstick in there?"

Tony tried to keep his voice even. "It's a satchel. Like a backpack. I carry my schoolbooks—"

"Check out the limp wrist." The two men from Table Ten emerged from the shadows of the parking lot. "Disgusting. Faggot car, too."

Tony tore through his bag, desperately searching for those keys. "Look, boys, I don't want any trouble."

The dark man came closer. "I saw the way you were looking at me. I know what you were thinking, too. Sick'ning, that's what it was. Flaming queen, coming on to me in public, in front of my friends."

"I didn't mean anything." Tony's heart was racing. Was anyone else in the parking lot? If he shouted, would they hear it inside the bar?

The dark man kept coming. "I know what you wanted, you butt-fucking pervert. Well, I'm gonna give you something a little different."

Tony threw back his shoulders. "Look, asshole, if you have some idea that because I'm gay, I'll be your punching bag, you got it wrong. I've studied Tae Kwon Do and I am one mean mofo, so the smartest thing you could do is just leave me alone."

The dark man laughed. "Listen to him, Johnny. The little cocksucker thinks he's tough. Gonna use his sissy boy kung fu on us." He laughed again, slow and ugly. "I'm quaking in my boots."

"We have security here," Tony lied. "All I have to do is yell."

"Then we'll have to make sure you don't."

The dark man pulled a Taser out from inside his coat and shoved it into Tony's gut. In one explosive burst, Tony felt the electric pulse ripple through his body, ripping it apart. His legs dissolved; a second later he hit the asphalt. The man applied the Taser again and again, torturing him, never letting him rest. Tony twitched and spasmed like a half-crushed bug. Even when the Taser was finally removed, he couldn't stop writhing. He was like a marionette on a madman's string, jerking one way then the next, his entire body convulsing.

While he was unable to resist, they dragged him into the back of their van. They Tasered him a few more times during the drive, just to keep him hurting and helpless, until they arrived at a dark, secluded vacant lot. No one could see what they did here. No one could hear, no matter how loudly Tony screamed.

They hauled him out of the van and threw him down on the concrete in front of a chain-link fence. When the spasming began to subside, they hauled him upright by his hair. A moment later, Tony felt the dark man's fist in his chest. The pain was searing, like a branding iron piercing his already weakened body. His attacker had hit him in the solar plexus, knocked the wind out of him. Maybe broken something. Tony couldn't breathe.

He wanted to cry out, wanted to attract some help, but he could barely muster a whimper.

"Let me help," the blond kid said. He lunged forward with a roll of duct tape and gagged Tony, then taped his wrists to two fence posts. He was immobile, pinned like a human sacrifice, arms splayed as if he were about to be crucified.

The first blow dislocated his jaw. The second cracked a rib. Tony was on fire; every nerve of his body had been electrified. The blows rained down on him, one after another, so many and so often and so hard that Tony could no longer distinguish where they landed or what part of his body had been broken. The dark man worked him over with a leather sap, pummeling his head and face and hands. Tony felt two of his fingers snap. And the blows just kept coming.

Consciousness began to fade. His vision blurred. He prayed for unconsciousness; nothing else could make the pain go away. Surely they would stop. Surely then they would stop.

The dark man saw him go limp and sneered. "If you think we're gonna quit just 'cause you don't like it, you got another think comin', faggot. We're barely gettin' started." He ripped the duct tape off Tony's face. "What d'you say to that, queer boy?"

Tony's eyes were so swollen he couldn't see. His lips were cracked and bleeding. But somehow he managed to muster the power to whisper: "Please don't kill me. Please."

"Beg me, you fairy. Beg!"

"I . . . am begging you. Please don't kill me. I'll do anything."

"Like what? Like maybe you'll suck my dick, is that what you're thinking? You'd like that, wouldn't you?" He shoved his fist deep into Tony's gut.

Tony was finished, he realized. There was nothing he

could do; he had no way to protect himself. He was entirely at their mercy. And they had none.

"Cut him down," he heard the dark man say.

His heart twitched. Was it possible—was this insane torture over? Were they finally done with him? The blond man whipped out a switchblade and cut the duct tape binding his hands—and cut his wrists in the process.

"Whoops. Guess my hand slipped."

"Never you mind, Johnny. I think he likes it. Give him another poke or two."

The blond man did. All over Tony's body. Treated him like a human pincushion. Tony felt blood gushing out of his body like water from a fountain, from his face, his abdomen—even his feet. Then he noticed the dark man was holding something—a five-pound iron maul hammer.

The two men continued their work for more than half an hour. And no one came to help Tony. His cries were heard by no one, no one except the person who had left the bar shortly after the assailants and witnessed the entire assault. And did nothing. But watched. And waited.

PART ONE

Times of Passion

CHAPTER

1

"I REALLY DON'T want to do this," Ben Kincaid muttered.

"You never do," Jones grumbled, as he pressed the camera to his face.

"Tell me again why this is necessary?"

"My duties as your office manager include marketing, true?"

"I suppose."

"That means it's my job to make sure you get out and network, an important part of modern-day law practice at which you are ridiculously pathetic."

"So that's what this is about? Networking?"

"The Tulsa County Bar Directory goes to every big corporation in town, Boss. Your face needs to be in it."

"So if someone sees my handsome face in a directory, they might decide to send some work my way?"

"You never know. You've got to stay above the radar if you want people to remember you."

Ben stood in the lobby of his sparsely decorated law office, trapped between Jones's workstation and the tacky sofa in the reception area. "I don't think I need new clients that badly."

"Take it from someone who has reviewed the monthly accounting books. You do. Now smile."

"I am smiling."

"That's not a smile. That's a grimace."

"It's the best I can do."

"You want to attract clients, not scare them off."

"I want to look like a lawyer, not a game show host."

"Would you just smile already?"

"Not in a million—" All at once, Ben's face lit up like a candle, with eyes wide and a hysterical grin.

Jones snapped the picture.

"Christina!" Ben whirled around.

The petite redhead standing behind him beamed. "How did you know it was me?"

"Who else would . . . would . . . do what you just did?"

"And that would be?" Jones inquired.

Ben's face flushed. "She pinched me!"

Jones arched an eyebrow. "Where exactly?"

"You don't need to know." He gave his law partner a long look. "Christina. You have a navel!"

"I hope that doesn't shock you." Her hair was done up in a professional-looking pinned-back hairdo, but she was wearing a brief fuchsia top that exposed her midriff, a short skirt, and pink lace pumps. Across the top of the shirt, written in sequins, was: MAIS OUI.

"Britney Spears, eat your heart out."

Christina did a little twirl. "You like, mon ami?"

"Of course I do. But Jones, as marketing director, shouldn't you give her a little lecture on professional deportment?"

"Hey, at least she knows how to attract attention. I got no complaints."

Christina blew him a kiss. "Merci, ma petite bagatelle. Oh, Ben, I'm sorry about last night."

Ben's reaction was so immediate Jones couldn't help but notice. His chin rose; his back stiffened. "Don't worry about it."

"How could I not? I don't know what came over me."

"Really, Christina, it's nothing."

"But I—"

"Really, you—"

"I wouldn't want—"

"Not another thought."

Jones's eyes narrowed. "So . . . what was this, Inns of Court or something?"

"Yeah," Ben said, much too quickly. "I mean, something like that. Right, Christina?"

"Right. Right." Was her face pinking up, or was it just a reflection from that outfit?

"Any messages?" Ben asked.

"Nothing new," Jones answered. "The same anonymous female we've been getting for weeks." He handed Ben the message slip. It contained only four words: PEANUT BUTTER AND JELLY.

"What on earth is that supposed to mean?" Jones asked.

Ben didn't answer. He crumpled the message slip in his fist. "Did you get that cable outlet installed, Christina?"

"Natch."

"Excellent. I told you the super wouldn't mind."

"The super moaned and groaned and told me he was much too busy to get to it anytime before Christmas."

"That would be a bit late for my purposes."

"So I informed him. And he agreed to move it to the top of his to-do list."

Ben was impressed. "Because he's such a good friend?"

Christina shook her head. "Because he knows better than to mess with me."

Cook County Criminal Courthouse
Chicago, Illinois
26th Street and California Avenue

KEVIN MAHONEY HAD visited the county courthouse many times since he began his law practice, but he had never seen it look like it did today. The sidewalks and courtyards outside were rarely crowded; at best a few skateboarders, panhandlers, and homeless people dotted the stone walkways. But today the area was so packed Kevin could barely find his way to the door. Maybe 2 percent of the throng had actual business in the courthouse; the rest were demonstrators, conveniently aligned east and west depending upon which side of the conflict they favored.

Kevin wasn't normally claustrophobic, but as he marched down the increasingly narrower gauntlet of protesters, it did seem to him as if the human walls were closing in. Did they know who he was? Who he was defending? He could only hope not. On the north side, the gay alliances and task forces stood in solidarity, passing out pamphlets and waving signs in the air. Kevin had read that they'd applied to the city council for the right to build a bonfire; denied, they had settled for a midnight candlelight vigil.

Kevin surveyed the array of signs, which ranged from the poignant to the pathetic. Perhaps the most moving placards were the simplest. EVANSTON—WORSE THAN LARAMIE, read a placard up front, where the evening news cameras would be sure to find it. Kevin had frequently seen the posters bearing the name and photograph of Matthew Shepard—1976–1998, underscored with one word: PEACE. Now he saw many similar displays, except that Matthew Shepard shared his space with a picture of Tony Barovick.

On the south side of the piazza, the opposition forces were chanting in the singsong cadence usually associated with boot camp. "I don't know but I been told . . . Jesus loves you young or old. . . ." The lyrics were probably clever, but the hubbub was so intense Kevin couldn't hear most of it. Instead, he focused on the signs swirling in the air: GOD STANDS AGAINST THE SODOMITES and WAGE WAR AGAINST THE HOMOSEXUAL AGENDA and YOU CAN BE CURED! Perhaps the most memorable came from a crew cut clutching a red, white, and blue poster with a simple, three-word message: AIDS CURES FAGS.

Kevin's Chicago-Irish, very Catholic instincts told him that he should avoid any possibility of conflict, but if he didn't get to the courtroom in the next five minutes, Judge Lacayo would be threatening to sanction him, which would be a lousy way to start the day. So he plunged into the thick of the gauntlet. The first few seconds were fine—no one noticed him—but that didn't last. He quickened his pace. Just as the front doors appeared in sight, one of the young men on the east side lurched forward. Kevin wasn't sure if it was an attack or if the man had tripped, but he darted out of the way, just the same. The man fell into the crew cut, and the inadvertent touching rapidly escalated into a brawl.

"Back off, fascist!"

"God hates faggots and so do I!" came the reply, and a second later the combatants were on the concrete trying to gouge each other's eyes out. More protesters jumped into the fray. As if from nowhere, a dozen police officers rushed in and pulled the factions apart, though not before several noses were bloodied.

Kevin doubled his pace, entered the courthouse, and passed through the metal detectors. The attendants were being particularly careful today, he noted. He entered the main lobby of the courthouse.

Lacayo's courtroom was full and then some, no great surprise. The gray-haired bailiff standing at the door, looking very official in his uniform and holster, nodded. "Biggest turnout I've seen in years." His name, as Kevin knew from countless prior court visits, was Boxer Johnson. He was in his late fifties and was definitely from the old school. By the book, firm, but salt of the earth.

"I assume security precautions are at a peak."

Boxer grunted. "These days, they always are. But yeah. This trial, we're taking no chances. Do you know how many people have called in threats against your clients?"

"I can imagine."

Kevin took his seat at the defense table, and the two defendants were led into the room shackled at the feet: Brett Mathers, eighteen, dark complexioned, and Johnny Christensen, seventeen, fair. The restraints were removed and the marshals stationed themselves outside the courtroom. The jury was led in—voir dire had finally ended the day before—and Judge Lacayo entered the room.

Kevin knew Lacayo had been on the bench about ten years. He tended to be conservative, at least by Chicago standards. Normally, he was one of the more relaxed judges in the building, but you couldn't tell it today. Whether it was due to the media attention or the huge crowd he must've passed through to get here, he presented a stony, all-business facade.

"I will only mention this once," Lacayo said, pointing his gavel toward the rear of the courtroom. "I will tolerate no disturbances. Anyone attempting to disrupt these proceedings will be immediately escorted out of the building. Now, if there are no further preliminary matters, let's get started."

"YOU DON'T NORMALLY go in for this couch potato stuff at work," Christina said, flopping herself down on the couch in Ben's office. Jones leaned against the armrest. "What's your interest?"

Ben shrugged. "It's a big case. It's on Court TV."

"There's always a big case on Court TV, at least according to Court TV. So what?"

Ben turned up the volume a notch. "I happen to have a light workday."

"Which, for you, would normally suggest the *New York Times* crossword and a Trollope novel. What gives?"

"I just thought it might be of interest to see how the Chicago big shots handle it. Might learn something." He pointed toward the screen. "There's Richard Drabble, the newly elected DA for Cook County. He was a law-and-order candidate. I bet he's salivating at the prospect of getting a piece of this trial."

"No doubt."

"The judge is Manuel Lacayo. Very conservative by all accounts."

"Who's the woman sitting just behind the defendant's table? A legal assistant?"

"No. Mother of one of the defendants."

"Really? How do you know?"

"I . . . must've seen her somewhere. So, Jones, Christina—don't you have some work you should be doing?"

"No," they both said.

"Then go update the files. Write a brief."

"Nah," Jones said. "I want to see this."

Ben folded his arms. "I thought I ran this office."

Jones patted him on the shoulder. "You believe whatever makes you happy."

KEVIN TOOK HIS seat beside his clients—careful to seem congenial and not give away how much he despised them—and listened attentively as DA Drabble began his opening statement. Drabble made all the expected points, generating neither surprise nor excitement. Kevin wondered if the extensive media coverage hadn't stolen some of his thunder. However hideous the details, there was nothing the man could say about this case that hadn't already been endlessly regurgitated on the evening news.

"Of all the motivations known to man," Drabble said, "hate is the one that is least tolerable, especially in a society as diverse as ours. What could be more vile than two young men who torture and kill, not out of necessity, not for profit, not for revenge, not because of anything the victim did, but because of what the victim was? The evidence will show that the defendants stalked Tony Barovick, forced him back to their fraternity house, attacked him without provocation, beat him mercilessly, then killed him. What kind of people could commit such a crime? What do you call two men so consumed with hate that they would commit such an atrocity, such an offense to decency and human compassion? I will tell you. You call them monsters. Monsters who need to be punished. Permanently."

Succinct—but eminently effective, Kevin thought. No doubt about where he was going. Or what Kevin needed to do in reply.

When it was his turn, Kevin took his position before the jury. He was a man of modest build but in possession of a voice three times his size. As soon as he opened his mouth, he had the jury's attention securely in his grasp.

"First of all, let me tell you what this case is not about. It is absolutely not a referendum on gay rights. During voir dire, I didn't ask any of you where you stood on the issue and, frankly, I don't care. It's not relevant. Whether you support gay people, tolerate them, or despise them, it doesn't change one essential fact—my clients did not commit this crime."

"Death to fascists!" someone shouted from the back of the gallery.

Judge Lacayo sprang into action. "I warned you I would not tolerate any inappropriate behavior. Bailiff!"

Kevin hoped Boxer would take the call—he knew how to handle minor-league troublemakers—but instead another bailiff, one he didn't recognize, stepped forward. "Yes, Your Honor?"

"Remove the offending person from the courtroom. Immediately."

"Yes, sir." He stepped up to the rail separating the gallery from the front . . . and removed his gun from his holster.

"Bailiff? What are you doing?"

"Removing the offending person." He swung his gun around to the defendants' table. "This is for Tony."

The gun fired. Blood splattered out of Brett Mathers's neck.

Someone screamed. Half the gallery rose to its feet; the other half dropped to the floor. Only a few remained stunned and frozen in place.

"You two work so well together," the man with the gun said to the remaining defendant. "Don't want to break up the team."

Johnny Christensen wanted to run, but there was nowhere to go. The woman sitting behind him cried out, "No! Please!"

Kevin crawled under the table while the shooter's attention was focused on Christensen. He knew he was supposed to zealously defend his client, but surely that didn't include serving as a human shield. And yet something told him that he had to act. The influence wasn't so much the law professors at Northwestern as it was the nuns at St. Gregory's, but he knew he was the closest, the one best positioned to do something. And he knew that if he didn't, this trial would turn into a bloodbath.

Without another thought, Kevin bolted toward the assailant. He tried to tackle the man, but was just a beat too late. The gun fired.

Kevin clutched his chest, feeling the blood spewing forth. It took a moment for the pain to register, but when it did, it was crippling. He cried out, embarrassed at himself but nonetheless helpless to stop it. Through teary eyes he saw the shooter hovering above him, the gun aimed at his head.

He heard a commotion at the rear, and a millisecond later, the voices of security officers on the move. They knocked the assailant to the ground and kicked away the gun. He struggled, but they soon had him under control. They cuffed his hands behind his back, then jerked him to his feet.

"Say no to hate!" the man screamed, as the officers jerked him toward the doors. "Say no to hate!"

Kevin heard someone talking into a cell phone. "Get an ambulance! Two men down in Courtroom Ten."

Judge Lacayo, back in his seat, pounded his gavel without effect. The courtroom was in turmoil and was likely to remain so for some time.

A medic rushed forward, first examing Brett Mathers, then Kevin. "We need to get you to a hospital as soon as possible."

The security guards fought the chaotic crowd, hauling their captive out of the courtroom. He did not resist. "For you, Tony," he said quietly, as they dragged him away. "And Matthew. And Claudia. And all the others."

CHAPTER

2

Sapulpa, Oklahoma
Ten miles west of Tulsa

"You heard what happened?"

"Oh yeah."

"Doesn't this change everything?"

"It does."

"What are we going to do about it?"

Manny turned off his four-bit drill and lifted his safety visor. He wished his visitor wouldn't come here. Spoiled the mood. He got enough of the dirty and seedy and ugly elsewhere. This was where he came to get away from it all. He didn't like it when "it all" came here.

This had always been his favorite room of his tiny house. Technically, it wasn't even a room of the house— it was the garage. But he'd decked it out like a first-class workshop. He had everything he needed to do his carpentry work and then some.

"What are you making?" his visitor asked.

"Oh, bookshelves." Manny turned the drill back on and finished making two more round bolt holes on the side of a thick piece of oak. "I sell 'em at the flea market over at the fairgrounds. Don't make that much, but it gives me somethin' to do. Something that doesn't involve pushin' or stealin' or snatchin'. And it gets me a little scratch. Just to tide me over till . . . you know."

"You should complain. You've cleared more than anybody."

"It ain't enough."

"It never is."

The visitor approached Manny's work-in-progress and ran a hand over the smooth-sanded wood. "I had no idea you were so talented. At anything legal."

"I love workin' with wood. Messin' around with my tools. It's the best part of my life."

"A man should have a hobby."

"Yeah."

They fell silent.

"What do you think we should do about it?" the visitor asked, finally.

"Well, I don't know exactly. Maybe nothin'. With one defendant down and the defense attorney in the hospital, there's no chance in hell the jury won't convict the other guy. Once they do that, this whole business goes away."

"Maybe."

"Don't you agree?"

The visitor paused. "I can still see a few loose ends."

"I think we're in the clear. In fact, I was wonderin' if maybe—"

"No chance."

"Aw, just—"

"I said no."

Manny hated that. The attitude, the arrogance. He'd been plying these trades for a long time. He knew what he was doing, and he didn't need some hawk looking over his shoulder, bossing him around like he was some kind of toddler. And the pressure just kept coming. Haunting his days and nights. He'd had all of it he could take. As soon as the transfer was complete, he'd have a little talk with this visitor of his. Like maybe a talk involving a snub-nosed .38.

"Something bothering you, Manny?"

"I been kinda worried about this whole thing. I guess you know that."

"Still having the nightmares?"

"Big time. Look, no matter what happens in court, I gotta blow the country. It's not safe for me here. You gotta come across with more money."

"You've already had more than anyone."

"If I can't get more, you know what I'll be forced to do."

"That would be bad. You worry me, my friend. Why don't you come up north and join the rest of us?"

"I prefer the warmer climate."

"Yes. That's what worries me."

"Now, if you could just speed up the transfer—"

"Not a chance."

"Are you sure? 'Cause I—" He threw the drill down on his workbench. "I gotta live, you know? And I'm tired of begging. I can't go on forever . . . like I have been."

"Meaning what?"

"Meaning maybe I need to have me a chat with someone right now."

The visitor grabbed his arm and clamped the bench-top vise around it, hard, then locked it.

"Hey! What the hell is this?"

"Think of it as therapy. You have dangerous information locked up in that head of yours, Manny. I'm going to help you forget."

Manny twisted his arm around, trying unsuccessfully to get free. "What are you talking about?"

"You've outlived your usefulness. You've become a risk. An unacceptable one."

"Hey—whoa now—wait a minute! Let's talk about this."

"We've talked long enough."

"If you think you can cut me out now, after I—"

All at once, Manny felt the wind literally choked out

of his throat. His visitor had pushed him backward, sprawled across the workbench, then pinned his neck down. The grip on his throat was even tighter than the vise.

"Just—wait!" he managed to choke out. "Let's . . . talk about this! What do you think you're doing?"

"Erasing those unpleasant memories." With his free hand, the visitor picked up the electric drill—and turned it on.

Beads of sweat broke out on Manny's forehead. He thrashed back and forth, but was unable to move. "What the hell are you going to do with that?"

"A little surgical procedure, I think." The visitor smiled. "Amateur lobotomy."

"You must be kiddin'! You can't—"

"I'm afraid I can." The sound of the whirring drill in Manny's ear was deafening—and terrifying. Slowly, the bit approached Manny's temple. "Here's the best part, though. I won't send you a bill. You won't have to worry about whether your medical insurance will cover it."

"Look! I'm sorry! I was just—I don't know—I just—" Manny thrashed frantically, but he was unable to get free. "Forget everything I said!"

"I wish I could. But it's you who will know the bliss of forgetfulness." The visitor pressed the tip of the drill against his skull. "Good night, Manny. Pleasant dreams."

CHAPTER
3

"COME ON. COME clean."

"I don't know what you're talking about."

"You do."

"I don't."

"Christina, I insist on knowing what's going on."

"If I had anything to tell you, Jones, I would already have done so."

Jones leaned over his desk in the front lobby of Kincaid & McCall. "I wasn't born yesterday, Christina."

"You're imagining it."

"Baloney. I saw the two of you, stuttering and coughing and getting all flush-faced. What's the big secret?"

"There's no secret."

"Then why did you see Ben last night?"

"We told you already. We had a . . . thing."

"There was no Inns of Court meeting. I checked."

"It was . . . that other thing."

"You two have been seeing a lot of each other."

"What else is new? We've worked together since he opened this office."

"Don't give me that. This is something different."

"Honestly, Jones, I don't have time for this nonsense. Shouldn't you be dunning debtors or something? Because I—"

"You're dating, aren't you?"

Christina froze. It took her more than a moment to recover. "Now you really are being ridiculous."

He threw down his pencil. "I knew it! I told Paula last night, 'Something weird is going down between those two.'"

"Jones, you're being silly—"

"How long?"

Christina took a deep breath, then slowly released it. "About three months."

"I knew it!" He pushed away from his desk. "And when were you planning to tell us?"

Her eyes moved skyward. "When there was something to tell?"

"Did you think this doesn't concern me?"

"Well, frankly—"

"The two lawyers in the office start getting all snoochy-gooches with each other? It's a recipe for disaster!"

"I think you're exaggerating—"

"How can I effectively administrate this office when you two are behaving like this? How do I know what's going on when you both stay in the office late working? Maybe you're prepping for trial, or maybe you're examining each other's briefs."

"Jones!"

"And what happens if you split up? What if you do a 'hell hath no fury' turn? Who has to leave the office? Who gets custody of Loving?"

"Jones! Calm down!" She checked the hallway outside Ben's office. His door was closed. "It's not that big a deal. I promise you."

"How can it not be that big a deal?"

"It's just . . . not . . . anything that . . ." She waved her hands in the air. ". . . because . . . nothing happens."

He paused. "Nothing?"

She shrugged. "Not so's you'd notice."

"Then what were you—"

"We played Scrabble."

He blinked. "You . . ."

"You heard me. That's all we ever do."

"But—" He ran his hand through his hair. "You were apologizing for last night."

"I laid a phony blank on him. Turned a *U* tile over and played it as a blank. Bingoed for fifty bonus points. Sneaky, I know, but the rules permit it, and I was behind, and . . . I hate to lose."

Jones stared at her. "So this big romance—"

"Scrabble."

"And there's been no—" He tilted his head back and forth.

"None."

"Not even—"

"Not even a good-night kiss, if you must know."

"How can you tell you're dating?"

She frowned. "I'm optimistic."

A FEW MINUTES later, the lobby doors opened, and a tall, attractive woman who appeared to be in her thirties entered. Christina was certain she'd seen the woman before, although she couldn't immediately place her.

The woman hesitated just outside Jones's desk. "Excuse me. Is this the law office of Ben Kincaid?"

Christina rose to her feet. "Yes. This is Kincaid *and* McCall."

"Wonderful." She clutched her purse with both hands. She seemed anxious about something. "I'm Ellen Christensen."

"That's it," Christina said. "I've seen you in the courtroom. I was watching on the television when . . . well . . ."

"Yes. Of course."

"That must have been terrifying."

"It was," she said, but Christina thought she seemed remarkably well composed.

"How is your son?"

"He's recovering. It's a trauma, seeing your best friend

shot just inches away from you. Not that the press has shown him the least bit of sympathy."

"No," Christina said. "I suppose not."

"I just thank God my Johnny wasn't killed." She was a thin woman, but her assured carriage gave her a bearing that exceeded her physical girth. She was actually much more attractive than she had appeared on television; her well-defined features had been blurred by the camera. "He's the one that psychopath from the gay rights group wanted, you know. Kevin Mahoney just got in the way."

Jones cleared his throat. "What brings you all the way from Chicago, ma'am? Is there some way we can help you?"

"I'm sure you've guessed why I'm here. Kevin Mahoney is stable, but he can't possibly try a case in his current condition, and the court insists on plowing ahead with this travesty. All the newscasters and politicians are bearing down, of course. Demanding swift justice. Meaning a hanging, the sooner the better."

Christina tried to steer her back on track. "So you're here . . ."

"To ask Ben Kincaid to be Kevin's replacement."

She stared at the woman, blank-faced. "You want Ben to take over your son's defense?"

"Yes, I do." She seemed confused. "Is there a problem? I've heard he's one of the top defense attorneys." She paused. "Which doesn't surprise me."

"No, no—there's no problem. You heard right."

"I know he doesn't normally work in Chicago—"

"That's not a problem. We can ally with a local lawyer. Get admitted to the Illinois bar *pro hac vice.*"

"I only hope he can fit it into his schedule."

"I can guarantee you he'll fit it into his schedule," Christina replied.

"That's wonderful. Ms. McCall, my son is innocent of

murder. I know that's not what you read in the papers. But it's true. I'm a bit pressed for cash at the moment— I took out a second mortgage just to pay Kevin—but if I can sell some of my jewelry, I might be able to put together a retainer. Do you really think Ben will take the case?"

Ben, Christina noted. Not Mr. Kincaid. Ben.

Jones appeared so excited he could hardly contain himself. "Well, let's consider the facts. The defendant is painfully unpopular and has been crucified in the press. The evidence is hopelessly stacked against him. The press is demanding a conviction. The case is impossible and unwinnable. And you—pardon me for saying so— don't have any money. Will Ben take your case?" He extended his hand. "I'd say it's a sure thing."

"If there's a problem . . ."

"Not at all," Jones added hastily. "Even if this case doesn't make Ben rich, it's enormously high profile. This is exactly what he needs. The preliminary work has already been done, so the expenses can't be too great. I'm all for it."

"Wonderful. Then if I could just speak to him."

"It's really not necessary," Christina interjected. "I'm his partner, and I know his schedule. He'll jump at this."

"That is splendid." She drew her purse in closer, holding it with both hands. "But I still think it might be best if I spoke to him . . ."

"I'll see if I can get him. But I'm telling you, it's a lead-pipe—"

The click of the office door down the hallway made them all pivot. Ben emerged from his office, necktie loose around his neck, and headed in the opposite direction, toward the kitchen.

"Ben!"

He turned, took one look—then stopped dead in his tracks.

"Ben, this is Ellen Christensen."

He stared a long time before answering. "I know who she is."

"Ben," Jones said, grinning from ear to ear, "she wants you to take over her son's defense. Can you believe—"

"No," he said succinctly. He turned back toward his office.

"Ben," Christina said quickly, "did you understand? She wants you to—"

"I'm afraid I'm not available." And he closed the door behind him.

HALF AN HOUR later, Christina entered Ben's office without knocking. "Ben, I want to talk to you."

"Look, if it's about that phony blank—"

"It's about Ellen Christensen's son. She says he's innocent."

"She's his mother."

She took the chair opposite his desk and scooted it up close. "I've been talking to her, Ben. She sounds pretty convincing. Shouldn't you at least meet with her?"

Ben continued reading his brief. "No."

"Could you please explain why not?"

"I don't have to justify my decisions."

"I'm not saying you have to. I'm asking if you will."

"Christina . . ." He leaned back and propped his feet up on his desk. "Could you for once please just leave it alone?"

"No, Ben, I can't. Think what that poor woman has been through these past few months—hearing the accusations against her son, mounting his defense on a limited income. She's a widow."

"I know."

Christina's brow furrowed. "Ben, this woman needs our help."

"There are lots of lawyers in Chicago. Getting one from Tulsa is crazy."

"I agree, but she's determined to have our firm represent her son." She leaned across his desk. "So why don't we give her what she wants?"

"Christina, I don't want to take this case. Let me be crystal clear: I *refuse* to take this case. Understand?"

She stood, obviously hurt in more ways than she could count. "No, Ben. I don't understand at all." She closed the door behind her.

IT WAS LONG past closing time, Ben realized, glancing at his watch. Time to go home? Safe to go home?

He pushed himself out of his chair and grabbed his coat. Maybe he should've just told Christina. It would've been simpler. But so much time had passed. He'd known Christina so long, he would've felt like a fool. She would've tried to make him think rationally. And he didn't want to think rationally. There was nothing rational about this.

Just as he approached his office door, he heard movement on the other side.

Christina was standing there.

"I'm leaving now," she said.

"I thought you'd already left."

"No." She looked one way, then the other. "Look, I don't think I'll be able to come over tonight."

"Sure."

"In fact . . . well, anyway." She shook her head. "This is stupid."

She started to turn away. Ben reached out and took her arm, holding her back. "Has Mrs. Christensen left?"

She looked at him coldly. "A long time ago."

"She'll find another lawyer, Christina. I promise you."

"She didn't want just anyone. She wanted the best."

"She'll have people lining up to take her case."

Christina shook her arm loose. "No, she won't."

"She will. I promise."

"She won't." She grabbed her overcoat off the hall rack and started for the door. "She doesn't need anyone else, Ben. I took the case."

CHAPTER
4

JOURNAL OF TONY BAROVICK

I ALWAYS KNEW I was gay. Always. As far back as I can remember, I knew I wasn't like the other kids. Maybe everyone feels that way when they're young, but with me it was something more, something profound. A real sense of distinction. And of danger. Because I knew what would happen if the other kids at Bradley Middle School ever got a whiff of my secret.

I'm probably not the only scrawny kid who didn't love PE class, but for me, the challenge was a lot greater than seeing if I could finish twenty-five sit-ups. Every single day we went through the same ritual—changing clothes, sweating, showering. The same exotic, erotic, intoxicating, and oh, so perilous routine. I practiced deep breathing, distracted myself, thought about someone ugly, whatever it took to make sure I didn't have a physical reaction that would betray my secret. At the same time, I couldn't help sneaking a peek every now and again. It was like throwing a straight fourteen-year-old into a bordello; the girls might not be all that great to look at, but they were girls, just the same.

Of course, all the boys I ran around with at that age were constantly talking about homosexuality. Looking back, it was such an obsession I can't help but wonder if I was the only kid on the block nursing a secret. All the talk was derogatory and hateful, to be sure, but it had a frequency that exceeded even nasty girl talk. You'd constantly hear someone shout, "Fag!" when someone did something wrong. "Back off, you fairy!" if there was an accidental touching. "Queer as a three-dollar bill!" for any nerds who weren't part of our particular nerd pack. At that age, most of the guys had no real understanding of homosexuality or even what these epithets implied—they were just words. That would change, of course. In time, I would become all too familiar with the venom that people both young and old could have for those of us with a sexual preference different from their own.

Even before I knew what being categorized as gay could do to you, I was going out of my way to make sure I wasn't. As a teenager, I observed and copied all the standard hetero moves. I asked girls to the school dances, I made suggestive remarks, I even took them out back and groped them like everyone expected, shoving my tongue down their throats and fumbling stupidly with the clasps of their bra. Even took a girl to the senior prom. I asked her, then I asked a friend who I suspected might be similarly inclined to double-date with us. Never mind that I was more interested in him than my date. We became a socially acceptable foursome. We bought the corsages, danced the slow dances, even went parking afterward. I was in the backseat going through the usual charade—with her skirt hiked up and her bra dangling around her neck—when a cop shined his flashlight through the window. I was secretly relieved, but damned if I was going to let anyone know it. "Did you see the way that pervert cop stared at us?" I remember grousing, as we drove our dates home. "He's probably some kind of faggot."

It would be a good long time before I stopped talking like that, even longer before I stopped thinking of myself in those terms. That may seem stupid to you, dear diary. After all, we don't live in the eighteenth century. But fear can be a powerful motivator. And the fear of being different is the greatest of them all. In the face of abject hate, even the most stalwart may become cowards.

CHAPTER
5

SERGEANT BAXTER FOUND her partner hunched over his desk, as usual. It was piled sky-high with paper, files, books, and about a week's worth of coffee cups. With his furrowed brow and intense eyes, he brought to mind those comics where Snoopy pretends to be a vulture.

"Still at it?"

Mike grunted.

"Metzger case?"

"Mmmm."

"Any new leads?"

"Nnnnnnn."

Well, this conversation wasn't getting her anywhere. Maybe she shouldn't barge in and start talking when he was obviously working, but it was hard to restrain herself. After the remodel five years ago, everyone on the floor worked in cubicles with no doors, no windows, and no ceilings, so privacy was hard to come by. "Morelli, I know you go for that brooding monosyllabic thing, and you do that somber Heathcliff look better than anyone I know, but if I'm going to be your partner, you're going to have to open up more."

He lowered his pencil. "You used a conditional clause."

"Excuse me?"

"You should have used the subordinate: Since I'm going to be your partner, you're going to have to open up more."

"Don't English major me, Morelli."

"But instead, you said *if*. As if there was some question about it." He looked up. "Is there?"

At least now she had his attention. "Why? Do you want there to be?"

"You tell me."

"I thought it was a done deal. We told Chief Blackwell we could work together."

"True enough. Just wanted to make sure you hadn't had a change of heart."

"Why? Have you?"

"I asked you first."

She crinkled her nose in disgust. It seemed as if every time she found herself almost liking him, he did something to remind her that she didn't. Sure, she was grateful; coming to Tulsa after that fiasco in Oklahoma City had salvaged her career. And after he got over his initial opposition—well, actually, it had lasted about a month—Mike had been quite kind to her. But she never forgot what a total pain in the butt he was to work with. "Look, I know obsession is your middle name and all that, but I think you need to give this Metzger case a rest."

"Never."

"It would be different if you were getting somewhere, but—"

"I let those murderers slip right between my fingers."

"It wasn't your fault."

"Whether it was or wasn't, it should've been my collar."

"No cop nabs every perp. It's part of the game. Don't ruin your life with this."

"This *is* my life." He returned his attention to his desk.

And if that was the way he wanted it, why not leave him to it? she asked herself, not for the first time. No skin off her nose, right? It's not as if they were dating. It was just a working relationship, pure and simple. Okay, there had been that one kiss. One and a half, if you counted the near miss in his office. But that had been an accident. Happened months ago, and he hadn't shown any interest since. They were partners, that was all. It was a professional relationship, and it would be best for all concerned if it stayed that way. Let him bust a gut over that kidnapping case.

Except that she couldn't.

"Been talking to Tomlinson," she said. "He told me you get like this."

"Did he now?"

"Told me about the Kindergarten Killer case. Said you were like a drooling Looney Tune during that one."

"He would know."

"And then there was the poisoned water case with the Sick Murder Method of the Month Club guy."

"You and Tomlinson must've had a long chat."

"I brought Starbucks." It had been a good talk. She knew how to bring people out. When she was growing up with her mom in Longdale—really more an expanded trailer park than a town—they'd had lots of time to talk. No money, but loads of chitchat. Her mother may not have been college educated, but she was quite the philosopher, in her own homespun way. Baxter's mama had taught her that she could do anything she wanted to do, could be anyone she wanted to be. Those had become the watchwords of her life. If her mama were alive, she'd be proud to see that the daughter of a small town beauty shop stylist had become a homicide detective. She'd done all right for herself, no doubt about it. Now if she could just get over this habit of falling for men she worked with—another legacy of her mother, come to think of it—her life would be perfect.

She peered at Mike through the tall stacks of books on his desk. He was working hard at giving the appearance of paying no attention to her. But she noticed he hadn't turned a page since she came into his office. "The point is Tomlinson says you always become intense and driven and monomaniacal when you've got an unsolved case. And that isn't healthy."

"It isn't?"

"No."

"Why not?"

"Just isn't."

"Gets the job done."

"Occasionally. But some cases can't be solved, you dunderhead. Ever."

Mike pursed his lips. "Are you suggesting this is one of them?"

"It has been a while since we had a lead."

"That doesn't mean anything."

"Of course it does. Unless you're a dunderhead."

"You know, Baxter, I always enjoy sparring with you. Really I do. But I am somewhat busy at the moment. Don't you have any work that needs your attention?"

"As a matter of fact, *we* do." She tossed a newly minted manila file on top of his littered desk. "Blackwell just sent this over. As of this moment, you're officially off the Metzger case. And on this one."

Mike frowned, fingered the edge of the file. "Where are we going?"

"Sapulpa, I'm afraid. I know you were probably hoping for Paris."

"What's the case about?"

Baxter pulled a face. "Do the words *power drill* mean anything to you?"

* * *

"THAT'S THE MOST inhumane killing I've heard about in my entire career. And I've seen some pretty damn bad ones."

Mike drove crosstown while Baxter read him the salient details of the murder. It would've been more sensible for him to read the file himself, but that would have required Baxter to drive, and only he drove his Trans Am. No exceptions.

This was the part of the job Mike hated most. After the crime scene—that was the fun part. Then it was all Sherlock Holmes logic and Popeye Doyle browbeating and all the other good stuff. But the crime scene itself! Well, the fact that he still got sick every time he saw a corpse—after seeing more than three dozen of them—told the whole story.

"Consider yourself lucky you can't see the pictures," Baxter said.

True, but he was about to visit the crime scene. And even if the coroner had preceded him, there was bound to be a mess. Something like this would take days to clean up. "Any likely suspects?"

"They don't even know who the victim was."

Mike swerved into the fast lane behind a Jag coupe. "This SOB is speeding." He reached into the back for his siren.

"Morelli. We're on our way to a homicide."

"But he's speeding!"

"Focus, Detective. Leave it to the traffic cops. We have pressing business."

He dropped the siren. "Spoilsport."

"This reminds me . . ." Her eyes drifted toward the passenger side window. "There's something I'd like to discuss."

Uh-oh. In Mike's experience, in a normal conversation, if people wanted to discuss something, they just did. When someone prefaced it by saying they wanted to discuss something, that was a sure sign of trouble. "Do we have to?"

"If we're going to work together." She corrected herself. "*Since* we're going to work together."

He sighed. He liked Baxter—really, he did. Sure, the first days had been rocky, but they'd come to a mutual understanding. Even more than that, you might say. But her penchant for overanalyzing everything and talking it to death made him crazy. He liked to think of himself as a sensitive soul, but he couldn't bear these constant exercises in personal relations mediation. "If we must."

"I think we need to establish some rules."

"We've already had this conversation, remember, Sergeant? On your first day. You gave me your rules. I remember it distinctly. 'No grabass in the patrol car.' "

"Well, I thought I should raise the issue again. After . . . you know. What happened."

He didn't need a more detailed reference. He knew what she was talking about. The Grand Lake stakeout. Late at night, in his car. Lots of coffee, nothing to do. They'd started talking, warming up to each other, for the first time. And the next thing he knew, their lips were touching.

Not that he minded exactly. Kate Baxter was a fine-looking woman, even if she was a pain in the ass as a partner. He went for that honey blond hair in a big way. But it did complicate the working relationship.

Baxter cleared her throat. "We need an agreement. That it won't happen again."

"We do? All right. We do."

"I'm not saying it was unpleasant. My lips went willingly. But we have to keep our heads clear. Unmuddled."

"Of course."

"There's no telling what Blackwell would do if he found out. Probably suspend us on the spot."

"Quite possible."

"But most important—I can't afford to let the word

get out about this. Not after what happened in Oklahoma City."

Mike had no problem placing that reference, either. She'd had an inopportune affair with the OKC chief of police—a man much older than she was and married to boot—and once it was known in the department, she was hopelessly compromised. Not to mention the butt of scurrilous jokes and sexist remarks.

"I understand entirely," Mike said. "So what are you thinking? We should ask Blackwell to split us up?"

"I'm just thinking there can't be any more smooching. Can you handle that?"

Sure, he thought. I'd rather skip ahead to third base anyway. "Not a problem." He kept his eyes dead ahead.

"Good. Well, I just thought we needed to get that established."

"Right you were." He turned the wheel hard to the left. "Break out the barf bags. We've arrived."

WHEN MIKE OPENED the door to the toolshed behind the house, he uncovered a grisly tableau that defied his powers of description. He had never seen anything like this before. And he'd seen a lot of homicide in his time.

After an initial glance, he excused himself, stepped outside, covered his mouth with a handkerchief, and did his level best to keep from being sick. When he returned, Baxter had already begun gathering some preliminary information. She seemed remarkably undisturbed by the scene around her. In fact—was he imagining it?—there was a tiny smirk on her face.

"You okay?" she asked.

"No, I'm not okay. If anybody can see this and be okay, they've got serious problems."

"I can cover if you want to wait outside."

"Thank you, Sergeant, but I think I'll do my job myself, just the same."

What had he expected anyway? A power drill inserted into the cranium—no way that was going to create a pretty picture. Like a firecracker tossed inside a jack-o'-lantern. Now the shattered shell lay at his feet, and the seeds and stuffing covered the walls.

Mike closed his eyes. "Philip Larkin was right. 'Man hands on misery to man / It deepens like a coastal shelf.' "

"God, not with the poetry again. I feel like I'm going to hurl as it is. Don't push me over the edge."

Happily, Mike didn't hear her. His eyes were fixed and all his other senses were focused on the tiny toolshed that surrounded him.

"Are you doing something?" Baxter asked, after enduring a minute or so of this.

"I'm listening."

"To what?"

"The room."

"Oh, cool. I love this part."

He stood in one place by the door, absorbing everything around him. "The best way to get a grip on what happened. Even better than forensics. Open your eyes and ears and drink it all in."

"Sure. So what are you drinking?"

Mike paused before answering, giving every syllable slow and deliberate emphasis. "This . . . is the victim's toolshed."

"That much I got."

"He loved this place. It was his favorite room. His retreat." Mike moved through the small space. "He came here to be alone. For peace of mind. To calm himself." Mike smiled. "He knew his killer."

"I'm glad to hear it wasn't a random drilling."

"It had to be someone he knew well." He paused a moment, lost in thought. "The killer let himself in, came back here, and found the guy working on his shelves."

"So it was a close friend."

"I doubt it."

Baxter frowned, arms akimbo. "You've lost me."

"I don't think it was a friend. I don't think it was someone he wanted to see at all."

"Given how it turned out, I don't blame him."

"Something bad was going on. Something that got him killed."

"And the room told you all this?"

"Yup." Mike did a small pirouette in the center of the room. "Do you smell anything?"

"Are you kidding? Someone was killed in here."

"Something else. Musk, I think."

"Musk?"

"Probably a cologne or aftershave. And if I can still smell it, he must've put it on pretty heavy."

"Who? The victim, or the killer?"

"That would be a good thing to know."

Baxter rolled her eyes. "Great. Musk. Now we've got a lead."

"Did anyone see anything? Hear anything?"

"We've got uniforms blanketing the neighborhood. So far they haven't turned up anything."

"The killer used a power tool, for God's sake. Someone must've heard something."

"Yes, but it wouldn't sound like a murder. More like someone . . . mowing their lawn. Nothing to get alarmed about."

Mike stood to one side and watched the crime scene technicians go about their work. He always tried to give them a clear field; he knew they wouldn't tolerate interference, not even from a senior homicide detective. There was a time when these guys considered themselves ancillary technicians, subordinate to the detectives, and behaved accordingly. Then that TV show—*CSI*—became a hit. Now they all thought Mike worked for them.

Which was not a problem for Mike. They had the hard job, as far as he was concerned—the videographers, the hair and fiber team, the prints man, the coroner. The guys in coveralls crawling around on their hands and knees looking for trace evidence. Their work paid off. More often than not, if a case didn't have an obvious suspect, it was forensic evidence that would lead him to one.

"Check his wallet?" Mike asked.

"What do you take me for? He didn't have one."

"No ID at all?"

"None. This house was being rented to a Philip Norton, but that appears to be a pseudonym."

"Any photos inside the house? Any photos of *him*?"

" 'Fraid not."

Naturally. That would've been too helpful. The victim's head was such a mess they couldn't possibly tell what he looked like now. So they had no face and no name. Great.

"Anything of interest in the house?"

"The place has been trashed. Still, I managed to find a noteworthy item or two."

"Wanna give me a hint?"

"Packed suitcase in the bedroom. Apparently the poor guy thought he was going somewhere."

Mike grunted. "He was right about that. He had a one-way ticket to 'the undiscovered country from whose bourn / no traveler returns.' "

"Morelli, if you keep going with the poetry, I might have to use a power tool myself."

"Any idea where he was headed?"

"North."

"Could you be more specific?"

"He didn't leave behind a bus ticket, Morelli. But I did notice that he was packing sweaters. So he wasn't hanging around here and he wasn't headed for Mexico."

Mike nodded. "What else was in the house?"

"Fifty thousand dollars in cash."

Mike did a double take. "Fifty thousand?"

"You got it, tiger. Hidden under a floorboard. Whoever tore the house apart never found it."

He pivoted and reluctantly glanced again at the mess on the toolshed floor. "Our poor victim must've pulled some sort of heist."

"Looks that way. I'll start checking the wire reports. See if I can figure out what he did."

"I don't know what to think. But it's very strange. Get some serial numbers off that money and run it past the FBI. They might be able to help you figure out where it came from." Mike took another long look at the toolshed. He wouldn't mind having a place like this of his own one day. Except not splattered with blood and brain matter. "Anything else?"

"Yeah—this." Baxter produced what appeared to be a photocopy of a newspaper article placed inside a clear plastic evidence bag. "Found this in the end table by the bed."

Mike scanned the headline. FBI PROBES PARTY DRUG RING. He couldn't tell what paper it had come from.

"Why was this of such interest that he made a copy?" she asked.

"Darn good question. Wish I knew the answer. But photocopies can yield information beyond the mere text."

"You think there's a connection between the murder and illegal drugs?"

"I don't know. God, I hope not." He looked one more time around the shed, then passed through the door. " 'And our little life is rounded by a sleep.' "

Baxter followed him. "Robert Frost?"

Mike shook his head. "Shakespeare. Again."

"He was a cheery soul. Aren't there any poets who are pleasant to read?"

Mike considered a moment. "You might go for Theodore Geisel."

"Really?"

"Possible."

"If I learned to spout poetry like you do, you think we'd get along better?"

"Possible."

"And you'd stop treating me like your ignorant secretary?"

"Possible."

"And you'd let me drive the Trans Am?"

"Not a chance."

CHAPTER
6

South Side of Chicago
near Jackson Park

CHARLIE THE CHICKEN was running scared.

That was why he blew town. That was why he was now back, albeit functioning under a different professional name. That was why he had buzzed his hair off, ditched his glasses, changed his look. He wasn't working the same neighborhoods and he hadn't haunted the old haunts. Hadn't gone anywhere near Remote Control. In short, he had burned all his bridges and forsaken all traces of his former existence.

And none of it would be enough.

Charlie recounted the change in his pocket. This was getting ridiculous. He couldn't make the pathetic fifty-dollar-a-week rent for this hellhole of a room in a part of Kenwood that urban renewal never touched. He couldn't even feed himself. He was a prisoner, just as much as if he were behind bars, except that behind bars he'd be a lot safer and better fed than he was out here. Safe or not, he had no choice. He was going to have to get out. Go to work. Earn some scratch.

But he had to be careful, too. Because his old friend, the one he had seen on that dark and rainy night, would be looking for him. He was sure of it.

He'd followed the case in the newspapers, of course. Who hadn't? Every dramatic development. So far, no one had a clue what had really happened. His friend had to be feeling fairly secure right about now. Impervious. About the only thing that could possibly go wrong would be if Charlie the Chicken opened his big mouth.

He wondered if that was what had happened to Manny. That hick had never had the sense God gave a carrot. Probably swapping testosterone with their mutual friend—until it went too far. And then—Charlie winced just to think about what had happened to the stupid slob. And to realize how easily it could happen to him. The smartest thing he could do was stay out of the way. Way far out of the way. Even if that meant there would be no transfer. He couldn't give their friend a chance at him.

If there was to be no transfer, then tomorrow he would have to start the job hunt. He had no choice. Back to the wonderful world of sex, oral and anal, licking and spitting, fancy French terms for things kids whispered about on playgrounds. Bathroom stalls. Adult parlors. Society cotillions. It's a wonderful life.

He wondered if he would ever be safe. When the trial restarted, that would help. A little. But would it be enough? Wouldn't his friend still be concerned about the havoc that could be wrought by skinny, hair-gelled, dimple-chinned Charlie the Chicken?

Would he ever be safe?

Somehow, he didn't think this was the life his parents had mapped out for him, back when they gave him birth and raised him in the Windy City's Cabrini-Green housing project. Good Catholic upbringing, decent schools. They'd thought he was going to grow up to be a doctor. Well, they'd missed that mark by a hell of a distance, hadn't they?

What had happened to him? He had always been rebellious, true, but this life was something else again. He'd always been fascinated by sex, too—but what teenage boy wasn't? Most of them didn't end up like him, doing the things he did. He couldn't even blame drugs or booze, like most of those in his line. He'd never been attached to either of them. Not an addictive personality. So what explanation did that leave? Just plain stupid?

His life was one big screwup, and he knew it. And it was about to be damned short, if he didn't do something to straighten himself out. So what was it going to be?

One day at a time, as the AA crowd liked to say. First work. Then money. Then food. Then flight. And keep the fear under lock and key.

Except the fear was already with him. Always with him. Time had not dulled its edge. And, quite possibly, nothing could.

Because a person capable of doing what had happened to Manny was capable of anything. Absolutely anything. At any time. To anyone.

Even Charlie the Chicken.

CHAPTER

7

**Cook County Detention Center
County Jail
26th and California Avenue**

CHRISTINA HATED THIS part of her job. She didn't know why, exactly. Objectively speaking, it wasn't that difficult. Didn't require much preparation. Didn't depend on quick reflexes, listening skills, or a mnemonic aptitude for arcane case law. Bottom line, all she had to do was show up and take notes.

So why did she hate it so much?

She stared at her reflection in the acrylic panel. Well, for starters, jails smelled. Always. Apparently it was a universal constant; even with its big-city budget, this Chicago joint was no better than the one she was accustomed to back in Tulsa. Possibly worse. The man at the front desk assured her that they scrubbed the place down regularly, but it didn't kill the stench. And she didn't like the paint, or the furnishings or, for that matter, most of the inhabitants.

But that wasn't the worst of it. The worst was seeing all these men restrained, locked up, trapped behind bars. The older she got, the more she thought she might be claustrophobic. Or maybe it wasn't a phobia. Maybe it was memory. She'd been locked up once, and it just about killed her. She never wanted to go through that again.

And she thought Ben understood that, even though they had never directly discussed it, which was why he always handled these lockup interviews and brought her along only if it was absolutely necessary. Except now, since he inexplicably refused to have anything to do with this case. What was up with that, anyway? It was so unlike Ben. She'd worked with him all these years; she'd never once seen him back away from someone who needed help, much less someone particularly asking for his help.

Jones thought maybe Ben wanted no part of it because the accused was obviously homophobic, violent, and thoroughly twisted. The press had crucified him; they would likely do the same to his lawyer. But that didn't ring true. Ben had agreed to represent an avowed member of a white racist militia group, for God's sake, not to mention a host of other undesirables. After all that, he's going to turn his back on some college kid? It just didn't make sense. There had to be something more.

The door on the other side of the acrylic barrier opened, and a moment later, her new client, Johnny Christensen, was escorted into the room. He was wearing the standard orange coveralls and leg restraints.

She picked up the phone. "Hello. I'm Christina McCall."

He looked strong, like he'd been working out while he was in lockup, which she supposed was possible, since he had little else to do. He had sandy hair and stubble, a strong, chiseled chin. All in all, a very appealing package. If it weren't for the murder thing.

"Yo," he replied, a small smile on his face. He was a flirt; Christina saw that immediately. A kid who was accustomed to using charm and good looks to win people over and get whatever he wanted.

"Your mother has hired me to take your case."

The smile increased. "Great."

"You're the client, though. You make the final decision. If you want someone else, just say so."

"No, this is great. I'm looking forward to working with you." The smile, the teeth, the cocked eyebrow—what a package. He must've had every sorority girl in the city at his fingertips.

"Your previous attorney, Kevin Mahoney, will be working with me as a consultant. But since he hasn't been released from the hospital, you need someone else to take the lead."

"I get that. Cool."

"You understand that the court has denied your motion for a further continuance?"

"What does that mean?"

"It means the trial starts up again Monday morning at nine o'clock sharp. We've chosen not to ask for a mistrial, and the judge hasn't done it *sui sponte*—he's probably concerned about double jeopardy. So it's same place, same judge, same jury. The only change is that you'll be a solo defendant and you'll have me sitting next to you at counsel table."

"Monday. Man." He stretched, flexing his biceps, which sent a ripple through the tattoo on his upper arm. "Are you going to be able to get ready in time?"

"I'll have to be. Fortunately, my predecessor kept good files and careful notes. I've already started devouring them. And Kevin may be feeling puny, but he's also bored to tears. So he won't mind helping. Don't worry, Johnny. I can handle it."

"You're going to try the case alone? By yourself?"

Christina drew in her breath. "I have a partner. But he's been unable to assist so far. Ben Kincaid."

"Kincaid? I've heard that name." He snapped his fingers. "That's who Mom wanted."

Christina leaned forward. "What?"

"Yeah. When I was first arrested. I remember Mom mentioning his name several times."

"Why?"

"I don't know. Ended up hiring that Mahoney guy."

Christina's brow furrowed. Curiouser and curiouser.

"Johnny, I've read Kevin's notes, and I read the transcript of your initial police interrogation, but could you please tell me what happened that night? In your own words."

A lot of the flash went out of his smile as she drew him back to the main subject. "I'd rather not. What do you need to know?"

"Well, I gather you don't deny that you and your friend beat up Tony Barovick."

"Hey, he was coming on to us. Right there in the bar!"

"And you thought that made it okay—"

"Oh, sure, it's easy to criticize after it's all done, but how would you feel if some guy came out of nowhere and started hitting on you?"

Flattered. "You thought he was making sexual advances?"

"And staring at me like I was a piece of meat. Really creeped me out."

Christina inhaled. "Johnny, I gotta be straight with you. The fact that a gay man supposedly came on to you in a singles bar is not going to fly as a defense. The prosecutor will crucify you."

"Well, it's sick!" He threw himself back against his chair. "I mean, why can't those people keep to themselves?"

"I'm sure he—"

"I mean, they always say they just want to be free to live their lives, but the truth is they're always out there promoting their lifestyle."

"He might've thought you were gay."

"I am not gay!" His words boomed out so loudly Christina didn't need the phone receiver to hear him. His face was transformed; all the charm drained out of it. She was suddenly glad there was an acrylic barrier between them. "I am 100 percent straight! Always have been."

"Johnny—"

"I want us to be absolutely clear on this, lady. I am not some goddamn queer."

"Johnny—"

"And I don't want anyone suggesting that I am."

Christina gritted her teeth. "Do you want to die? As in, lethal injection?" He fell silent. "Because that's what's gonna happen if you go into that courtroom talking like this. I guarantee it. The press has been demanding that someone pay for this crime. The DA has lost one defendant. He'll do anything possible to avoid losing you. And if you go up on the stand behaving like this, he won't even have to try hard."

Johnny thrust his hand against his forehead, staring at the ceiling. "Man. This whole mess sucks so bad."

"Yeah." She thumbed through her papers. "So would it be safe to say you were the one who instigated the attack?"

"No way, man. It was Brett—Brett all the way. He was a firecracker."

Christina didn't know if that was supposed to be good or bad. "He was the one who started it?"

"Absolutely. I think he went a little nuts, to tell you the truth. Lost it. I mean, I just thought we'd rough the kid up a little, you know? Teach him a lesson. But that wasn't enough for Brett. He wanted the kid to hurt. He brought the Taser. He insisted on breaking his legs."

"And you just stood there and watched?"

"Kinda. I mean, I'm not saying I did nothing, okay? But it was mostly Brett."

Christina didn't know whether to believe him or to assume this was the usual game of blame-the-dead-guy. Putting the blame on a codefendant was a standard defense maneuver. But would the jury buy it here, when the codefendant has been executed on national television? It might seem too convenient.

"Brett would've never stopped. He wanted to keep at it, even after he did both legs. I was the one who pulled him off, finally got him out of there."

"Now that's something I wanted to ask you about," Christina said. "You say you left Tony in that vacant lot?"

"Right."

"And when you left him, he was still alive?"

"Abso-fuckin'-lutely. He was hurtin', to be sure. But alive."

"Then how did his very dead body end up in your fraternity house?"

"Don't you think if I knew that I would've said something before now?" He thumped his hands against the acrylic. "Somebody else must've come along."

"A third man? Who also had a psychopathic hatred of gay men?"

"Something. Someone who could get the kid back to the frat house."

"But you have no idea who it was?"

"No."

"Or why anyone would do such a thing?"

"No."

Christina puffed out her cheeks. She wished to God Ben were here. He was good at handling the impossible ones. She was considering switching to a wills-and-estates practice. "I've read the M.E.'s report, Johnny. She says what you're describing is impossible. She says Tony was killed in the fraternity house shortly before the body was found."

"I don't care. She's a liar."

"The coroner? Hard to imagine."

"Are you sayin' I'm lying?"

"I'm saying the physical evidence doesn't support the

testimony you're presenting. If you appear before the jury with that, you'll go down in flames."

"It's what happened."

"You're going into that courtroom with multiple strikes against you, Johnny. The city is up in arms. The gay alliance groups are demanding action. The national news agencies are outraged. Basically, everyone wants to see you convicted, and the jury knows it. If they even get a hint that you're lying to them—"

Johnny sprang out of his seat. "Why does everyone care so much about a goddamned fag! It isn't fair!"

"Johnny, calm down."

"Explain it to me, would you? Why some fuckin' queer has more rights than I do?"

Christina eyed the door. If the guard outside heard this, their interview would be terminated but quick. "Johnny, please sit down."

"If we'd beat up some white Christian guy, no one would care. A woman, even. Big deal. But because we took out a pervert, suddenly I'm public enemy number one."

"Johnny, you can't talk like that."

"Why not?" he bellowed. "Don't we have the First Amendment anymore?"

"You're right, Johnny. We do." She banged against the window to get his attention. "So I guess you're going to have to make a choice. Do you want to express your constitutionally protected opinion, or do you want to live?"

Johnny lowered himself back into his seat, glaring.

Where did this kid come from? Christina asked herself. What could give birth to enmity of this magnitude? Normally, she would blame his parents, but Christina had met the guy's mother and she seemed like a perfectly nice, well-educated person. Where had he gotten his indoctrination into hate?

"This is the sort of thing I should expect from a lawyer. Hell, not even Jesus loved lawyers."

"Excuse me?"

" 'Woe unto you, lawyers! For you have taken away the key of knowledge.' That's what our Lord and Savior said. In Luke."

Thanks so much for making my day . . . "Look, kid, I'll level with you. I don't know if I can win this case or not. I've read Kevin's files, and what little defense he was planning to put on won't cut it. This story about someone else coming along and moving the body won't cut it. We need something more."

"Like what?"

"Like proof that you didn't kill Tony Barovick." But only mangled and mutilated him. That's all.

"How are we going to get that?"

"I don't know. I'll get my investigative staff on it immediately."

"You think they'll find something?"

"I can't possibly predict that. But I know this." She leaned forward. "If you don't cooperate with me, we will lose."

He stared through the acrylic at her.

"If you start spouting off in court, we're history. You've got to do what I say, when I say it. Including keeping your mouth shut. And be nice about it. Got it?"

He saluted. "Yes, ma'am."

She began stuffing her notes back into her briefcase. "And one last requirement. You absolutely positively cannot keep secrets from me. None. I don't care how bad it is. If there's anything you haven't told me, anything at all, I want to hear about it. Before the DA does."

"Understood. I mean, I will."

"I hope you mean that. I really do." She rose. "I'll be back tomorrow. There are some papers I need you to sign. In the meantime, your assignment is to search that little brain of yours for anything that might help your case. Even the tiniest detail. Maybe something you never told the police or Tony or anyone."

"Well, I'll . . . try."

"Good." She stood. "Can I give you one last piece of advice?"

"Sure. Shoot."

"Don't talk."

He craned his neck. "You mean . . . to the police?"

"I mean to anyone. Not the cops, not the guards, not your cell mate. No one." She smiled. "You're in serious trouble, Johnny. So don't make it worse than it already is."

CHAPTER
8

As CHRISTINA TOOK the elevator up to Kevin Mahoney's twentieth-floor office in the heart of the Magnificent Mile, all she expected was a pleasant pneumatic ride. And Kevin's office! Compared to what she was used to working out of, it was like setting up shop in Taj Mahal. Gorgeous bay windows in every office looking down on Michigan Avenue. Nice clean carpet, modern art prints on the wall. The way a law office was supposed to look.

Except not today.

In the elevator lobby, covering the brass nameplates and the rest of the wall, was a spray-painted drawing of an upraised clenched fist. Beneath it were the words: NO MORE HATE. DEATH TO FASCISTS!

She took a deep breath, then slowly released it.

In the corner, Christina spotted a man with a digital camera photographing the display. He was obviously a professional.

"*Tribune,* or *Sun-Times*?"

He looked up from his viewfinder. "*Tribune.*"

"How'd you know?"

"Anonymous call. Group called ANGER."

"And you really think this is newsworthy?"

"Are you kidding? This is front-page art. My editor loves a strong graphic. Hey, do you work here?"

"For the moment."

"Mind posing in front of the fist?"

"As a matter of fact."

She pushed past him and entered the lobby. Jones was sitting out front, having totally taken over the space normally occupied by Kevin Mahoney's receptionist. He had a phone in each hand and a stack of pink message slips as thick as a sandwich.

"There you are!" he said. "Thank God. The phone has been ringing off the hook."

"Why?"

"Morning papers announced that you've taken over the Christensen defense. You wouldn't believe how angry some people are about it."

"Because, of course, bad men aren't entitled to attorneys."

"That's pretty much their view, yeah." He passed her the messages. "Here's more than twenty protests."

"I saw some of that in the elevator lobby. What's ANGER stand for?"

"Act Now for Gay Equal Rights."

Christina pondered a moment. "Why is that name familiar?"

"The guy who shot your client's codefendant was a member of ANGER. One of the local leaders, actually."

"So we're talking major extremists."

"A lot of these people are threatening violence if you don't drop the case. Not against the hatemongers—against you. Us. Letter bombs and stuff. Paula's pretty concerned." He wiped his brow. "I know I was in favor of taking this case, but now I'm wondering if we need to give this some more thought."

"I gave his mother my word, Jones."

"Nonetheless—"

"I've filed papers with the court. It's a done deal." She scanned the messages. "I don't suppose any of these are supportive?"

"Actually, there was one. Even offered to help finance the defense."

"Super! ACLU?"

"Nah. Some ultraright fundamentalist group. God's Chosen, or something like that. Wants to support Christensen the holy crusader in his battle against the sodomites."

Her eyelids fluttered. "Holy crusader. More like ignorant putz who joined the wrong fraternity." She tossed the messages into her briefcase. "Has Loving's plane come in yet?"

"Yeah. And Paula came up with him. They're in the kitchen scarfing doughnuts."

"Good. Team meeting in ten minutes. Main conference room."

"Sure. Will Ben—?"

"Has he left Tulsa?"

"Not to my knowledge. What's up with that, anyway?"

"Don't know. But I've got some suspicions. I've got a call in to his mother."

"In Oklahoma City?"

Christina shrugged. "Something my client said made me think there might be some history on this."

"But—isn't she kind of . . . frosty?"

"Says Ben. I adore the woman. Who knows, if I can squeeze in a visit, we might have time to go shopping."

SHE KNEW SHE was wasting her time, even as she dialed the phone. But she couldn't help herself.

"Ben, would you please reconsider—"

"No."

"You don't have to go to court. Just stay in the background. Give me the benefit of your wisdom."

"No."

"Ben, who's gonna know?"

"Will she be there?"

Christina hesitated. "You mean Mrs. Christensen? Well, of course she—"

"My answer is no." There was a staticky pause on the line. "Now I have to get back to my work."

"Ben, I've known you since the day you started practicing, and you've never behaved this way."

"What way? Smart?"

"As if you don't care. About"—don't say it, she told herself—"anything."

"I don't know what you're babbling about."

"Ben, don't shut me out. Tell me what's going on."

"What's going on is that I have a lot of work to do. And so do you, apparently."

She hesitated. "Ben—I missed you last night."

After a painfully protracted silence, she hung up the phone.

A GIRL HEARS the strangest things when she walks into a conference room unannounced.

"Cutter-Sanborn? No one uses Cutter-Sanborn."

"Well, they should."

"You can't turn your back on two hundred years of library tradition."

"Times change. The U.K. is way ahead of us on this."

"It's a losing battle, Paula. Dewey Decimal is here to stay."

"I'm not trying to junk it. I'm just saying Cutter-Sanborn is a viable alternative."

Christina cut in between Jones and Paula, his wife, who worked as a reference librarian at the downtown Tulsa City-County library. "Is this another one of those fascinating library science debates?"

"Can you believe it?" Jones said. "She's advocating a whole new system of cataloguing."

"A much better one," Paula insisted.

"Has poor Linda Saferite in a tizzy. What an idea! I mean, I'll admit there are advantages. But any change would be unforgivably burdensome to the rank-and-file librarian."

Christina shook her head. And they called lawyers nerds. "Look, team, we've got a major case on our hands and less than a week to get ready for it. I need everyone's cooperation."

"Ain't the work mostly done already?" This came from Loving, their investigator. He was a large, physically imposing man. When she'd first met him, Christina assumed he'd be able to extract information from people just by hovering over them and snarling. And although he never ruled that out, as it happened, he was usually far more subtle. And successful. There was a brain rattling around somewhere in that massive downhome frame. "Mahoney'd already started the trial when that wacko broke into the courtroom with the gun."

"I've read through Kevin's files," Christina said. "And here's the bad news. He didn't have squat. He was going down in flames and he knew it."

"Why didn't he plea-bargain?"

"None offered," Christina said. "Too much publicity. The DA was sure of his case. I've been reading Tony Barovick's journal. He was a fascinating young man. I keep hoping I'll find a clue in there somewhere—but so far nothing."

Jones threw up his hands. "Then what are we going to do?"

"That's what we're here to discuss."

"Christina, think for a minute," Jones said. "I'm used to this never-say-die attitude from Ben. But you've always been the sensible one. So do the sensible thing. Ditch this case."

"I told you already. I can't."

"Give the court some excuse. Temporary insanity or something."

"Sorry."

"Why should we risk letter bombs? I'm not even sure

it will be good publicity. Getting creamed in a case that's getting national attention is not going to attract clients."

"We have to be tough. To boldly go where no lawyer has gone before."

"Split infinitive, Christina," Paula said. "You know I think we girls should stick together. But I have real concerns. This kid killed a man in cold blood."

"He says he didn't."

"Well, of course he—" She drew in her breath. "Listen, Christina. I know everyone is entitled to a fair and able defense. But this is a hate crime."

"I remember a very similar discussion a few years ago. When Ben insisted on representing that racist in Arkansas. I told him I wouldn't be any part of it. But Ben insisted he was the only chance the kid had at anything like a fair trial. And he was right."

"So where's Ben now?"

Christina closed her eyes. "Look, people, I can't waste time. Are you with me or not? I need to know."

The three other people sitting at the table looked at one another. It wasn't long before Loving spoke. "We're with ya."

"Absolutely," Paula said. "No matter what."

"Right," Jones said. "Even if we go bankrupt. Even if we all get blown to smithereens."

"Thanks, Jones."

There was a knock on the door. Ellen Christensen stepped in. Christina showed her to a chair and introduced her to everyone. "Thank you for coming."

"Thank you for taking the case." Christina was impressed by how gracious she was. Quite a contrast from her son. "I—saw what they did. Out in the lobby. I'm sorry."

"No big deal. Happens to us all the time." Jones opened his mouth. Christina cut him off. "Mrs. Christensen, you know your son better than anyone. Can you give us any insight into what happened?"

"I really can't. Johnny is my late husband's son—my stepson—but I've been with him so long I feel as if he is my son, and I think he feels the same way. His biological mother died when he was quite young. We used to be very close, till he went off to college."

"You lived in Toronto?"

"Until a few years ago. My husband was an executive in a major energy firm. Was eventually transferred to Chicago. Johnny's grades were never great, but my husband's friends managed to get him into U of C."

"How much do you know about this fraternity he's in?"

"Not much. I wasn't crazy about the idea, but Johnny's father had been Greek, so Johnny was determined to do it, too. Do you think it's been a problem for him?"

"Maybe. When I was in school, frats were mostly hotbeds of sexism. But Johnny's clan seems to have favored homophobia. Some of them, anyway."

"You think he fell in with a bad group?"

"Well, his former codefendant, Brett Mathers, sounds as if he was a real hard case. According to Johnny, he did most of the brutal beating."

"Then Johnny should not be charged with murder."

Christina shook her head. "Sorry, ma'am, but according to the DA, he participated in a felony that led to homicide. That's felony murder."

"But surely a lesser penalty—"

"Felony murder is still murder one. And Illinois has a hate crimes statute on the books—which has been upheld by the Illinois Supreme Court. Maximum penalty is death by lethal injection. And I can promise you, the DA plans to go for the maximum."

"Do you think . . . Is there a chance . . ."

Christina was never one to pull punches. "If the jury thinks Johnny killed that kid out of pure malice against homosexuals? I'd call the death penalty a certainty."

Mrs. Christensen pressed her hand against her forehead. "I just don't understand it. Larry and I were very involved in Johnny's education. We taught him to be tolerant, not prejudiced. We're actually very liberal."

"There's no explaining these things, ma'am. They're kids—not photocopies."

Mrs. Christensen's eyes started to water. What an ordeal this must be, Christina thought. The sole remaining parent, dealing with a crisis of this immensity. Facing these accusations against her oldest son. Facing the possibility of his death. Christina wondered how she could bear it.

"Is—is there anything you can do?"

"Yes," Christina said, gazing around the table. "And we're going to get started immediately. Paula?"

"Yes?"

"Hit the stacks. Get me background on the victim—Tony Barovick."

"Okay . . . but if he was an essentially random target for a hate crime—"

"Make no assumptions," Christina cautioned her. "If we accept all the DA's assumptions, we'll end up with the DA's result. I want to learn something new."

"Okay . . . I'll look, but—"

"Jones? Get on the Internet and check out this fraternity. See what you can find out about it. See if anything like this has ever happened before."

"You got it."

"Then run a deep background check on this ANGER group. And its members. Especially the local leaders."

"Okay . . . but why?"

"It may be nothing. But having a member pop up out of nowhere and take out one of the defendants? I don't know. Something about it makes me suspicious."

"I'll check it out."

"Loving?"

"Aw, hell. You're gonna give me the bar, aren't you?"

"You got it."

"Ben always gives me the bars. I thought you'd be more enlightened."

"Sorry to disappoint. But there's a reason why we give you these assignments. You excel at them."

"Flatterer."

"I want you to become a regular at Remote Control. That's the singles bar near campus where Tony Barovick worked. He was leaving there when he was attacked. It's apparently a frequent hangout for the local college coeds, and kids slumming from the University of Chicago—like members of Johnny's fraternity. Sniff around and see if you can learn anything useful."

"For you, dear, anythin'."

"Remember, Johnny says they left Tony—alive—in a vacant lot not far from the bar. That means someone else carried the body to the fraternity house."

"But—wouldn't the coroner—"

"If so, there's a good chance there was a witness to the move. Find me that witness, Loving."

"I'll do my best."

"I'll handle the pretrial motions and trial prep, obviously."

Mrs. Christensen looked up tentatively. "And Mr. Kincaid?"

"Will not be involved in this case."

"I see."

"But I can guarantee you we'll do everything there is to do, ma'am."

"Oh, of course. I didn't mean to—" Polite to a fault, Christina thought. "I have great confidence in you."

"We appreciate it. I'm afraid bail is an impossibility— Kevin already tried and lost—but I can arrange some visitation. If you want to see your son before the trial."

"Yes, I'd like that." She wiped her eyes dry. "May I say something more?"

"Of course."

"I know what you all must be thinking. About my

son. I know it looks bad. The reports in the newspapers have been gruesome. And even though you've agreed to represent Johnny, you must be thinking . . . well, it certainly looks as if he's . . . a horrible person. A beast. But he *isn't*." She said the word with such emphasis it stung Christina's tear ducts. "I've known him since he was little, and I know that he has a good heart."

The four staffers at the table looked at one another, but remained silent.

"I don't know what happened at college, but the little boy I knew could never have changed so much. He was insecure, and subject to peer pressure. I could conceive of him watching and maybe not helping—but murder? It's not possible." She clenched her fist tightly. "It is simply not possible."

She fell back, emotionally exhausted. "Please help him."

"We'll do everything we can, ma'am. Everything possible. I guarantee it."

And Christina meant every word she said. But she couldn't help wondering if this wasn't a case in which everything simply wouldn't be enough.

CHAPTER
9

"ALL RIGHT, MORELLI, much as it pains you, it's time for a spot of pleasure. Pull your head out."

He didn't.

Sergeant Baxter entered his cubicle and dropped a lightweight cardboard box on the edge of his desk, in one of the few uncluttered corners. "I'm serious, partner. You can't avoid this. The time has come for a respite revered by law enforcement officers everywhere."

His neck craned upward, if only slightly. "And that would be? . . ."

She beamed. "Doughnut break."

His eyes returned to his desk. "That is so cliché . . ."

"I've got Krispy Kremes."

Mike dropped his pencil. "Well, why didn't you say so?"

"I got an assortment. Try the cherry cream."

"Aww, Baxter. You know I don't like the cream-filled stuff."

"You do not like them, so you say, but try them, try them, and you may."

"Excuse me?"

"Try them and you may, I say!"

The corner of his lip turned upward. "Been to the library, have we?"

Her eyes darkened. "I guess you thought that was pretty funny, huh? Suggesting that I might be able to handle the poetry of Theodore Geisel. Alias Dr. Seuss."

Now Mike craned his neck. "It was . . . just the first thing that popped into my head."

"Uh-huh. And you weren't suggesting that I was . . . what's the word I'm looking for? Stupid?"

"Not at all. I love Dr. Seuss."

"So did I. When I was two."

"It was just a joke."

"At my expense."

"Not at all. I was just—"

"You were saying I was an uneducated boor."

"No, no . . ."

"Or maybe you were just sulking, because I told you to lay off with the romance."

"Huh?"

"I know how barren your love life is. Small wonder you're always making moony eyes at me and breathing hard whenever our toes accidentally touch."

"What in—"

"I'm not saying you're not a handsome-looking dude. Decent, anyway. But we can't be partners if there's even a whiff of romance in the air. It was no reason for you to run off at the mouth and insult me."

Mike found himself breathing hard, but it wasn't because of any whiffs of romance. "Baxter, I was not insulting you. I have a lot of respect for you. Promise." He paused. "Especially when you bring me Krispy Kremes."

Her eyes narrowed. "Really?"

"Absolutely."

"And you don't mind the no-romance rule."

"Not remotely. I'm relieved, actually."

"Well, that's a little more acceptance than was strictly necessary."

"I'm just saying—"

"Good." She pointed to the box on the desk. "The glazed doughnuts are under the cherry ones."

Mike's eyes brightened. "Yeah?" He dug deep and grabbed one. "Wanna split it?"

She shook her head. "I will not eat them in a box. I will not eat them with a fox . . ."

BEN HAD TOLD Christina about this unique experience, but she rarely thought it was necessary that she experience it for herself. As with the jailhouse jaunts, when in the course of their cases this visit became necessary, Ben always did it. Once or twice she'd tagged along, but that was okay, because she just kept her eyes closed and pretended she was in Maui. Ben did all the work. And she was happy to let him.

She pushed open the glass-paned door lettered COOK COUNTY MEDICAL EXAMINER. My God, they never covered this in law school.

As soon as she stepped inside, Amber Wilson, the coroner, dropped everything—knives, sawtooth blades, and dismembered arm—and greeted her. "Kevin Mahoney phoned and told me you were coming."

Christina forced a smile. "Dr. Wilson, would you be terribly offended if I didn't shake your hand? I don't mean to be rude. But . . . I know where it's been."

"I understand entirely." Christina was having a hard time adjusting to the idea of this woman as a coroner. A coroner should be gray-haired and remote and perhaps slightly whacked. Amber Wilson was young and outgoing. She didn't fit the mold at all. Except it looked as if she might be slightly whacked.

"What can I do you for?"

"Can I ask you about Tony Barovick?"

She nodded, returning to the main operating theater. "I thought that might be it. Let me tell you, Christina— your guy's alibi is hopeless. Not even tenable. From a medical standpoint, it's really a boring case."

Wilson dug through a file cabinet until she came up with one marked BAROVICK. "So what's your question?"

Christina considered how best to phrase it. "The thing is my client insists that he and his buddy did not kill the kid. Just roughed him up."

"They broke both legs."

"Would that necessarily be fatal?"

"No, but common sense tells me—"

"Right, right. The point is when they left him, at around 9:30, my client says he wasn't dead. And he wasn't in the fraternity house, either. He says they left him in a vacant lot, so crippled he couldn't possibly move. Meaning someone else came along, killed him, and moved him. Or vice versa."

Wilson shook her head. "Sorry, Christina. But I can positively guarantee that didn't happen."

"How can you be sure?"

She flipped through the pages of the file, refreshing her memory. "Medical science."

"Are you so certain the body wasn't moved?"

"No, that isn't it. The corpse was in such bad shape, I couldn't make any determination on that score. Not for certain."

"Then what?"

Wilson closed her file. "The first thing I did at the crime scene was take decomposition readings to establish the time of death. Not that I enjoyed it. It was midnight, I was cold, and the joint had more posters of naked women than I've seen in my entire life. The DA was being an asshole and trying to tell me what to do and when. But I performed the tests, just the same. And the time of death was well after 9:30—more like 11:00, 11:15."

Christina shook her head. "I don't know. My client is pretty convincing."

"Christina, if the beating took place in a vacant lot, don't you think the police would've found traces?"

"The boys didn't remember where it was. They said they were drunk and drove and drove—and stopped at a deserted place chosen at random. Of course, the cops never looked too hard, since they think Tony was killed in the frat house. And even if the vacant lot were found, it could've been cleaned up."

Wilson dropped the file back in its drawer. "Christina, I realize you don't know me, but I'm a straight shooter. If the DA's case sucks, I'll say so. But you're barking up the wrong tree."

"You're sure?"

"Absolutely. Scout's honor. Girl-to-girl. Your client killed the poor kid. There's simply no other possible explanation."

"HELLO, HANDSOME."

Mike sighed, eyes still glued to his desk. "Look, Baxter, if this is—"

He stopped short. Wrong voice.

"Special Agent Swift! What the hell are you doing here?"

Mike rose to his feet and crossed his office to greet her. Just like the last time he'd seen her, she was wearing a black turtleneck. And looking fine in it, too.

"I'm on special assignment. How ya been, you big teddy bear, you?"

"Oh, all right. Nothing to—"

"Don't just stand there. Give me a hug." She wrapped her arms around him and squeezed. And did not let go.

"Hey, Morelli, shouldn't we be leaving to—"

They both turned to see Sergeant Baxter standing in the doorway.

"Oh, excuse me," Baxter said. "I didn't know you had . . . company. I'll come back later."

"No, no," Mike said, "come on in. We're just . . ." What the hell were they doing, anyway? "Baxter, this is

Special Agent Swift. With the FBI. I told you about her. We worked on the Metzger kidnap case together. Before your time."

Baxter looked at the other woman levelly. "Right."

Mike turned back to Agent Swift. "And this is Sergeant Baxter. She's my partner. For the time being."

Swift extended her hand. "Glad to meet you, Baxter. Got a first name?"

"Yeah. But I think Morelli is afraid of them."

"I noticed that. I'm Danny. Short for Danielle."

"Kate." They shook hands, but Mike noticed that Baxter seemed very tentative. "What brings a Chicago white shirt out to our lowly cop shop?"

"Special assignment," she explained.

"Anything I'd know about?"

"Well, yes, actually. The drill bit boy."

"That's a homicide. What's the FBI interest?"

"Sorry. I'm not at liberty to say."

"You're going to be working with us. But you can't say why?"

"For the moment." She leaned forward and spoke in hushed tones. "Don't sweat it, Kate. I'll spill something as soon as I can. I'm not much for the rule book—ask Mike. I just like to get the job done. And the best way to accomplish that is for us all to get along."

"I think maybe we need to talk to Blackwell."

"Don't bother. I've just come from his office. He's on board."

Baxter frowned. "I won't pretend I'm happy about this. These interjurisdictional things always turn out to be a headache. And I'll be honest—I don't much like working with Feebs. Neither does Morelli." She paused. "Right, Morelli?"

Mike's shoulders rippled. "Well, as a rule, working with the Bureau is not my idea of the good life. But I guess I don't have any problems with this." Baxter looked at him as if he'd just sold her into slavery. "At least I have some history with Agent Swift."

"That's right," Swift said, jabbing him in the ribs. "And we got along pretty well, didn't we, handsome?"

"Yeah. Except for the minor detail of the bad guys getting away."

Baxter looked as if the top of her head were burning. "Just so you know, Swift, we don't usually go in for that overly familiar flirtatious stuff."

"Lighten up, Kate. We're just joshing."

"There's nothing funny about inappropriate office conduct. Sexual harassment is not a joke."

"Sexual harassment?" Swift looked at Mike. "Did I harass you? I don't recall you complaining." She helped herself to a chair. "Why don't one of you tell me what you've got on this case so far?"

Mike wanted to sit behind his desk, but that would leave Baxter standing, and that was too rude, even for him. "We don't know much about the victim. Not even his name. We checked the mug shots. Didn't find a match."

"Check the DEA records?"

An interesting question. "No. We've been interviewing people who knew him, neighbors and such, but there aren't many. They say he mostly kept to himself."

"But you're not buying that, right?"

"Right. No man is an island, entire of itself."

Swift turned to Baxter. "Don't you get shivers when he does the poetry thing?"

"Love it," Baxter deadpanned.

"I appreciate you two being so reasonable about this," Swift said. "Sometimes local law enforcement just goes ape when we Feds come in. Get more territorial than most jungle primates." She checked her watch. "Wanna go somewhere for a cup of java?" She smiled in a way that was uncommonly inviting. "We could catch up."

"Yeah. I think I'm about finished here." Mike fiddled

absently with the stapler on his desk. "Baxter, care to join us?"

"Thanks, but I've got some paperwork to take care of. Why don't you call me when you're actually ready to work? Partner."

"No problem." Swift grabbed his arm. "So, isn't there a Java Dave's within walking distance?"

CHAPTER
10

BEN CAME HOME from the office as depressed as he remembered ever being. That's what you always say, he told himself. Which said something about his life. Something fairly pathetic.

He had stopped by Weber's for takeout—cheeseburgers, fries, and chocolate milk. Comfort food. With luck, he would make it up the stairs of his boardinghouse without being accosted by tenants complaining about the air-conditioning or explaining why they couldn't possibly pay their rent this month. Sometimes both at once.

He entered the boardinghouse where he lived—which he now owned—and walked up the stairs to his room without interruption, dropped his food on the kitchen table, then stopped to check in on the felines.

A big wicker basket with a cushion was the current home of Giselle, the huge mama cat, and her kitten Melisande. Ben had eventually given away the rest of the litter, but he couldn't bear to part with them all, regardless of what people said about two cats in a small apartment.

He opened several cans of Feline's Fancy and scooped it into their individual bowls, stroked their fur, talked baby talk—then heard a sound coming from his bedroom.

He stiffened.

He removed his shoes so he could walk more quietly

on the squeaky hardwood floors. He tiptoed across the living room, then slowly made his way down the corridor.

What he found in his bedroom was a beautiful young woman wearing nothing but a pink string bikini.

"I thought you'd never get home," the woman said, brushing her curly brunette locks behind her round and radiant shoulders.

"Joni?" Ben said, almost choking on the words. Of course he'd seen her many times before. She did live here, and had been serving as his building superintendent to work her way through college. But she was normally wearing baggy overalls or jeans with holes in the knees.

"I tracked down the plumbing problem," she said, pointing to the hole where floorboards used to be. "Leaky pipe. Just below your bedroom."

"So . . . I assume you're working on it?"

"Like, you thought maybe I was going for a swim under your bed?"

"Well . . . I didn't . . . I—"

"Yes, I'm working on it. I knew I'd end up soaked—I always do when I handle these plumbing jobs for you. Don't worry. I'll mop up the mess."

Now that he noticed, she did appear to be wet, which certainly had an effect on the adherent qualities of her suit.

"So I thought—be smart for once, Joni. Switch into your suit before you start the job. Hope you don't mind."

Ben managed to speak even though his tongue was thick and cottony. "I can live with it."

"Good. I was afraid you might have a stroke or something."

"What? Since when—"

"I know how uncomfortable you are with some things. Like human physiology."

"That's . . . not at all . . ."

"I told my mom what I was doing when I changed. She asked if she could come, too."

"Oh?"

"Yeah. Wanted to see the expression on your face."

"I don't see why that would be at all amusing."

"Me neither. You were totally stoic. Cool and debonair." She looked away, smiling. "Anyway, the plumbing job's just about done. I'll be out of your hair soon."

"Good." He loosened his tie and tossed it down on his bed. "I have some things to do."

She grabbed a wrench and went back at it. "Really? Hot Scrabble game?"

The weird thing was she said that like there was something wrong with it. "No."

"Don't tell me—you and Christina are going to do something else? Monopoly, maybe? I guess for you that would be, like, second base."

He popped open his briefcase. "Christina's in Chicago."

"Why?"

"She's working on a case."

"But you're not?"

"It's her own deal."

Joni's eyebrows knitted. "I didn't think she had her own deals."

"Well, she does."

"Is there, like, something wrong between you two?"

"Not at all. She's just working."

"Hmm." Joni gave the pipe a final twist, which required flexing her biceps and creating a rippling effect that Ben thought he was unlikely to forget anytime in the near future. Then she began putting the floorboards back into place. "Well, it's none of my business. But can I give you some advice?"

"I need a college junior to be my spiritual adviser?"

"Ben, you know how I love and respect you. And you

know what a mentor you've been to me. But despite my relative youth, there are a few things I know more about than you."

"Such as?"

"Life." She hammered the floorboards back into place. "Maybe you should give Christina a call."

"She's busy."

"Couldn't you help?"

"Absolutely not."

"I don't suppose you're inclined to tell me why."

"Not in the least."

"Same old Ben." She grabbed a towel, then walked right up to him, wet bikini and all. "Could you at least do me a favor? Dry my back. There's a spot I can't reach."

Reluctantly, Ben took the towel. Damn, but being a landlord was hard! The responsibilities were overwhelming.

MIKE DROPPED BY around eight, using the excuse of a hot *Xena* rerun and bearing a New York-style pizza from Mario's. Actually, the *Xena* thing was a pretty good excuse as far as Ben was concerned. He hadn't seen this episode before; Xena was in top form, hacking away in her black leather.

"So, you're really going to take this Chicago case?" Mike asked.

"Christina is," Ben replied. "I'm not having anything to do with it."

"Word is lots of people are out to get that Christensen kid. Anyone associated with him is in danger."

"Swell. I like this case even better now."

"Why don't you let me call someone at Chicago PD? Maybe they can send an officer over to keep an eye on Christina? At least during the trial."

"Don't bother. You know Christina won't allow it. The jurors would assume Christina thought she needed protection from her client. Which would not exactly improve her chances."

"Maybe they can send someone low-key. Plainclothes."

"I don't think it will make any difference."

"Oh, well. It's not as if she's ever gotten herself in trouble before." He popped open a beer. "So, why is she in Chicago while you're here?"

Ben's forehead creased. "I assume she's working on her impending trial."

"But you're not."

"No, I'm not."

"And there's nothing unusual about that."

"No, there isn't. We're two separate human beings. We have separate lives. Separate identities."

"Fine, fine. Don't go all I-did-not-sleep-with-that-woman on me. You want the last slice of pizza?"

Ben cast his eyes down to the nearly empty cardboard box. "Not enough to arm wrestle you for it."

"Good call. I'd cream you."

"I've been working out."

Mike dangled the tail of the last Combo Supreme over his lips. "Success is counted sweetest / By those who ne'er succeed . . ."

MAYBE HE SHOULD call her, Ben thought, as he sat in his overstuffed chair staring at nothing. Forget that he had turned the case down, that she had gone over his head. She had been practicing for almost two years now; it was not unusual for her to handle a case on her own. Joni had said he was a mentor. Maybe he should take that attitude. Offer her that kind of assistance, just like when he was starting out and he'd had—

Well, okay, he pretty much did it on his own. But that didn't mean Christina had to. He should just pick up the phone and—

But he couldn't. Not this time. Not this case. It went

too deep. The hurt was too ingrained. He couldn't make himself do it. And even if he did, how could he know he was doing a good job? He couldn't possibly be objective, not here, not with—

He stretched his feet out on the ottoman. His stomach was churning, and it wasn't because of the pizza, either. This was tearing him apart. He played the piano for a while, but it didn't calm him. He tried to work the *New York Times* crossword, but couldn't focus. All he could think about was Christina.

He had known her for so long now, cared about her so deeply, he felt closer to her than anyone he had ever known in his life. Not that he would ever tell her that. But it was true. He hated leaving her dangling in the wind like this. What was that kid's mother doing, anyway, giving a case of this magnitude, with this much media saturation, to a lawyer of Christina's relative inexperience?

Of course he knew exactly what she was doing. And that was why he couldn't give in.

He gripped the arms of his chair resolutely. This was the way it had to be, like it or not. He could not help Christina with this case. Not at all. Not a bit. Absolutely not. Never.

THE NEXT MORNING, Ben unlocked the front doors and tiptoed into his office. As far as he knew, everyone else was in Chicago, but he was taking no chances.

With great stealth he made his way to Christina's office. Her desk was a mess, as usual, but this time she had a pretty good excuse. He was glad, because it made it all the easier for him to execute his plan.

He punched on the computer monitor at Jones's workstation. He knew Christina had a laptop and would check for e-mail periodically. First, he forwarded a hyperlink to a Web page on the University of Chicago Law School's

Web site: STUDENTS SEEKING INTERN POSITIONS. Next, he sent a link to the Lexus database that keyed up the text of *State v. Harmon*. Christina was brilliant when it came to arguments in equity, which were the heart of any motion for a continuance, but she sometimes forgot about the more arcane legal precedents; what's more, Ben's sources had told him that Judge Lacayo was a sucker for public policy arguments. Since he was using Jones's e-mail program, Christina would assume the case had come from Paula. Which was good.

After all, it was important that everyone understand that he would not help Christina with this case. Not in the least.

CHAPTER
11

JOURNAL OF TONY BAROVICK

THE DAY OF my high school graduation I decided I was coming out. This was no small decision. I lived in the suburbs, after all, deeply traditional, conservative suburbs, dominated by huge churches, Democrats who always voted Republican, and trailer trash who measured success by the size of the wheels on your pickup. To say that gay men had to remain in the closet is to state the obvious. Oh, there were probably worse places—we did at least have some gay bars and a small gay underground network—but it wasn't exactly Greenwich Village, if you catch my drift.

And my father. Since I'm treating this journal more like a third-rate autobiography than a diary, I should make the point up front that my father was not a bad person. More than once he surprised me with his kindness, with his startling gentility. But he had not exactly been raised with a progressive attitude, and it showed. At heart, he was still the kid from the projects raised by poor white laborers, and as a result, he carried around the baggage of every kind of prejudice there was: prejudice against foreigners, minorities, Catholics, aggressive women and, predictably enough, homosexuals. I remember once in the seventh grade when I got the lead in the middle school musical. My mother was delighted, but I noticed that Dad's reaction was much more subdued. Late that night, when Mother wasn't around, he made a rare effort to talk to me. "I guess being in plays is all right," he said in that awkward sputtering drawl of his. "Problem is you gotta watch out for the fags." He said it as if it were a two-syllable word.

I didn't know what he was talking about, or pretended I didn't, but he reinforced my later determination to keep my secret to myself. He was right, of course; there were plenty of guys who shared my sexual inclination treading the boards, but that didn't make it any easier. In the early Eighties, when the AIDS plague started making the papers, I remember my father throwing down the *Sun-Times* in disgust and saying, "Who the hell cares about a bunch of queers?" Quite a statement, coming from a man who I knew had a good heart, who really had no meanness in him. Imagine what you'd get if you combined all those inbred prejudices with someone who did have some meanness in him. Maybe a lot of meanness.

That and countless similar remarks told me exactly where my dad stood on this issue that was of crushing importance to me. Which explains why I put off telling him for as long as I did. Mother was a different matter— she wasn't going to like it, just as she didn't like it when I wouldn't try out for the tennis team. But bottom line— she loved me, and she always would, and if it turned out I was gay, she'd learn to live with it. Father was different. I couldn't predict how he'd take it.

Not well, as it turned out. I don't believe for a minute it came as any great surprise. He wasn't a stupid person. I'm sure he'd seen the signs. About the only time in his life he gave me money without my asking for it was before that senior prom. I found an envelope on my bed with a hundred-dollar bill in it and a note that read: TAKE A GIRL OUT FOR THE TIME OF HER LIFE. He knew, or at least suspected. But I guess that isn't the same as being told.

The weird thing was he seemed to take it as a reflection on himself, not me. "Too much time with his mother," he muttered, turning his eyes skyward. "Never had to work for anything. Not like I did." I didn't know what that had to do with anything, but it seemed to make sense to him. Mother was okay till he spewed out, "You had to push him into all those plays, didn't you? Singing lessons? My God, it's no wonder." Mother broke down at that point—and I left. I already had an apartment lined up for the summer, and a job. I didn't need this crap. Not from the people who brought me into the world.

Things got better with my mom. After about a month, we started meeting on the sly—having lunch together at the Art Institute or window-shopping on the Magnificent Mile. But I haven't spoken to my father in years. The few times I've seen him, he just stares at me, examines me like some awful black blot, like I'm a stain on his shirt. He never says anything. Not even hello.

A few months ago, I went to the funeral for my friend Gary's father. He held it in till everyone went home, then cried like a baby all night long. *You can't imagine what it feels like,* he kept saying. *I mean, you've known your father all your life. He's a part of you. And then, one day, he's gone. It changes everything.*

I held Gary all night long, trying to comfort him, because I think I understood what he was going through better than he realized. It's even worse, I thought to myself, when you've lost your father—and he only lives about two miles away.

CHAPTER

12

CHRISTINA BERATED HERSELF all the way to the courtroom. *Good grief, girl. It's not as if this is the first time
you've ever come to a courthouse by yourself.* But Chicago was a very different city; skyscrapers towered all
around her, and everyone seemed so busy, busy, busy.
She dodged taxicabs seemingly intent on murder as she
crossed the street, avoiding well-dressed panhandlers on
her way up the courthouse steps. Yes, there was something different today, but it wasn't just the fact that she
was away from home. It wasn't the pressure, the imminent trial date, the parade of protesters camped outside
the courthouse. She had been spilling files and dumping
coffee on her briefs and generally acting like a flibbertigibbet all morning long. It wasn't her usual leitmotiv,
and she didn't like it a bit.

She intentionally arrived early so she would have a
chance to meet the district attorney, Richard Drabble, in
his office—not in the courtroom. She still hoped she
could talk some reason into him; there was no reason
for a protracted trial played before all America. Surely
they could reach some sort of understanding. And she
wanted a chance to size the man up, to get some idea
who she was up against. She'd seen him on television, of
course, but it wasn't the same. When she met someone
face-to-face, looked into their eyes, shook their hands—
that's when she started to get a picture of who this person really was.

She found the DA's office near the door and introduced herself to the receptionist. She was surprised—and impressed—when the man himself appeared barely more than a minute later.

"A pleasure to meet you, Ms. McCall. Thank you for stopping by."

She took his hand. "I'm sorry I couldn't drop in sooner."

"Very brave thing you've done—taking over this case on such short notice. And with so little prep time."

"Well, you have to play the hand you're dealt."

"Isn't that the truth." He chuckled. He was a handsome fellow, Christina thought—intense blue eyes, a square jaw, salt-and-pepper hair. Early fifties, she guessed, but the years were making him look stronger and more distinguished, not less. "Is there anything I can do for you?"

"Well," she said, clearing her throat awkwardly, "I did wonder if you'd consider any sort of deal that—"

He held up his hand. "I'm sorry, Ms. McCall, I can't. There's just too much pressure bearing down on us, demanding a conviction. And frankly—our case is too strong. I don't envy your position at all. I know you can't win, but I sincerely hope you can save face and not appear incompetent."

"Or perhaps I prefer cases that come with built-in excuses because I really am incompetent."

He flashed some teeth. "Don't be modest, Ms. McCall. You've had a distinguished little career. Not many legal assistants make it to your level."

She hesitated. "But—you understand—I'm a lawyer now."

"Of course. But that's a recent development, right?"

"Well, relatively speaking, I suppose." And your point is?

"Most of your death penalty cases have actually been handled by your partner. What's his name again?"

"Ben Kincaid," she said slowly.

"Right, right. You two handled that cop killer case. Very impressive."

"Well . . . thank you."

"I'm glad I haven't had anything like that on my watch. This Barovick case has been my highest profile gig yet, and I'm glad of it. I just want to do my job, without all the interference you had to brook in that case. Of course, Tulsa is not Chicago by any means. You don't have our resources. I'd like to think we could've taken care of that here in one trial and a lot less time. But it all worked out in the end, right?"

"Riiiiight."

"Have you met Judge Lacayo yet?"

"Haven't had the pleasure."

"Well, he hasn't always been the most open-minded about women lawyers. Especially as lead counsel in important cases. But I'm sure it will be fine."

So was this guy deliberately trying to psych her out, Christina wondered, or was it just the effect of her own insecurities impinging on an innocent conversation? Didn't matter—time to bring this conversation to a close.

"I should probably be getting to the courtroom."

He checked his watch. "Oh, me, too. Gotta meet a reporter first, then I'll be right there."

"Can you give me directions?" Christina asked. "This is my first time here."

"No problem. Lacayo's courtroom is not in this building. Cross over on the catwalk to Building Two, then keep going to Building Three. Take the elevator down to the basement and turn left. His courtroom is the last one on your right."

"Got it. Thanks."

"Sir," the receptionist said, interrupting, "here are the briefs you wanted."

He appeared mildly distressed. "Oh, geez, Mona, I

can't carry those to my interview. What would the reporter think? I told you to have them couriered to the courtroom." Again he glanced nervously at his watch. "Now it's too late."

"No problem," Christina said. "I'll take them." She held her briefcase horizontally in both hands, taking the tall stack of manila envelopes on top.

"Are you sure?" Drabble said with concern.

"It's a snap. See you in a few minutes."

"Yes, see you."

FIFTEEN MINUTES LATER, she was five minutes late, still hauling all those papers, sweating profusely, and nowhere near the courtroom. She had found Building Two with ease, but somewhere along the way to Three, she'd gotten lost. She'd ended up on the wrong side of the building and had to go down to the ground floor and reenter in order to get to the catwalk. It took her forever to find the elevator; her arms felt as if they were about to give out. With great relief, she punched the button marked B.

And stepped out to find nothing.

Not nothing in the strictest sense, but no sign of life. Before her was a dirty, dank corridor filled with cleaning supplies and a floor waxer. Certainly no courtrooms. Not even close.

She glanced at her watch again. Ten minutes late, now. She'd been hometowned.

Summoning her strength, she got back in the elevator and ran all the way to Building One. She got directions from the man at the newsstand. Turned out Lacayo's courtroom was near the front door—just down the hall from where she and Drabble had had their little conversation. By the time she finally arrived, she looked as if she'd just run the marathon and was almost twenty minutes late. She assiduously avoided the throng of reporters and spectators and made her way to her table.

"You look as if you could use a hand," Drabble said, offering to take some of the paper load.

"Imagine that," Christina said, as she dumped it all on the defendant's table.

"I take it you're Ms. McCall?" Lacayo said, leaning down from his bench. He looked almost reptilian, hovering, his beak nose pointed downward, and was obviously unhappy.

"I am, sir."

"You're not a member of our bar, are you?"

"No, sir. But Kevin Mahoney has filed a brief on my behalf to be admitted *pro hac vice*."

"Apparently local counsel failed to give you adequate instruction, Ms. McCall, so allow me to fill in the gap. I'm not a stickler for much, but there is one thing I absolutely insist upon. And that is punctuality."

It would be. "Yes, sir. I'm sorry, sir."

"Ask any lawyer in this county and they will all tell you the same thing. Judge Lacayo is a tolerant, patient man. But he will not put up with dillydallying. Everyone knows that."

Of course they do, Christina realized. That's the whole reason for this little prank. Poisoning the well before I have a chance to take a drink.

"Maybe they do things differently in—" He glanced down at his papers, then made a face as if he'd just sucked on a lemon. "—Ok-la-homa. But here in Cook County, we expect our lawyers to behave as professionals."

"Yes, sir."

"It's more than just nit-picking. It goes to the whole caliber of representation. A tardy lawyer is a sloppy lawyer. That's what I always say."

"Certainly, sir." Should she tell the judge what happened? Of course not. Then he would consider her a whiner—and a stooge—in addition to a dillydallyer.

"I'll overlook your flagrant misconduct this one time, Ms. McCall, but only this once. If it happens again, there will be consequences. I'll be watching you."

She glared at Drabble, who studiously avoided her gaze. He'd won this round and they both knew it. He'd ensured that she got off on the wrong foot with the judge—and the client as well, since Ellen Christensen was in the gallery. All she could do was grit her teeth and bear it—and plot her revenge.

"Are you ready to move forward, Ms. McCall?"

"I am, your honor."

"And you are death-qualified?"

"Yes, sir." Though perhaps not in the way that he meant . . .

"Very well. We shall proceed." Christina had no experience with Judge Lacayo, but she couldn't believe that he normally behaved this way. He seemed uncommonly stiff and formal, doing a stern paternal routine that almost seemed like an *SNL* send-up of a judge. Probably the influence of all the reporters in the courtroom, she speculated. Not to mention all the protesters outside.

Judge Lacayo called the case and got right to the nitty-gritty. "Ms. McCall, I have your motions before me. Normally, I would not allow what are essentially pre-trial motions at this stage of the proceeding—when the jury has been selected and the trial is simply in recess—but as we all know, there have been some extraordinary circumstances, so I granted this hearing."

"Thank you, your honor."

He turned his attention to the papers on his bench. "Predictably enough, your first motion is another request for a continuance of the trial date. I thought I had already made clear—"

"If I may, your honor." Christina grabbed her notes and headed for the podium. "I know the court is anxious to get this trial moving, but as you're aware, I received this case only a few days ago."

"We're all aware of the regrettable circumstances that required Mr. Mahoney to step down."

"Exactly. So given the magnitude of the penalty potentially faced by my client, I'm requesting a three-month continuance in order to have time to thoroughly prepare—"

"Do you have access to Mr. Mahoney's notes?" the judge asked, cutting her off.

"Well, yes, sir, I do." The problem was, there was nothing there.

"And I believe you even have access to Mr. Mahoney himself."

"That's true, your honor. He's been very good about—"

"So I don't see the problem."

"The problem, sir—" Christina took a deep breath. The trick was to make her point without suggesting that Kevin Mahoney had been negligent in preparing the defense the first time around. "—is that every attorney has his or her own style, and while the materials that Mr. Mahoney was prepared to use at trial might have worked for him, I'm finding them somewhat . . . ."

"Yes, counsel?"

"Unavailing. If the court would simply allow me adequate time to prepare my own defense, I think the results would be far more salutary."

"If I may, your honor," Drabble said, rising to his feet, "the State would oppose giving the defense additional time to fish around and see if they can come up with something better."

"It's not a matter of fishing around," Christina insisted. More like praying for a miracle. "But in a case of this magnitude—"

"If I understand what you're saying," Judge Lacayo said, "you're essentially asking for more time because Mr. Mahoney had a different defense style than you do. I'm sure you take great pride in your style, Ms. McCall, but if the defense has had adequate time to prepare—and this one has—I see no need to extend it. Furthermore, the speedy trial provisions of the Constitution mandate that we proceed."

"But your honor—"

"If, on the other hand, as I suspect, you just want more time to see if you can dig up a better defense, it would be positively unfair to allow you more time. So if you have nothing else . . ."

Christina rifled through her notes. Where was that case? "Your honor, I would direct the court's attention to *State v. Harmon*." Thank goodness for Paula. Christina had found this case in her e-mail this morning, with the rest of Paula's invaluable research. It was exactly what she needed.

"I know the case, counsel."

"Then you know that the Harmon court established that in addition to the needs of the defense and the interests of fairness, public policy considerations should be examined when determining whether to grant a continuance."

Judge Lacayo sat up at attention. "Are there public policy issues here, counsel?"

"Yes, sir. Needless to say, there has been an enormous amount of public interest in this case." She glanced back to both sides of the gallery, making her point. "It's more than just a murder case. In the eyes of many, it has taken on a symbolic mantle. It's become about tolerance, diversity, and the effectiveness of the American criminal justice system. People are looking to this case, this courtroom, to give them a sense of resolution and, if I may say so, a sense of justice. It is important that we don't fail them."

Lacayo appeared to be listening intently. "Go on."

"If I am required to proceed with haste, there will always be some who will say the result was tainted by the circumstances in which the defense was prepared and presented. In order to give people a sense of resolution, we must assure them that the trial was conducted in such a manner as to give the truth a full and fair opportunity to arise."

"So what I hear you saying, counsel," said Lacayo, inching forward, "is that in order to keep people from claiming your client was railroaded, I have to give you everything you want."

Christina felt the prickly heat creeping up her collar. "I wouldn't put it like that . . ."

"And how far does that go, Ms. McCall? I notice you've also filed a motion to suppress. Do I have to cave in on that one, too? In order to assuage the public need for resolution."

"Your honor, equity always plays a larger role in continuance motions, and here—"

"No, I'm sorry, counsel." He eased back into his black leather chair. "When you raised the public policy concerns, you had me going for a moment. But you have to realize there are many factors that favor going forward—principally an increasingly clogged criminal docket. Also, if I continue this case for three months, the jury will have to be dismissed and a new one impaneled. And for what? So you can appease the public? So you can develop a defense that's more in your style? I'm sorry, Ms. McCall, but you just haven't given me adequate grounds for a continuance. Motion denied."

"But your honor, the needs of—"

He looked at her harshly. "Here in Cook County, Ms. McCall, when the judge says he's ruled, it's over. Move on."

Christina reluctantly turned to the next page. That

was by far her best shot—the motions to suppress evidence were major-league long shots.

After Tony Barovick's body was found in the frat house, the Chicago PD put out an APB and began rounding up every member. They found Johnny and Brett, along with several other frat boys, at Remote Control, the bar where Tony had worked. A visual inspection showed that both Johnny and Brett had scraped knuckles and blood splatters on their clothing. They arrested the two and read them their rights. Johnny stayed cool for a while, but the police continued to needle him, hoping he would do exactly what he did—display some of the temper that would've been necessary to exact the punishment visited on Tony Barovick. He pushed the officers away, screaming, "Who the fuck cares what happened to that flaming faggot?"

It was not a confession, but to the jury, it would have the exact same effect.

"First of all, your honor, we move to strike from the prosecution's witness list all those persons who overheard statements made by Johnny Christensen and Brett Mathers at the bar the night of the murder. Allowing them to repeat what was said by a third party is, by definition, hearsay."

"We don't disagree," said Drabble, rising once again. "But it falls within acknowledged hearsay exceptions. The defendant's statements are admissions against his interest. His partner's statements are admissible because the declarant is obviously unavailable—being dead."

"Hearsay exceptions are allowed at the court's discretion," Christina rejoined, "and should only be permitted where the circumstances suggest reliability. Here, there are no such assurances. The men were all drinking heavily. The two suspects were both puffing, trying to impress their friends."

"By bragging about mercilessly beating a man," Drabble added.

"The point is that nothing about this scenario suggests trustworthiness."

Lacayo shook his head. "I'm sorry, counsel. Once again, I can't agree with you. The statements combined with the close proximity in time to the murder suggest trustworthiness to me. The fact that they even knew a beating had taken place so soon after the event, only minutes after the body was found, suggests that the statements were truthful. And, frankly, if someone's stupid enough to make remarks of that nature in a public place, they deserve to hear them repeated in court."

"Pardon me, sir, but it sounds as if you're punishing my client for being stupid."

"No, ma'am. Life punishes the stupid. No need for the courts to get involved."

Christina felt her knees weakening. She was bombing out here, and she damn well knew it. If she couldn't do better than this, Johnny Christensen was a dead man.

She glanced over her shoulder to the front row of the gallery. Since her client hadn't been released for this hearing, his mother—as the woman who had hired Christina—was the most important person in the room. Ellen Christensen sat with a remarkably stoic expression.

"Your honor," Christina said, trying to pull herself together, "if I might direct your attention to one statement made by my client after he was taken into custodial arrest."

"That's the one we like to call 'the confession,' " Drabble said.

Christina flashed him an evil look.

"You're talking about the"—Lacayo cleared his throat, then spoke in lowered tones—"the 'flaming faggot' remark?"

"Yes, your honor. Contrary to being a confession, this statement isn't even relevant to the crime. It doesn't indicate what he did or did not do, only his . . . opinion regarding persons of different sexual preference. It should be excluded, since it is potentially damaging and not probative of the matter at issue."

"I greatly disagree," Drabble said. For the first time, his voice rose. "This statement is uniquely probative of one important fact—the defendant's venomous hatred of homosexuals. This was a hate crime. And this statement evidences that hate more clearly than I could do in a thousand closing arguments."

"I'm sure the DA would love to have this statement in his closing argument," Christina said, "but that doesn't make it relevant."

"It goes to motive," Drabble said. "More than that, actually. It proves motive."

Lacayo shook his head. "I'm afraid that once again I'm inclined to agree with the prosecutor."

Christina tore desperately through her notes. "What about Miranda rights?"

Lacayo glanced down at his briefs. "I have an affidavit stating that the rights were read and that the defendant waived them."

"The defendant had been drinking," Christina insisted. "His table was littered with tequila shot glasses. The police saw that. They knew he was in a vulnerable mental state. So they read him his rights real quick and started pounding him with questions."

"Again, counsel, I'm not willing to give the man special privileges because he voluntarily engaged in foolish conduct."

"Your honor, if the police can do this, they could pick up any kid who's had a few too many and start hassling him till he says something incriminating. No one would be safe."

Lacayo removed his glasses. "I think this is getting a bit far-fetched."

"It goes to consent, sir, and the Constitution and the rulings of the U.S. Supreme Court require that Miranda rights be knowingly waived before the police may question. In his state of mind, he couldn't possibly—"

"Let's just cut through the baloney, could we?" Lacayo said, revealing another spark of temper. "Do you have any evidence indicating that your client did not understand his rights when they were read to him?"

Christina hesitated. "Well, the whole scenario—"

"I thought not. And if this man had his wits about him enough to brag about a hideous crime, he was able to understand the rights which he's probably heard on television a thousand times before. Forgive me for saying so, counsel, but this argument is weak."

"Your honor—"

"I don't normally try to advise counsel, but I'm going to make an exception here, Ms. McCall, because you're new to our court. I know this case has been thrust upon you in difficult circumstances. But you do not do your client any favors with these desperate arguments."

Christina's lips parted.

"To the contrary. By making it seem as if you're floundering about, grasping for any straw no matter how feeble, you disincline the court to grant any relief in your favor and make a bad situation worse."

Christina was speechless. Chewed out in open court, in front of the woman who hired her and a host of state and national media. Of course Lacayo was grandstanding for the reporters, but that made no difference. This was devastating.

"The best thing you can do now," the judge continued, "is to stop making motions, go to trial, present what evidence you may have in a calm and reasoned manner, and let justice take its course. That public policy you were so concerned about earlier is not served by these frivolous attempts to suppress the truth."

Christina fell into her seat, so choked she couldn't speak.

"Your motion is denied. All your motions are denied. So if there is nothing else—"

"If I may, your honor," Drabble cut in. "The state has a pending motion to bifurcate the evidentiary portion of the case from the sentencing portion. I filed a brief."

The judge nodded. "I don't have any problem with that."

"Wait just one moment," Christina said. "I didn't get his brief."

Lacayo peered across the room at her. "You have not received a copy?"

"Excuse me," Drabble said, "but isn't that your copy on your table, Ms. McCall? In the manila envelope." He turned back to the judge. "I handed it to her myself."

Christina ripped open the top envelope he had given her a few minutes before—that she had volunteered to carry for him. Sure enough—a motion to bifurcate.

The man had suckered her. Not once. But twice.

"So when you told the court that you did not have the brief, Ms. McCall," the judge said, obviously angry, "that was something less than the truth?"

"I—I guess—I had it. I just didn't—"

"Ms. McCall," Judge Lacayo said, "this court feels just as strongly about truthfulness as it does about punctuality."

"Of course, but—"

"Perhaps the least appealing quality of the unprepared lawyer is the tendency to make excuses for her failures."

"But your honor—"

"The motion to bifurcate will be granted. This hearing is adjourned. Have a nice weekend, and I will see you all again Monday morning when we begin this trial." He glared at Christina. "And I will expect rather better preparation and performance than I have seen in this courtroom today." He slammed the gavel.

As soon as Lacayo was out of the courtroom, the

noise level in the courtroom became deafening, at least to Christina. She just hoped to God that Drabble didn't come over to extend his sympathies. That would be too much. She might have to slug the man. The reporters would be waiting for her outside, but she knew if she sweet-talked the judge's clerk, he might let her exit via chambers.

So this was what it had come to—sneaking away from the courtroom, head hung in shame. What the hell had she thought she was doing when she took this case? She might sneak away from the reporters, but she knew she would still have to face Ellen, if not here, then back at Kevin's office. What would she say?

She needed help. She didn't like to admit it, but it was true. She was in over her head. As she packed away her materials, she noticed an e-mail she had printed out this morning. INTERNS SEEKING PART-TIME POSITIONS.

If Ben refused to help her, he couldn't complain if she found someone else who would, right?

By the time she'd made it back to the street, Christina was already on her cell phone setting up interviews. As far as she was concerned, she had no choice. After a performance like today's, she had to do something. Anything. Because when this trial started, it would be about a good deal more than her professional reputation. It would be about whether a young man who insisted he hadn't committed a murder would be sentenced to death—because his attorney blew it.

CHAPTER
13

CHARLIE THE CHICKEN sat opposite the desk and stared at the man in the gray, off-the-rack JCPenney's suit. He was the natty sort—everything in its place. You could see it on his desk; you could see it in his clothes. A hanky tucked in his jacket pocket. Even wore a tie tack, for God's sake.

"Tell me about yourself," the man said, folding his hands into each other.

"Sure." It was a tiny office with plywood walls; the man shared space with a bail bondsman. "I grew up on the South Side. Dropped out of high school, moved downtown. Adventures in the big city—you know how it goes. Had some idea I was going to get involved with a theater company, but so far that hasn't happened. I had to take a trip out of town recently, and . . . unfortunately, that caused a break with my previous employer. Now I'm back and looking for something to do."

"Are you still interested in theater work?"

"Yeah. But at the moment, I need to earn some bread. But that's okay. I mean—it's all performing, isn't it? When you get right down to it. Playing a role. Assuming a character. Trying to please the audience."

Charlie had to fight to keep from laughing. Even a grin would probably be a mistake at this juncture. Who knew how much of a sense of humor this guy had, given what he did for a living? He came off as such a starched shirt. Charlie had expected a significantly higher sleaze factor—silk shirt, or perhaps Hawaiian, open at the collar, collar flared. Fat, feet on the desk, leaning back in the chair. Like a porn film producer, maybe. Instead, he got the man in the gray flannel suit.

"As you might imagine," the man continued, "our hours are at times somewhat irregular and unpredictable. Would that be a problem?"

"Not at all."

"Afternoons are common. And sometimes late nights. Very late."

Charlie spread wide his hands. "Hey, I'm at your disposal."

"Splendid. Do you have a cell phone?"

"No. Unfortunately, I've had to scale back a bit of late. Cut out the nonessentials."

"I understand entirely."

The most remarkable part, all things considered, was how utterly respectable this office seemed. From all outward appearances, he might as well be interviewing for a job as church secretary, perhaps the mayor's aide. But this sort of thing had to be low-key, he supposed. Couldn't attract attention. A big neon sign reading PIMP would probably be a mistake.

"Do you have any hobbies? Other than your theater work?"

"Well, I haven't had too much time for it lately, but, yeah, I love to read. Haunt the libraries, you know. Learned most of my best tricks and techniques there, courtesy of the Cook County taxpayers. And I make boxes."

"Boxes?"

"Hard to explain. I got the idea last time I was in Santa Fe. It's kind of like painting, except on a three-dimensional surface. Sometimes I follow a theme, sometimes I go more abstract. I got one in a gallery on Michigan once. Never sold, though."

The man smiled pleasantly. "My late wife was fond of miniatures. Little dollhouses, I called them."

Charlie tried to suppress his urge to barf. "Well, that's . . . somewhat similar, yeah."

"Where are you living?"

"I'm kind of between places at the moment. I'd been rooming with a guy for years but . . . well, you know how these things shake out sometimes. It didn't work anymore. Then I left town and, since I've been back, I've been squatting in a real dive. One of those rent-by-the-week joints. I think some of my neighbors may be renting in five-minute increments."

"Oh, dear."

"Yeah. So you can see why I'm interested in making some cash. I got things to take care of."

"But of course you do." He scanned a form that lay on the desk before him. "Just a few more things we need to cover . . ."

None of this get-to-know-you BS fooled Charlie for a moment. The man cared about only two things: how much are you willing to do, and how big is it? And if Charlie wanted work, it'd better be big.

"Are you active in sports?"

"Oh yeah. You may not be able to tell—I've always been on the skinny side—but I love to get outdoors and work up a sweat. I play racquetball several times a week." Which was total bull, but it was the most big-dickish answer he could come up with off the top of his head. "We were in the state finals last year."

"Impressive. Could we talk a moment about your professional qualifications?"

Here we go. "Of course."

"You say you've done this sort of thing before."

"Oh yeah."

"So you wouldn't be uncomfortable with the general parameters of escort work."

"Not a bit."

"Then let me ask. Are there any activities you wouldn't be willing to engage in?"

Charlie hesitated. "I'm not sure. Perhaps if you could give me some idea . . ."

"For instance, many of our clients are older women. Considerably older than yourself. Would that be a problem?"

Charlie's face brightened. "I love older women. Bring on the grandmas."

"And some of our clients are rather . . . large."

"Fine, fine. More to love."

The man did not crack a glimmer of a smile. "What about men?"

"Men?"

"Yes. Would that be a problem?"

"I'd . . . probably prefer not to do men. I just . . . it's not my thing, you know?"

"Are you certain about that? We get many requests from male clients. With relatively few outlets for that sort of thing or places to meet men with similar interests, many do find themselves turning to us for assistance. If you were willing to take male clients, we could provide you with a great deal of work. And you did say you needed funds . . ."

Charlie thought long and hard. It was tempting, no doubt about it. If he could score some big money, fast, he could buy some fake ID, get his records altered. Make himself untraceable. Maybe even fly off to Rio and disappear once and for all.

But then he thought about Dean, and that first hideous, painful night . . .

"No. I'm sorry, I can't do that. But bring on the women, and I'll give them something they never dreamt—"

"Are there any acts you would not be willing to engage in? Any positions?"

"With the grandmas? Nah. I don't care."

"Well, then, that just about covers it, I think." He

stacked his papers and punched a perfectly placed staple in the upper left corner. "I don't see why you can't start immediately."

"Great."

"My secretary will issue you a pager. Please keep it on your person at all times. If we buzz you, proceed to a telephone as soon as possible for your instructions."

"Roger."

"Now there are a few rules we should review. First—"

"Get the money up front."

The man's lips thinned. Was that what passed for a smile with this guy? "Yes. There are others, however. Our clients must always be treated with respect. Be punctual. Never argue. The customer is always right. And most important—"

"Get the money up front. I understand. Believe me— I've been there."

"Good. We shouldn't have any problems. May I validate your parking?"

"Uh, no. I took the bus." Which was true, even though it didn't leave often and never went exactly where he needed to go. But he felt safer in a bus than he did walking the streets. Anything could happen to you when you were walking alone on the street, Charlie thought, a sudden chill running down his back. Like with Tony Barovick. He knew what had happened to that poor kid—like no one else did.

Well, almost no one. One did. The one who was undoubtedly searching the streets of the city, night and day, looking for Charlie the Chicken. So he could do it again.

CHAPTER
14

CHRISTINA AND LOVING sat in a booth, casing the joint as they huddled over two longneck beers and a video monitor. Loving preferred to get the lay of a place before he barged in asking questions. And it was just as well, because Remote Control was not your average singles bar.

"So this is how they do it in the big city," Christina said. "Back in Tulsa, they'd just have a debutante ball."

"That would be an improvement," Loving replied.

"I suppose this is better than trying to meet someone in an online chat room."

" 'Fyou say so."

"You can tell if a guy is really a guy."

"Mebbe."

"I suppose you preferred it when you could just club a woman over the head and drag her by the hair back to your cave."

He shrugged. "Did simplify things."

Christina scoped out the crowded bar. It was filled with people using video monitors, all of them hooked up to a single camera network. From the relative privacy of your booth, you could channel surf—for people. Keep switching from channel to channel till you saw someone you liked, then push a button to let your obscure object of desire know you're watching. If there is no objection, you pick up the phone and chat. A meat market for the Nintendo generation.

"I know we're working," Christina said, "but I won't object if you want to try it out. After all, a good investigator has to get a feel for the environment."

"Pass," Loving said.

"Too chicken?"

"Too smart."

There was a buzzing sound, followed by a pop-up message on their screen. "Channel 42 says, 'Hi!' Would you like to reply? Press A to initiate contact. Press B to send them packing."

Christina gave Loving a poke. "C'mon. Go for it."

"Nuh-huh. The message is from someone named Adam. He doesn't wanna talk to me. Or if he does, I don't wanna talk to him."

"Well, I'm game." Christina pushed the A button. A head shot of a dark-complexioned man in his early thirties popped onto the screen. "Ten-four, Adam. This is Becky Sue."

Loving arched an eyebrow. Becky Sue?

"Hi, Becky Sue," the face on the screen replied. "I've been watching you."

"You yellow dog, you."

"I'm in one of the back caverns. Got a bottle of champagne and a chaise longue. Would you like to join me?"

"I don't know. Whatcha got?"

Christina found his attempt at a seductive look all too amusing. "More than you can handle, sister." He unbuttoned the top button of his shirt.

"I dunno, pardner. I can handle a lot."

Adam was still unbuttoning. "That's good to hear. Because I've got a lot for you."

"Tell me more."

"Why talk at all? Come back to my cavern and I'll give you a taste of my all-night sucker."

Christina pressed a hand to her throat. "Oh, my."

"Come on, gorgeous," Adam cooed. "Let me show you what you're missing. We'll relax, pour a few shots."

"Sorry, slick. I don't do hard liquor."

"Do you smoke? I've got some joints."

Loving stiffened.

"It's quality stuff. Just in from Mexico."

Loving began to slide from their booth. Christina grabbed his arm. "Hold on, Starsky."

"What's the problem?" Adam asked. "He doesn't smoke?"

"No, dear. The problem is he hates drugs and the people who promote them. Last guy who tried to pass him a joint ended up in the hospital for a week."

The screen went black.

Loving got up. "I'm going after him."

"Don't bother. He'll be long gone."

Loving grimaced. "I got enough atmosphere. Let's try some actual investigatin'. They're expecting us. You want the owner?"

"Aye, aye, Cap'n."

"I'll do the barmaid. Word on the street says she was a close friend of Tony Barovick's." He moved toward the bar. "Don't make anyone mad or go anywhere I can't see you. I'm only lettin' you in on this 'cause we're so pressed for time. Push hard. Don't let him weasel around with half answers. We'll meet back here when you're done."

"No doubt," Christina said. "Unless I find a dark cavern with a chaise longue."

CHRISTINA HATED BEING made to wait, but she might tolerate it from, say, the president of the United States. But from a greasy, overweight club owner? It didn't sit well.

Fortunately, she had the overhead monitors to amuse her. One was scrolling through a montage of images from throughout the bar: couples kissing, men's butts in tight jeans, women's cleavage—had a camera been pointed at her chest while she sat in the booth with Loving?—a rapid-fire succession of faces howling with gaiety or rapturous with passion. If this wasn't a television commercial, it should be.

At long last, Mario Roma put down his cell phone. "So you're defending the guy who killed Tony."

"Accused," Christina clarified.

"We had cops and lawyers crawling all over the place, after what happened. I don't remember you."

"I'm new to the case." Christina took the open stool—then immediately checked to see if there were any cameras zooming in on her cleavage. "So you own this place?"

"I do. My pride and joy."

"How's it doing?"

"It's turned into a nice little moneymaker. I'm talking to some people about turning it into a franchise."

"I'm not surprised. It's a unique concept. You deserve your success."

"Thanks, lady, but I can't take credit. It was all Tony's idea."

"Tony? Tony Barovick?"

"Yeah." Roma waved, and a waitress brought him what looked like a microwaved burrito. "You want something?"

Christina gazed at the mass of congealed cheese and refried beans. "I already ate. Thanks, though."

"When Tony came on as manager, this was a perfectly ordinary singles joint. People flirting and dancing and coming on to each other just like they have for the last fifty years."

"And Tony Barovick came up with the idea of modernizing it?"

"Exactly. He was into computers and video and stuff. Understood all this high-tech jazz. Couldn't figure out why it had never been used to help people get together. We use technology to improve our businesses and transportation and television reception, so he thought: Why don't we use it to improve the mating process?"

"Good point, if a little clinical. So you went for it."

"Almost immediately. I can't take credit for the idea, but I know a good one when I hear it. I took out a loan and invested a million bucks in all these cameras and computers and stuff. We've been booming ever since."

"That's great."

"Have you checked it out? It's fabulous. You can scope the action—without embarrassment or awkward situations. Everyone's more relaxed. It's a great way to hook up with someone. I mean, compared to this, computer dating services look like something from the Stone Age."

"And Barovick also managed the club?"

"Yeah. Did a bang-up job, too. He was on top of everything. Whatever the patrons wanted, he made sure they had it. They loved him."

"So if Tony was your manager—and idea man—you must've known him pretty well."

"For two years." Roma took a huge bite, smearing some bean sauce on his gray mustache. "He was a great employee. And friend. I loved him like a brother."

"You must've been pretty torn up after what happened."

Roma's cheeks sagged. Hard lines formed across his forehead. "Lady, there ain't no words for what I felt when—when I found out."

"Bad?"

"Let me put it this way. I'm not a rich man—but the second I heard what happened, I put it out on the street that I'd pay fifty thousand dollars to anyone who could catch, hurt, or kill the men who did it. Or better yet, all of the above."

"You put a bounty on their heads? You know that's illegal."

"So put the cuffs on me." He hefted a tall, cold mug of beer. "I did what I had to do."

"They were caught very quickly. Right here in the bar?"

Roma clenched his teeth so hard his head seemed to shrink. "Yeah, they came back here. Bragging about what they did. How bad they hurt Tony." His voice became quieter. "If I'd had the chance, I'd have ripped their heads off with my bare hands."

Looking at the man, his physique, his evident anger, Christina didn't doubt that he could do it. "I guess you knew Tony was gay?"

"Sure. Everyone knew."

"And you were okay with it?"

"Didn't see what business of mine it was who he slept with. Long as it's between consenting adults, who cares?"

If only we all saw the world through the eyes of Mario Roma. "Did you know the two boys who were arrested? The frat guys?"

"I'd seen 'em before. But I didn't want anything to do with them."

Christina made a mental note. "And why is that? Don't like fraternities?"

"More than that." Mario shrugged. "Could be wrong. But the skinny dark one looked like mob to me."

"And that was bad because—"

"I have to explain what's bad about the mob? Or maybe you thought that since I'm Italian-American I must be Mafia."

"I was just asking questions."

"I've kept my nose clean my whole life, lady. I put my life together without any help from anyone, including mob bosses. And I'm proud of it. So don't start in with your insinuations."

"Wouldn't dream of it." Christina peered intently at the man's face. Methinks he doth protest too much.

"My club's a clean joint. We don't allow people to stumble out and drive drunk. We don't permit drugs—not even a hint."

Christina decided not to tell him about Adam and the back cavern.

"Remote Control is a good place where a guy or gal can go to meet someone. Safe. Wholesome."

"Sort of a Disney singles bar."

"Well, yeah, in a way. I mean, there's a need for this. Used to be, you'd meet a nice girl at church, or a neighborhood dance, or whatever. But those old communities have disintegrated. Hell, with computers, some people never leave home. We got more people, but it's harder to meet them."

Christina couldn't disagree. Being single in Tulsa was like being an atheist in, well, Tulsa.

"We provide a valuable community service. So I was mad as hell about what happened to Tony—not only for Tony but for Remote Control. I don't like hoods running around. For that matter, I'm not crazy about lawyers."

"Well, I don't want to bring the neighborhood down." She put away her legal pad. "You'll be around, if I have more questions?"

"I'm not going anywhere." He gobbled down the last of his burrito. "You know my motto: At Remote Control, you're only a click away."

"C'MON, BABY. DO something sexy."

"I don't know . . ."

"Please. Who's going to know?" His voice dropped. "I'll strip if you'll strip."

The woman tentatively unfastened the clasp of her dress. The man started on his shirt.

"Now shake 'em, baby. Shake 'em!"

Without warning, both participants burst out laughing.

Loving turned off the monitor. "Ain't that gonna spoil the mood?"

"They were both kidding all along," Shelly explained. "It was sort of a video truth or dare, seeing who would crack up first."

Shelly Chimka, a petite auburn-haired young woman with an effervescent personality, had been showing Loving the inner workings of Remote Control. "Most of the patrons don't realize that we can monitor all video conversations. Although I'm not sure it would change anything if they did. Tony and I used to come back here and eavesdrop for hours. We had more fun than any of them."

"You and Tony were close?" Loving asked. They were standing in the manager's office, behind the kitchen and bar—the office that used to be Tony's. There was not much there—a few chairs, a desk, and a lot of audio, video, and computer equipment.

"I adored him. I mean it. I'm not just saying that because he's dead." She reached instinctively to wipe her eye—but her arm wouldn't reach. Her right arm was in a sling. "He gave me my big promotion, you know. I was just a lowly waitress with the slow afternoon shift when Tony became manager. He put me behind the bar and gave me the best shift. Used to say sales doubled once the boys knew I was going to be tending bar."

"Don't doubt it," Loving replied.

"When Tony was here, work wasn't work. You know what I mean? He made everything fun."

"How?"

She ransacked her memory. "The last night, before . . . We'd heard this rumor that there was an undercover cop here."

Loving's chin rose.

"So we tried to pick out who it was. Tony always had

the most absurd theories. 'That mild-mannered grandmother is really a twenty-five-year-old male Lebanese
bodybuilder in drag.' That sort of thing."

"Sounds like a great boss."

"He was. And a great friend. I could tell Tony anything."

"Did you have any . . . hint? 'Bout what happened?"

"Not at all. Sure, sometimes the frat boys acted like
assholes. But I never dreamed—" She looked down,
squinting to fight back the tears. "I mean, everyone
knew Tony was gay. So what? I didn't think anyone
cared about that anymore. And then—" She pressed her
hand against her mouth. "And then you blink for a
minute, and one of the loveliest men to ever walk the
earth has been killed. Just because of what he was."

"Tony was lucky to have a friend like you." Loving
waited a moment before proceeding. "Has anythin' bad
been going down here at the club lately?"

"We still have frat boys, if that's what you mean."

"I don't know. Mob contacts? Hit men?"

"No. My boss won't have anything to do with the
mob."

"Gambling? Illicit sex? Drugs?"

She shook her head. "We don't permit any drugs in
the bar. Zero tolerance."

"You sure about that?"

"Roma won't stand for it. If he gets even a hint, he's
all over it."

That was the official policy, anyway, and she seemed
sincere about it. "If you think of anything else that
might help, ma'am, gimme a call, would you?"

"I will."

"One more thing—would you mind if I ask how you
hurt your arm?"

Shelly tensed. "It—it isn't relevant. It happened after
Tony . . ."

"Still. If you wouldn't mind."

Shelly took several deep breaths, trying to calm herself. "You already know, don't you? I can see it in your face." She tossed her rag down on the bar. "Well, you're right. I tried to kill myself. Slashed my wrist. Had to go to the hospital. The sling is just to cover the wrist bandages. I didn't want it to be obvious."

"Was this after Tony was killed?"

She nodded. "I just . . . I didn't understand how anyone could have so much hate. So much cruelty. How they could torture a good, sweet man. When I read in the papers that Tony begged for mercy, pleaded for his life, and they ignored him, I—I—" She pressed a hand against her forehead. "Well, I didn't want to live anymore. Couldn't."

"And how do you feel now?"

"It still hurts, but . . . I'm not suicidal."

"That's good. Thank you for your time."

"Sure. Oh—"

"Yes?"

"I know you're working for the lawyers representing that Christensen kid, but—they are going to convict him, aren't they?"

Loving shrugged. "Certainly looks that way."

"Good. Good." She peered down at a tiny point on the floor. "I don't want to sound vindictive, but someone has to pay. When someone as beautiful as Tony is taken, in such a . . . brutal way. He suffered so much. And we're still suffering—all of us who loved him. Shouldn't the bastards who did it have to suffer, too?"

CHAPTER
15

SPECIAL AGENT SWIFT raced into Mike's cubicle, waving a message slip in the air. "Woo hoo!" she squealed. "I got lucky!"

"Why am I not surprised?" Baxter groused, sotto voce.

Mike raced to her side. Baxter arrived at a somewhat more leisurely pace.

"Can I cook, or can't I?" Swift continued. Mike noticed that her Southern accent seemed to become more pronounced in moments of great excitement.

"We got a positive print ID on the photocopy," Swift explained.

Baxter squinted. "I don't understand. There was a fingerprint on the photocopy we found in the victim's pocket?"

"No. The photocopy was a fingerprint."

"I'm lost."

"Don't feel bad," Mike interjected. "A lot of people—including those in law enforcement—don't know that photocopiers leave a fingerprint—due to the tiny scratches and dirt on the copier's glass and optical system."

"And this can be traced?"

"You bet your sweet bippy," Swift said enthusiastically. "The odds against two copiers having exactly the same pattern are astronomical."

"Our victim didn't have a copy machine in his apartment," Mike explained, "so I sent plainclothes officers to all the copy shops in town, checking for the same pattern. And it paid off." He glanced at the message. "Kinko's. Memorial and 51st. Shall we?"

MIKE WAS NOT surprised to learn that Sergeant Tomlinson was the man who had tracked down America's Most Wanted Photocopier, or that he had pored through three months of credit card receipts before Mike arrived. Tomlinson had always been the king of go-the-extra-mile. That was how he had ended up as Mike's partner, until Kate Baxter came along.

"Actually," Tomlinson said, "I've been through them twice. Working from the approximate date and cost. But nothing even comes close."

"If he just made a single copy, he wouldn't use a credit card," Mike reasoned. "Probably just small change." Which was too damn bad. Because a credit card receipt would've given him a name. And, more than likely, an address.

He addressed the clerk, a pimply teenager named Sid. "Any record of cash purchases?"

The kid shook his head, stiff-necked. Mike couldn't decide if he was intimidated because this was his first encounter with law enforcement—or because it wasn't. "People come in all the time to make one or two copies. There's no way to trace them."

And you're not likely to recognize any of them, either, Mike thought, but he was going to give it a try, just in case. He pulled out a digitally reconstructed photo of the victim. "Ever seen this guy before?"

It didn't matter what the kid said, because Mike could tell the moment his eyes lit on the photo that he had.

If nothing else, the boy had the sense not to lie. "Yeah. I recognize him."

"He's been in the store before?"

He hesitated only a moment before answering, but

it was a moment that told Mike everything. "A few times."

"But that's not how you know him."

Sid glanced over his shoulder, as if hoping some photocopy emergency might extract him from the interrogation. "I've just . . . seen him around."

"You've bought drugs from him, haven't you?" Agent Swift asked, out of the blue.

"What? God, no. I don't do drugs."

"What about Ecstacy? You probably don't consider that doing drugs. Right?"

"Well . . ."

"Come clean, kid. It's the smart thing to do."

The kid looked at her, but didn't answer, which spoke volumes. Mike was impressed. Chalk up one for the FBI.

"It's all right, son," Mike said. "We're not looking to make a drug bust. We need information about this man."

The boy remained silent.

"Of course, if you don't help us, I'll have to consider what I might do to persuade you. Like maybe a search of your work locker. Your car. Your apartment."

"His name's Manny," Sid said. "Manny Nowosky. And I've only seen him a few times."

"You know anything about him?"

"Not much. He was holed up in a rental house not far from where I live. Used to run into him at the pool parlor. I haven't seen him lately."

And there's a reason for that. "There must've been something else," Mike said.

"I wouldn't know what it was."

"Did you hear any rumors? Even hints? Maybe about something big going down. A big score. A big bust. Manny coming into a big wad of dough. Anything."

Sid shook his head adamantly. "No, nothing. I never had that much contact. We just . . . did business a few times."

"And that was all?"

"He was a carpenter, I remember. Took his stuff up to the flea market sometimes to sell."

"And?"

"Sometimes we . . . talked about cars."

"Cars? Just cars?"

"Race cars. Kind of a hobby for us. We were both into drag racing."

Swift blinked. "Drag racing? Like—zoom-zoom? *American Graffiti*?"

"Right. We could rattle on for hours, talking about mag wheels and stick shifts and stuff. He seemed a little old for that sort of thing. But as I learned, he raced pretty regularly."

"On the street? When the cops weren't looking?"

"No, man. On designated drag strips. It's safe. Legal. When he talked about his favorite strip, he called it—what was it?—'the happiest place on earth.' "

"And you're sure he wasn't talking about Disneyland?"

"Positive. Drag racing."

"I didn't know there were any strips around Tulsa."

"Tulsa?" The kid was incredulous. "He wasn't from Tulsa. He was just passing through. Taking care of some business. His strip was near Evanston."

"Evanston?" Swift's eyes widened. "As in the suburb of Chicago?"

"That's the one."

Swift gave Mike a long look. "Well, guess what, boys and girls? I think you're going to be paying a visit to my neck of the woods."

Mike nodded. "Sounds that way. We can't get a flight till tomorrow morning, though." He gave Sid his card. "If you think of anything else you know about this guy—anything at all—give me a call."

"Okay. Sure."

They prepared to leave. "And kid?"

"Yes, sir?"

"The federal penitentiary in McAlester is a really ugly place. Take my word for it. You don't want to go."

"No, sir."

"So keep your nose clean. Tomlinson?"

"Yes, Major?"

"Nice work." He slapped his old friend and protégé on the shoulder. "Wanna grab a sandwich? You can fill me in on what you and Karen and that girl of yours have been up to. And what's going down with the uniforms. Especially the gossip. I love the gossip . . ."

CHAPTER
16

"CHRISTINA!" LOVING BELLOWED. "You're needed in the conference room. There's like—thirty of 'em in there!"

"I'll be just a minute." She met him in the hallway. "I've been reading your reports. You've covered a heck of a lot of ground."

The burly man tipped an imaginary hat. "I aim to please, ma'am."

"I really appreciate your tracking down all of Johnny Christensen's friends and frat brothers."

"Yeah. Too bad none of 'em knows nothin.' " He shook his head. "I gotta tell you, Christina. No one saw Tony in the vacant lot, and no one saw him moved to the frat house."

"I know. But it was late, and there was no reason for anyone to be there. Keep on it, okay?"

"Natch."

"You might get with Jones and see what he's got on this ANGER group. Maybe a little infiltration would turn up something useful."

"I'll check into it."

"Good. Get a copy of Paula's report on Tony and the man who shot Brett Mathers. It's very thorough. Good starting place."

"Will do."

Christina started for the conference room. "Wanna help me in here?"

He grinned sheepishly. "You don't want my help, Chris. I'd just hire the cutest one."

"Right." She pushed the door open and entered the conference room—which was packed solid with young law students. And Jones.

"Have you talked to Ben about this yet?" he asked.

"No. He doesn't want to be involved."

"He might want to be involved in acquiring new staff! We don't have the money to hire an intern."

"Find it."

"Where? It's not as if you're getting paid big bucks."

"I don't know. There must be someplace."

"I could take it out of your salary."

She paused. "Someplace else." She laid her clipboard on the table and addressed the sea of eager young faces. "Good morning, and thank you for coming. As I'm sure you all know, we've been handed a major case with an extremely tight deadline—and we need help. If you're looking to make a fortune overnight or to get another line on your résumé, leave now. But if you want to knuckle down and do some seriously hard work—and maybe get a crash course in how criminal cases are tried—line up over here. Be prepared to tell me what your goals are—why you wanted to be a lawyer in the first place. We'll start the interviews immediately."

AFTER AN HOUR or so, the faces blurred together and Christina had a hard time differentiating the words of one candidate from another's.

"I guess it was *Perry Mason* that did it for me. I mean, watching the show, somehow you just knew Della was the brains of the outfit. But did she ever get any credit? Nooooo."

"I think the American criminal justice system is in sorry shape. I became a lawyer so I could reform the system from within. And get a swimming pool. I live to swim."

"My mom always said, 'Carrie, the way you argue, you ought to be a lawyer.' So here I am!"

"I used to watch you on Court TV, every afternoon, during the Wallace Barrett trial. And I thought, Man, can that girl dress! I wanna get me some of that action."

"Doesn't it drive you crazy when people talk about the Founding Fathers? I mean, how sexist is that? There were women in those colonies, too."

"Mostly, I want to be a lawyer so I can give speeches. I give seriously hot speeches. When I talk, people melt like butter."

"I hate it when creeps tell lawyer jokes. I mean, that's so bigoted. Negative stereotypes, based on someone's profession. It's disgusting. Now, Aggie jokes—those are funny."

And worst of all, in Christina's estimation: "I just want to be an attorney so I can help other people."

"Ugh." Christina rolled her eyes. "No, thanks. We've already got one of those."

AND THEN THERE was one. By the end of the morning, Christina had narrowed the field to: Vicki Harmon. On the plus side, she was smart, energetic, and appeared to work out regularly—a good quality given the rigors of trial preparation and courtroom proceedings. Furthermore, she was personally recommended by the dean of Northwestern, and she had the best résumé of the lot. On the minus side, Christina thought, she's probably smarter than I am, is even shorter than I am, and by all indications is even quieter than Ben. If such a thing is possible.

She hired the girl anyway. "I assume you can start immediately."

Vicki spoke softly—more like a mouse squeak than

a human voice. "Oh yes. I'll be here first thing in the morning."

Christina shook her head. "When I say immediately, I mean immediately. As in *now*."

Vicki blinked. "Oh."

"This trial starts Monday, remember? And I don't want to scare you off—but you'll be my right-hand man. My Number One."

Another blink. "Oh."

Despite her quietness, the girl was seriously cute— which was kind of a strike against her. Christina was used to being the cute one in the office, but there was no way she could out-cute this little slip of a thing who was twelve years younger. Oh, well. The sacrifices she made for her clients . . .

"And not that this is immediately relevant," Christina continued, "but I see on your résumé that you speak French."

"Oh. Yes."

"Not just clichés, but really, truly speak French?"

"It was my minor in college. Can I still have the job?"

Christina batted her lips with a finger. "Let me think. You're young, pretty, smart, ambitious, have good grades, are well dressed, almost a lawyer, free of entanglements, and you speak French. Vicki—you're living my dream."

Vicki leaned forward timidly. "If you'd like . . . I'd be happy to give you French lessons. When there's time."

Christina extended her hand. "Girl, I think this is the start of a beautiful friendship."

"STOP RAVING AND just tell me what happened," Christina said, trying to calm him. "You say you got a letter bomb?"

"I wish," Jones replied, pacing in front of Christina's desk. "That would've been better. I said the package exploded when I opened it. Right in my face. Tons of excelsior."

"And you're bringing this to my attention because . . ."

"Because it's a threat, Christina. It's got a brochure from ANGER. 'Stop hate now,' it says."

"Doesn't seem like that big a deal to me."

"It would if you'd seen the doll."

"The . . . doll?"

"Right. Mutilated. Cut up. Smeared with red paint."

Christina drummed her fingernails. "I suppose we have to acknowledge that Johnny is likely to become a target of—"

"Would you just listen for a moment?"

Christina couldn't think when she'd ever seen him so upset. "This wasn't a Ken doll they mutilated. It was short and female. With long flowing red hair."

Christina's lips drew together wordlessly.

"They've moved way beyond making Johnny a target. He's under lock and key. They can't get to him." Jones looked at her grimly. "But they can sure get to you."

CHAPTER
17

EVEN THOUGH IT was contrary to her nature, not to mention the established practice of many years, Christina actually knocked before entering Ben's apartment.

Only a few seconds later, Ben opened his door. "Christina! But—I thought you were in Chicago!" His face was a mix of unreadable emotions. Christina preferred to think he was happy to see her.

"Caught the red-eye. Had to make a few visits, collect a few things before the trial starts Monday morning."

"Collect a few things? Such as? . . ."

"May I come in?" She looked as if she'd come straight from Tulsa International; she was carrying luggage. "I brought cookies. Chocolate milk. Travel Scrabble."

"Of course." Ben preceded her into the living room. She'd been here so many times she could find it blindfolded. Same threadbare sofa, same coffee table. Same enormous cat curled up in his chair. "I'm surprised to see you."

"Well, surprises are the spice of life, right?" she said casually, as she sat in an overstuffed armchair.

"I'm surprised you're not working tonight."

"I needed a break. I've been pulling down twenty-hour days. And that pretrial hearing . . ."

"Yeah, how did that go?"

"Not well."

Ben crossed his legs and clasped his hands around his knee; as body language went, he was a million miles away. "You didn't expect that judge to give you a continuance, did you? With half the world waiting for this trial?"

"It was a long shot. But I had a fresh angle. I made a public policy argument."

"Really," Ben said, barely reacting. "Brilliant."

"Yeah. Found an obscure local precedent. Didn't fly. I had him going—he thought about it for a few seconds before turning me down. Rejected all the motions to suppress, too."

"It might've been different if you'd been the first attorney on the case. You can't expect him to turn back time and make evidentiary rulings after a jury has been selected."

"Yeah." They fell silent. Christina looked around the room, gazed at the pictures on the wall—there were two—scrutinized her shoelaces—until she couldn't stand it anymore.

"Ben . . . I really need your help."

"Christina—"

"I think there's a lot more to this murder than people think, but I can't possibly track it all down in time."

"Nonetheless—"

"If you won't do it for me, do it for Johnny Christensen."

"That's—" Ben stood, then turned away. "That's exactly what I can't—won't do."

"Why?"

He walked to the window and stared out at the back alleyway. "I don't want to discuss it."

"I . . . didn't know that we had . . . secrets . . ."

"It's not a secret. It's just too complicated to explain."

"Ben, do you have any idea how much attention this murder case is getting?"

"Well, I saw pictures of the redecorations in your Chicago office lobby on CNN."

"That's just the tip of the iceberg. We're getting threatening calls by the hour. The Chicago papers and talk radio hosts have been running op-ed pieces condemning us for taking the case. You know the rant—'some lawyers will do anything for money.' That kind of crap."

He continued staring out the window. "We've seen all that before."

"Yes, we have, and that's why I find your refusal so unfathomable. You've always said the unpopular cases are the most important ones to take. Anyone can represent a sympathetic client. But the dirty, unpleasant, unpopular ones—that's when you prove that a lawyer's oath isn't just words, that everyone—*everyone*—is entitled to a fair trial."

"All true."

"Then where the hell are you?" Her voice rose much louder than she had intended. "Where's your oath now that I need it?"

Ben turned, his arms spread, his head shaking, as if he were groping for words that would not come. "I . . . can't do it, Christina."

Christina felt so many emotions coursing through her—anger, confusion, disillusionment—she couldn't possibly give voice to all the thoughts raging in her head. And she didn't want to be here any longer.

She gathered all her belongings. "I'm leaving."

Ben stretched out a hand. "Don't."

"What's the point?"

"We could . . . play a game of Scrabble. I've been studying up on the three-letter words."

"I'm not in the mood to play with someone who would . . ." She didn't finish her sentence. "As long as I've known you, Ben, you've always done the right thing. That was what I've always admired about you most."

She could see his body tensing. "There are some things . . . no one should be expected to do."

She headed for the door. "We've been through some tough times together, you and me, Ben. We've had good cases and bad. Good clients and bad. Won some, lost some. But no matter how they came out—I was never disappointed in you." She grabbed the doorknob and flung the front door open. "Until now."

CHRISTINA'S EYES WERE flooding and her head was boiling and as a result she almost crashed into Ellen Christensen and knocked her down the stairs.

"Oh, I'm so sorry," Christina said, wiping her eyes. "I didn't—" She stopped for a moment, letting her brain come back into focus. What was Mrs. Christensen doing in Tulsa? At Ben's house, no less? "I didn't realize you knew Ben. I mean, outside the office."

Ellen's lips thinned. "Ben and I know each other very well."

They did? "I'm sorry. I didn't know. I mean, not that's it's any of my business."

Ellen smiled slightly, then passed her on the stairs.

Christina ran across the front yard to her car, feeling stupid and betrayed. She'd been suspicious before, but now it was all starting to make a twisted sort of sense. Small wonder their relationship was going nowhere. Small wonder he didn't want to talk about it. What a fool she was. The combination of running, fresh air, and heartache was clearing the cobwebs out of her muddled brain.

Oh, my God, Christina realized. She's the one. *She's the one!*

She got into her car and checked her pocket calendar. She had to fly back to Chicago tomorrow morning, but there was still time for a road trip to Oklahoma City. She wouldn't put it off this time. She was going to clear up this mystery, once and for all.

Even if the answers killed her.

CHAPTER
18

ANOTHER DAY IN the exciting life of Charlie the Chicken, he thought, as he strode through an elegant North Side neighborhood. Lovely homes—big palatial mansions, large enough to house everyone in his apartment complex with ease. The lawns were all perfect, as if they had been mowed with cuticle scissors. Rose bushes seemed to be the thing this year; everyone had them, in some cases in sickening abundance.

It was a lovely stroll, but Charlie wasn't enjoying it. For one thing, he was working, so it would be a mistake to act as if he were out on some pleasure jaunt. Moreover, this was the first time he'd been outside, exposed, for more than ten minutes since he'd returned to Chicago. Not that he thought the person who was looking for him was likely to be hanging in this neighborhood. But you never knew. You couldn't be too careful, not with someone like that. When he remembered what had been done to Manny—

He mentally erased the chalk from his brain. He needed to get in a happy mood. This was his first gig for the new service, and he wanted to do a first-rate job of it.

When he arrived at his destination, he had to stop and gape. This place was immense! Not just a house—more like a walled city. The lot had to be two acres, maybe more. It went on and on as far as the eye could see.

Must've been oil, Charlie reasoned, made back in the days when oil tycoons were practically printing money. No one could afford to build a palace like this today.

He glanced down at his clothing, wondering if he had erred. He was wearing tight jeans, as usual—so tight they clutched the crotch and, quite frankly, made it difficult to walk. He couldn't wait to get them off. Fortunately, he knew he would not have long to wait. And he'd gone with a white muscle T-shirt. Not exactly the standard attire for this part of town—unless maybe you were the gardener. Perhaps he should try to find the servant's entrance?

Hell with it. This lady would be glad to see him. He'd checked himself out in the mirror before he left, and he looked damn good, if he did say so himself. He marched up a long paved walkway that led to the massive front door. He wondered: Would the door open, or would it lower like a castle drawbridge?

It opened.

"Are you Charlie?"

"Yes, ma'am."

"Then come in."

She was pitifully thin—these rich wives tended to be—but at least she wasn't decrepit. He wasn't a good judge of age, but she couldn't be older than her mid-fifties. And he supposed if he had to choose, he'd go with egret-frame before he'd tackle big-pig fat.

She led him directly to her bedroom, which did not surprise him. He wouldn't have minded spending some time checking out the ungodly expensive furniture and art objects that cluttered every square inch of the house, but she hadn't invited him over for a grand tour. Like most of the women in her social strata, she was all business.

She instructed him to remove his clothing, which he did. Then she tucked an envelope under his shirt. That was the cash up front, presumably. He supposed it would be gauche to count it.

"I'm fifty-two years old and I've never had an orgasm," she said, sitting on the edge of the bed, still dressed. "I think it's about time. Don't you?"

Isn't this a chat you should be having with your husband? But Charlie knew that probably wasn't an option. Scattered about the room were pictures of at least three kids so, Charlie surmised, it wasn't that sex didn't exist. More likely that Mister Big Business Missionary Position You're Here to Service My Needs never bothered to ask his wife if she was enjoying herself down there. "I'll do my best, ma'am."

That wasn't good enough. "I explained very carefully to your superior that what I wanted was an orgasm. That's what I paid for."

"And I'll do my best."

She still wasn't satisfied, but happily she didn't push it. "What should I do?"

"I'll take care of everything, ma'am. You just lie there."

Of course, he hadn't meant it literally, but she took it that way. Or perhaps she was always like that, which might explain why her husband didn't kill himself trying to bring her to sexual ecstasy. Whatever the reason, for the succeeding hour and fifteen minutes, the woman never moved. The Ice Princess lay flat on her back, elbows over her breasts, rigid. She *was* enjoying herself. He could tell that from the involuntary responses of her body. She was melting in all the right places. But she didn't move. Only once did a small, high-pitched peep escape, and she immediately squelched it. Must've done something powerful there, Charlie thought. Make a note.

By using his experience-born powers of insight, he did get some glimmer of what the woman was into. She liked dirty talk, for instance. Once he started with that, her body gave unmistakable signs of being seriously turned on. And once he'd managed to forklift her under the covers, he took advantage of the Louis Vuitton silk sheets to slither around and across her body. She liked that.

He did, at long last, manage to deliver the Big O. He would've preferred to hear her cry out in ecstasy, but her wide-eyed, stunned expression was almost as gratifying. When at last he rested, flopping down onto the bed, she left. He was to give her ten minutes—presumably so she could dress without being seen—then let himself out. Which he did.

Talk about your noblesse oblige—the lady even left him a tip. A five-dollar bill tossed casually on his clothes.

Five dollars? He started to get very worried about what was in that envelope. Breaking away from tradition, he ripped it open right then and there.

Fifty dollars? Fifty frigging dollars? That was half of what he understood was the minimum. What was going on here? He works for more than an hour delivering her first taste of sexual pleasure and she stiffs him?

Goddamn it! He shoved the money into his pocket. He was going to have a talk with the boss. He felt certain he'd never find the woman; she was probably showering all traces of him off herself, assisted by six handmaidens and a eunuch or two. His share of the fifty dollars wouldn't get him jack. And he'd wasted his whole day. He was tempted to grab some damn antique on his way out, but he knew that would only get him in worse trouble, perhaps thrown in jail. Or with this lady's connections, maybe he'd just be executed on the spot.

Damn!

He threw himself out the front door, slamming it behind him.

And found himself staring at a smiling face. And a deadly weapon.

Charlie jumped three feet into the air. He fell back, clutching his chest, moving as far away as possible.

"I know what you are," said the man holding the electric hedge cutter.

The gardener, Charlie said, trying to calm himself. Not the one he was running from. Just the gardener.

"If you came to talk to the missus, she's busy. Try again later."

The big man with the stubbled face continued to leer.

"I know what you are. I know what you did. I see you, through the big window outside the greenhouse."

"There are laws against that sort of thing, pal." He tried to push past the man, without success.

"Whore," the man said, placing a finger on Charlie's chest. "That's what you are."

"Look, if I scream, your mistress will come running, and you'll be—"

"Cheap piece of ass." Before Charlie knew what was happening, the man had slapped his hand against Charlie's crotch and squeezed. "Get me some of that."

"Leave me alone!" he said, futilely trying to push the man away.

"What you want? Money? You already got paid. Now deliver." He squeezed all the harder. "I can hurt you, boy. Better if you cooperate."

"Go—to—hell!" Charlie brought his fists up under the man's chin and ran, ran as fast as he could manage in his too-tight jeans. He was almost a mile away before he checked to see if the gardener was following him.

He was alone.

Jesus Christ, what a day. And for what? Fifty frigging dollars? Fifty-five, technically.

He ran his hands through his hair, trying to catch his breath. The sudden shock had reminded him of how vulnerable he was. This was life and death, and he wasn't talking about the sex pervert gardener, either. He knew he was being hunted, just like a fox at an English country house. He could run and run and run, but eventually, like all foxes, he would be caught. His only chance was to get himself out of the race.

Before it was too late. Like it was for Manny. And Tony Barovick.

CHAPTER
19

"WHO ARE WE?" shouted the man at the front of the small auditorium.

"We are the Minutemen," came the thunderous response.

"What is our job?"

"To sound the alarm."

"Where is the danger?"

"Here, now, all around us."

"What are we going to do about it?"

"We will fight!"

Loving rubbed his weary brow. This had been going on for half an hour, and he'd had about as much of it as he could take.

He'd read somewhere—maybe in a *Reader's Digest* article in a dentist's office—that insanity could be contagious, and he supposed it must be true. And he was enduring this for what—this case? Not exactly his favorite. He'd almost been proud of the Skipper when he'd declined to take on Johnny Christensen. It certainly looked like the sort of loser Ben would jump at. But he'd said no, and Loving realized they'd dodged a major-league bullet. Until Christina caught it and inserted it in their collective hearts.

He was sure there was some reason why he should care whether the pig who'd beat the hell out of that poor college kid got the death penalty or not, but he was having a hard time figuring out what it was. He didn't know where a kid like that could come from—so full of hate, so ready to act on it, at the expense of others. But now that he'd sat through this Christian Minutemen crap, he was beginning to think it was a miracle there weren't more like him.

As near as Loving could tell, the Christian Minutemen were the product of some sort of weird crossbreeding experiment between the Promise Keepers and the Moral Majority. All of the members appeared to be men, most of them young, most of them from a lower tax bracket, or with roots in one. His kind of people, Loving would normally think, but after listening to some of the drivel he'd had to put up with since he'd showed up at the YMCA tonight, he wasn't so sure. He gathered that the organization normally encompassed a wide variety of social and political issues, but tonight, not too surprisingly, the only topic was homosexuality.

"They sayyyyy that it's just a different lifestyle," the speaker on the stage intoned, with all the fervor of a Baptist preacher which, as it turned out, he was. "They sayyyyy they can't help themselves. That's just the way they are. They have no choice. But do we believe they have no choice?"

"No, sir!" the crowd shouted back.

"That's right. Our Savior blessed each of us with the right to choose. Since the serpent came into the Garden of Eden, our Lord has given us the chance to choose between a life of sin or a life of Godliness. God does not create sinners. Sinners create sinners."

"A-men!"

"Amen, indeed, brothers. Make no mistake about it, permissive homosexuality is the last and greatest portent of the end of civilization as we know it. It brought down ancient Greece. It brought down Rome, the greatest empire the world had ever seen. And it will bring down this great nation as well—if we let it. Are we going to let it?"

"No, sir!"

He paced back and forth across the stage, working the crowd, acting as a conduit for the energy bubbling up in the room. "I'm glad to hear it, my brethren. Because the time for action has come. This is the day when we must all stand up and be counted. This is the day when we must all be willing to fight!"

In a notebook hidden in his lap, Loving made notes. He recognized several of the men in attendance as members of Johnny Christensen's fraternity. That didn't surprise him. He knew there was a close relationship between the two; that was what had brought him here tonight. Apparently the frat president was high in the Minutemen hierarchy, and there were links at the national level as well.

One of the frat boys, a shortish, sandy-haired kid named Gary Scholes, caught Loving's interest. Not just because he belonged to the club. And not just because Loving knew the kid's name was on the prosecutor's witness list, although that was certainly a point of interest. But mostly because he looked as if he really didn't want to be here. Most of the others were eating it up, chanting back, playing the parts of true believers. But not Scholes. He was much more sedate. Something was bothering him.

And Loving really wanted to know what that was.

Less than ten minutes later, he saw Scholes make an unobtrusive exit. Loving decided to follow. He was happy to have an excuse to escape this chanting. And he had a hunch there was a lot more cheese down Gary Scholes's tunnel.

LOVING WAS NOT surprised to learn that ANGER—the militant gay rights group—held its meetings in the parish hall at St. Crispin's. He had been told this Episcopal church was generally considered one of the most liberal in the greater Chicago area. What did surprise him was that he had trailed Gary Scholes all the way from the Christian Minutemen meeting to this one.

It only took about two seconds to realize that this was a group that would probably not have been welcome at the YMCA. ANGER was well named, because Loving had rarely seen so much of it packed together in one room. Good thing he didn't subscribe to any of the stereotypes of gay men as weak and effeminate, because this visit would've seriously disillusioned him. Most of these hotheads were ready to start a revolution—World War III, if necessary.

Loving wandered around the room, making small talk, drawing people out, starting conversations on any topic other than the one he wanted to know about. In his experience, conversations like these—he liked to call them "unofficial interrogations"—went better if the subjects had no suspicions that he was interested in a delicate subject. So he tried to find a neutral topic that they were comfortable with, maybe even eager to talk about—their children, last night's ball game, their dog. Dogs were best. If he could get people talking about their dogs, he could own them.

As the meeting was called to order, everyone took a seat in the folding chairs arranged in the center of the room. The arrangement was deliberately nonhierarchical. The chairs were placed in a circle; leadership was all but invisible.

Scholes was sitting next to a stout Latino named Jesus Menendez who, according to the scuttlebutt Loving had managed to gather, was thought to have been the best friend of Paul Allen Metheny—the man who had stolen the bailiff's gun and shot Brett Mathers.

"If we let this happen once, it'll recur a thousand times," one of the men in attendance said.

"They've hit us—hard," said Menendez, who Loving thought was the leader. "We have to strike back. Not just against the friends and family and lawyers. Against the hatemongers themselves!"

This sort of dialogue continued for a good long while. There was a time, it occurred to Loving, when sitting in a room with three dozen guys, all of whom were probably gay, might've bothered him. But he liked to think he was past that. He didn't much care what people did with each other anymore, as long as they didn't hurt anyone. He tried to stay out of people's business, and hoped others would show him the same courtesy. Problem was—sometimes they didn't.

"This your first time?" asked a young black man sitting behind him.

"Yeah," Loving said. "I'm the newbie."

"Don't let it get to you. These boys talk tough, but they're all pussycats deep down."

Well, that was a relief. Because at the moment, Menendez was talking about burning down the courthouse in the event a not-guilty verdict was rendered in favor of Johnny Christensen.

"Listen to me," the black man said, addressing the group.

"Hey!" Menendez shouted, hushing the crowd. "Roger wants to talk."

"Many of you know me," he continued. "I knew Tony Barovick. Well. Closely." The room fell silent. "And I can tell you this. Tony would not have approved of violence of any sort. Tony loved everyone—even those who didn't return the affection. He would never have condoned shooting defendants in the courtroom or targeting their lawyers or burning down courthouses."

"We're not doin' it for him," someone growled.

"You're doing it in his name," Roger shot back. Loving was impressed at how articulate he was, how well he managed to keep cool under fire. "You're shaping his memory, his legacy. Don't make it a nasty one. Don't let it be tainted by the same kind of ugliness that took my

Tony away." Roger scanned the room, almost daring them to defy him. "Tony was not a perfect person. There were times when . . . we had our problems. Who doesn't? But I know this—Tony believed in love. He thought love could change the world." He paused again, giving his words time to breathe. "Wouldn't it be nice if we gave that a chance?"

After the meeting was adjourned, Loving made a bee-line toward Gary Scholes, catching him just outside the church doors. He was talking to Jesus Menendez. As soon as they concluded their conversation, he shouted, "Hey, wait up!"

Scholes stopped. "Do I know you?"

"Nah. I—" Thinking . . . thinking . . . "I just recognized your face. You're in the same frat Johnny Christensen was in, aren't you?"

His eyes narrowed. "And you know this because? . . ."

Loving put on his best aw-shucks expression and dug his hands into his pockets. Given his size and profound west Oklahoma accent, it usually sufficed to assure the other party he was a hopeless dullard who couldn't possibly be a threat. "Geez . . . this is embarrassing. Since I got laid off, I've been . . . kind of a Court TV junkie. Watch it all day long. I've been especially caught up in the Tony Barovick coverage. You knew Johnny Christensen, didn't you?"

Scholes frowned. "Yes. A little."

Loving acted as eager as a lonely puppy. "Really! Tell me about him. What's he like?"

"I should get back to my room . . ."

"Aw c'mon. Just a little somethin'."

Scholes seemed torn. "Well . . . he isn't the monster the media is trying to make him. But he's got a lot of issues."

"Who doesn't?"

"Yeah. But he's way above his quota. He's been—"

Scholes must've thought better of it, because he stopped himself midsentence.

"Were you with him . . . that night?"

"Yeah. After."

"Did you know what he did?"

"Couldn't help. He bragged about it for damn near an hour."

"And you heard?"

"Yeah. I also heard him—" He stopped, then turned back toward the parking lot. "Look—I gotta go."

"I gotta thousand more—" But it was too late. Scholes was out of there.

Heard him say what? Loving wondered. And why was he at this meeting in the first place? And why was a supposedly loyal fraternity brother so quick to diss his brother? Something strange was going on here. Loving didn't know what it was. But he intended to find out. If he had to hear about every dog in the Windy City.

CHAPTER
20

JOURNAL OF TONY BAROVICK

MY FIRST REAL job was waiting tables at a bar called the Black Dahlia in the ritzy Wicker Park area. First I took drink orders, then I tended bar, then I became the night manager, which meant I did both and then some, only more so. There was a reason I rose through the ranks so fast, even though I was taking classes part-time. I loved it. Everything about it. The freedom of being on my own, making a decent living. The exhilarating nightlife. The chance to hang out with people of all kinds, all walks, even people my father might not approve of. For the first time, I felt as if I'd left the artificial worlds of school and family and church and found something real.

This was not a gay bar, but everyone who worked there knew I was gay. I never made any big announcement or anything, but for once, I didn't try to hide it either. I don't know why, exactly—the time just seemed right. No one minded. The boss was a big old gruff macho guy, but he didn't care. Every now and again he'd make some remark about "managers who were light in the loafers," but I didn't sense any malice in it. At least it wasn't an obsession with him. And it certainly didn't prevent him from treating me well. I worked for several months, till I moved on to Remote Control. It was comfortable. Most of the time.

We started to attract more of the biker traffic that frequented the suburbs. I'm not talking Hell's Angels, at least not most of the time. This was yuppie biker stuff—doctors and lawyers in midlife crises, tooling around on absurdly expensive, perfectly polished Harleys and wearing designer leather jackets. Despite their education and relative affluence, some of them could be harsh, especially when they left the wives and girlfriends at home and it was just big alpha males gathered around the table, all of them jockeying to prove that despite his age and the spare tire around his gut, he was the biggest stud puppy of them all.

"I bet you're desperate to suck my dick, aren't you?" one of them said to me one evening when I came to take their order. I didn't know what to say. Nothing was necessary, as it turned out, because they all started laughing so hard—and checking their friends to make sure they were laughing, too. At home that night, I thought of a thousand brilliant comebacks, but when it happened, I was too stunned to speak. I was still transfixed when he added, "If I catch you looking at me like that again, I'll stuff your balls in your mouth. If you have any."

Objectively, I realized the jerk was only revealing his own insecurities, but it hurt all the same. Just when you think you're safe, you're not. Just when you think people accept you for what you are, they don't. How long would I be hated for being the way I was born? For being the way God made me?

"I had a buddy down at the penitentiary who hit a fag with his hog doing ninety miles an hour. Know what he got?"

"Eight to ten?"

"No. The Congressional Medal."

Bad as they were, I'd take them any day over the holy rollers who sometimes wandered into the bar. Sometimes it was just kids on a church outing; sometimes it was a group determined to save my soul. It was to be expected—what with politicians talking about "waging war against the homosexual agenda" and preachers teaching from the pulpit that "the acceptance of homosexuality is the sign of the Beast."

Imagine standing there with your little pad, asking if you can take their order, only to hear, "Did you know that studies have proven that homosexuality can be cured?"

"It's not a disease," I said weakly.

"Don't be afraid," said a small woman with dark eyes. She took my hand and pulled it to her breast. "We just want to help you."

I shook her hands away. What, was this supposed to turn me on? Spark my interest in chicks with a messiah complex? It didn't work. I brought them coffee and stayed away from their table until they finally departed. They left tracts on the table. I threw them away.

How many times did I have someone read that nasty little verse from Leviticus to me, the one passage in the entire Bible that arguably, subject to differing interpretations, may come down on gays? I'd point out that it was right next to the verse that says children who are disrespectful to their parents should be executed. For that matter, Leviticus prescribes the death penalty for house burglary and adultery. How many of us would still be around if we started enforcing these laws? I'd ask. But I never got anywhere with them. Leviticus also dictates that a mother must make a burnt offering after bearing a child, that a father must prove his daughter's virginity by displaying a bloody sheet in the town square, that you can't sow your field with two kinds of seed or put on a garment made of two kinds of material. Who would suggest that these passages should be taken seriously in this day and age?

The antigay passage rubs shoulders with passages condemning masturbation, or sex during menstruation. For the ancient Jews, reproduction was survival, so any form of sexual activity that didn't produce offspring was met with disapproval. How long are we going to let ourselves be ruled by four-thousand-year-old laws concocted by primitive Jewish tribes running around in the desert? I'd ask. But they didn't listen to anything I said, and even if they did, they wouldn't admit it when they were hanging around with their holier-than-thou friends. Truth was, as I soon realized, that passage in Leviticus was just a smokescreen—a convenient excuse to justify their own prejudice which had its basis in fear and xenophobia, not the Bible.

"Sodomy is still a crime in some states," one young tough told me. He was clenching his fists, looking as if he'd enforce the law himself. "God doesn't like it when you pervert the natural order."

Then why the hell did he make me this way? I wanted to scream. It's not as if I chose to be gay. But you can't explain that to these people. You can't explain what it's like, being constantly judged. Having people suggest that there's something wrong with you because you're not just like them. Feeling as if you're on the outside looking in, when all you really want in the world is to belong. To feel part of the gang. Not to be alone.

CHAPTER
21

MIKE WAS SO unaccustomed to letting someone else drive that he didn't know what to do. He fidgeted with the lighter, played with the electric windows, and scanned the radio dial—Chicago had a lot of stations. He found a Billy Joel song he remembered from college, smart and oh-so-catchy. Now he'd probably have the tune running through his head for days.

"You know, Swift," Mike said, "I'm starting to get excited."

"Want me to hose you down?"

"That won't be necessary, thanks." Mike gazed at the towering buildings on either side of them, the throngs of people crowding the sidewalks, the hustle and bustle of famed Michigan Avenue. "This is my first time in Chicago and I'm pretty pumped."

"I'm excited about the drag racing. Who'da thought? It's like something out of *Grease*."

Mike watched as Swift steered her car down the busy street. Letting someone else drive went totally against the grain, but it was her car and her city, so he was just going to have to bear it. "Are you the good girl, or the naughty girl? Olivia Newton-John or Stockard Channing?"

"Who do you want me to be, big boy?"

Mike smiled. "Why do you do that?"

"Do what?"

"All the innuendo. I know you don't mean it."

"Don't be so sure, slick. I think you're a darn fine specimen, as men go. And I figure in a job like this, a girl's got to take her pleasure where she can find it."

"Uh-huh." Mike watched as the skyscrapers whizzed by his window. "You're aware that you're driving Baxter crazy, right?"

"Because we left her at headquarters to do the grunt work?"

"Because she thinks you're coming on to me. Constantly."

A sheepish grin crossed the agent's face. "You got a problem with that?"

"I'm just saying."

"That woman's got more repressed desire than I've ever seen. I can't help but toy with her. It's my nature."

"Well, I'd appreciate it if you'd lay off her a little."

"What's it to you?"

"It isn't helping the investigation."

"Don't give me that BS. Do you have feelings for her?"

Mike bit his lip. He had made Baxter a promise. "She's my partner."

"Don't hide from the question. Answer it."

"I just don't think you need to be needling her all the time."

"Look, Mister Tall, Dark, and Dense, if you and Baxter are romantically involved, or want to be, you should get a new partner."

"That isn't—"

"And if you aren't, sugah," she continued, "I'm available. And my apartment is only a few blocks away."

ABOUT AN HOUR later, Mike stood at the edge of a drag strip in the middle of an open field pondering the nature of the enduring relationship between a boy and his wheels. Small wonder guys love cars, he mused, as he watched two of them tear off into the distance. It's all there. Sleek polished hoods, rubber tread, big noisy engines. The thrill of adventure, the hint of danger, the strong scent of sex. Nothing sexier than chrome.

"Amazing how the automobile has changed human society," Mike commented.

"More amazing how the automobile has changed human courtship," Swift replied. "Did you lose yours in the backseat, too?"

"I'm afraid that information is classified."

"Whatever. Have I mentioned yet that I find this all kind of a turn-on?"

"Probably. But not to these children, I hope."

As Mike gazed around him, he felt as if he were swimming in a sea of teenagers—or people who wanted to pretend they were. Who else would come to the Windy City Sizzlin' Speedway, which was basically a long paved strip out in the middle of nowhere, surrounded by undeveloped brush and red clay. According to some of the boys in Swift's office, a local farmer had gotten the inspiration to pave a strip across some uncultivated land. It was a huge success. Drag racing in the city streets sharply dropped overnight—and thanks to the small entrance fee, the farmer made a tidy profit.

"How many kids have you talked to so far?" Mike asked.

"I dunno. Seems like a million or so."

"And you showed them the picture?"

"Right. If dear departed Manny had friends, I haven't stumbled across any of them."

Mike nodded. "Keep at it." He plowed into a nearby group of young people. He made no attempt to be subtle; he knew they could make him a mile away, so why pretend to be anyone other than who he was? Besides, some of these kids had seriously cool cars.

"So you come here often?" Mike asked a sweet young thing named Tanya. He guessed her to be about sixteen, with hair that looked like a kindergarten finger-painting project.

"Almost every day when school's out." Talk about enthusiasm. She almost bounced when she spoke. "It's so bad. Totally phat."

"I notice you're one of the few females on the premises."

"I don't know why that is. I live for it. It's like, you know, like, duuuuude." She laughed.

"Yeah, but . . . why?"

"Hey, you gotta do something, right? What else is there? This beats going to the mall. Or drinking or doing drugs."

"Can't argue with that."

"My car is great—I got a 350 V-8, Tranny, slick as ice, and enough r.p.m. to handle the Indy 500. Where else am I going to get the chance to challenge every would-be macho stud in the city—and win?"

"I can see the appeal."

"It's a great way to prove yourself. Once you're behind the wheel, it doesn't matter if you're big or small, male or female. All that matters is how good you are. You turn the ignition—and thirteen hundred feet later, you know who's hot and who's not."

Mike watched as two more cars approached the starting line. One of them was apparently being driven by a friend of Tanya's. "Come on, Hootie! Show 'em your struts!"

Hootie was the lanky boy in the Thunderbird. He glanced at the driver in the neighboring yellow Camaro, then punched it. And they were off—at something like 100 m.p.h.

"Kind of dangerous, isn't it?"

"Better here than on the streets. I have seen a few wrecks, though. Nothing too bad. Some of the slicks bet on the races. Then they start taking it way too seriously."

Hootie, alas, did not win his race, which did not surprise Mike, being a former Camaro owner himself.

"That's tough. Hootie's gonna be bummed. I better go."

"Just a sec." Mike had been so absorbed in the racing he almost forgot that he was technically supposed to be investigating. He pulled the photo out of his pocket. "Ever see this guy before?"

She looked for only a moment. "Yeah, I've seen him. I think I raced him. Has an '89 Mustang, right? Modified engine. Big wheels." She grinned. "I knocked his socks off."

"What was he doing here?"

"Far as I know, he was just racing, like everyone else. We get some older guys, sometimes. Fogies trying to recapture their youth with big, souped-up race cars. You know the kind."

Mike was suddenly glad he had left his Trans Am back in Tulsa. "Know anything else about him?"

"Well . . . I don't know it for a fact. But some of my homeboys said they thought he was pushing."

"As in drugs?"

"That's what they said."

"Pushing what?"

"I couldn't tell you. Nothing too serious, I think."

"X?"

"I don't know. I'm not into that at all." She turned back toward the strip. "I just love to race!"

Tanya scampered away. Mike talked to several of the other kids in attendance, but no one knew more about Manny Nowosky than she had. Mike did, however, learn a lot about drag racing.

"You're dying to try it, aren't you?" Swift said, coming up behind him.

"I don't know about *dying*," he mumbled.

"Put it on hold for a minute, Top Gun. There's someone here you need to meet."

Standing beside her, Mike saw, was a young black man, maybe in his mid-twenties. He was solidly built, with strong and well-shaped features.

"Roger Hartnell," Swift explained.

Mike shook his hand. "So you knew Manny Nowosky?"

"Yes, I did."

"What do you do?"

Swift answered for him. "He's a head honcho in the Chicago office of ANGER."

"Regional director, actually," he corrected.

"That's the gay activist group, right?"

"Gay and lesbian," he corrected.

"Isn't that like saying, 'people and women'?"

Swift laughed. "Sorry, Mr. Hartnell. Major Morelli was an English major. He gets like this."

Mike ignored her. "Mind if I have a few words with you?"

Hartnell shook his head. "Sure. I've been quizzed by so many police officers and reporters I could do it in my sleep."

"Oh? And why is that?"

"My close friend was killed. Murdered brutally. Because he was gay."

Mike's eyes widened. "Are you talking about Tony Barovick?"

Hartnell nodded.

Mike pulled the man away from the roar of the crowd. Swift followed behind. "How well did you know Tony Barovick?"

Hartnell thought a moment. "Very well."

"Meaning?"

"We were lovers."

"How long had you been together?"

"About six months. From last November until . . . We had an apartment near campus."

"Must've come as quite a shock."

"You could say that."

Hartnell remained remarkably stoic, but Mike supposed he had talked about his lover's death so many times he could do it without flinching. Better switch to the investigation at hand. "And you knew Manny Nowosky?"

"I recognized his picture. I've seen him here. And I've seen him at Remote Control—that's a bar where Tony worked and where I used to spend a lot of time. Tony and I used to speculate about what his deal was. Tony thought he was an undercover cop. I thought he was a pusher. Either way, we didn't like having him around."

"Well, I'm happy to inform you that's not going to be a problem anymore." Mike gazed at the photo. "I can guarantee he isn't an undercover cop. The rest I'm not so sure about. Know anything else?"

"Sorry, no."

Mike decided to run with a hunch. "Ever see him talking to Tony?"

"I think maybe Tony took his order once or twice. He used to help out sometimes on the floor."

"Ever see Manny with anyone else?"

"No. Always alone."

"So I don't suppose you have any idea why someone might want to take him out."

"No. I wouldn't."

Mike pursed his lips. This guy was tight-lipped—more monosyllabic than most guilty people he interrogated. Was there a reason for that? Or had he just learned to be careful?

"And you work for this ANGER group?" Swift asked.

"It's a volunteer position, but, yes."

"May I ask why?"

"I just think it's important that we all make a contribution. Do something to make the world a better place. After what happened to Tony—how can anyone deny the need for this group's work? I absolutely believe this is the defining issue of our time. A hundred years from now, history will look back on people who disparage homosexuals the same way we look back on slave owners. As primitive, ignorant hatemongers. Bigots. I want to be remembered as one of the good guys."

"But this isn't just altruism," Swift said, cutting to the heart of it, as usual. "You have a personal interest in this crusade."

"Because I'm gay? True enough. Doesn't make the cause any less important."

"What exactly is it you ANGER folks do?" She had to shout to be heard over the zoom-zoom; another race was starting.

"Our main goal is the dissemination of information. Educate the public, that's what we're about. We may be too late to get the old boys who grew up on the farm and learned to hate everyone who's different from themselves, but there's a lot we can do with their children. The world is changing."

"Is it?"

"Absolutely. You know how many schools started gay clubs after Matthew Shepard's murder? Hundreds. Most of the kids in them aren't even gay—they just want to show their support."

"I'm all for education," Mike said, "but ANGER has done a lot more than that. You guys are the ones who put the *active* in activism."

"We're not much for sitting on our hands, if that's what you mean."

"You're not above resorting to violence, either."

"What choice do we have?" Mike could see the phlegmatic exterior fading a touch. "We live in a violent world. Do you know how many hate crimes are committed against gay people in this country every year? More than a thousand. The Matthew Shepard case got all the publicity, but that was just the tip of the iceberg.

There were a dozen other hate-based murders of gay people that year. People you never heard about."

"It does seem to be on the upswing," Mike admitted.

"There's nothing new about hate. Do you know about Claudia Brenner? She was out hiking the Appalachian Trail in Pennsylvania with her girlfriend, back in 1988. They were minding their own business, having a great time. Too great for some people. Some backwoods hoods showed up with shotguns. They killed her girlfriend. Seriously wounded her."

"She became a gay activist, didn't she?" Swift said.

"Damn straight. Wouldn't you? We got killers out there. Frat boys who think hate is cool. Preachers telling young people that God sends hurricanes because of gays. Or that it's a mental disease that can be cured. That gays will be the downfall of civilization. Hell, one of the kids who killed Tony was a church choirboy! The other one was an Eagle Scout! It's all around us, and always has been. There's nothing more hateful than prejudice, whatever its brand. We have to take action—strong, decisive action!"

Mike had the sense that Hartnell had delivered this speech more than once. "Is that what you told Paul Metheny? Just before he went to the courthouse and shot two people?"

Hartnell raised his hands. "Hey, I had nothing to do with that. ANGER has officially condemned his act."

"But he was a member of your organization?"

"He was a loose cannon. Paul had always been a little unbalanced. He was bipolar, and had strong sociopathic tendencies. I'm not even sure that was his real name. He was on medication, but I guess he stopped taking it. So he lost his head in the courtroom. Tragic."

"Come on. You must've applauded when you heard what happened."

"I've told you. We publicly condemned his action. Immediately."

"But you must've been privately pleased."

"No way."

"Those two kids killed your lover!"

"And I wanted to see them pay, too. I'll admit it. But not like that. Not vigilante style."

Swift cut in. "I've read about the graffiti your group inflicted on that law office downtown. The one that's representing the surviving defendant."

"That was not our act, either."

"ANGER took credit for it."

"No, we released a press statement approving of the sentiment behind it. That's a vastly different thing."

"If you say so." Mike had done his best to needle the guy, pressure him into saying something he might not otherwise, but it wasn't working. He checked Swift to see if she had anything more. She shrugged. "So what brings you here today?"

"Are you kidding? I love to race."

"You seem a little intellectual for this scene."

"What, because I went to college I can't have a little fun?" He paused. "Tony and I used to come out here all the time. It was one of the few places where he could just cut loose and be himself." He shook his head, eyes glistening. "Who ever thought he'd be killed for that? Being himself."

AFTER THEY'D TALKED to everyone on the premises, Mike reconnoitered with Special Agent Swift. "I think we've done everything we can out here."

"Just as well. The thrill is gone."

"And by my watch, it's five o'clock. I'm officially off duty."

"And that means? . . ."

"I think you know. You won't tell Chief Blackwell, will you?"

"Depends. Can I ride shotgun?"

"I don't know. How much do you weigh?"

"Excuse me!"

He grinned. "All right, but try to sit lightly." He started sprinting toward the parking lot. "I'm going to show these kids what an old fogy in a borrowed cop car can do."

CHAPTER

22

AT PRECISELY 12:05, Charlie the Chicken spotted the person he feared most, the one he knew was hunting him.

The one who would stop at nothing to silence him.

The day had started like so many others. He'd hitched a ride out to Michigan and One Hundred and God-Knows-What where all the new houses were going in. He'd rung the bell and been introduced to Stacy. Stacy was a contrast to the Ice Princess in about every way possible. He'd complained about the princess's stick figure, but Stacy cured him of that quick. She was at least a hundred pounds overweight—one of those poor girls who are so short they never really have a chance once middle age sets in and the pounds refuse to go away. She wasn't quiet like the princess either; she was a big girl with a big noise . . .

"Oh, baby baby baaaabay . . . Yes! Oh God yes. Yes yes yes yes yes! That's how you do it, baby. Just keep doing it just like that keep it coming. Oh, don't stop. Don't ever stop. Oh, you feel so good. Oh, baby. Oh, baaaabay . . ."

It was like having the radio on in the background, except he had no means of turning it off, no matter how desperately he wanted to. Stacy differed from the princess in the movement department, too. Meaning, she knew how to. And did so. With great gusto. When she started whipping those huge hips around, she started tidal waves rippling through the mattress, one way then the next, a kinetic sculpture seen from the worst possible angle. Did it never occur to this woman that it was hard to hit a moving target? Probably not—she was too deep in the throes to be aware of anything. He had to wonder, though—was he really turning her on? Or was she doing it to herself?

Under the big top, he thought, as he crawled beneath the big pink muumuu she was wearing. And that led to the endless portion of tonight's program. Men talk about women who can't get enough, but in reality, Charlie had rarely experienced it. Until now. Stacy could not, under any circumstances, no matter what he tried, get enough. She had him where she wanted him, and she was determined to make sure he stayed there, too. With her ample knees pressed against both sides of his head, he couldn't possibly escape. Minutes seemed like hours. Death by asphyxiation became a real possibility.

"Strangest thing I've ever seen," the coroner would say. "He suffocated to death."

"Suffocated?" Agent Mulder would ask.

"You heard me. A clear case of death by vagina."

Perverse, yes, but he had to amuse himself somehow, until at long last, the ordeal ended. The knee lock broke and he came up gasping for air.

Well, at any rate, he didn't have to wonder whether Stacy liked it, and he didn't get stiffed either. Two hundred big ones, tip included. A few more gigs like this and he'd be home free.

Or so he thought. Until he saw the face, the one that haunted his nightmares. That changed everything. Until then, his plan had been to lie low, scrape together some cash, and use it to make sure he was never found.

Too late.

It couldn't be a coincidence—that face, out here, driving around in a car, obviously looking for something. He didn't think he'd been spotted, but even so—how long would he be safe here? Or anywhere? If he could be traced to his work location, then what he did and who he did it for was obviously known. Probably where he had been living. He could no longer pretend that he was safe for the moment. He wasn't.

And if he didn't do something quick, he never would be again.

CHAPTER
23

CHRISTINA WAS SO busy talking on her cell phone during the walk up the drive that she almost didn't notice where she was. She fired off a long list of instructions to Vicki, the new hire—whose voice was so soft Christina could barely hear it on the cell—then sent Jones off on several new research quests, then conferred with Loving on various schemes to break through the wall of silence he was getting from her client's fraternity. By the time she finally rang off, she was already on the front porch.

And what a porch it was. She couldn't kid herself—just being here made her edgy. She was dead in the heart of the richest section of Nichols Hills. Driving down Sixty-third to get here was like driving through Hollywood Hills; without exception, every house was huge and fabulous—multistoried, pillared Federals and plantation-style estates—with sprawling, perfectly cut green lawns.

And the Kincaid manor was no exception. It was more than a little startling. She sometimes forgot how utterly different Ben's upbringing had been from her own. He seemed like such a regular guy—too regular on occasion. And the way that he chose to live—insisted on living, actually—was a marked contrast to the way he was apparently raised.

She rang the bell. A few moments later, it was answered by a woman who was dressed in essentially the same style as Christina—a professional assistant, perhaps. Christina was escorted into an inner parlor, where Lillian Kincaid awaited her.

The older woman stood and extended her arms, the picture of graciousness. "Christina! How good to see you again."

Christina took her hands. "Great to see you, too, Mrs. Kincaid."

"Please call me Lillian." She guided Christina to a chair. "Cup of tea? It's Earl Grey."

"Um, sure."

Her hair was grayer than the last time Christina had seen her, but that didn't mean much, since Christina knew she colored her hair. It was a fashion choice, not a sign of aging. To the contrary, she looked wonderful. She was well into her seventies, but she looked much younger. The only signs of true age were stylistic; she still wore big beauty shop hair, as she probably had done since the Fifties.

After she poured the tea, Lillian leaned forward and squeezed Christina's hands. "I haven't seen you since you received your law degree. I am so proud of you."

To her surprise, Christina found herself blushing. "Well, thank you." Ben had always described his mother as remote and austere, but Christina had never found her so. Formal, perhaps. But there was definitely a soul in there.

"And I was pleased to learn you'd joined Ben's practice."

"Really? You didn't feel like I was trying to horn in on his business?"

"Please. I was relieved. You know how I worry about Ben, and his practice, if you can call it that. With you there to look after things, I thought there was a chance he might, well . . ." Her fingers danced in the air. "See some improvement."

"I know exactly what you mean. I've encouraged Ben

to focus on marketing. To get out and network. But—you know how that goes."

"I can imagine."

"Things are looking up, though," Christina said. "This has been our best year yet. We're actually making some money. If we can just keep Ben from spending half his time on clients he knows can't pay."

"That must be intensely frustrating."

"Well, I'm used to it. Ben has a good heart." She laughed suddenly. "As if I need to tell you that."

"No, please do. You know how little he gives me. We talk more frequently now than in years past. I think he's finally gotten over . . . well, his troubles with his father. But he still doesn't open up. Doesn't confide. Not like his sister."

"How is Julia doing, by the way?"

Lillian's eyes went heavenward. "Oh, don't ask, please. Sometimes I think I must've been the world's worst parent."

"Don't be ridiculous. Julia will work her life out in time. And even if he doesn't say it, I know Ben loves you very much."

Lillian looked down at her teacup, smiling faintly. "Perhaps so." She leaned forward, and her eyes sparkled. "Anyway . . . you know what I want to hear. Have you and Ben? . . ."

Christina knew her face was flushing now. "I'm not sure . . ."

"Has he asked you out?"

Christina craned her neck. "Oh." She swallowed. "Ye-es . . . in a vague sort of way." She sighed. "We play Scrabble."

"Scrabble?"

"Scrabble."

Lillian shook her head. "I blame Edward for this one. I told him a million times. Talk to your son. Give him the facts of life. Take him to New York and buy him a high-dollar hooker."

Christina's eyes ballooned. "Lillian!"

"But of course he never did. Too busy with work. Saving other people's lives and tinkering with his inventions. And you know what that got us." She set down her cup. "As much as I'd love to swap girl talk with you, I know that isn't why you've come. What's happening?"

Christina's eyes wandered about the exquisitely furnished room. The matched burgundy sofas flanking the Oriental table were perfectly chosen, perfectly arranged. The objets d'art on the end tables were placed with precision, each oriented just so. On the other side of the room, the black Steinway was polished and glistening. Is that where Ben learned to play the piano? she wondered. What must it have been like, growing up in this house?

"It's Ben. He's been acting very strangely lately. I've got a new case that he refuses to have anything to do with."

Lillian's long fingernails tripped along her cheekbones. "Must be potentially profitable."

"No, that's just it. The client has no money, the defendant is incredibly unpopular, all the evidence indicates he's guilty, and the DA is desperate to convict. It's a textbook Ben Kincaid case. But he won't come anywhere near it."

"Did he say why?"

"No. He won't talk about it."

"Do you have any idea what his problem is?"

"Not really. Well . . . a suspicion." Christina paused, gathering her strength. "Do you by any chance know a woman named Ellen Christensen?"

She pondered. "Christensen . . . Christensen . . . No, I don't think—" She stopped abruptly. Her hand pressed against her lips. "Oh, no."

"What? What?"

"That must be her married name. I didn't realize . . ."

"Then you do know her."

"I've never met her. This all happened years ago, when Ben was living in Toronto on that Rotary Fellowship." She paused. "But eventually I found out what happened—what she did. To Ben. And why he's been suffering ever since."

NOTHING WORSE THAN going over the quarterly statements. All this accounting mumbo jumbo gave Ben a throbbing headache. Jones had tried to teach him how to read these things, but it never took. For all he understood, they might as well have been written in Urdu. Which would explain why his firm was in the financial shape it usually was.

He heard the door open and threw down his pencil. "Paula, you can just leave the report—"

He stopped short. Mistaken identity.

Ellen Christensen was standing in his office, just inside the door.

He did not get up.

"Do you mind if we talk?" She didn't wait to be invited to sit. "It's been a long time, Ben."

"Yes."

"I came by your apartment. I knocked on the door for several minutes."

"I must not have been home."

The room fell silent, so silent Ben could hear the plumbing, water rushing through unseen pipes, air-conditioning hissing through the vents.

"I suppose you're here to meet Christina?" he said finally.

"Actually, no. I understand she's in Oklahoma City."

Ben raised an eyebrow.

"I wanted to talk to you."

"To me? After all this time? Why?"

She looked at him levelly. "I think you know why."

"I can't imagine."

"I'd like for you to get involved in my son's case."

"There's no need. Christina has it well in hand. She's a superb attorney."

"I don't doubt it. But you've got years of experience on her. Everyone says you're one of the best. You know the courts, the judges, how the system works. It was clear to me, when I watched Christina at the pretrial hearing—"

"You shouldn't judge anything by that," Ben said, cutting her off. "That hearing was lost before it began. The fact that Christina got as far as she did shows how resourceful she is."

"Nonetheless," Ellen continued, "everyone I've talked to tells me you're one of the most gifted criminal trial attorneys working today."

Ben snorted. "Christina must've paid bribes."

"I heard that even before I hired Kevin Mahoney. But I—" She frowned. "Well, to be truthful, I couldn't bring myself to call you. It would be so . . . awkward. But this is different. It's crunch time, as my late husband used to say."

"True enough."

"There are obviously some forces who want to see my son dead. They almost succeeded once. And how many others are there out there, maybe lurking in the jury or in a judge's robe?" She paused, gathering her breath. "I need the best there is, Ben. I need you."

Ben drummed his fingers on his desk, not even realizing he was doing it. "Well, now. This is quite a role reversal, isn't it?"

Her head fell. "Ben, isn't there any way we can . . . let the past be the past?"

"That would be the noble thing, wouldn't it? Pity I'm not that noble."

"Please, Ben. I'm begging you."

"I recall doing a little begging myself."

"Ben . . ." She pressed her hand against her forehead. "I did the right thing. At least—I thought I did. You don't know what would've happened if—"

"I know you wouldn't have a hatemongering bastard for a son!"

Ellen looked as if she had been slapped in the face, which in a very real sense, she had. After a long while, she spoke. "Is there nothing I can do to change your mind?"

"Nothing short of a miracle."

"I believe in miracles," Ellen said quietly. "And there was a time when you did, too."

Ben made no reply.

"I wish I could tell you, Ben, that you haven't changed. That's what people always say. You haven't changed a bit." She stopped, her eyes not quite reaching his. "But you have."

"It's been a long time," he answered. "Everyone changes."

"Perhaps. But you were so sweet and innocent and trusting and . . . and . . ." Her eyes wandered helplessly. "And I can't help but ask myself if this is my fault."

"Don't be ridiculous."

"I know I hurt you, Ben. I understand that. But if you could just try to understand what I was going through."

"I don't want to have this conversation."

"But I can see that you're still hurting—"

"You're making too much of this."

"Ben, please! At least—" She paused, her face twisted with emotion. "Peanut butter and jelly, Ben."

"Stop."

"Peanut butter and jelly."

"That was stupid."

"You didn't used to think so."

"That was a long time ago."

"Not that long," she said quietly. She held out her arms toward him. "One embrace. Just to remember."

"I'm sorry, Ellen. I'm not trying to be mean or vengeful. I just—can't."

Her arms fell, and she looked as tired as a person could possibly be and still go on living. "Is there nothing I can do?"

"No. I'm sorry."

"I'm sorry, too." She took her purse and rose. "But I wish you the best, Ben. I mean that. I always have. I—I understand. Really I do."

A moment later, she had disappeared down the corridor. And Ben's office door was shut tight. And locked.

If only he could shut his mind as easily. If only he could block out the thoughts, force himself to forget. What she was, what she had become.

What her face looked like, smeared with blood.

He remembered everything. Especially that day on the subway. What he thought would be the last time he ever saw her.

ONE OF THE great advantages to living in Toronto, in addition to the clean streets, the cultural opportunities, and the low crime rate, was the subway system. The best in the world, some said. You could get anywhere you needed to go in no time at all.

Except sometimes Ben wished it wasn't so easy to get so far so fast. Sometimes he wished the whole world would slow down. And give him a chance to catch up.

"I don't care what the doctors say," Ben said. He was not a child, damn it, and he was not going to cry. "I want to be with you."

"It won't be the same."

"I don't care if it's the same. I don't care if it's a day."

"I'm not planning to drop dead tomorrow." Ellen checked herself. It was a crowded subway car; she lowered her voice. "Maybe not at all."

"Then what—"

"I'm going to be sick, Ben. Very sick."

"I don't care. I want to be with you."

"Would you stop thinking about yourself for one damn minute?"

Ben felt his heart pounding, as if beating a path out of his chest. "I—I don't understand. I thought we loved each other."

"Ben—"

"You said you loved me. You said you'd marry me."

"Ben—"

"My family is coming up in three days for the wedding. My grandmother is coming from her farm in Arkansas. My father has already paid for the tuxes!"

"Ben, would you just listen to me!" She gripped his wrist, and as she did, he could feel the tension radiating through her. "I have encephalitis, Ben. Viral encephalitis."

"I don't even know what that is."

"It's a viral infection of the brain. It can cause brain cell death. Swelling. Seizures. Brain damage. And death."

"But not every time."

"You're not listening to me, Ben. It could change me."

"I don't know what you're talking about."

"I'm talking about brain damage!" She raised a hand, pressing it against her forehead. "What do you think happens when your brain cells die? Even if it doesn't kill you, it can change your personality. Already I feel . . . different. I wake up in the morning and I'm not sure who I am."

"I don't care. I want to be with you."

"*I don't want to be with you!*" She fell backward, exhausted, pale. "I don't want you to see me like this."

"But we were—"

"I can't marry you, Ben. I can't marry anyone! Don't you get it? It wouldn't be fair, not to you, not to anyone."

"There must be some way. My father is a doctor and he has friends and—"

"Go away, Ben. Please go away and leave me alone."

"Ellen, no."

"Yes. I'm getting off at the next stop. And you are not going to follow me."

"Ellen, I can't."

"Please!" She was shouting, the veins rising in her neck. *"Leave me alone!"*

That's when it started. She fell to the corrugated metal floor with such velocity it was as if she had intentionally launched herself. She writhed back and forth on the floor. Her nose bled like a hose. Spittle bubbled up from her mouth.

"Ellen! Ellen!" He felt paralyzed, unable to move. She had become a spasmodic rag doll, twitching and thrashing in an unnatural manner. Her eyes rolled up into her head. "Ellen!"

She was barely able to speak; her face merely a reminder of what it had been before. But she still managed to spit out a few syllables. "Beeeen . . . gggg-go a-wayyy!"

He watched helplessly as a middle-aged man pushed him aside and knelt beside her. He loosened her collar and put something in her mouth to hold down her tongue.

Ben gaped at the hideous transformation. She was not at all the girl he remembered, was she? Could this possibly be the woman he loved?

"G-g-g-go . . . a . . . wayyy, Ben! *Go a-way!*"

WHEN LILLIAN FINISHED telling the story, Christina felt as if she'd been flattened by a truck. She'd always suspected there was something like this. Only three days away and everyone he loved coming. And in the middle of the subway . . .

"I'm sorry I can't tell you more about it, but as you know, Ben isn't much of talker. I've had to pick up most of what little I know from third parties."

"That's all right," Christina said, still feeling shell-shocked. "So they broke up because she was sick?" She shook her head. "I mean, that's tough. But why would that make Ben so bitter? Surely he'd understand . . ."

"Christina." The older woman grabbed her hand and gripped it tightly. "You've got to keep that woman away from him. No matter what. Even if it means dropping the case."

"I can't do that. The judge would never allow it. Not so close to the trial date."

"Christina, please listen to me. I'm his mother. I know what he was like when he returned from Toronto. You don't know how long it's taken him to get where he is now. I don't want to erase all that."

"I—I—" Christina was at a loss for thoughts, much less words. "I hear you. I'll—I'll do whatever I can."

"I know you will." Lillian looked at her earnestly. "Because I know you care about Ben. Just as I do. And you don't want—"

"Of course not." She rose. "If you'll pardon me, I need to get back to Tulsa before dark. I've got an early flight to Chicago tomorrow morning."

"I understand." Lillian smiled, as best she was able, and wagged a finger. "But next time you're in town, young lady, I want to go shopping."

"You don't like my outfit?"

"Don't be silly. Now you're starting to sound like Ben."

"Well, I just thought—"

She put her arm around Christina and walked her to the front door. "I think it's a splendid outfit. Red is your color, Christina."

"You don't think it makes me look like a big tomato?"

"Nonsense. I just wanted—" She paused, and Christina thought she saw her eyes glisten. "I don't get many opportunities to take anyone shopping anymore. Especially not someone I like as much as you."

Christina was starting to feel a little itchy-eyed herself. "Thank you. For everything."

Lillian nodded. "Let me know what happens. And Christina?"

"Yes?"

Her voice fell to a hush. "If Ben gives you any trouble, play Rachmaninoff's 'Rhapsody on a Theme of Paganini.' He's a total sucker for it. Turns to butter."

"I'll remember that."

CHAPTER
24

"SO HAVE YOU slept with her yet?"

Mike was not entirely surprised to look up from the desk—temporarily assigned to him at the Chicago office of the FBI—and see Sergeant Baxter hovering overhead. "I assume you're not talking about Gwyneth Paltrow."

Baxter had her fists pressed against her hips, feet spread. For some reason, she reminded Mike of those old commercials for Mr. Clean. "You know damn well who I'm talking about. The FBI bimbo."

"Bimbo seems a bit harsh for someone with a master's degree in criminology."

"Just cut the crap and give it to me straight. Are you doing her?"

Mike stretched out his arms, pushing away from the desk. "Would it bother you if I was?"

"Damn straight it would. Are you?"

"I'm confused. I thought you made it very clear you weren't interested in having an intimate relationship with me."

Her face was taut and lined. "I didn't say I wasn't interested. Exactly. Not that I am. But what I said was that it would be inappropriate."

Mike shrugged. "Okay. And Special Agent Swift—Danny—obviously feels differently. So what's your beef?"

"My beef is that you and I are supposed to be partners!"

"But you said—"

"Not that kind of partners. Professionals—as in, doing our job. Remember that? I'm not talking about . . . about . . ."

"Grabass in the patrol car?"

"Right. I'm talking about doing our job. Properly. And I can't do it when my partner is constantly cutting me out. Treating me like the little sister no one wants to play with."

"I wasn't aware that I was doing that—"

"Well, you are."

"—so I guess I'll let you come along when we go bike riding after school. If Mom makes me."

"Don't be such an asshole." She leaned across his desk. "You know what I think? I think you're punishing me because I won't sleep with you."

"Get over it already."

"You can't get what you want from me, so you're giving me the dirt assignments while you go off with your new playmate."

Mike had to bite his tongue. Sarcasm wasn't going to calm her. He did enjoy seeing her get worked up, though. She was a lot sexier when she wasn't being all cool and professional. "None of your assignments have been dirt. Every interview is important. I can't predict which ones will pay off and which ones won't."

"But you always pair off with her."

"It makes no sense for all three of us—"

"But *I'm* your partner!"

"But she's working with us, too." He lowered his voice. "And I would like to know why."

"Maybe you should just ask *me*."

Mike and Baxter both pivoted. Swift was in the doorway. She was wearing another black turtleneck, with black cords and her piece holstered over her left shoulder. She looked hot, and Mike wasn't thinking about the room temperature, either.

"As I recall," Mike said, "you told us you couldn't reveal the reason for your assignment to the Nowosky murder."

"And that's just eating you alive, isn't it, sugah?" Swift strolled across the office. "Only thing you hate worse than the FBI is a mystery you can't solve."

"Who says I can't solve it?" Mike shot back.

"Oh, my. Does the big bad policeman have a theory? Let's hear it."

"Okay, I'll play." It would be hard to be more self-assured and in-your-face than this woman, Mike told himself. This should be a gigantic turnoff. But it wasn't. "I've got a few connections in Hooverland myself, and they tell me it's all very hush-hush, but there's a good chance that since the Metzger kidnapping fiasco, you've been reassigned to some kind of drug task force specializing in designer and recreational drugs targeted toward kids. What a surprise then that Manny Nowosky, among other enterprises, turns out to have been pushing Ecstasy." He paused. "How am I doing so far?"

"I haven't fallen asleep yet."

"So come clean, Swift. Is that why you're horning in on our little small-town homicide investigation? Are we tracking a drug connection?"

"If we are, we have a right to know about it," Baxter said. "Drugs change everything. Those people play for keeps."

Swift stared at Mike, then at Baxter, before speaking. "You can keep your mouths shut? Because this is important. I'm under strict instructions not to share with local law enforcement."

Mike raised three fingers. "Scout's honor."

Swift frowned. "Yeah. It's drugs. Big time. Ecstasy ring. You know what X is, right?"

"MDMA," Mike answered. "Methylenedioxymethamphetamine."

"I'm impressed. So you also probably know that it's a

billion-dollar market, now almost entirely controlled by professional criminals. It's cheap and easy to make. Kids love it. It's the 'hug drug.' Makes you feel all warm and fuzzy and euphoric—without the wired feeling that comes from amphetamines or the confusion that comes from LSD. Requires no tools—no dirty infected syringes, no coke spoons. So the kids go to these clubs, roll around in their little cuddle puddles, and are stupid enough to think it doesn't do them any damage."

"And you think Manny Nowosky was pushing it?"

"Given the kind of money these guys play for, I could see someone getting the drill-bit treatment. Actually, as drug executions go, that could be considered mild."

"So your interest in Manny is only peripheral. You're tracking the drugs." Mike nodded. "Thanks for leveling with us."

"No prob. I didn't like keeping secrets from a hunk of manhood like you."

Baxter burned.

"Just keep it to yourself. And grab your coats."

"Where are we going? If I may ask."

"To a local bar, Remote Control. Remember—Roger Hartnell mentioned it. He saw Manny Nowosky there. And if he did, someone else might have as well."

THE THREE OFFICERS took a booth near the front of Remote Control, shouting at one another to be audible over the very loud, very live band. "I can barely hear myself think in here," Swift complained. "Why do these places always play their music so thumpingly loud?"

Baxter held up a finger. "Music hath charms to soothe the savage beast."

Mike smiled. "Breast."

"Excuse me?"

"Breast."

"Morelli, I think you need to pry your eyes away from that video monitor."

"It's *breast,* Baxter."

"I mean, God knows I've seen how you sneak a look when you think I can't see, but it's totally inappropriate for—"

Mike was forced to raise his voice. "It's poetry, Baxter!"

"Is that supposed to be some kind of compliment?"

"You were quoting—misquoting, actually—a line from Congreve. 'Music hath charms to soothe a savage *breast,* / To soften rocks, or bend a knotted oak.' Not beast. Breast."

"Oh." She fell silent for a moment. "So who was this Congreve dude? Some kind of pervert?"

"Yeah," Mike said, exchanging a look with Swift. "He's doing eight to ten at Leavenworth." He gazed around the crowded bar and its wide array of computers and video terminals. "So this is an Ecstasy outlet?"

"That's what my people tell me," Swift replied. "This is where they're getting the stuff. They take it away, then hold their raves somewhere else to keep the heat off this place."

"And Manny Nowosky was one of the main men."

"Not according to my informants. He was a low-life punk. That's why he was on the premises, moving and shaking, making it happen. The big boys would never come near an actual point of delivery."

"None of which explains what he was doing in Tulsa. Or why he got rubbed out."

"I could only speculate. Maybe he did something that displeased his masters. Maybe they knew we'd made him. Maybe he knew too much about something that was none of his business."

Mike pondered the possibilities. He didn't have nearly enough information to draw any definite conclusions.

But some disturbing possibilities were beginning to coalesce in his brain.

"I talked to the owner of this joint, Mario Roma," Baxter said, joining them at their booth. She pointed at the man back behind the cash register. Mike also recognized the person to whom Mario was speaking. It was Roger Hartnell—ANGER's regional director and Tony Barovick's former lover. "He insists that he has nothing to do with the mob. Or drugs."

"It's possible the mob is not involved," Swift said. "I can't say for sure. His denials certainly don't prove anything. But more and more of these prestige drug operations are being handled by independents."

Mike nodded. "Even if there's no mob connection, how likely is it that the magnitude of drugs you're talking about could be distributed here without him knowing?"

Swift followed his drift. "I can't guarantee that the owner is in on it. Or even aware of it. But someone would have to be. There's no way this thing could grow to this size without the help of someone on the inside."

"That's about what I thought. Excuse me, ladies and germs." Mike slid out of the booth, crossed to the bar and introduced himself to Shelly Chimka, the perky auburn-haired woman who was on duty. She was wiping down the bar, a little awkwardly. Mike suspected she was right-handed, but since her right arm was in a sling, she had to make do with her left.

"Major Morelli," she replied. "Are you here to see my shining face? Or are you hoping for a little video romance?"

"My idea of video romance is a six-pack of beer and a rerun of *Xena: Warrior Princess*. Can I talk to you?"

She put down her rag, suddenly serious. "I suppose. What about?"

"Sorry to be the bearer of bad tidings, but I have it on

good authority that drugs are being distributed here. Big time."

"I haven't seen any of it."

"I believe you. You're stuck behind the bar. You don't get out into the secluded caverns. How easy would it be to arrange a sale here, with all the video gizmos? Everyone would think you were just lining up a rendezvous, and they'd be right—except the purpose of the rendezvous wouldn't be romance."

Shelly seemed disturbed and more than a little frightened. "Listen to me, Major—you gotta believe me. I am not involved in drugs. Not in any way, shape, or form."

"Okay." Mike whipped out the computer-generated photo. "And what about Manny Nowosky?"

She didn't have to look at it long. "I've seen him around. Quite a bit, actually."

"Did you know him?"

"No. But I've seen him here. Talked to him a few times."

"What about?"

"Oh, just small talk. Stuff you say to barmaids while you wait for the next round. I don't recall anything specific."

"Did he come with anyone?"

She thought for a moment. "No, he wasn't part of a group, and he never really seemed interested in playing with the gizmos or scoping out the chicks. He came alone." She passed back the photo. "Haven't seen him around lately, though."

Mike glanced at Swift. "There's a reason for that. Any idea who might've been out to get him?"

She stared stonily, as if transfixed by the thought of the horror. "I'm sorry, but I don't."

"What about Tony Barovick?"

"Tony? I don't follow . . ."

"Did he know Nowosky? Was he involved with drugs?"

"That's ridiculous. He wouldn't have had the chance—"

"He was the manager. He was all over the place."

"Tony was the sweetest man who ever lived. I can't believe—"

"Did he have any secrets?"

She seemed taken aback. "Secrets?"

"Most people do. Did Tony?"

She hesitated. "He would sometimes lock himself up in his office. Like for hours. He said he was writing in his journal. But sometimes, he wouldn't be in there alone. He'd take in other guys, guys I didn't know. Not Roger. It seemed weird. You don't take in a friend to write in your diary, right? The joke around the office was that . . . well, you can imagine."

"So he was up to something. You just don't know what it was."

She tilted her head slightly. "I guess."

"You never answered my question. Did Tony know Manny Nowosky?"

Shelly fell silent.

"Well? Did he?"

Her words came slowly and carefully. "Major, you have to understand. Tony was like a brother to me. He gave me this job. He took care of me."

"Yeah, and they may have taken care of him."

Shelly's eyes widened like balloons. "You don't think—"

"That stupid frat boy has been saying from the start that he didn't kill Tony. I know at least one person who actually believes him. Wouldn't it be a damn thing if he was telling the truth?" Mike leaned across the bar. "One more time, ma'am. Did you ever see Manny and Tony together?"

She licked her lips before answering. "Once."

"And that was?"

"The last night. The night—" Her eyes fell. "The night Tony was killed."

"Nowosky was here! What did they talk about?"

"I don't know. They were arguing about something. That guy—Manny—was mad at Tony."

"Did they leave together?"

"I don't think so. I'd already knocked off. But I was told that Tony got a call—I don't know who from. Then he left." She paused. "But the girl on duty told me she saw Manny leave just a few moments after he did." She covered her mouth with her hand. "Oh, my God. I never put the two together. I never imagined—"

"Any other criminal types here that night?"

She thought a moment. "Now that you mention it, there was another guy. The chicken."

"Excuse me?"

"Oh, sorry. Chicken. That's street slang for a hooker. Gigolo. Whatever you want to call them. I mean, I didn't know for a fact that he was, but that's what everyone told me."

"You know his name? Where he lives?"

"Sorry, no. He wasn't a regular."

"And he left at the same time as Tony?"

"That's what they told me. Just a little while after Manny. He'd been watching the door all night. I thought he was waiting for a john. Jane, whatever. But maybe it was something else."

"Yeah, maybe. Thanks, Shelly. You've been a big help." He slid a card across the bar. "If you see this chicken in here again, I want you to give me a call. Immediately. And don't let him leave till I get here."

He returned to the booth where the other officers were still talking.

"What happened?" Swift said, smirking. "Strike out with the coed?"

He shook his head. "No. I struck pay dirt."

"Does that mean my chances of getting lucky tonight have diminished?"

"No," he said, staring grimly off into space. "I think maybe for the first time I'm beginning to understand what this case is really about."

CHAPTER
25

JOURNAL OF TONY BAROVICK

WHEN I GOT a shot at the manager position at Remote Control—except it wasn't called that then—I jumped at it. I mean, gee-whiz, this was a place even my mother could visit. Not that she would. But she could.

The main adjustment I had to make related to the clientele. The Dahlia had been a drinking bar, with a lot of toughs and all-guy groups, bikers, and general carousers. Remote Control was a singles bar and everyone knew it. That changed everything. It also guaranteed—being so close to the Phillips campus—that it would never be empty. And it wasn't. But I thought it could do better. Not just that we could make more money, but that we could provide a greater service to the community, by combining my love of gadgets with my love of, well, love.

When I first presented my ideas to Mario, he laughed. "Singles bars don't provide a service," he explained. "We're in the meatpacking business. We help people find someone to help them get through the night. It never lasts. Why should it?"

I wasn't satisfied with that. The reason singles pairings don't last, I reasoned, was because they aren't based on anything but physical appearances. We could change that. It seemed ridiculous to me that here in the twenty-first century, with the vast technology we had at our disposal, none of it had been employed to improve the courting process. About the only attempt I could even think of was so-called computer-dating services, which more often than not were a complete scam. We could do better.

All the technological innovations we eventually implemented were my idea. Mario kicked and screamed—but he always ponied up the money. We changed the name to Remote Control—my idea again—and started marketing ourselves in the campus newspaper. And it worked. *If you build it, they will come!*

We never talked about it, but I'm sure Mario realized that my being gay gave me insight into how this whole process could be improved. Sure, most of our clientele was straight, but that didn't mean they didn't have their secrets, too. People really grooved on the idea of putting themselves out there—via video cameras—without making fools of themselves. People loved the idea of being able to check out a prospect surreptitiously before meeting them. More than check them out—to actually get a sense of who that person was. When they finally met, the "first dates" always went a thousand times better because the participants didn't feel like it was a first date. They already knew this person, right? At least a little bit. And that made all the difference. About a year after we changed the name, we had our first—of several—weddings right in the bar—a couple who had met each other there, thanks to my whizbang gizmos. I felt vindicated. I felt as if I had finally given something back to the world. I had proven my father wrong. I might be gay, but I was not a pervert. And I was certainly not a loser.

There's been talk about franchising Remote Control. Mario has always been a hustler, and he knows a good thing when he sees it. He promised me I wouldn't be forgotten if the chain made the big time. I don't think I'd better bet the farm on that, but whether he takes me along or doesn't, he has given me a place to shine, and for that I will always be grateful. Best of all, he's given me a home, something I haven't had for a long time. I look forward to going to work. Shelly has been behind the bar for almost a year now and I love her. I consider her the sister I never had. I'd do anything for her. The customers love her, too, and she's able to handle some of the financial stuff that is frankly way over my head. She takes care of me. And I do my best to take care of her.

That's what being in a family is all about, isn't it?

CHAPTER
26

AFTER HE GOT the page from his boss, Charlie the Chicken found the nearest pay phone and gave him a call.

"Got something special for you this time, Charlie."

Well, that can't be good.

"You're going to enjoy this." Even when Charlie couldn't actually see the man's tacky gray suit he could see the man's tacky gray suit. It was in his voice, in his carefully suggestive phrasing.

"What is it?"

"Do you remember our conversation? When I first interviewed you? We talked about your . . . likes and dislikes." There was something particularly creepy about the man's voice today, which immediately put Charlie on his guard.

"I don't do men. Absolutely. It's a rule."

"But Charlie . . ."

"No."

"But consider—"

"I'm not going to change my mind, so give it up."

"You wouldn't have to actually . . . you know. Think of it more as . . . an acting job."

"The answer is still no, and nothing you can say will—"

"He's willing to pay triple your usual rate."

Charlie felt his jaw drop. Triple?

"And I for one am willing to double your usual commission. To help you overcome your reluctance. Think of it as hazard pay."

"Still, I don't do—"

"Come now, Charlie. Be sensible. You told me you needed money. I'm trying to help you."

Yeah, sure you are. Help me to an early grave.

But the man did have a point. Charlie needed a stake—fast. If he didn't raise some more scratch, he'd never get out of this town. And if he took too long about it, he'd end up dead.

"And you're sure I won't have to . . . you know."

"Positive. That's not what he's into."

"Well, I might consider it."

"Good boy, Charlie. You're doing the right thing—and the patriotic thing."

"Patriotic?"

He could hear the smile in the man's voice. "You know what they say. Support your local congressman."

He was wearing a corset. Or maybe it was a bustier. Charlie always got those two confused.

"I've been bad," Congressman Tweedy said, looking repentantly at the carpet. "I need to be punished."

And I need a new line of work, Charlie thought. "All right, you bad boy—"

"Girl."

"Girl. All right, you bad girl. Bend over."

Tweedy assumed the position, clutching the back of a leather recliner. He had a nice house, well furnished. Charlie wouldn't mind meeting the little lady who had done this place up, but somehow he felt certain that wasn't going to happen. Congressman Tweedy's wife had to be a million miles away. And when the cat's away . . .

"Take that," Charlie cried, smacking the man on his all-too-exposed posterior. It was hairy and rippled with cellulite and almost as protuberant as the sagging gut on the other end. He tried to keep his eyes on the furniture. "And that!"

"Harder," the congressman gasped. "I've been very bad."

Turned out, Charlie swung a pretty mean ruler. He'd brought his own. He'd brought a dog collar, too, but it was beginning to appear that he wasn't going to need it.

Charlie continued swinging, making a satisfying smack as the wood hit the flesh.

"Harder," the man grunted, between squeals. "I need—"

"Shut up, bitch," Charlie said, and thwacked him so hard the blow almost knocked him into the chair.

"Oh yes. Yeeeesssss."

Shouldn't be too much longer now, Charlie observed. Good. Then he could get out of here, get back to his apartment where he couldn't be spotted by his roving stalker. Besides, he was really getting into the swing of this, and he was afraid if he did it much longer, he might start to like it.

"Repeat after me," Charlie commanded. "I am a fat ugly little girl."

He whimpered. "I am a fat ugly—"

"Shut up, bitch!" He thwacked him again, and this time, just for good measure, grabbed the congressman's arm and thwacked the back of his hand. Tweedy trembled with pleasure.

"Now listen up, you sorry excuse. Do you think you can learn how to behave like a proper little lady?"

"Y—yesss."

"Yes, *sir,* bitch!"

"Yes, sir!"

"I'm not convinced," Charlie bellowed, thwacking all the way. "I think I'm going to have to keep on beating you. Harder and harder. Over and over. Until you just can't take it anymore."

"Oh, noooo," the congressman said, meaning oh yessssss . . .

Tweedy was breathing hard and fast now, gasping for each breath, sweating like the pig he was. Charlie knew the man was close; all he needed was a finishing stroke, something creative and effective and . . .

"On the floor, bitch!" He pushed the congressman down, then put his boot on the side of the man's face and crushed it into the carpet. And thwacked him some more.

"Oh yessssss! . . . Yes, yes, yes, yes, yessss!" Groaning, the congressman rolled over on his side. "Oh, thank you, sir. That was—"

"For me, too," Charlie said, grabbing the cash on the coffee table. "Parting is such sweet sorrow. Let's not make a scene, okay?" He stopped at the door. "Oh, and Congressman? Good luck in the November election." He gave a little salute. "You certainly have my vote."

CHAPTER
27

EVERYONE SHOULD HAVE a place where they can go to get away, Ben mused, as he sat down with his Trollope novel and a cup of hot tea and stared at the specials board at Novel Idea. It was a great place to have lunch, and since it was, technically, a bookstore, when you were finished, you could look at the new releases. Of course, Ben rarely read anything written after 1901, but still. The best of it was, he came often and regularly enough that people knew and recognized him. There was even a sandwich named after him on the menu. It was like Cheers for Ben—the place where everybody knows your name.

Even on his busiest days, he tried to slice away a half hour to relax, nourish his body with tortilla soup, and nourish his brain with nineteenth-century lit. It was a chance to refresh and recharge.

Usually.

"Ben, we've got to talk."

Somehow, here in his sanctum sanctorum, Christina was sitting at his table. And she'd closed his book. And she'd taken his tea.

"Christina, I'll be back in the office in—"

"And you'll shut your door and blow me off. And I have a flight for Chicago leaving in ninety minutes and I can't mess around with you anymore."

He grabbed for his book, but she pulled it away. "And what makes you think I'll listen to you here?"

"Because if you don't, I'll create a big scene. And I know how you hate scenes. Especially here, where everybody knows your name."

Scott, the owner, stopped by. "Can I get you anything else, Ben?"

"Yes. A new table. With one chair."

He grinned. "You two. What kidders. French onion soup, Christina?"

"Yes, that would be lovely." Scott returned to the kitchen. "Looks like I'm here to stay, Ben."

He folded his hands. "You know, Christina, you've done some bad things before, but this is truly evil."

"I know. I feel horrible about it. But we have to talk."

"If it's about the Christensen case—"

"You know it's about the Christensen case. Specifically, it's about Ellen Christensen."

Ben's movements slowed. "What about her?"

Christina leaned across the small round table. "I know, Ben."

"You know what?"

She looked him right in the eyes. "I know."

Dee, the manager, passed by their table. "Saw you on TV the other night, Christina. Loved your hair."

"Thanks."

"Smart move, Ben. I'd let her do all the press conferences from now on."

Ben grabbed his tea and pulled it back to his side of the table. "I'll bear that in mind."

"I'm serious," Christina said, once they were alone again. "I know all about it."

"You couldn't possibly—"

"I've talked to your mother."

Ben was floored. "What! How dare you—"

"I knew she'd shoot straight with me, and she did."

"She couldn't know everything that—"

"She knows more than you realize. She had a private

investigator look into it, after you came back from Toronto acting like an escapee from the lunatic ward."

"She didn't!"

"She did. I'm sure he didn't learn everything, but believe me, he learned enough."

"She had no right."

Christina reached out instinctively and took his hand. "Ben, I'm so sorry that had to happen to you. I guess I've always known there must've been something, something in your past, but I never dreamed . . ."

He pulled his hand away. "I don't want to talk about it."

"And I don't blame you. I mean, my ex-husband left me, but it was nothing like—"

"I don't want to talk about it!"

She held up her hands. "I just wanted you to know—that I know." She drew in her breath. "And I understand. But I still need your help."

He shook his head. "Christina, please don't ask me to—"

"Frankly, Ben, I'm not asking you anything. I have two things to *tell* you."

"Oh?"

"First, I've hired an intern."

"What?" he said, doing his best to appear shocked. "What did you think you were doing? We can't afford that!"

"We'll manage somehow. Don't worry—Vicki is smart. You're going to love her."

"What's the second message? You're moving our office to Park Avenue?"

"No. You're joining the Christensen defense."

"The hell I am."

"That's right. The hell you are."

"So you think that just because you've talked to my mother, I'm going to relent and take over your case?"

"I don't want you to take over."

"Excuse me?"

"I want you to help. But it's my case. You can second-chair."

"Me? Second-chair?"

"I've done the pretrial work and it is my case."

"*Second-chair?*"

"I know you have more experience in the courtroom, but frankly, Ben, I'm much smarter."

"Is that so?"

"I just need help, and I'm bright enough to get it when I need it. So you're going to join the team."

"Christina, I will not have anything to do with that woman."

"You don't have to. She's not the client. Her son is."

"I will not have anything to do with this case. I told you before—"

"And I accepted it, before," she said, cutting him off, "because I didn't know what had happened. But now I do. I understand how you must feel. But joining in this defense is probably the last best hope you have to get over this. And if you refuse to help and this defense tanks, you will regret it for the rest of your life. You'll be guilt-ridden and . . . well, pretty much just as you are anyway, only more so. Because you'll know you could've helped, but didn't. Because of something that—"

"I can't believe that you would ask me to do anything for her!"

Christina looked up at him. "I'm not asking you to do it for her, Ben. I'm asking you to do it for me."

Ben fell silent.

"We've been through a lot together, you and I. And I felt as if we'd gotten to know each other pretty well. All things considered." She tossed back her curls. "At the same time, I've always felt there was some sort of—I don't know—barrier between us. Something that prevented us from ever . . . oh . . ." She threw down her hands in frustration. "Whatever. The point is, I never knew what it was. But I do now. And I will never let it come between us again."

"Christina . . ."

"Please, Ben. Please. For me?"

As they looked at each other, decades seemed to pass in the space of seconds.

After a while, Dee reappeared. "Another cup of tea, Ben?"

"No," he said slowly, speaking to Dee but looking at Christina. "We need to get out of here. We've got a flight to catch. And a ton of work to do."

CHAPTER
28

THE MAN SITTING on the other side of the desk was wearing that same gray suit. "I don't understand what the difficulty is. I've had nothing but good reports about you."

Well, that was good to hear. Charlie the Chicken could still deliver.

"Do you have some complaint about the hours?"

"No, nothing like that."

"I admit, I have kept you busy, but I thought that was what you wanted."

"It was."

"Is it the kind of work? The clients?"

"No. All that has been fine."

"I know that last job was . . . somewhat unusual."

That would be one way of putting it. If the words sick, twisted, and demented weren't available.

And what a job it was. He'd known something was up from the moment he'd opened the door. For one thing, she wasn't nearly as old or as unattractive as most of his new lady friends had been. And what was that thing she was wearing? Pink and diaphanous, it was like a sarong designed by Victoria's Secret. She was very direct, forward, not a bit embarrassed. She took him not to the bedroom, but into the main parlor.

Where another woman was waiting.

"Would you mind taking off your clothing?" the first

woman said, while the second, a brunette wearing a black teddy, giggled.

"I aim to please," Charlie answered, and he complied. He'd thought they were ready to start the action, and was already envisioning how he would arrange things so he could delight them both simultaneously, dealing with the complexities of multiple breasts, a plethora of private parts . . .

"And would you mind putting this on?"

Charlie stared at the limp rag she held in her hands.

"If it's not a problem. The man on the phone didn't seem to think it would be."

He took the thin leopard-skin loincloth from her and wrapped it around his hard thighs. Jungle-man suit, that's what it was. Tarzan of the Bordello.

"Oh, wow. He looks good in it," said the woman on the sofa.

"He looks good, period," her friend replied. "Check out that six-pack."

Would you like me to open my mouth so you can examine my teeth? he wondered.

"Just stay right there," the woman on the sofa said. "Where I can see you." She squealed. "Oh, Marcia. Did you see those muscles ripple?"

Her friend grinned. "Do you work out?"

"When I get a chance."

"Well, your chance has arrived."

"You want me to work out?"

"Sort of." She handed him a long pink feather duster. "Start with the top shelves, would you? Work hard. Get all hot and sweaty."

Ooo-kay . . . He went to work on the bookshelves just behind him. He wasn't used to working in a costume, but he liked to think of himself as open-minded. "Hey, if you want, I can—"

The two women were shoving their tongues down each other's throats.

If they wanted something, they'd let him know. Maybe a Tarzan yell or two. Whatever they needed.

Not much, as it turned out. As his workout—and theirs—progressed, he came to feel increasingly irrelevant. Not that they would let him leave. But they didn't want him on the sofa. So he dusted down the living room for an hour or so while the two women pleasured themselves with a variety of techniques and implements, then collected his loot and got the hell out of there.

"They did pay you double," the man behind the desk reminded Charlie. "One hundred each. Plus a very generous tip. Even after we remove our share, that still left you earning a per hour wage of—"

"I know," Charlie said. "It's not the money. I'm still desperate for money."

The man made a minute adjustment to the lie of his desk blotter. "Then I'm afraid I don't understand."

"I'm sorry. If you could just pay me what I've earned."

The man sighed heavily and passed him the money. "All right, then. I'm sorry, too. Best of wishes."

Charlie stared at the disappointingly small stack of cash. "Could you possibly loan me some money?"

"Pardon?"

"I have to blow town—and make sure I'm not followed."

"Ah. Trouble with the law."

"No, it's not that. It's just—"

"Charlie, I've offered you some wonderful opportunities to earn money."

"I can't wait. I've already screwed around way too long."

He held up his hands. "Then I don't see how I can help you."

Damn everyone! he thought, as he made his way to the bus. How did he ever get started in this stupid business?

That question was easy enough to answer. Dean. He was the man who put me on the road to chickendom.

When Charlie had first left home, he'd had no idea where to go or what to do. The friend of a friend he was supposed to stay with bailed, and he couldn't hook up with any theater groups. He was trying to decide whether to give up and go home when he heard that ultradeep voice behind him.

"You got a place to stay, kid?"

Dean was a big man, tough, wiry, with a voice like the Grand Canyon. He took Charlie to the Sizzlin' Sirloin for a great meal. He was so warm, so sympathetic. Listened to all of Charlie's stories—why he had to leave home, how he just couldn't live with his parents any longer. Dean understood. Told him he could stay at his place. Which seemed like a great deal.

Until Charlie woke up in the middle of the night. In pain.

Dean was on top of him, hurting him, pinning him down, punishing him, tearing him. Charlie felt paralyzed; he'd never experienced anything so intense, anything so ungodly painful in his life. Dean's hot breath was on his neck and his body was all over him and there was nothing Charlie could do about it.

When it was over, Dean rolled over and sighed. "Thanks, punk."

Charlie should've left then and there. But where would he go? He had no money, no place to stay. Maybe those were just excuses. Maybe there's always an alternative, but he sure as hell couldn't come up with one.

A week later, Dean invited Charlie to meet some of his friends. Friends with similar interests. After a while, it didn't hurt anymore. After a little longer, he was barely aware it was happening.

It had been maybe a month, living with Dean, when the man said, "Charlie, do you know what a chicken is?"

"Yeah. They sell 'em at KFC."

"That's not what I mean. On the street, a chicken is a young punk like you who sells his body for money."

"You mean, like a hooker?"

" 'Cept it's a good-lookin' hunk of a boy. Like you."

"Why are you tellin' me this, Dean?"

"Well, Charlie, you been livin' here for more'n a month now. And I've took care of you. Took good care of you. Haven't I?"

Charlie remained silent.

"But time comes a boy's got to be a man. Got to take care of hisself. That time is here, Charlie. You got to carry your share of the load."

In time, he moved out of Dean's place, but never changed his line of work. It was just so easy, and it left so much spare time for other things. And he was good at it! He made women happy. There wasn't anything trashy about it, not most of the time. He loved those ladies, and they loved him. What could be wrong with that? If only he'd stuck to the chicken work, and not gotten tangled up in the other mess . . .

But he had. And now that mistake could cost him his life.

He'd been trying to make enough scratch to get somewhere, but he didn't have time for that now. The savings plan was on hold—it was fly or die. Even if he had to leave town on foot, he had to go. Because this person was smart. This person had some amazing resources.

He had to get to the bus station. He had enough to get somewhere, anywhere.

He climbed onto the city bus. He was beginning to feel calmer now. He wasn't out of the woods, but at least he had a plan of action. He had options. He had hope.

All of which died the instant he sat down and looked out the window. The bus pulled away, but the face he dreaded most was back at the bus stop, smiling at him.

He'd been found.

CHAPTER
29

"So you're the guy my mom wanted in the first place?" Johnny Christensen said, peering through the protective acrylic panel.

Ben didn't reply.

"Mr. Kincaid will be acting as my second-chair, Johnny. He's doing it as a favor to me."

"I see." He rubbed a hand against his stubbled chin. "As opposed to doing it for me."

"Or your mother," Ben said, in a low tone.

"So how do you think our chances look?"

"I won't lie to you," Ben said. "The evidence has been stacked against you from the start, and we haven't found much to counteract it. As I told you before, my cop friend is in Chicago and he has some interesting theories, but so far nothing that's likely to help us in court."

"Then you think . . . I'm gonna lose?" The color drained from Johnny's cheeks. "You think they're gonna fry me?"

"I can't predict the penalty—"

"Well, I can. I've read the papers. If they find me guilty, I'm gonna be executed. I know I will."

Ben couldn't argue with his conclusion, especially given the Illinois hate crime statute. "Johnny, we'll do everything we can."

"I'm only seventeen. I don't want to die."

"We'll do everything—"

"I'm so scared. All the time, scared. I can't sleep. You

know how much weight I've lost?" His eyes began to well up. "I don't want to die."

"You should've thought of that before you attacked Tony Barovick."

"I didn't kill him, man."

Why pull punches? "Even if your story is true, the things you and your friend did were cruel beyond measure. You tortured a poor boy who never did anything to you."

"I can't help what I am," Johnny said, his voice surprisingly tender. "The way I was brought up."

"Your mother would never—" Ben choked his words off. "I can't believe anyone ever taught you to hate people just because of who they are."

"Are you kidding? At my church, the preacher used to come down on fags every other week! He told us homosexuals are all going to hell. That as Christians, it was our duty to try to lead people away from lives of sin."

"So that's what that beating was? A Sunday school lesson?"

"Since when were Christians ever afraid to use force? Even Christ tossed the moneylenders out of the Temple."

"Did he break their legs?"

"Look, opposing homosexuals is part of my religion. You can't criticize me for following my religion."

I might, Ben thought silently. "Is religion important to you, Johnny?"

"Hell, yes. I sang in the church choir, you know. Even taught a Sunday school class. The Bible specifically speaks out against homosexuality. A hundred years ago, no one would've questioned it."

"Yeah," Christina said. "And schools were segregated. And women weren't allowed to vote. And children went to work at the age of eight." Having been down this road before, Christina knew it was a dead end. "Look, Johnny, we don't have a lot of time, and we didn't come here for a socioreligious debate. I just wanted your approval to add another lawyer to the case. And to ask you if you remember seeing anyone else at Remote Control the night you confronted Tony Barovick. Maybe someone who left the bar about the same time you did? Or Tony did?"

"There was another guy. He was hanging around the bar for a long time. I remember because . . . well, we talked about going after him. What he does is almost as disgusting as what Tony Barovick did."

"What's his name?"

"Probably not his real name. But everyone at Remote Control called him Charlie the Chicken."

"Do you know where Mr. Chicken lives?"

"Nah. Why?"

Christina craned her neck. Talking into a phone receiver for so long made it stiffen up. "Just following every possible lead. If there's anything else . . ."

"Look—" Johnny said, before she hung up the phone. "I know what the score is. I know you two don't like me. You think I'm an ignorant putz. But I'm telling you—I did not kill that guy. Brett did not kill that guy. He was alive when we left him. I promise you. I *promise*." His eyes began to well up again. "I'll pay the price for what I did, but please don't let them kill me for something I didn't do. Please. *Please*."

"I JUST DON'T get it," Ben said as they emerged from the detention center. "How Ellen could raise a kid like that."

"She's only his stepmother," Christina replied. "Maybe the damage was done before she was involved."

Just as she had during the flight out of Tulsa, Christina continued to bring Ben up to speed on the case as she led him across the parking lot to their temporary offices in Kevin Mahoney's suite. "I've got angles on all the prosecution witnesses," she explained, "and I think I can deal with, if not totally defuse, most of them. But what I don't have is a real defense. An alternate explanation. Kevin didn't have one, either."

"Any theories?"

"You know what Mike said. There may be a connection between his murder and ours—and it may have something to do with drugs."

"That's not much to go on."

"Agreed. Without concrete evidence, the jury will just think we're grasping at straws, trying to complicate an open-and-shut case. I've asked Vicki to go over the arrest records for—"

"Excuse me!"

Across the parking lot, Ben saw a young black man waving at them. "Could I speak with you?"

"I'm sorry," Ben said, "but I'm really pressed for time and—"

"Don't mean to interrupt," the man said, as he caught up to them. "But it's the lady I want to talk to. Are you Christina McCall?"

She nodded.

"You're handling the Christensen case?"

"We both are," she answered.

"I'm Roger Hartnell," he said. "I—I knew Tony Barovick. Well."

Christina remembered reading about him in one of Loving's reports. "Do you know something about what happened to him?"

"No, sorry—I didn't mean to mislead you. I haven't come as a friend of Tony's. I came in my capacity as regional director of ANGER."

"You're the creeps who redecorated our elevator lobby."

"We're not responsible for that. Our press release merely said that we sympathized with those who did it."

Ben frowned. "So you're not here to help us with this case?"

"No, sir. I'm here to ask you to drop it."

Ben took Christina by the arm. "I'm sorry, but we don't have time for—"

"Listen to me. What you're doing is wrong."

"Sure," Christina replied. "We should just let the posse string Johnny up."

"I don't mean that he should have no representation. Let the court appoint someone, if necessary. But when it comes from attorneys of your stature—it seems like an endorsement."

"It's how the legal system works. Now if you'll excuse me—"

"Please just give me one minute. You don't understand everything that—"

"I'm sorry," Ben said, "I think I do understand your position. And I admire you for trying to combat hate and prejudice—up to a point. But we have a job to do—"

Ben was cut off by a sudden crack of thunder—except the skies were clear. It was a gunshot.

"Get down!" he shouted. He grabbed Christina and pushed her behind a low retaining wall.

Another shot followed. Where was it coming from? Ben scanned the horizon, while simultaneously scrambling for cover behind a parked car.

"Get out of the way!" he shouted at Roger, a moment too late. A bullet caught the man in the right leg. He tumbled to the ground.

"Ben," Christina asked, clinging to the pavement, "have you got your cell phone?"

"Left it in my bag," he said bitterly. He tried to pull Roger to safety, but another shot fired; the bullet bounced off the sidewalk just inches from Ben's hand. He gave it another try and this time managed to pull Hartnell behind the car. The three of them huddled there, pinned in place.

"Any idea where the shooter is?" Christina asked, huddling close.

"Somewhere in the parking lot. Not far. Not far enough." Another shot rang out. Ben raised his head just enough to see movement about four rows of cars away. Their sniper was even closer than he'd imagined.

"Give me your briefcase," Ben said.

"Why?" She didn't comply. "Don't do anything stupid, Ben."

"Hartnell is bleeding to death."

"We're just off a busy street in downtown Chicago. Someone will call for help."

"Maybe. But help won't be able to get to him as long as there's a killer trying to pick off anyone who comes close. Give me the briefcase."

With profound reluctance, Christina passed him the hard-shelled attaché case. Ben took it to the front of the car, aimed himself toward the next row, and dove.

Just after he appeared in the open space between rows, another shot rang out, but by that time Ben had already scrambled behind another sedan. Still not close enough to do anything.

His heart was pounding so intensely it was hard to think. "Here goes nothing," Ben muttered, then dove again.

This time the sniper was ready for him. The shot came much sooner. Ben heard the shrill whine, then felt it rip through his suit jacket.

"Damn!" He rolled behind the next row of cars, patting himself down, making sure he was still intact. His right side stung. He pulled up his shirt and saw that he was bleeding. Just a scrape, but that was way too close. If he tried that stunt again, the sniper was bound to get him.

He knew it wasn't safe to peer over the top of the cars, so he crouched down and looked beneath. Sure enough, one double row away, he spotted a pair of sneakers: blue-striped Nikes.

Mustering all his strength, he threw the briefcase forward, aiming for where he knew the sniper had to be. He heard a grunt, followed by a sudden clatter. A quick check under the cars told him the sniper's weapon had fallen to the ground.

This was his chance. Ben raced forward, barreling around the cars. He poured on speed, whipped around the line of parked cars . . .

The sniper was gone. The gun lying on the pavement was the only evidence that he had ever been there.

Ben scoured the parking lot, trying to get a lead on him, but found nothing. He collected the gun and returned to Christina.

"I think we're clear," he told her. "Let's get help." He ran up the steps and through the front doors of the office building—then froze.

The lobby had been trashed. Shattered glass was everywhere. The information counter had been destroyed, hammered to bits. Phones had been ripped out of the walls. Tiles broken. Lights ruined. Elevator doors destroyed.

But what most commanded Ben's attention was the display in the center of the room, hovering where the information counter used to be. A tableau dangling from the ceiling, two figures hanged in effigy, obviously constructed from department store mannequins, so crude that they didn't really resemble anyone. But one was branded with Greek fraternity letters.

And the other had a red-dyed mop on its head for hair.

LIVE BY THE SWORD; DIE BY THE SWORD read the placard dangling from the feet of the figure that was supposed to be Johnny. The one hanging beneath the representation of Christina read: YOU'RE NEXT.

THE OWNER OF the mail-order revolver purchased under an assumed name watched Ben Kincaid and his friends scurry about from a safe distance. Everything had gone as planned, except that the lawyer turned out to be considerably braver than word on the street suggested. No matter. The point had been made. They'd be looking over their shoulders constantly now, wondering if this was the magic moment when the sniper would reappear and give them the drilling they had barely escaped.

And with good cause. Because the sniper *would* return—sooner than they expected.

CHAPTER
30

HURRY! CHARLIE THOUGHT as the bus driver dawdled in the turn lane.

Did he not understand that this was a matter of life and death? Of course, he didn't. You're not thinking rationally, he told himself. But who would expect him to think rationally at a time like this? His stomach was in knots and his hands were trembling. He'd been a basket case since he saw what he saw—who he saw—when he got on the bus.

Think it through, Charlie. Having seen me get on this bus, it would be no trick to find out where it's going. Follow it, make sure no one gets off. Or head for downtown. Anyone with a car could move faster than this bus. And therefore . . .

He gazed out the window, searching in all directions for the face he most dreaded. There were no more stops before the bus arrived at the downtown terminal. He had considered creating a disturbance, forcing the driver to stop the bus so he could get off. But in the long run, what would that get him? Where would he go? What would he do? He'd been found once. He could be found again. He had to get off the city bus and onto one that would take him far, far away.

It was the Chicken's last stand. All those days of servicing Chicago's high-society dames were done. They'd have to find someone else to fill the slot in their leather-bound Filofaxes between getting their hair done and making the society tea. His illustrious career was drawing to a close. Maybe he'd even go back home, go back to being just plain old Charlie.

It was hard to imagine, after all this time. Could he possibly return to his former life? Did he want to? Would his parents accept him? It might sound all sweet and bucolic, but he suspected he would soon miss life in the big city. The glamorous world of palatial mansions and Henredon furniture and . . . and . . .

And the Tarzan suit. Most of all, he would miss the Tarzan suit.

When they arrived at the terminal, Charlie stepped cautiously off the bus. He scanned the parking lot, the station—everything and everyone. He was so close. If he could just get out of town—surely that would bring this horror story to an end.

He went inside the station and got in line for a ticket. He didn't have that much money, given the paltry share the escort service let him keep, but he had enough to get somewhere. Anywhere.

After purchasing his ticket, he took a seat in one of the clamshell chairs near the ticket booth. These seats must've been designed to discourage loitering, because they were as uncomfortable as anything he'd ever experienced. He had almost half an hour before his bus left. If he spent it here, he might incur permanent spinal injury.

He wandered over to the vending machines, bought himself a Coke and a Snickers bar. Comfort foods for the underprivileged, he told himself. And they tasted good going down, too. Maybe it was just the sugar rush, but his mood was definitely improving.

Any minute now, he'd see his bus roll up outside the front door and hear the caller tell them all to get on board. Best to take a quick bathroom break while he had a chance. He detoured into the men's room, went to the urinal, took care of business, zipped up, turned around.

Surprise.

"Hello there. Long time no see."

Charlie was so stunned he couldn't think straight. He stuttered like an idiot. "W—w—what are you doing in here?"

"Looking for you, Charlie."

He glanced at the door. A broom had been wedged through the handle. No one else could get in. No one could help him. He tried to edge away, but the obstruction in his path wasn't budging.

"Look, I'm leaving town. I haven't spoken to anyone and I don't plan to. Keep the money. You can trust me."

"My experience with trusting others has not been very good."

Charlie could feel himself failing. His knees were wobbling so badly he could barely stand. "Just let me get on the bus. I promise I'll be out of your life forever."

"So you say. But what happens when you've been drinking too much at the local tavern, desperately trying to elevate the sex drive of some rich bitch in her late seventies? Perhaps you talk too much, say something you shouldn't. What happens if the rich bitch trade dries up and you find yourself short of cash? Would blackmail occur to you?"

"I wouldn't do that. I wouldn't."

"Unfortunately, I can't take that risk."

Backed up against the urinal, porcelain jammed into his back, Charlie had nowhere to go. "If you try anything, I'll scream!"

A second later, the butt of a gun cracked his jaw with such explosive force that he was stunned. His legs disappeared; he crumpled to the floor and lay there, his shattered jaw pressed against the foul-smelling tile. His head felt as if it were on fire; all he could see was white. He couldn't move his mouth. Or anything else.

A perfectly aimed kick caved in his abdomen, smashing several ribs. Pain rippled through him like a river. Then he felt hot breath beside his cheek. "Just a tip, Charlie. If you're going to scream, just do it. Don't give the killer a warning."

Somehow, from somewhere, he managed to find words. "Please . . . please don't do this."

"I recall a time when I was asking for your cooperation, Charlie. You were not so forthcoming, then. And now the time for discussion has passed."

Another unbearable blow to his rib cage, then he felt himself being twisted around, turned onto his back. The pain was excruciating. Nothing could possibly hurt more, or so he thought, until he felt the hand on his face, forcing his shattered jaw open.

"Hungry, Charlie? Here's a snack."

Charlie felt cold steel pressed into his mouth, overwhelming his gag reflex. He tried to muster what remaining strength he possessed to do something, anything, cry for help, push the gun away. But he couldn't. He clenched his eyes shut, bracing himself against the inevitable.

In his final nanosecond of life, he was thinking about home.

PART TWO

Crimes of Passion

CHAPTER
31

"LADIES AND GENTLEMEN of the jury, this is a crime that—"

DA Drabble hesitated. It was a slight pause, but Ben noticed, just the same. The DA could be forgiven this bobble. The last time this court had heard opening statements in this case, they had been interrupted by a fanatic with a gun. At some level, Drabble's subconscious mind had to be searching the room, looking for any indication of danger.

"This is a crime," Drabble continued, "of the worst sort—cold-blooded murder. And as the evidence will show, it was committed for the worst possible reason. Not for love, money, jealousy, revenge, or any of the baser emotions that normal people can understand, if not condone. This was a crime of hate—pure, blind, unreasoning hate. Johnny Christensen did not take this life because of anything Tony Barovick did. He committed murder because of who Tony Barovick was."

Drabble was good. As before, when Ben had seen him on television, Drabble impressed him with his unforced yet deliberate manner. He didn't come off as rigid and self-righteous, as so many DAs did. He didn't insult opposing counsel. He didn't resort to melodrama—well, not much—and he skipped most of the cheap theatrics, waving bloody photographs in the air and such. It was probably not a sign of any innate superiority; truth was, Drabble didn't need to resort to any of that. He knew how to communicate, how to make the jury listen and, hardest of all, how to make them believe.

"On that chilly spring morning just a short time ago, Tony Barovick left his place of business and headed for home. He was probably thinking about the usual things—getting some groceries for dinner, what he might watch on television that night. What he didn't know—what he couldn't possibly know—was that he was being stalked—yes, stalked—by two students, two fraternity boys he had served back at his club. What had he done to offend them? you might wonder. Had he insulted them? Stolen from them? Hurt them? No, Tony hadn't done any of those things. Tony hadn't so much as mixed up their drink order. They were out to get him simply because he was a homosexual. And they didn't like homosexuals. Indeed—they hated homosexuals."

Ben scanned the courtroom. It was packed, as he'd expected. A few of the spectators were the usual thrill seekers, but most of the gallery was taken up by the press. CNN and FOX News and some of the other national outfits had set up camp in the hallway outside, so it was no surprise that they were allocated many of the choice seats. Several on-air personalities and celebs had been spotted in the courtroom. Rumor was that Dominick Dunne had a contract to write a book about the case, and John Cusack was negotiating for the movie rights. Everyone wanted a piece of the action.

Boxer Johnson, the bailiff who'd been clubbed over the head by the killer of Brett Mathers, was back on the job. Ben knew he'd taken a lot of grief after the execution; the shooter had knocked him out in the men's room and stolen his uniform and gun. He seemed none the worse for it today; he stood at attention at the rear of the gallery, calm, watchful. An assured, strong presence.

In addition to the media reps, Ben also spotted a few people he'd read about last night, after he and Christina

recovered from the shooting incident and finished with
the police and the medics and he began cramming every
bit of relevant information about this case into his head.
Many of the people Tony Barovick had worked with
and the potential witnesses were here, including the
owner of the club, Mario Roma, and Tony's barmaid
and friend, Shelly Chimka. Scott Banner, the president
of Johnny's fraternity, was sitting behind her. Roger Hartnell was in a wheelchair, thanks to the bullet wound, but
he was here, against doctor's orders. He said it was important that he make an appearance, both as the local
director of ANGER and as Tony's former partner. They
all sat together, behind the DA's table, presumably to
show their support for Tony.

Only one person sat behind the defendant's table by
choice. And Ben had spent the entire morning studiously
trying to avoid eye contact with her.

"They were driven by one motive and one motive
alone," Drabble continued. "Blind, unreasoning hate.
Hate born of fear, of ignorance. The same kind of hate
that sent six million Jews to the gas chamber. The same
kind of hate that killed 168 people at the Murrah Building in Oklahoma City. The same kind of hate that killed
thousands at the World Trade Center. The kind of hate
that cannot be tolerated in any civilized society."

Vicki, the new intern, whispered into Ben's ear. "This
seems unduly inflammatory. Are we going to let him get
away with this?"

Ben eyed Christina carefully. They were both tempted
to object—this was pretty over-the-top. But Kevin Mahoney had told them that Judge Lacayo was usually le-
nient about what he'd allow in openings and closings.
And they couldn't deny that this was a hate crime—a
critical part of their strategy was to acknowledge up
front what Johnny had done, and what he had not done.
They both decided to let it pass.

"This is what they did," Drabble continued, his voice

darkening. "First, they beat him mercilessly, giving him no chance to defend himself or escape. Then they used a Taser to torture him. Then they cut him. With a knife. And finally, when Tony must have felt that he couldn't possibly feel any more pain, when he was crying out for mercy, they put wooden blocks under his knees and ankles, took a five-pound iron maul hammer and shattered his legs—first his left, and then, after the initial shock wave of pain had subsided, the right."

Ben checked Johnny's expression. He was holding up pretty well, all things considered. He'd been a wreck when the marshals brought him into the courtroom this morning. Crying like a baby, shaking visibly, begging for help. Christina had taken him to a rest room to scrub him up and get him back in control before the jury arrived. She'd been largely successful, though he had no idea how she'd managed it. No one was going to leave this trial with a good impression of the kid, but at least now he didn't look like guilt incarnate.

Ben wondered what was going through Johnny's mind as he heard the DA recount the list of horribles in which he had participated. Was he remorseful? Ashamed? Or was he secretly proud of himself, of what he had done in the name of his holy cause?

"Do you know what it feels like to have a thousand volts of electricity run through your body?" Drabble asked. "It isn't pleasant. Your legs turn to rubber. You lose all control of your bodily functions. You can't stop twitching. You can't control your bladder. You lie on the ground and flop back and forth like a jellyfish." Drabble leaned in closer. "But as bad as it is, it probably doesn't compare with seeing someone take a knife to your flesh and cut it while you watch helplessly. And it certainly doesn't compare to having your knees braced by two wooden blocks and seeing your legs destroyed with a five-pound hammer. Is it even possible for those of us who didn't experience it to know what that would feel like? To measure the intensity of the anguish that poor boy suffered? To conceive of the magnitude of hate that would be necessary to commit such acts on another human being?"

Okay, Ben thought, so now he was being a little melodramatic. But it was an extraordinary crime—a brutal, hideous, inhuman one. It would be difficult, if not impossible, for any DA to discuss it without sounding intense.

"When Tony Barovick was found, just a short time after his destruction at these hands, in the fraternity house of which the defendant is a member, he was dead. Now the defense attorneys may try to suggest that Tony was killed somewhere else—but the evidence will show otherwise. The defense may suggest that the defendant beat Tony Barovick but didn't quite kill him—but the evidence will show otherwise. What the defense will not deny is that Johnny Christensen attacked Tony Barovick, cruelly and mercilessly—because he did. Did Christensen want Barovick to die? Was that his intent?" Drabble paused. "I think his actions speak for themselves.

"Now I still remember the voir dire we did several weeks ago," Drabble continued, "and I know many of you have mixed feelings on the subject of homosexuality. Some of you have deep-seated reasons, religious reasons, and we are not here to challenge those. But what I am here to say is—" At this point, Drabble whirled around and pointed at Johnny. "—what this man did was not an acceptable protest to another man's lifestyle choice!"

He fell silent, letting his words reverberate in the jurors' ears. "And it is important that we, as a society, make it clear that we will not accept this kind of conduct. As jurors, you swore to uphold the law, and that duty was never more important than it is today. Why? Because there are some people who hate women. Who hate children. Who hate people of other races, other religions. Who hate fat people. Bald people. There will always be those who hate. But this—this!" He grew quiet, finishing with barely a whisper. "This must never happen again. Never!"

After a measured moment of silence, Drabble took his seat. Judge Lacayo nodded in Ben's direction.

"Here's your outline," Vicki whispered.

Ben smiled. Christina was right—he liked the new kid on the block. She was quiet, a bit timid, so unaggressive he wondered if she could ever possibly survive as a trial attorney—which was exactly what people used to say about him. Small wonder he liked her.

"Thanks, but Drabble didn't use notes, so I won't either."

"You know what you have to do?" Christina whispered to him.

He nodded. "I'm going to be brief."

"I think that's best."

Ben took his position before the jury. He knew he didn't have the slickness, the imposing presence or, for that matter, the good looks of his opponent. But he had managed to learn a thing or two about talking to juries. He'd learned, for instance, not to lie to them, because contrary to popular belief, most jurors were not stupid, and they would pick up on a lie immediately—and never trust him again. And he'd learned that, for the most part, jurors weren't really impressed by hyperbole or dramatic surprises or courtroom theatrics. The stuff that made good television did not necessarily make a good trial. In his experience, what juries really liked was someone who would just tell them what happened, tell it straight, and let them draw their own conclusion. Of course, as he also knew, if the story was told properly, the conclusion could be artfully predestined—without giving the impression of doing so.

"First of all," Ben said, echoing the words he had

heard Kevin Mahoney speak all those weeks ago, "let's establish what this trial is not about. It is not a referendum on gay rights. It is not a campaign for more hate crimes legislation. It is not a forum for sending messages to the populace at large. Nothing you do here will alter the history of World War II or alleviate the tragedies born of terrorist acts. You have been brought here to do one thing, and one thing alone—to determine whether this man's guilt has been proven beyond a reasonable doubt. As the judge will later instruct you, any other consideration is grossly improper."

Ben took a moment to size up the jurors. He hadn't had his usual opportunity to get to know them during the voir dire, but he'd read the transcript and reviewed Kevin's notes. Now he needed time to read the lines of their faces. He sensed that a few of them were wary of him, perhaps even suspicious. That wasn't a great surprise. Some people were naturally suspicious of defense attorneys, usually those on the right side of the political fence or with a strong law-and-order bent. Many assumed anyone accused of a crime was probably guilty, that trials were a waste of time, that attorneys only existed to put the guilty back on the streets. The best way he could win them over would be to come clean about his client's flaws.

"Second, I am not here to convince you that my client, Johnny Christensen, is a great human being. He isn't." Ben could almost feel Ellen's eyes boring into him, not to mention Johnny's. Never mind. He knew what he was doing. "He was neither good, nor kind, nor nice the day Tony Barovick was killed. He was mean and brutal and ignorant, and in many respects he represents the very worst part of this country, the faction that finds it acceptable to commit acts of cruelty and violence in the name of some higher cause. My partner has been trying to convince me Johnny's not that bad, just misguided and poorly educated, but I'm not buying it. Frankly, I don't even like sitting at the same table with him."

Ben watched the eyebrows of more than one juror rise. Well, at least now he had their attention. "And you know what? I don't mind telling you that, either. Know why?" He leaned over the rail. "Because it doesn't matter. None of it matters. Whether you like him or you don't *doesn't matter*." He paused. "I know you're not stupid people. I know you won't be led by your emotions. If you convict—and that is an *if*—it will be because of the facts presented to you at this trial, and not because you do or don't like someone."

Ben walked slowly to the opposite end of the rail. "Now let me clearly state that we do not disagree with much of what the district attorney has said. We will not try to dispute the undisputed facts. Johnny Christensen did participate in the beating of Tony Barovick. We acknowledge that. But he was not the principal actor in that crime and, most significantly, he did not kill Tony Barovick. His cohort, Brett Mathers, did not kill him. Nor did Tony Barovick die from the beating. They left him in a vacant lot seriously injured, to be sure, but very much alive."

Ben didn't detect much reaction from the jury. Many probably thought he was splitting hairs. Okay, Johnny beat him to the edge of death but didn't deliver the finishing stroke—big deal. But that kind of thinking was exactly what Ben wanted. Because the charge brought by the district attorney was not aggravated assault, not even manslaughter. It was murder—murder in the first degree. If he could convince the jury that Johnny did not deliver or participate in the delivery of the death stroke, there was just the tiniest chance he might come out of this trial alive.

"You may have noticed that the DA didn't say anything about how Tony got to the fraternity house—because the investigators don't know. They've scrutinized the vehicles belonging to Johnny and his partner—and found nothing. The DA didn't say anything about what actually caused Tony's death—because they're a little fuzzy on that point, too. They can't tell you to what extent the illegal drug trade at Tony's club—which Johnny Christensen had nothing to do with and played no part in—may have created a motive for murder.

"The DA would suggest that this is an open-and-shut case, but there are, in fact, many unanswered questions. And that's a problem. Because you can't convict a man just because you don't like him, or because he did something else that was bad. You can't convict when you don't really know what happened, or where, or who did what. In order to convict my client of the crime with which he has been charged, you must find him guilty beyond a reasonable doubt. Think about that. Beyond a reasonable doubt. That's a very high standard. And it's one that the district attorney, for all his good intentions, simply can't make."

Ben buttoned his jacket, turned and took his seat, careful not to let his eyes wander toward his client—or his client's mother.

It had started. Let the games begin.

CHAPTER
32

IF TELEVISION LEGAL dramas were required to play out a trial in real time, Ben mused, there would never be another lawyer show. In fact, there would never have been a first; *Perry Mason* would have sunk into obscurity. Because even with a case as dramatic and extraordinary as this one, 75 percent of the trial was dull as dust. The endless procedural rigmarole could bury any viewer's interest—all the procedural hoops the law required, the painfully protracted process of establishing foundations and complying with the increasingly complex rules of evidence. The constant interruptions for bench conferences, jury breaks, the judge stepping out to attend to other business. Small wonder every legal drama he'd ever seen had taken outrageous liberties with reality. Jury trials need a good editor to keep them interesting.

And this trial was no exception. Despite the packed room full of spectators desperate for action, Judge Lacayo first went through his preliminary instructions to the jurors, parties, and counsel, making a record of everything the appeals court might want while the court reporter took it all down. Even after Drabble started putting on the prosecution's case, the excitement level did not increase much. His first three witnesses were purely pro forma types, establishing elements everyone knew and no one disputed but that were necessary to lay a proper foundation in the event of an appeal: such as establishing that a person had died, and that the person was Tony Barovick.

It was not until the fourth witness, called after the lunch break, that the witness stand began to heat up. And even that was not immediate. First the prosecution had to establish the police officer's experience, years of service, flawless record, qualifications, yadda, yadda, yadda . . .

"Officer Montgomery," Drabble said eventually, "please tell us what you were doing shortly after midnight on the morning of March 22."

"I was patrolling in my vehicle with my partner, Officer Raymond, in the area of Phillips College when I received a call on my radio."

"And what was the call?"

"An anonymous tip about a possible 510 at a frat house on campus."

"Did you respond?"

"Of course." Montgomery was a slim man with an erect, almost stiff, bearing. He struck Ben as an honest man, and he conveyed that sense to the jury in his testimony. "We were the closest vehicle in the area. I notified campus security and proceeded to the fraternity house."

"When did you arrive?"

"A few minutes after midnight. We approached the front door. I knocked and called out, but there was no response."

"What did you do?"

"The door was open, so we went inside. We soon entered one of the side rooms—a den or sitting room or something. That's where we found him."

"And by *him* you mean . . ."

"Tony Barovick. We didn't know that was his name at the time, of course. All we saw at first was . . . the mess."

The transformation of the officer's face was, Ben did

not doubt, unintentional, but quite evident just the same.

"Would you please describe what you saw?"

Despite his obvious reluctance, the officer answered the question. "You could see at once that something was very wrong—the boy's legs were twisted back at unnatural angles. His clothes were torn and soaked with blood. His face had been cut. There was some kind of burning on his face. Like he had been . . . cooked or something. And his legs . . ." The officer shook his head, taking a deep breath to maintain his even tone. "Well, his legs were like hamburger meat. All pulped and shattered and . . . gone."

"Could you tell if he was still alive?"

"There was no way that poor kid could be alive. But I took his pulse—standard procedure. He didn't have one."

"What did you do next?"

"Called homicide, naturally. Called the coroner's office." He grimaced. "Sent my partner out to get my coat. It was warm outside, but it was cold in that frat house. Or maybe it just seemed like it—with that mutilated body. Gave me the chills."

"Understandable, I think, given the circumstances. Did you do anything else before you left the premises?"

"While I waited for the detectives to arrive, I looked for members who might be able to tell me what happened."

"Did you find any?"

"Not at first. The house was empty. Apparently some big fraternity function was taking place elsewhere on campus and most of the members were there. But I did find an e-mail message left up on one of the computers in an upstairs bedroom that talked about an 'after-glow'—that was their word—taking place at midnight at Remote Control. So I radioed that information into

HQ and they sent officers to the bar. After the detectives arrived, my partner and I returned to our vehicle and went back out on the street to resume our duties. But to tell you the truth—it was a struggle."

"You couldn't get back to work?"

"No. I just kept thinking about what I had seen. That horrible scene. Couldn't get it out of my mind. I ended up having to knock off early. I can't explain it very well but when you've seen something like that—" He shook his head. "I mean, it isn't just that it's so visually disgusting, although it was that. It's the thought that someone—anyone—would be capable of doing such a thing to another human being. Who could be so heartless?"

Ben felt the eyes in the jury box turning toward Johnny.

"I thought about applying to be on the investigating team looking for the assailant, but I put it out of my head. And you know why? Because I'm a big believer in the law. Law and order. And I knew that if I ever found the man who had done that, I wouldn't be interested in reading him his Miranda rights. I'd just want to make sure that bastard never had a chance to do anything like that to anyone else ever again."

Ben objected, of course, but it was pointless. The officer wasn't delivering evidence, and the jury had already heard his commentary. There wasn't much he could do on cross, either, since he didn't doubt anything the officer had said, and his testimony didn't yet link the crime to Johnny. It would be a tactical error to browbeat a witness who was just delivering the undiluted and unquestioned facts. So he contented himself with trying to lay a foundation for the future.

"When you entered the fraternity house, did you see any signs that a beating had taken place?"

Montgomery looked at Ben as if he'd lost his mind. "I certainly saw the results of the beating."

"You know what I mean, Officer. I'm trying to determine where the beating occurred."

"There was blood under the body."

"Although perhaps not as much as you might expect if this extensive beating had actually taken place there."

"I couldn't say. I'm not the coroner."

"Did you notice any overturned chairs or furniture?"

"No."

"No scuffs, no dents, no broken lamps, no bits of duct tape, no damage whatsoever."

Montgomery frowned. "Maybe the boys were careful not to hurt their house when they tortured their victim."

"I can think of a more likely explanation, Officer. And I bet you can, too." Ben glanced at the jury, hoping to see their brains whirring. Some defense lawyers tried to spell everything out in capital letters during cross. He always thought that it was better if he gave the jury the necessary information but let them reach the conclusions on their own. If they thought they were being clever—thinking ahead of the game—they were more likely to go where he wanted them to go. "Now, after you found the corpse, you assumed that the assailant had been a member of the fraternity, right?"

"It seemed a logical conclusion."

"But in fact you never saw any member of the fraternity with the victim, did you?"

"Obviously not."

"And in fact you testified that no members were in the house at that time, right?"

"Right."

"What's more—the front door was open."

"That's true."

"So anyone could've brought the boy into that house. As far as you know."

"The coroner's re—"

"As far as you know, Officer. You're here to tell the jury what *you* know."

Montgomery sat back in his chair. "I didn't see who brought him into the house."

"Good. Thank you for clearing that up for me."

DURING THE BREAK, Ben asked Vicki if she had any suggestions. She might be a bit on the meek side, but she was very organized, and organization was by far the most important asset when trying a case. Her notes were detailed and accurate; her files were systematically arranged and accessible.

"Anything I left out?" Ben asked.

"I thought you were great," she said, not quite making eye contact. "I didn't see how you could do anything with that witness. But you did—without being confrontational or alienating the jury. I could see where you were going. I think the jury could, too."

"Let's hope. I'm going to get some coffee. Can I get you anything, Johnny?"

He shook his head. For a boy sometimes given to great bursts of Sturm und Drang, he had been quiet, almost invisible, since the trial actually began. Ben had seen this phenomenon before. Pretrial—it never seems quite real. More like some crazy TV movie-of-the-week that's sure to have a happy ending. But once testimony begins, it becomes very real. As do the potential consequences.

"I could use some coffee. Assuming I can't have anything stronger."

"A safe assumption. Okay, that's three coffees and one chocolate milk."

Vicki put down her legal pad. "I'll come with you."

"There's no need—"

"I want to," she said, looking down toward his shoes. "I'm going to stick to you and Christina like glue. I want to get the full trial experience."

Ben gave Christina a look. "Maybe we should let her take the next witness."

CHAPTER

33

SERGEANT SASSER WAS one of three officers who went to Remote Control the night of the murder, following up on the lead from Sergeant Montgomery. He was a middle-aged man with a bushy salt-and-pepper mustache and hair that reminded Ben of praline pecan ice cream.

"What did you do when you entered the club?" Drabble asked him.

"We made a few inquiries and soon found the group of young men from the frat house. There were six of them, all sitting together in a corner booth around a table. They were laughing and drinking, hooting and hollering. They weren't hard to find."

"Are any of the men who were at that table in the courtroom today?"

"Yes," he said, nodding toward the defendant's table. "Jonathan Earl Christensen."

"Did you confront the men?"

"Not at first. The other two officers and I took a seat at an adjoining booth. I wanted to hear what they were saying."

"And were you able to overhear anything?"

"Oh yeah. They didn't seem to care who heard."

"What were they saying?"

"Objection," Ben said, rising to his feet. "Hearsay."

Judge Lacayo nodded. "Sustained."

Drabble frowned, then rephrased. "What, if anything,

did you hear the defendant say?" Admissions by the defendant against his own interest constituted an exception to the hearsay rule.

Sasser did not hesitate. "He was bragging about beating up Tony Barovick."

"Did he call Mr. Barovick by name?"

"No. He called him 'that flaming faggot' and 'that sick queer' and—well, other harsher terms."

"The court appreciates your discretion," Judge Lacayo said speedily. "And it does not believe any further detail is necessary. We get the idea."

"Did he provide any specifics about what he had done to this . . . victim?"

"Yes. He specifically mentioned using a Taser. In fact, he showed it to his friends. He talked about cutting him. And he talked about swinging a hammer. His exact words were—pardon me, your honor—'we broke that little cocksucker's legs into a million pieces.' "

Several members of the jury gasped—literally gasped. In a split second, Ben knew that the "magnitude of hate" about which Drabble had spoken in his opening had been transformed from the theoretical to the all-too-real.

"Did he seem regretful or remorseful about what he had done?"

"Objection," Ben said. "This is a fact witness, not a psychiatrist."

The judge frowned. "Well, the witness can describe the defendant's demeanor or emotional state, as he witnessed it. Perhaps you should rephrase, Mr. Prosecutor."

Drabble nodded. "Did you hear the defendant say anything that suggested that he showed any remorse about what he had done?"

"No. As I said, he was bragging. He and his buddy were proud of themselves. That was evident. The whole group was laughing it up."

Ben felt the eyes burning his way—and past him—to

Johnny. He knew what the jurors had to be thinking. What kind of monster was this?

"How long did you listen to the conversation?"

"As long as we could. As far as I was concerned, it was the easiest way to obtain rock-solid evidence. Sit in a chair and listen while the perp inadvertently confesses in front of three police officers. But after a while, one of them started to leave. That's when I moved in."

"What did you do?"

"I put the defendant and his friend Brett Mathers under arrest. We had heard more than enough to justify it. Pursuant to the arrest, we searched them."

"Find anything?"

"On the defendant, we found the Taser. His friend had the hammer in his car. They both had split knuckles with blood smeared on them. Later tests showed that—"

"Objection," Ben said. It was an easy win. The jury would have to wait and hear from a forensic expert what the later tests showed—namely, that the blood and skin fragments under Johnny's nails came from Tony Barovick.

"Did you participate in the later custodial interrogations of the defendant?"

"Yes, I did. Christensen was tight-lipped at first, didn't want to talk. Used his phone call to contact his mother, denied doing anything wrong. Claimed he'd been lying to his friends, that it was some sort of hazing game they played to scare new members. But he cracked pretty quick. Before the sun came up, he'd begun confessing. He admitted to participating in the assault on Tony Barovick. Using the knife, the Taser. Shattering Barovick's jaw. Helping his buddy with the leg fracturing. Pretty much everything."

"Thank you," Drabble said solemnly. "Pass the witness."

Small gains, Ben reminded himself as he approached the podium. That's what you strive for. This was the prosecution's case, not his, and Drabble wasn't putting people on the stand to make Ben happy. If he could accomplish any little thing, it was a successful cross.

He didn't waste any time. He knew a police witness would never warm up to him—they were specifically trained not to—so there was no point in trying to win him over.

"You testified that there were six men sitting around the table where you eavesdropped. But you only arrested two of them, right?"

Sasser was nonplussed. "Jonathan Christensen and Brett Mathers were the only two who talked about assaulting the victim. The other four were just the audience. They seemed to think it was a wonderful thing the boys had done and a great cause for merriment, but they didn't admit to participating."

"Did you ever consider the possibility that Johnny Christensen might have been exaggerating?"

"That he might be claiming to have hurt the victim more than he really did? Why would he?"

"You said yourself that his audience seemed to enjoy this talk. Maybe he was trying to impress them."

Sasser shook his head. "You know, counsel, I might be willing to go along with you on that—if I hadn't seen the corpse upon which every disgusting act they described had been perpetrated."

Ben knew better than to let a cop witness take the ball away from him. "Sergeant Sasser, you're supposed to be testifying as to what you saw and heard—and nothing more. And you didn't see Johnny Christensen strike Tony Barovick, did you?"

"No."

"And the fact that he talked about it afterward doesn't prove that he did, does it?"

"Well . . ."

"Have you ever heard anyone say something that wasn't true?"

"Sure, but—"

"Especially when they're trying to impress someone, right? You might've told a lie or exaggerated details on occasion to make a good impression yourself."

"I never bragged about pummeling someone with a five-pound hammer. That's for damn sure."

Well, Ben told himself, I certainly opened the door for that one, didn't I? He tried to press on quickly.

"Did you overhear anything that would indicate where the beating took place?"

"Not that I recall. I might've forgotten. Since we'd already found the body, there didn't seem to be much question—"

"You're assuming the beating took place at the fraternity house, where the body was found. But wouldn't that be a rather odd place to attack and kill someone?"

Sasser shrugged. "Not especially. I assume they lured the boy there or forced him to come. It would afford privacy. They could turn up the stereo to drown out the screams."

"And wouldn't it be even stranger to leave the body there? Where the crime would certainly be traced back to them."

"I never claimed these guys were geniuses. I expect they thought they had some time before they had to dispose of the body."

"So you're saying they killed the man right there, in their own home, left the body in the den, and went out for a beer?"

Sasser started to get agitated. "You can't judge these people by normal standards. Anyone capable of doing what those two did clearly does not think like a normal person."

This was getting him nowhere, Ben realized. Time to shift gears.

"You've admitted that the late Brett Mathers was also involved in this alleged beating, right?"

"Right. He'd be sitting at your table now, too, if he were still alive."

"How can you know exactly what Johnny did and what Brett did?"

"I can't. And fortunately the DA tells me it doesn't matter."

"Objection. What is the relevance of this questioning?" Drabble asked, addressing the bench. "We all know that when the commission of a felony results in a homicide, felony murder charges may be brought against all participants. And the last I heard, beating someone with a sledgehammer was a felony. So what difference does it make who did what?"

A huge difference, Ben thought, if not now, then for sentencing purposes. But he couldn't argue that. "The point, your honor, is that two people were involved, and the prosecution doesn't know which of the two—if either—actually killed Tony Barovick."

"I'll allow further questioning on this point," Lacayo said. "But I warn you, Mr. Kincaid, that I will be instructing the jury on the elements of felony murder at the conclusion of the evidentiary phase, and if your client participated in any felony that resulted in a death, he is liable on this charge."

Ben nodded, then returned his attention to the witness stand. "You mentioned your initial questioning of Johnny Christensen. I've had the pleasure of reading the transcript of that interrogation several times. Did Johnny ever confess to beating Tony Barovick with a hammer?"

"He talked about it in great—"

"Answer my question, sir. Did Johnny ever confess to using the hammer? Did he confess to even touching the hammer?"

Sasser exhaled slowly. "No."

"In fact, he specifically said that it was his buddy Brett who used the hammer, right? And come to think of it, you found the hammer in Brett's car, right?"

"Right."

"In fact, according to Johnny, Brett was the one who committed all of the most brutal parts of the beating. Brett was the one who broke Tony's legs. And used the Taser. And Johnny says he tried without success to get Brett to stop."

"It's no big surprise, after we've got him dead to rights, that he would try to pin everything on his friend."

"Move to strike," Ben said, "and I'll ask the court to instruct the witness not to engage in speculation about motives."

Lacayo nodded, without much enthusiasm. "The witness will limit his remarks to what he actually saw or heard."

The flaw in this argument, as Ben knew all too well, was that Brett, before he died, had tried to pin everything on Johnny. But, happily, that transcript wasn't coming in. "The bottom line, sir, is that you don't know where the victim was killed, or how, or by whom. At best, all you know is that a beating took place. But that does not equal murder."

"You ever had your legs shattered?" Sasser shot back.

"I'm sorry, Sergeant, but in cross-examination, I get to ask the—"

"Because I have." He turned toward the jury. "In the war. Vietnam. You can't imagine how that hurts."

"Objection," Ben said hastily. "Nonresponsive. Not relevant."

"It is relevant!" Sasser shouted. "The only reason I survived is that I got medical attention fast."

"Move to strike!" Normally, law enforcement witnesses were well behaved and by-the-book. Something inside this guy had snapped.

The judge pounded his gavel. "The witness will refrain from—"

Sasser ignored him. "But Tony Barovick didn't get

medics. They just left him lying on the floor to die. To bleed to death. They didn't care."

Lacayo shouted across the room. "Mr. Drabble, take control of your witness!"

"This witness is dismissed," Ben said. "Move to strike his irrelevant statements. In fact, I move to strike his entire testimony."

"Why?" Sasser growled. "Because you're afraid of the truth?"

Ben rushed to the bench. This emotional outburst might have an impact on the jury, but it could also give him a mistrial, or possibly even grounds for appeal.

"I'll go," Sasser said, stepping down from the stand. Then suddenly, he whirled back around on Ben. "But don't tell me we can't call it murder because we don't know who did what or which of the many tortures actually killed that poor boy. It was brutal, cold-blooded murder. And anyone—everyone—who had anything to do with it deserves to die!"

CHAPTER
34

"WHAT'S HE DOING?" Swift asked Baxter, under her breath.

"Listening to the room."

"What?"

"Don't ask."

The two female law enforcement officers stood silently and watched as Mike stared off into space—or at least as far as it was possible to stare in this small and sordid public rest room. Crime scene technicians swarmed around them. A man in yellow coveralls was on his hands and knees picking up bits of trace evidence with adhesive strips. Another was rubbing Luminol on the tile as if it were floor wax, looking for errant blood traces in a sea of red. And Mike appeared oblivious to it all.

"How long does this usually take?" Swift asked.

"No telling. Until he comes up with something. Sometimes not long. And sometimes . . . well, let's just say we might want to adjourn to that deli I spotted outside and get lunch. And dinner, if necessary."

Swift grimaced. "I hope it doesn't take that long. This place smells."

"Most murder scenes do."

"Thanks, Sergeant, I have worked a crime or two. But this joint is way above average on the stink scale. It probably smelled bad even before it contained a corpse. But now we have that all-too-rare combination of urine, decaying flesh, and copious amounts of blood. A whole can of Glade couldn't freshen this place up."

One of the local Chicago crime techs, a man named Grayson, perked up. "Actually, it isn't any of those things. It's the cranial gases."

"Cranial gases?"

He nodded. "Released when the gunshot blew off half the guy's head. Stinks to high heaven. Worse than colon dissections."

"So we're all carrying around little stink bombs in our heads?" Baxter pulled a face. "Remind me not to put a gun in my mouth."

Swift approached Mike and gave him a slap on the shoulder. "All right, Yoda. Enough communing with the universe. Whaddaya think?"

Mike slowly diverted his gaze to her. "He thought he was safe."

"Come again, slick?"

"He thought he was in the clear. He knew someone was out to get him, but he thought he'd managed to escape whoever it was or whatever he'd done. Probably going to catch the first bus out of town and never come back."

"I can confirm that," Grayson said, pointing at the materials he had carefully removed from the victim's satchel and wrapped in plastic. "Bus ticket. Unused."

Mike nodded. "Must've been a hell of a shock when he turned around and saw . . . whoever."

Baxter's eyes narrowed. "How do you know he did?"

Mike pointed to a red smudge on the steel flush handle above the right-side urinal. "Blood—but no fingerprints. He must've been standing right here, facing away, when the killer smashed his head back. Probably taking a leak, turned around—and there he was. He recognized his killer."

"How can you be sure of that?"

"Because he didn't scream immediately. If a stranger

had come this close, he would've shouted. But he recognized the assailant. He probably tried to talk his way out of it. Didn't work. Judging from the lacerations on the jaw and the chest, the killer knew how to fight. He put the victim out of commission fast. And then blew his head off."

"Okay, Sherlock," Swift said, "I'll buy all that. Got a theory on *why* the poor slob was killed?"

"If I knew that, I'd know who did it. Unfortunately, I don't." Mike thumbed through the contents of the dead man's travel bag. "Twelve-inch ruler. Zircon-studded dog collar."

"Guy must've had a big dog, judging from the collar," Swift said. "My mama always favored Great Danes, herself."

Mike didn't reply. He turned to Grayson, who was testing something with his pocket-size lab kit. "What's that?"

"A white creamy substance I found inside the victim's satchel."

"Yes, but what is it?"

"I can't be sure. I'll need to get it back to the lab."

"Grayson, I saw you test it. Tell me what it is."

"I can't be positive until—"

"Grayson."

"My professional integrity requires—"

"Grayson!" Mike jerked the man toward him by the collar. "Are you aware of how much I outrank you?"

"Sir . . . you're not even a member of our force. You're out of your jurisdiction."

"Which won't help your sorry ass one little bit if I tell your supervisor you disobeyed a direct order from a superior officer. Understand me?"

"Yes. Sir," he added.

"So I'd appreciate it if you'd answer my question. What is it?"

"Nonoynol-9," he answered sullenly.

"And what the hell is that?"

"It's . . . most commonly used as a spermicide."

"Thank you, Grayson. Dismissed."

Grayson left the bathroom as quickly as possible.

"Bit hard on him, weren't you?" Swift asked. "Since he was basically right. You're out of your jurisdiction."

"Details, details . . ." He grabbed Baxter's arm and pulled her over. "Let's test your deductive reasoning powers, Sergeant. What did this poor schmuck do for a living?"

She stared at the contents of the bag. "Dog collar. Ruler. Little bracelets."

"And spermicide," Mike added. "They all add up to? . . ."

She shook her head. "I don't get it."

"That's all right. It's not a sign of inferior detective skills. More like a sign that you're a wholesome person. Now, Special Agent Swift here probably got it a long time ago. Am I right?"

Swift grinned. "My mama didn't raise her girls in a convent."

Baxter looked annoyed. "So spill already. What does it all add up to?"

Swift batted her eyelashes. "Sex, sugah."

"Sex? I mean, I get the spermicide, but—" She stopped short. "Ohhh. I am so embarrassed."

"I would say kinky sex," Swift added, "but that's so judgmental."

Mike smirked. "You may recall that Shelly—the bartender at Remote Control—told us about a chicken? A male prostitute, for the unenlightened. Charlie, I think she called him. She said he was at the bar the night Tony Barovick was killed. Left not long after Tony did."

"Just like Manny Nowosky."

Mike nodded. "These people are all linked—and not just by the fact that they're now dead. They're being systematically picked off because they are all connected to . . . something. And the most likely candidate?"

Swift agreed. "The Ecstasy ring."

"Wait a minute," Baxter said, trying to catch up. "If the victims were all involved in a drug ring, that would mean that Tony Barovick—"

"Was not exactly the saint the popular press has made him out to be."

Baxter's eyes widened. "If you're right, a lot of protesters currently camped out in front of the courthouse are going to have to repaint their placards."

"Yeah. And find a new martyr." Mike grabbed his trench coat. "Come on, gang. Let's check out this loser's apartment."

"Right behind you, tiger."

"Oh, and Baxter?"

She stopped at the door. "Yeah?"

Mike smiled. "Those weren't little bracelets."

She covered her face with her hand. "Oh, geeeez . . ."

CHAPTER
35

As CHRISTINA HURRIED down the long courtroom corridor, she listened intently to the words coming over her cell phone.

"I really do think there may be a connection, Chris. Between Tony Barovick, and the drill bit through the head guy, and this new victim. I know the evidence is slim, but my instincts tell me there's something there."

"Like what?"

"I have no idea. But I intend to find out. So let's stay in touch with each other, okay? And exchange information. I'll show you mine if you show me yours."

"Sounds good. Thanks for keeping me informed, Mike. I really appreciate it."

"Least I can do. Hey—do me a favor. You and Ben be careful."

"Okay. Why?"

"Someone tried to off your client once, remember? Trashed your place, took a few potshots at you. From what I hear, these ANGER dudes are seriously militant. I don't want you to get caught in the cross fire like the last lawyer did."

"Understood."

"Not that I normally think taking out defense attorneys is a bad thing. But I make an exception for you."

"Thanks, Mike. You're sweet."

"I suppose there's no point in trying to talk you into dropping the case."

" 'Fraid not."

"Right. Can't be sensible. You get that from Ben. I could probably get the local PD to assign a security detail."

"I can't do my job with security dogs hanging over me."

"Yeah. That's what Ben said, too. Give my best to that former brother-in-law of mine, okay?"

"Will do, Major. Talk to you again soon."

CHRISTINA GAZED AT herself in the mirror. No matter how many times she tried a case, she knew she would never get used to it. The pressure, from the first smash of the gavel to the last, was unrelenting. And it was worse when the stakes were so high. Worst of all when she knew the next witness was a critical one, perhaps the critical one. And she had to cross-examine.

Life was simpler when she had been a legal assistant. But not as much fun.

Before she left the ladies' room, she made the traditional last-minute glamour check. Hair all properly pinned back. Check. No makeup smears. Check. Lipstick not on teeth. Check. Lunch not in teeth. Check. Everything as it should be.

She took a deep breath and smiled at that cute freckled face in the mirror. Showtime.

Roger Hartnell was waiting for her in the corridor outside the courtroom. He was using a cane today but seemed to be able to get around reasonably well. "Ms. McCall! I need to speak to you."

"I'm surprised to see you up on your feet so soon."

"Turned out it wasn't as bad as it looked. Bullet just winged me."

"Hurt much?"

"Only when I move."

"Then why aren't you at home in bed?"

"Because I need to talk to you."

"Look, if it's about my dropping the case—"

"I've just come from a meeting of the ANGER steering committee."

"Mr. Hartnell, I understand how you feel about our representation. I'm sure if I'd known Tony I'd feel the same way. But I can't drop the case. So no matter what you and your committee think—"

"Miss McCall, you have been targeted."

Christina felt a cold grip at the base of her spine. "You mean—the sniper—the figure hanging in the lobby."

"I don't know anything about that. We don't condone violence. What I'm talking about is . . . publicity."

"I'm not following."

He reached into his briefcase and pulled out a display mounted on stiff cardboard. "Starting tomorrow morning, these ads are going to run in major newspapers and magazines all across the country."

The layout contained four photos. The top and largest bore the caption: THIS IS TONY BAROVICK. Below, in a photo that appeared to have been taken at Remote Control, were seven people, including Roger and Shelly and the club owner, Mario Roma. THESE ARE HIS FRIENDS. The third photo was captioned: THIS IS THE MAN WHO KILLED TONY BAROVICK. Johnny Christensen, dudded out in his prison coveralls. And the final row of photos was captioned: THESE ARE HIS FRIENDS.

There were only two. Ben and Christina.

Christina felt her jaw stiffening. "You can't do this. This is slanderous."

"Our attorneys assure me it is not. All we say is that you have befriended your client, which you clearly have done."

"I'm not talking about me. I'm talking about Johnny. This ad calls him a killer—which has not yet been established in a court of law. He could sue you."

"But by the time that case comes to trial, this murder trial will be over, and he will be a convicted killer. Imagine a convicted killer crying because we called him a killer a week early. I just don't see him raking in the dough."

Christina pushed the layout away in disgust. "You're determined to see that Johnny is convicted, aren't you?"

"Of course I am. I loved Tony. I want his killer punished."

"No, you want Johnny punished. You have no idea who killed Tony. All you know is what the police tell you. And take it from me, Roger—sometimes they're wrong."

"Not this time. I'm certain of it." He put the layout back in his briefcase. "And soon the rest of the world will be certain, too."

As SOON AS Christina saw DA Drabble coming through the metal detector, she stepped forward. "Oh, Richard! Glad I bumped into you. The courtroom assignment has been changed."

He looked at her warily. "It has?"

"Yeah. Apparently a larger room opened up when Judge Pennington finished a big rape trial. We're going to take over his space."

"And that's? . . ."

"Top floor. End of the corridor."

A slow smile spread across his face. "Vengeance is sweet, huh?"

"I don't get you."

"But he who laughs last, laughs best."

"You're just a bundle of clichés this morning, aren't you?"

He laughed. "Nice try, Ms. McCall, but you're not going to throw me for a loop on my own home court."

"You don't believe the court has been moved?"

"Oh, I can believe that easily enough. I was in the clerk's office last night and heard them talking about a reassignment. But they were discussing the possibility of going to Judge Cantrell's courtroom. In Building Three."

"But there was—"

"So nice try, little lady, but it'll take a better scam than this lame bit of business to make me late for Lacayo's court." He grabbed his briefcase and hurried merrily down the corridor.

Ben came up behind her. "We really are going to Judge Pennington's courtroom, aren't we?"

Christina nodded. "Cantrell's has to be fumigated. Someone saw a rat."

"And you knew Drabble wouldn't believe you when you told him."

"Which is why I met him at the door. Before he had a chance to hear it from someone he trusted." She checked her watch. "He's going to be fifteen minutes late. At the least."

Ben whistled. "You know, Christina, you are just evil."

She held up her hands. "I can't help it if he's a suspicious person." She smiled. "Who needed to learn a lesson about the consequences of messing with me."

AMONG THE REASONS Christina wasn't looking forward to this cross was the fact that Amber Wilson seemed like a nice person who was, after all, only doing her job. But in this case, the coroner's testimony was too important to give her a pass. She had to cross the lady as if she were a combination of Satan, Hitler, and Richard Nixon combined.

Once court finally got under way—and Judge Lacayo finished tongue-lashing Drabble and his entourage for being late—the DA began his direct examination.

"Dr. Wilson, would you please tell us when you became involved in the Tony Barovick case?"

Wilson twisted around to face the jury. "I arrived soon after the body was discovered."

"And what did you find?"

"A severely damaged corpse. As was immediately apparent, the victim had a shattered jaw, two shattered legs, and numerous cuts and abrasions. The body was covered with blood."

"He was dead?"

"Very."

"Were you able to determine a cause of death?"

Wilson ran a hand through her brown hair. "Technically, the cause of death was cranial asphyxia—technically, that's the cause of almost every death. What caused oxygen starvation of the brain is more difficult to say. In this case, the victim had been so mistreated, had been so . . . damaged in so many ways, it's impossible for me to say exactly which blow killed him. It could have been the one to his neck and jaw causing a closure of the respiratory passages in the neck, or a compression of the major blood vessels in the neck—the carotid arteries and jugular veins. The blows to the legs could have caused shock, leading to heart failure."

"Are there ways to determine which blow resulted in death?"

"Not reliably, not in this case. The body was too severely damaged. I did detect evidence of heart failure—but he had been beaten so severely that he had two cracked ribs. He'd been subjected to intense electric shock. Any of those things could have been lethal. It's really just a matter of which one kicked in first."

"And you can't say for certain which did?"

"Not reliably." She glanced at Christina. "And I feel certain the defense counsel wouldn't want me to speculate. Bear in mind—contrary to what some people believe, the human body's physiological and muscle systems do not immediately shut down at death."

"But you can reliably say that the beating caused the death."

"Absolutely. That was evident."

Christina could see that Wilson had prepared carefully for this testimony. She also appeared to have anticipated Christina's planned line of attack; she was very carefully delineating what she could be certain about and what she couldn't. While at the same time making sure she gave Drabble what he needed to get a conviction.

"Dr. Wilson," Drabble continued, "the defendant has raised some questions regarding when death occurred. Is it possible for a medical examiner to make a determination as to the time of death?"

"Yes, it is. There are several methods of doing it. Liver mortis—which is the discoloration of the skin to a pinkish color caused by the settling of blood cells in the small vessels of dependent skin and tissues—does not begin until one to two hours after death, and rigor mortis—the progressive stiffening of the body caused by chemical changes in the muscle tissues—does not begin until two to four hours after death. Since only a short period of time had passed, neither of those were very useful. Fortunately, there are other indicators of the stage of decomposition—body temperature, analysis of the stomach contents, and so forth. Immediately following death, the human body begins to decompose. The rate of decomposition is steady, predictable, and measurable, and barring extraordinary circumstances, will provide a reliable measure for at least the first two hours after death."

Drabble nodded. "I see. Did you reach any conclusions regarding time of death in this case?"

"Absolutely."

"So the time of death would be . . ."

"Eleven P.M. Eleven-fifteen at the latest."

Drabble nodded thoughtfully. "The defendant has suggested that the beating took place at another location at around 9 P.M.—just after Tony Barovick left the club—and was over by 9:30."

"No. Not possible. The beating might have begun then, but the killing stroke—the death of Tony Barovick—came later." She was adamant, and with good reason, Christina knew. Johnny was with fraternity brothers who could alibi him from about 9:30 to 10:45. Wilson was placing the murder at a time when Johnny was alone, before he rejoined his friends at Remote Control.

Christina watched carefully as several of the jurors shifted around in their chairs. They'd been hoping medical science could tell them with certainty who was lying. And that was what they were getting now—or so they thought.

"And you're sure of this?"

"Beyond a doubt. To a medical certainty."

"Thank you, Doctor. Your witness, Ms. McCall."

Christina slowly made her way to the podium. She hated experts. Cross was bad enough with normal people—it was all but unbearable with someone who was only on the stand because it was an accepted fact that she knew more about the matter at hand than you did.

"First, Dr. Wilson, I'd like to talk about the cause of death."

"Very well," she said, all forthright and chipper. Christina knew that wouldn't last long.

"I appreciate your honesty in telling the jury that you really don't have the slightest idea what the cause of death was. Very forthcoming of you."

"Ye-ess," Wilson said, waiting for the other shoe to drop.

"I was troubled, though, by your assertion that the death must've come as a result of the beating by Johnny Christensen and Brett Mathers. Since you don't know what the cause of death was, how can you pretend to know who caused it?"

"I believe he has admitted beating the boy—"

"Yes, but not to killing him."

"And I saw the results of the beating. Given the severe trauma of the body, it would be ridiculous to suggest that anything else could've caused the death."

Was that a challenge, Doctor? "My point is that you don't know exactly what Johnny did. The killing stroke—to use your own words—could have come from another person."

Wilson shook her head. "Even if it was his fraternity friend—"

"But what if it was another person altogether? A third person."

"I've heard no evidence of a third person."

"But you can't rule out the possibility."

"When we have two self-confessed perpetrators who conducted an extensive torture and beating, it seems absurd—"

"Dr. Wilson, could Tony Barovick have been strangled?"

Christina's sudden switch threw the coroner off balance. "Uh—strangled?"

"Sure. You said he died of oxygen deprivation to the brain. You hypothesized that a jaw or neck injury might've caused asphyxiation. Wouldn't a simpler explanation be that someone strangled him?"

Wilson hesitated. "I haven't heard anything about any strangling . . ."

"And that's the problem, isn't it? You don't want to attribute the death to strangulation—because Johnny never confessed to any strangling. You want to attribute death to one of the things he did confess to. But that doesn't make it the cause of death. Especially if a third person was involved."

Wilson was beginning to squirm. "I think it's pointless to speculate when we know the victim endured a hideous assault."

"You've read the transcript of Johnny Christensen's so-called confession, haven't you?"

"Of course."

"So let me ask you, Doctor—is it possible that a person could have endured all that Johnny described and still live?"

"Oh, anything's possible, but—"

"In fact, judging from Johnny's description, the beating—although horrible, to be sure—did not involve anything that would absolutely, positively cause death, right?"

"I assume the defendant downplayed the intensity—"

"Well, now assume he told the absolute to-the-letter truth. Despite the severity of the injuries, those wounds were not necessarily fatal, right?"

"I agree that survival was possible. But given that he didn't—survive, that is—and that we know this horrible assault occurred, to speculate about third parties and intervening causes is just indulging in fantasy."

"Were there contusions on Tony Barovick's neck?"

Again, the switch caught her flat-footed—which, of course, was exactly what Christina wanted. "It's true, there were abrasions on the anterior neck, but—"

"And streaking arethema on the lateral aspect of zone one?"

Wilson did a double take. "Ye-esss . . ."

"And the cartilaginous tracheal rings were crushed?"

Wilson sighed. "Been doing some reading, Ms. Mc-Call?"

"I try to stay informed. All of those factors are possible indicators of strangulation, aren't they?"

"True. But just the same," Wilson continued, "with a body so severely tortured and mutilated, those injuries could have been caused by any number of things."

"Including strangulation by a third person?"

Wilson's frustration was mounting. "This whole speculation about a third person is useless."

"Useless to the prosecution, yes. You don't want to suggest strangulation as a possible cause of death, because in his confession Johnny didn't say anything about strangulation. You want to pin it on something he confessed to doing."

"No, that isn't—"

"Nonetheless, simple strangulation, subsequent in time to the beating, is a possible cause of death. Correct?"

Wilson took a deep breath. "As I testified, the time of death was shortly before the body was found. There wasn't time—"

"Well, let's talk about that," Christina said, flipping a page in her notebook. "You say the time of death was about 11:15—and in no case earlier than 11:00."

"That's correct."

"And you base this conclusion on the body's decomposition, which you tell us is steady and predictable."

"Absolutely."

Christina snapped her fingers. "Come to think of it, what you actually said was that *absent extraordinary circumstances,* the rate was steady and predictable. What would some of those extraordinary circumstances be, Doctor?"

"They are all wildly improbable."

"Try me."

"If the body was exposed to radiation—which it wasn't. If he'd been feverish at the time of death—which he wasn't."

"What about if he'd been refrigerated?"

"Excuse me?"

"Refrigerated. What if?"

"But the body wasn't refrigerated. It was found in a fraternity house."

"Was it terribly cold in that fraternity house?"

She looked at Christina as if she'd asked to see her knickers. "Not that I recall."

"Think harder, Doctor. When I visited your office last

week, you mentioned that the room was cold. And Officer Montgomery told us it was so chilly he sent his partner after his coat."

"If you say so."

"But it was you who said so, Dr. Wilson. And you were right. Do you know how cold it was? When the doors and windows in the room were shut? Before the police arrived?"

"I couldn't possibly know. No one could."

"Well, actually, Doctor—I could." From the defendant's table, Vicki passed her a photo that had already been admitted into evidence. "The crime scene technicians photographed and videotaped the entire room where the body was found—including the north wall, which is where the thermostat is located. I took the liberty of having that section of the photo enlarged." She slid it across the witness stand. "Let me ask you again, Doctor—what was the temperature in that room?"

Wilson frowned. "Sixty degrees."

"Sixty? Now that's pretty cold, especially in a small room with all the doors and windows shut. Wouldn't have taken long to cool to that temperature."

Wilson tossed down the photo. "I will admit that it is an abnormally low temperature, but it's hardly a refrigerator."

"So how much effect do you think that low a temperature would have on the body's decomposition?"

"I couldn't say exactly. Not much."

"I might have to argue with you there, Doctor." Vicki passed Christina a large and heavy leather-bound book. "This is called *Principles of Forensic Science and Criminology* and was written by the late Dr. T. S. Koregai. It's generally considered one of the definitive works on the subject. In fact, I think you have one in your office, don't you, Doctor?"

"You know I do."

"Dr. Koregai provides a chart in which he sets

down the effect of increasingly low temperatures on postmortem decomposition. According to him, if the temperature is sixty degrees, you can expect decomposition—get this—to happen a third as fast as normal. He says the entire process would be slowed." She pondered a moment. "You know, I'm no math whiz, but I think that means that instead of the time of death being an hour before you arrived, it was more like 9:30 or 10:00—when Johnny Christensen was in the company of several friends."

"I suppose it's theoretically possible—"

"Thank you, Doctor. No more questions."

There was quite a stir in the courtroom after she finished. Half the reporters in the gallery ran out the back doors clutching their cell phones; the others were scribbling furiously in their notebooks. They seemed to think this was a breakthrough. And it had been a good cross—if she did say so herself.

But Christina didn't kid herself. She might have established that Johnny *could* be telling the truth—but not that he *was* telling the truth. Unless she could come up with an explanation of who killed Tony Barovick and why, it was all too likely that the jury would conclude that the beating Johnny admitted to caused the death. Or that anyone capable of doing such a horrible thing to another human being deserved to die whether he delivered the killing stroke or not.

ONE OBSERVER WHO was not a reporter nonetheless headed out the back doors as soon as the judge called for a recess, thinking this was not supposed to happen. Johnny Christensen had to be convicted. If these two shysters kept doing what they were doing—well—this case might never be put to rest.

Should've killed them before, back when they were pinned down in front of their office. Before they had a chance to stir up more trouble than they could possibly imagine.

Never mind. There were many more cheap, readily accessible handguns in the world. If the case continued to progress in this manner—and there was any chance at all of Johnny Christensen escaping punishment—the sniper scene would be reenacted. With more positive results.

Warning had been given—and ignored. There would be no more warning shots. Now it was time to shoot to kill.

CHAPTER
36

OUTSIDE THE COURTROOM window, four stories down, Christina could hear chanting. Some of the gay rights protesters were getting rowdy, it seemed. "Don't wait—punish hate!" they chanted, over and over again. Probably heard about what just happened in court today, Christina mused. Just hope they didn't bring their snipers this time.

"Christina?" It was Ellen Christensen, standing just behind the rail. She saw Ben flinch the instant the woman spoke. "That was wonderful, what you did up there."

"Well, thank you."

"Will the jury believe Johnny now?"

"We still have a lot of work to do. But we're off to a good start."

A new voice barked in her ear. "You should be ashamed of yourself, you cheap little hustler!"

Christina instinctively ducked. She froze. Then, not hearing any gunfire, stood back up. Was she getting jumpy? Considering all that had happened, she thought she had good cause.

It was Mario Roma, the owner of Remote Control. "Tony was a good boy!" he bellowed. "He deserves better than to have some two-bit lawyers playing tricks to put his killer back on the street!"

Ben ran to her side. She was aware that her knees were knocking. All this turmoil was really starting to get to her. "Sir, all we're trying to do is bring the truth to light."

"Bullshit!" From the corners of the room, the bailiffs were advancing. "I know exactly what you're trying to do. You should be ashamed of yourself!"

One of the bailiffs—Boxer Johnson—tapped Roma on the shoulder. He did not stop.

"There's a word for a woman who will do anything for money. You're nothing but a cheap, two-bit whore!"

The bailiffs took one arm each and forcibly removed him from the courtroom, still screaming. "Remember this, lady, everyone gets theirs in the end. What goes around, comes around. Count on it!"

"THAT WAS BIZARRE," Ben said. "Talk about coming out of nowhere. Why would that guy want to—" He turned and saw that Christina was trembling.

"Hey." He took her by the arms without even thinking about it, then did and let them go. "What's wrong?"

"I don't know," she said, with a tremor in her voice. "I'm just . . . tired of all these threats." She put a hand on the gallery railing to steady herself. "I'm starting to get a bad feeling about this case. This whole mess. Like something horrible is going to happen."

"Buck up, Chris. We've still got a long way to go."

"I know," she said, her voice grim. "That's what worries me."

BEN HAD HANDLED psychiatrists in the past, so Christina asked him to take this one. He wasn't sure he was the best choice; he might have a slight edge on Christina in the psychojargon department, but she had it all over him when it came to understanding people. But it was her case and her call, and he knew that for whatever reason she was feeling a bit on edge. He could do it this time for her.

Drabble's decision to call a psychiatrist to the stand during his case-in-chief was an interesting and some-what unusual choice born of one central reality of trial practice: The prosecution never knows what the defense is going to do. They can guess, but they can't be certain. The prosecution is supposed to tell the defense every de-tail of their case, their evidence, witnesses, everything. But the defense doesn't have to reveal anything. Often the prosecution has no idea what the defense case will be till they hear it live and in person in the courtroom. Prosecutors have many other advantages—most notably the tight connection with law enforcement, the institu-tional resources, and usually, the judge. But in the de-partment of foreknowledge, they were vulnerable.

Which led to the psychiatrist. Drabble couldn't be certain Christina wouldn't try some sort of insanity defense. The violence of the beating would certainly support it. She could argue that Johnny had been tem-porarily insane, or that he had been brainwashed by peer groups. Not their best shot, in Ben's view, but a def-inite possibility. And Drabble couldn't count on being able to call the psychiatrist later in rebuttal. Kevin Ma-honey had advised Ben that Judge Lacayo adhered to the "heart attack" standard—he allowed the prosecution to call additional rebuttal witnesses only if some surprise development in the defense case had been of such mag-nitude as to induce a heart attack. Suggesting that a man who mercilessly beat a homosexual to a pulp was crazy wouldn't qualify. Thus, the psychiatrist—now. The fact that he was also an expert in hate groups was a bonus.

Ben didn't know the doctor, didn't know if he was the type who'd say anything, and frankly, didn't care. If Drabble wanted to put him on, it couldn't be good for their case, so he did his best to keep him off the stand.

"Your honor, this is not relevant," Ben argued in chambers.

"It is rather unorthodox," Lacayo said, leaning back in his chair, his fingers pressed against his lips.

"Yeah," Ben said. "Especially when we're not running an insanity defense."

"I don't know that," Drabble said calmly. "But even if they don't use the word insanity, they will no doubt argue that this nice boy from a pleasant middle-class family couldn't possibly commit this awful crime. We're entitled to rebut that."

"That is not what he's doing," Ben insisted. "He's suggesting that because a man is a member of a certain organization—"

"Two, actually."

Ben grimaced. "That his association with these groups incriminates him. It's a First Amendment issue."

Drabble waved his hands in the air. "All the witness will say is that the fact that the defendant was in antigay groups demonstrates that he was predisposed to harbor hatred toward gay people. Duh."

"You know it won't stop there," Ben said. "The witness'll be suggesting that because he went to some meetings where the use of violence was espoused, that meant he acted in conformity on the night in question. A clear evidentiary violation."

"I will not argue that," Drabble said, getting a little hot. "I don't have to. Your client has confessed, remember?"

"Not to the murder."

"Close enough."

"This is like the O. J. Simpson prosecutors suggesting that because O.J. dreamed about hurting his wife that meant he did."

"As I recall," Drabble said, "the prosecutors lost that case big time. Maybe you shouldn't protest so much."

"You'll go beyond that," Ben said. "You'll turn it into a—"

Lacayo held up his hands. "Quiet! I've heard enough. I'm going to allow the testimony."

"Your honor!" Ben started.

"I said, quiet! I'm ruling. I'll allow the testimony, but only for the purpose of showing that the defendant was psychologically capable of the crime. I want no assumptions that he did anything more than what he has confessed to doing."

"Understood," Drabble said.

"And I don't want a lot of psycho mumbo jumbo that will only confuse the jury, either." He peered across the desk at Drabble, and Ben felt certain a pointed message was being communicated. "I don't think this is a complicated case. Let's not turn it into one."

"DR. PITNEY," DRABBLE said, after exhaustively establishing the man's professional credentials and that he had spent ten hours examining Johnny Christensen, "would you call the Christian Minutemen a hate group?"

"Absolutely." The man had a bushy red beard which he seemed to have a hard time keeping his hands off of. "They deny it, of course. They justify all their beliefs in terms of carefully chosen scriptures. But by my standard, and that of most of my colleagues, an organization that opposes people based on who they are, based on being members of a discrete group, is a hate group."

"Is there any documentation backing up your view on this point?"

"Of course. You've already admitted the group's printed principles and tenets into evidence. I would invite the jury to read it when they have a chance. Pay particular attention to the passages about 'the plague of homosexuality,' the equation of 'consensual sodomy' with child abuse, the suggestions that homosexuality is a mental disease adopted by choice by the ungodly. Homophobia is all over the document—and this is something that is handed out to all prospective and new members of the organization."

"Is this . . . unusual?"

Pitney shifted around in his seat. He was doing a good job, Ben noted, of making eye contact with the jury, but not in such a direct and obvious manner that it made them uncomfortable or feel they were watching a performance. "Depends on what you mean. When this organization was first created, about sixty years ago, its principles also included equally vehement passages about people of other races. That has fallen away, of course. In our modern world, that wouldn't be tenable; they'd be perceived as a KKK—another supposedly Christian group. And the principles still have many incredibly sexist antifemale passages. As with many fundamentalist groups, they are very fond of the New Testament scriptures about a wife cleaving to her husband and being subservient to him. That, too, is falling out of favor, even with extremists. Homosexuality is another matter, however. Although times are changing, prejudice against homosexuals is still acceptable in many quarters, particularly with some religious groups. From the standpoint of an organization, it's still a viable basis for hate."

"And the Christian Minutemen have been involved in hate crimes against gays?"

"Its members have. More than thirty in the past five years. Of course, the organization always disavows any responsibility for the crimes, just as it has in the present case. But it still happens. Repeatedly. You draw you own conclusions."

"Where do these people come from? How do they become the way they are?"

"It's hard to explain. Because it's always a combination of factors. Almost never a single linear event. I've yet to meet a member of one of these groups who was actually harmed in some way by a homosexual. But there is a great appeal in some psyches to having someone to hate. Some cause to rally around, some mission. And in some cases, an excuse for violence."

"In your experience, Dr. Pitney, is this an example of failed parenting?" A pointed question, Ben knew, because Johnny's mother was listed as a witness for the defense.

"Sometimes. But you know, I've examined large families where one of the parents—usually the father—promoted prejudices to his children. Some of the offspring adopted it lock, stock, and barrel, and even as adults engaged in the same racist slurs and attitudes. And some of the children reject the hate education while still in their teens. By the same token, I've interviewed young people who grew up in good homes with well-educated, non-prejudicial parents who ended up joining radical militia groups. That's not the most common scenario, but it does happen."

"What makes the difference?"

"I don't know." Ben looked up; that was something he didn't hear often from an expert witness. "It's a combination of nature and nurture. Sometimes it's a part of teen rebellion, either to adopt or to refuse to adopt these prejudices. Sometimes it's personality—some people, happily, are just not predisposed to hate, no matter what the situation. Some young people are exposed to a forceful personality at a critical juncture who transforms their way of thinking. Education is obviously a factor, as is wealth. But you know what I really think makes the difference? And I'll admit up front I have no way of proving this. But I think in the long run it has to do with the subject's . . . how to say it? . . . exposure to ideas. Never once have I encountered a well-read man who was also a hatemonger. There are no Ph.D.s in the KKK. I truly believe that people who expose themselves to the arts—fine arts, visual arts, poetry, literature—people who expose themselves to *good ideas* will not end up adopting bad ones. It's the guys who don't come into contact with new and better thoughts—who do their work and pay the bills but aren't exposed to new ideas in any way that influences them—who are most likely to hang on to the old bad ideas they learned as a child." He paused. "Or in a keenly bigoted fraternity house."

Drabble nodded, turning a page in his notebook. "Now, Dr. Pitney, you've had a chance to examine the defendant, Jonathan Christensen, haven't you?"

"Yes." Pitney detailed the hours he spent, the tests he performed, records he reviewed, laying the foundation for the testimony to come.

"Did you reach any conclusions regarding the man's sanity?"

Pitney nodded. "John Christensen is all too sane. Plagued by hate. More than ready to act upon it. But unfortunately, that does not make him insane. Not even temporarily."

"Based upon your time with him, why do you believe he committed this horrible crime?"

"Objection," Ben said, grateful to have an excuse to interrupt. "It has not been established that Johnny committed any crime."

Drabble smiled. "I'm so sorry. I'll rephrase. Why do you believe he committed the horrible beating to which he has confessed?"

"It all comes down to the one word: hate. I believe he nurtured these antigay sentiments for some time. He attended an ultrafundamentalist church and no doubt heard some of it there. But it really mushroomed when he joined the fraternity and started going to the Minutemen meetings. He was totally indoctrinated."

"How so?"

"Historically, Jonathan has not been an especially bright student, nor has he been good at sports, nor has he been very popular. He was one of the kids who slip through the cracks. Till he joined the Minutemen. I believe he was so glad for the companionship, so pleased to feel a part of something larger than himself, that he was particularly susceptible to hate teachings. Fraternity houses have historically been hotbeds of sexism—guys playing macho for their friends by talking trash about women. That sort of language, of course, has become politically incorrect in recent years. In many respects, homophobia has filled the gap."

Drabble looked puzzled. "The problem is, Doctor . . . it's one thing to privately harbor some prejudices. But to snatch someone from a public place and quite literally beat him to a pulp—that's something else again."

"True, this was an extreme case—but that's not all that uncommon, unfortunately. These things start small— just some guys sitting around talking. The tension builds, the need to act upon their words becomes more urgent. And the next thing you know—someone's swinging from a rope. In this case, Johnny has admitted he was in the company of a like-minded friend who had performed violent acts in the past, and he claims that the victim made sexual advances to them. For two people in this mindset, that could be more than sufficient provocation to trigger a violent episode."

"In his statement, the defendant has always claimed that his friend, Brett Mathers, was the principal actor."

"And that may well be. But what difference does it make? I wouldn't have done what he did, or permitted it to happen, no matter what a friend did. Neither would you. But John Christensen did. Not out of insanity. Out of cold-blooded hate." He shook his head, at once moved and disgusted. "John Christensen isn't crazy. But he is evil."

"Objection!" Ben said, rising.

Judge Lacayo craned his neck. "The man's an expert, and he's entitled to his opinion."

"But that had nothing to do with psychiatry. I hardly think that's common jargon in his field!"

"Overruled," Lacayo said. "Please continue, Mr. Drabble."

Ben sat down beside Christina and whispered into her ear. "I'm not going to cross this guy."

"Agreed. Just get him out of the jury's face as soon as possible."

Drabble continued his direct. "And you're sure about this conclusion, Doctor?"

Pitney paused, gathering his thoughts. "Remember that the beating is acknowledged to have taken something like half an hour. Now imagine being beaten, knifed, hammered for that long a period of time. You know that poor boy cried out for mercy. The defendant has acknowledged that he did. Probably offered to do anything if his assailants would only stop hurting him."

Pitney wiped his brow, visibly shaken. "Frankly, most people, even if they started, couldn't have gone on after that. Even most deranged psychopaths couldn't have continued. John Christensen wasn't fueled by insanity in any way, shape, or form. He was driven by his selectively sociopathic hatred. Even now he believes what he did was justified. Maybe even believes it was some sort of divine intervention. Someone like that isn't crazy. But he is absolutely without question the most dangerous element in any society. The one capable of unspeakable evil. The one most important to stop."

CHAPTER
37

JOURNAL OF TONY BAROVICK

ROGER CHANGED MY life. He really did. I can't claim that he was my first lover, or even my first male lover. But he was the one who mattered. He always will be.

He came in on Friday night with a bunch of other guys from a drag racing strip. Most of them grabbed one of the video consoles and started scanning the pictures, not so much looking for love as entertaining themselves. But Roger held back. I saw him, sitting at the table, quietly sipping a margarita. And the more I watched him, the more I had a sense that although he was part of the gang, he wasn't. That he didn't belong. And that started me thinking . . .

As I've mentioned before, I don't have perfect radar, but it didn't take me long to figure out that he was gay. I waited on his table attentively, made a few casual remarks, dropped the names of a few gay haunts, felt him out. When the rest of his buddies left, he stayed. I went off duty, had Shelly make us another round, sat down with him and talked. And talked and talked and talked. It was easy—we had so many of the same interests and preoccupations. We agreed on almost everything. And made a date to meet the next Thursday for lunch. So we could talk some more.

The first time Roger spent the night, I thought that might feel strange, but I was wrong. It felt terrific, calming, thrilling. Not just sexually, although that was certainly part of it. But it was more. It was feeling, for the first time in my life, that I didn't have to hide anything, that I didn't have to put on a show. That I could just be who I really was, without repercussions. That's a wonderful, freeing feeling.

Roger wants to meet my parents. Well, I have to be honest—I'm not ready for that. And what would be the point? My father wouldn't speak to him any more than he will speak to me. I'm not sure my mother would be much better, no matter how hard she tried. Roger isn't just gay, he's black. Not that that should have anything to do with anything. But I lived with those folks for seventeen years. I know how they think, and I'm very afraid of what they might say. It's sad that I can't share the most glorious thing that has ever happened to me with my parents, but that's the way it is. You can take the hard line with your kids and feel very self-righteous about it, but it always results in a division. A lack of closeness. And a lack of trust. And things are so good with me and Roger right now, I just don't want that intruding upon our happiness.

Knowing Roger has been such a transforming, liberating experience for me. I don't know if I can possibly explain it to someone who hasn't been there. But before Roger, no matter where I went, no matter what I did, indeed, no matter how happy I might have been, I always felt . . . apart. Alone.

But not now. With Roger, I know I've made a connection, one that matters. I know we are together, that we will always be together. No matter what happens. How can I not? I'm in love. For the first time in my life, I am truly head over heels in love. And it feels great.

CHAPTER
38

IT WASN'T AS bad as visiting the scene of a homicide, Mike told himself, trying to bolster a sunnier outlook. It wasn't as bad as a trip to the coroner's office. It wasn't as bad as root canal surgery.

But who was kidding whom? It was pretty damn bad.

"Contents of a dead man's apartment. If you can call it that," Baxter said, dictating into an imaginary recording device. "Two half-eaten pizzas. Sour milk. Tacky shag carpet. The pungent aroma of human waste. Cockroaches. Lots of dirty—make that stale and crunchy—underwear. And here in the cupboard, more sex toys than can be found in most adult bookstores." She slammed the cupboard shut. "Charlie the Chicken was one class act, wasn't he?"

Mike tilted his head. "He was working with a limited income, I think."

"That," Baxter said, "plus he was slime. Bad combination." She got too close to the sofa and the smell of— she didn't want to know—almost gagged her. "Thank goodness he had a rent invoice in his bag. Otherwise, we would've never found this hellhole. Although at the moment, I'm thinking it's a dubious blessing."

Special Agent Swift entered from the rear bedroom. "Hey, kids! Back here! Water bed."

Mike winced. "Too trite."

"How could this guy afford a water bed?" Baxter wondered aloud.

"Maybe he got it from an old lady as a tip."

"It's the only thing I could call actual furniture," Swift said. "All indications are that he hadn't been here long."

"And didn't plan to stay long, either," Mike added, "judging from the bus ticket in his pocket. He knew someone was after him."

"You're sure of that, Sherlock?"

"Sure enough. See the muddy footprints beneath the front window? The wear on the floorboards? He knew his killer was after him. He was watching for him. Probably scared to death."

"Hey!" Baxter shouted. "Over here!" From an open drawer on a spindly end table that looked as if it would collapse if you blew on it hard, she withdrew a framed photo. "I think we have a shot of our victim."

Mike scrutinized the photograph. He was a young man, probably early twenties, if that. He had dark hair and slightly chubby chipmunk cheeks. It conformed in all respects with the face they'd found in the bus station men's room. What was left of it.

"This is excellent," Swift enthused. "It may not be all that current. But it beats running around with another one of those computer-enhanced jobs."

Baxter nodded. "Pretty unlucky that both our victims had half their faces erased."

"It's not luck," Mike said firmly. "It's design. Our killer is smart—probably experienced. He's trying to hide the trail. Prevent us from identifying the victims. So we don't recognize the connection."

"Which is?" Baxter said, eyebrow arched.

Mike didn't answer. He stared at the photo. It gave him a much better picture of what the deceased looked like than he had gotten from the shattered remains in the men's room. "You know, I've seen this face before. But I can't quite place where."

"Ever work vice?" Swift asked.

"Not for any length of time."

"Drugs? DEA files?"

Mike batted his fingertip against his lips. "Maybe. I don't know. It'll come to me. I hope."

"Maybe you should see the department hypnotist," Baxter suggested.

Mike shook his head. "Memories recalled under hypnosis aren't reliable. You can almost never get them admitted in court. Judges are really down on it."

"Where do they stand on massage therapy?" Swift asked, her full-lipped grin spreading. "I've heard mine is very stimulating."

"I'm not surprised," Baxter said, "given how much practice you must've had."

"R-r-r-r-ar." Swift made a cat claw in the air. "So whaddaya say, handsome? Haven't you held me at bay long enough?"

"Not that I'm not tempted," Mike said, "but I'm heading back to your office. Give me enough time, and possibly enough beer, and I'll remember." He tucked the photo under his arm. "This could be the break we've been waiting for."

CHAPTER
39

AFTER THE DISASTROUS testimony from the psychiatrist, Ben comforted himself thinking that it couldn't get any worse, not with the innocuous list of witnesses left to the prosecution. Once again, he was dead wrong.

"The state calls Gary Scholes."

Ben whispered to his client. "You sure this is going to be okay?"

"I'm tellin' ya—nothing to worry about," Johnny insisted. He seemed more upbeat than he had since the trial began. "Gary and I are brothers. We took a pledge of loyalty. He wouldn't do anything to hurt me."

"Then why is he testifying against you?"

"He was subpoenaed, man. He can't help it. But he'll make 'em sorry, once he's up there. We stick together."

Ben watched as the gangly college student ambled to the front of the courtroom. All witnesses were nervous, but he seemed particularly unhappy to be where he was. And Ben noticed that the man did not look at his pal Johnny as he passed by their table.

In the first few minutes, Drabble established that his witness knew Johnny Christensen, that he was a member of the same fraternity, and that he had attended some of the meetings of the Christian Minutemen. "Were you a member of that organization?"

"Yes. Have been for years."

"Even though it's an antigay group?"

"The Christian Minutemen aren't anti-anything."

Scholes ran a hand through his hair. He was wearing a suit and tie—standard courtroom attire—but looked ferociously uncomfortable in them. "We are opposed to homosexuality. Homosexuality is a sin, as the Bible makes explicitly clear. But we embrace all people. We try to help gay people find the way. We help them find a cure for their problem."

Drabble tilted his head. "A cure?"

"Yes. The Christian Minutemen believe that homosexuality is a disease, possibly a mental disorder, and I might add that many well-known and respected authorities support our position. We believe that with therapy and conditioning and spiritual counseling, people can overcome this disease and lead wholesome, natural lives."

Ben tapped the end of his pencil on the table. He never liked it when he was unsure where the prosecutor was going. Why was Drabble going to such pains to establish his witness's position on gay issues?

"So you bear no enmity toward the homosexual community."

"No. I may not approve, but I bear them no malice. I believe in counseling, therapy. I do not believe in violence. The Minutemen do not officially promote violence, and we've done our best to squash the rumors that some of our members were involved in . . . gay-bashing."

"How long have you known the defendant, Jonathan Christensen?"

"Since he joined the fraternity."

"Were you friends?"

"I'd say so. We spent a lot of time with each other, along with the other frat guys."

"Did you ever hear him express his opinions regarding gay men?"

"Oh yeah. He—"

"Objection," Ben said, approaching the bench. Drabble followed. "Hearsay. Not relevant. More prejudicial than probative."

"Goes to motive," Drabble replied. "Obviously."

"My client's position regarding homosexuals is well established," Ben rejoined. "Anything more on this subject is just cumulative. Worse, the prosecutor is implying that Johnny's disapproval of homosexuality proves he committed murder."

"It does seem to me as if we could skip this part," Judge Lacayo said. "Let's move on to the heart of the man's testimony."

Drabble grudgingly complied. "Mr. Scholes, were you with Johnny Christensen on the night in question?"

"Part of the time, yeah."

"Which part?"

"I saw him around eleven P.M. in a club near campus called Remote Control."

"And not before?"

"Absolutely not."

"Why were you at Remote Control?"

"It was a regular hangout for the guys in our frat house. You could probably find some of us there any night of the week. An e-mail had gone around inviting members to meet there after a sorority function taking place earlier that night."

"Did you know Johnny Christensen would be there?"

"Not till I arrived, with three others. We saw Johnny and Brett, so we joined them."

"How long were you with them?"

"Until the police arrested Johnny and Brett."

"What were the topics of conversation?"

"There was only one." His lips puckered, as if he had an unpleasant taste in his mouth. "Johnny and Brett were describing how they'd just beaten up some . . . homosexual."

"Were they bragging about it?"

Scholes took a deep breath. "Yes. They were very proud of themselves. Played it all out for us, practically in real time. Made a big joke of it."

"Wait a minute," Johnny whispered, back at the defendant's table. "What's going on here?"

Ben didn't answer. Seemed the fraternity of brothers wasn't as tight as Johnny thought.

Drabble continued. "It was a joke?"

"Yes, they thought it was very amusing. They were particularly delighted by their victim's pleas for mercy, his begging for his life. Johnny would kind of imitate the boy's voice, you know, real high and effeminate-sounding. 'Please don't kill me. Please. I'll do anything.' " Scholes licked his lips. "He thought that was hilarious."

The courtroom fell silent. All eyes were on the defendant, not the witness.

"Did Johnny reenact the beating?"

"Oh yeah. He was high as a kite, you know? Irrepressible. Showed us his mean right, his uppercut. 'This is the swing I used to break his jaw,' he said. And he showed us all his tools—the knife, the Taser. Brett told us about the hammer." He shook his head. "They were so proud of themselves."

"What was the reaction from the rest of the group? Did they laugh?"

Scholes shrugged. "Some of them did. A little. Especially after they'd had a few beers. But mostly Johnny and Brett were entertaining themselves. They were oblivious to the rest of the world."

"And what was your reaction?"

"I was sick. I stayed because I didn't want to create a scene, but the whole thing repulsed me. Bad enough to torture another human being like that—but then to take so much pleasure in it. To laugh and brag about it. I thought I was going to vomit."

Back at the defendant's table, Johnny held his head in his hands. "I can't believe this."

"Shhh," Ben whispered. "The jury is watching."

"But—he's a brother! Why would he turn on me like this?"

Because he has a conscience? Ben thought. He couldn't believe what he was hearing, either, but for entirely different reasons. Why would Drabble risk putting one of Johnny's friends on the stand, just for this? All this grotesque braggadocio had been related by the police witnesses. Another version wasn't necessary. There had to be something more.

"How long were you at the bar?" Drabble continued.

"About an hour. Maybe a little more. By that time, Johnny and Brett were starting to wind down, and I thought I could leave without taking any grief from anyone. I started to go and others followed my lead—and that's when the police moved in."

"Were you questioned?"

"For a time. They eventually let me go. Johnny and Brett were the only ones they arrested."

Drabble closed his notebook, gripped the corners of the podium, and leaned forward, an earnest expression on his face. "Now, Mr. Scholes, I'm going to ask you another question, and this is very important, so please take your time before answering. During this entire sordid conversation—the bragging, the reenacting, the laughing and joking—did Johnny ever say that he had killed his victim?"

"No. He never used that word."

"Did Brett?"

"No. They talked about how bad they hurt him, but never said they killed him. In fact, early on, I remember specifically hearing Brett saying, 'We shoulda just killed him.' Which of course suggests that they didn't."

Ben and Christina looked at each other, eyes widening. What was going on here? Why was Drabble making their defense for them? Christina seemed faintly pleased, but Ben knew Drabble would never intentionally have his witness buttress a defense theory, even if it was the truth. There had to be more to this. And whatever it was, he felt certain he wasn't going to like it.

"Was there any reaction when Brett made that statement?" Drabble asked.

"Yes. Johnny fell strangely silent, for the first time. He seemed to kind of withdraw inside himself. His head drooped."

"What did you make of that?"

"Well, at first I just thought the booze was wearing off. You know—he was coming down from the buzz. Then, out of nowhere, I heard him say, real quiet like, 'Brett is right.'"

A buzz rose from the gallery of the courtroom, a mixture of whispers and scratched pencils and shuffling and craning. All eyes were fixed on the witness stand.

"He said that?"

"Yeah. And I said, 'What are you talking about?' He answered right away. He said, 'We should've killed that filthy faggot. I should take care of that myself. I should go back and finish what we started.'"

The buzz grew. Eyes widened all around the courtroom.

"Objection!" Ben said, not because he had any grounds but because he thought he had to. "This is hearsay—"

"Admission against interest," Drabble said calmly.

"—and was obviously invented by the prosecution to counteract our defense. This testimony does not appear in any of the witness's prior statements!"

"I just remembered a few days ago," Scholes said. "When I read in the paper that Johnny was claiming he didn't kill that kid."

"The objection is overruled," Lacayo said.

"But your honor," Ben continued, trying to break the spell these deadly words had cast over the courtroom, "this is an eleventh hour switch obviously concocted to—"

"You'll have a chance to expose any perceived faults in the testimony during cross," the judge said firmly. "The objection is overruled. Proceed."

"It's not true," Johnny whispered, as Ben retook his seat. "I don't remember saying anything like that."

Ben motioned for him to be silent. The last thing they needed was for the jury to see him desperately protesting his innocence. Stay calm, he mouthed.

Drabble resumed his questioning. "And what if anything did the defendant do after he made that statement?"

"Nothing at first. But about a minute or so later, he got up, with this really weird expression on his face—and left the bar."

Now the noise in the gallery was so intense Judge Lacayo had to clap his gavel a few times and order silence. Sitting behind the defense table, Ellen Christensen's eyes closed, her face contorted in pain.

"He left?" Drabble said, acting surprised, although Ben knew perfectly well he wasn't. "For how long?"

Scholes tossed his head to the side. "Hard to say exactly. Maybe fifteen minutes."

"And this would be when?"

"Around 11:10, I think."

Ben felt a cold chill grip his spine. Eleven ten—still within the window of the coroner's estimated time of death.

"And how long does it take to get from the bar to your fraternity house?" Drabble asked.

"Only a few minutes. You can walk it in five."

"So let me get this straight. At 11:10, the defendant says, 'I should finish what we started,' leaves the bar for fifteen minutes, then returns."

"Objection, your honor," Ben said. Thank God he finally got an opening. "He's leading the witness."

"True enough," Lacayo replied. "Sustained."

"What's more, I object to this entire line of questioning. It's all supposition based on hearsay. The witness can't testify about what my client did after he supposedly left the bar. This evidence isn't probative of anything."

Drabble arched an eyebrow. "Then it shouldn't pose any threat to you."

"I move to strike," Ben continued, advancing toward the bench. Drabble joined him. "In fact, I move for a mistrial."

"On what grounds?" the judge asked.

"On the grounds that this speculative and irrelevant testimony has permanently tainted this jury."

"Tainted them with the truth?" Drabble asked.

"The mere fact that the man left the table for a little while doesn't prove he killed anybody."

"And I'm sure you'll make that point on cross and in closing," Lacayo said. "Anything else?"

"Yes! At the very least, I move that the jury be instructed to disregard this line of questioning."

"That will be denied," Lacayo ruled.

"Your honor, he's lying!"

"That's why God made cross-examination, counsel."

"If nothing else," Ben pleaded, "strike the testimony on grounds of fundamental fairness. The prior defense attorney interviewed the witness extensively, but he didn't hear anything about this."

"Maybe he didn't ask the right questions," Drabble said.

"That is another issue you can address on cross," the judge added.

"What's more," Ben said, glaring at Drabble, "the prosecution has a legal obligation to come forward during the pretrial period with any damaging evidence they intend to use at trial. But we never heard about this."

"We gave them the witness," Drabble said. "Good grief, do we have to give them a list of questions to ask? We can't lead them by the hand every step of the way."

"Defendants are supposed to be tried by evidence, not by ambush."

"Gentlemen, please!" Lacayo held up his hands, clearly indicating he wanted the discussion to end. "I'm sympathetic to what you're saying, Mr. Kincaid—and I know the appeals court will rip me a new one if I allow anyone to be tried by ambush. But I don't feel this one detail varies that much from what you already knew the witness was going to say—"

"It destroys our entire defense!"

"—and you did have access to the witness before-hand. It would be different if he lied to you, but there's no indication before me that he did—only that you failed to cover an important area of potential testimony. We can't do everything for you, you know. Sometimes counsel has to stand on their own two feet."

Ben bit his tongue.

"We're burning daylight, gentlemen, and I'm still hoping we can finish the prosecution's case today. Let's move along."

The attorneys returned to their positions. Drabble passed the witness. Ben launched in on him immediately. "Mr. Scholes, do you consider yourself a good person?"

The witness was understandably perplexed. "I guess."

"Are you a loyal person?"

Scholes's lips tightened. Now he knew where this was going. "I try to be."

"And I believe you've said you considered Johnny Christensen your friend?"

"True, but—"

"Do you think he considered you a friend?"

"I like to think so."

"And when you sat together in that bar last March and he was talking, do you think he expected you would repeat what he said to third parties?"

"Probably not, and normally I wouldn't. But this is murder!"

A fair point, Ben thought quietly. "Nonetheless, he was speaking to you in confidence."

"Well, not really, because as it turned out, the police were listening at the next booth."

"But neither of you knew that. He must've thought he could trust you." Ben had no idea whether this would fly or not, but it had to be to their advantage to portray the witness as a traitor and a snitch rather than a whistle-blower.

"I guess."

"But as it turns out, your loyalties were somewhere else altogether, right?"

"I . . . don't know what you mean."

"How long have you been in the Christian Minutemen?"

He seemed taken aback by the sudden shift in topic. "I've already said—for some time."

"Over three years, to be more precise."

"Y-yes. That's right."

"You're rising up the ranks in the local chapter, aren't you?"

"I'm the assistant deputy director."

"And what's the position of your organization regarding the murder of Tony Barovick?"

"We have publicly condemned the actions of the accused."

"Even though he's one of you."

"Even so."

"The fact is," Ben said, "Johnny has become something of a liability, hasn't he?"

"I'm . . . not sure what you mean."

"Oh, come on now, Mr. Scholes. You've been to the meetings. It must've been discussed. If Johnny Christensen is linked to the Minutemen, it could really mess up that supposed nonviolence position of yours."

"Attacking that boy was his idea, not ours."

"So you say. But in any case, Johnny has become a political liability, and you've gone out of your way to distance yourselves from him. That's why you've cooperated with the police, isn't it? You'd be happiest if Johnny disappeared from the face of the earth. Not because of what he did—but because he got caught."

"I'm just telling you what I know."

"And then some. You and your little gang of hooligans want to see Johnny convicted, and you're not afraid to make up a story to see that it happens!"

"Objection," Drabble said. "This is just harassment and speechifying."

"I didn't hear a question in there anywhere, Mr. Kincaid," the judge said sharply. "Do you need instruction on how a cross-examination is to be conducted?"

"No, sir. Could we get the witness some instruction on the difference between the truth and a great big lie?"

"Objection!" Drabble boomed.

Ben winced. Shouldn't have done that . . .

"Mr. Kincaid!" Lacayo pointed his gavel. "I'll only warn you once. I will not have this kind of behavior in my courtroom."

"My apologies, your honor."

"Consider yourself sanctioned. You may deposit five hundred dollars with the clerk of the court on your way out today."

Great. Looks like I'm taking the bus home. "Sorry, sir. I'm just . . . frustrated."

"May I answer his question?" Scholes asked. "Because I'm not lying!"

Ben readdressed himself to the witness. "Then why didn't you mention this hot little tidbit about Johnny leaving the bar before?"

"I told you. I didn't think of it."

"Until just before your courtroom appearance. After you've been interviewed by the defense attorneys. After the prosecution has learned about our defense."

"I remembered reading in the *Trib* that Johnny was claiming—"

"What about the other three men at the table?"

"I—I'm not following you."

"All the frat boys at the table that night were interviewed by the police and by the defense attorneys. Why is it that none of them—*not one*—recalled hearing Johnny say anything about 'finishing what he started'?"

"I was sitting closest to Johnny. And at that time, he was speaking quietly."

"And no one else noticed that he was gone for fifteen minutes?"

"It might not have been that long. I'm not sure. They probably just thought he'd gone to the bathroom and didn't keep track of the time. But I did."

"And why is that?"

"Because I'd heard what he said just before he left."

Ben took a deep breath, trying to collect his thoughts. He was getting nowhere with this witness—worse, he was giving the man a chance to repeat and reinforce everything he had said. He needed to extract what little he could from this witness and get him out of here.

"Mr. Scholes, you don't know where Johnny went when he left the table, do you?"

He hesitated. "I . . . don't know for a fact."

"And you don't know what he did while he was gone, either, right?"

"I didn't see what he did. No."

"And did he at any time say that he had killed anyone?" Ben presumed that if he had, it would've been mentioned already.

"Not specifically. Mostly he just bragged like before and massaged his hand."

Ben blinked. "His hand?"

"Yeah. He kept rubbing his fingers and palm. He seemed to have strained it or something."

Strained it—strangling someone?

"Thank you. No more questions." And good riddance.

Lacayo addressed the prosecutor. "Any redirect?"

Drabble shook his head. "No. And the prosecution rests."

Christina made the usual motion for a directed verdict, which the judge denied without even thinking about it. The prosecution had more than made its case, and everyone in the room knew it. The judge dismissed the jury for the day, instructed the defense to be ready to begin tomorrow morning, and adjourned the court.

Pandemonium ensued. Reporters pressed against the rail, trying to get quotes from Ben and Christina, from Drabble, from Johnny. Christina declined their kind offers to preview her defense to them and started packing.

Ben felt a tugging at his wrist. Johnny.

"This isn't goin' so hot, is it?"

Ben wasn't sure how honest to be. "Things rarely look good for the defense after the prosecution rests. If they don't have a solid case, they don't go to trial. But now we get our chance."

"But we don't have anything. Do we?"

"We have you."

Lines formed around Johnny's eyes. "Do you think they'll believe me?"

After one look into those eyes, there was no way Ben was going to tell him what he really thought. "I hope so." He nodded toward Christina. "Team meeting?"

"Definitely."

The marshals took charge of their prisoner, and Ben and Christina bundled all their materials together and charted a course for the rear of the courtroom.

What Ben had told Johnny was absolutely true—things never looked good for the defendant at the conclusion of the prosecution's case. But at the same time they rarely looked this grim. Usually he had some ace up his sleeve, some trick or theory or angle. But this time Drabble had seen him coming. He'd deflected their intended feint like a master swordsman, literally destroying their defense before they'd had a chance to put it on.

If the jury thought Christina had called into question the coroner's estimated time of death, Johnny's disappearance at 11:10 might not be so incriminating. But if they didn't . . .

They had to come up with something new—something different. But what could it be? What could possibly make the jury forget what they had heard, forget the horrible punishment Johnny had visited on another human being—and then laughed about? This case had more aggravating circumstances than all of Ben's previous cases combined. If Johnny was convicted, any plea for mercy in sentencing would be laughable. The death penalty was a dead cert.

PART THREE

What Is False Within

CHAPTER
40

"LET ME CARRY that catalog case, Mr. Kincaid."

"I'm fine. Call me Ben."

"Can I get you something to drink, Mr. Kincaid?"

"Not right now. *Ben.*"

"Do you need any supplies? Legal pads, Post-it notes?"

"No, thanks."

"Anything at all? Fresh coffee? Sharpen your pencils?"

Fetch your slippers? Ben took Vicki firmly by the shoulders. "Vicki, I admire your zeal. I know you're trying to do a good job. But seriously—relax. We hired you to be a legal intern. Not a gofer."

She flushed, then looked away shyly. "I just know how much stress you and Christina are under. I want to help in any way I can."

"You are helping. And doing a great job. So don't worry about it. We'll get this meeting started, then maybe—"

"Chocolate milk!" the young woman said, snapping her fingers. "Christina told me how crazy you are for it. I'll get some out of the fridge."

And she was gone before he could say another word.

Ben took a seat beside Christina at the office conference table. "Have I mentioned how much I like your new intern?"

"At least she talks to you. She gets so bashful around me she can barely finish a sentence. I think she must be a little sweet on you, hard as that is to imagine. You really like her?"

He nodded. "I've always gone for those quiet, subservient types."

"Well, that explains—" She thought better of it. "Jones? Loving?"

"Present or accounted for," Loving replied.

Vicki returned with the chocolate milk. "I hope it's okay cold. I didn't know whether I should warm it."

Ben grimaced. Warm it? "This will be fine."

"All right," Christina said, addressing the troops, "I don't suppose I need to tell anyone that this trial is going against us in a big way. We have to face facts: Drabble saw us coming and headed us off at the pass. Those last two witnesses were disasters."

"Those last two witnesses just told the truth," Jones grumbled.

"I don't know that. And for our purposes, it's beside the point. Johnny is in trouble."

"Because he's a murderous, hatemongering creep."

"Jones! That's our client you're talking about!"

"Don't I know it! I've had to clean up the mess outside the offices twice now, thanks to him. And he's not even paying his bills!"

"Whether you like it or not, we took the case. And we're losing."

"Maybe we *should* be losing."

Christina pointed a finger. "What's wrong with you, Jones? As I recall, you were all for this case when Ellen Christensen first came into the office."

"Did you hear what he did?" Jones replied. "Did you hear what that kid from the frat house was saying? How our client just . . . destroyed poor Tony Barovick? And laughed about it?"

"We can't sit in judgment of our clients," Ben interjected. "No one is guilty until a verdict is rendered. And for that matter—I talked to Mike earlier today. He asked if I'd send him a copy of Tony Barovick's journal. He thinks maybe Tony wasn't quite the sainted martyr the media has painted him."

Jones slapped the table. "Don't tell me we're going after the victim! That's got to be the all-time sleaziest tactic."

"Not if it's the truth."

"The truth! What are we going to say—that he deserved to have his legs shattered with a hammer?"

"As you know, Mike has been investigating the murder of two low-level criminals. Mike believes they were involved in some kind of drug-pushing deal that operated out of Remote Control. And he thinks Tony Barovick may have been in on it."

"That's total bullshit."

Ben disagreed. "It makes sense. Tony was the manager, after all. He was in every night. How long could something like that go on without him knowing about it?"

"It's a crock." Jones swung around in his chair. "I don't buy it, and the jury won't, either."

"I have similar concerns myself," Christina said. "If we start talking about drug-running at this stage of the game, the jury will think we're just conjuring up bogeymen to create reasonable doubt."

"Which would be more or less the case," Ben answered. "Except Mike says there's really something to it."

"But how do we prove it? Does Mike have any evidence? Any witnesses?"

"Not so far. Nothing that would hold up in court."

"It would take a lot to make the jury forget what Johnny has admitted he did. And failing some concrete proof of a third party, he's always going to seem like the most likely suspect." She pushed away from the table. "No, I have to agree with Jones on this one, even if he is a temperamental, irrational hothead."

"Hey!"

"Until we have a bona fide witness who can take the stand and explain what was going down, this drug-pushing theory is a loser for us."

"Christina," Ben said, "think about—"

"And since this is my case," she continued, "my decision is final."

Ben dropped his chin.

"Jones," she continued, "I've been reading your reports. You've done some great work digging around the nooks and crannies of this case. But I haven't seen anything that gives us a defense."

"Guess why?" He folded his arms across his chest. "Because there is no defense. Everybody knows he did what he did."

"Admittedly, distinguishing between a torturous bone-breaking beating and a murder is a tricky argument. But it's the one we're stuck with. Loving?"

He sat up. "Yes, ma'am!"

"I've read your reports, too. You've really gotten tight with those frat boys."

He smiled slightly. "I know how to speak their language."

"Just act sexist, self-centered, and irresponsible?"

"Aww, they're not all bad."

"Neither was Hitler."

"And they're easy to talk to, once you know the magic words."

"Which are?"

" 'This round's on me.' "

"I'm not seeing that you've found anything that gets Johnny off the hook, though."

" 'Fraid not. I got the same story at the frat house that I got from the Minutemen. Some of them might've had an ax to grind against gays, but none of them liked what Johnny and his buddy did to Tony Barovick. The Minutemen think it set their cause back; they don't want anythin' to do with him."

"Then why do they keep trashing our offices?"

"They claim they had nothin' to do with that, too."

"Judging from that last frat boy witness," Ben said, "the Minutemen are hoping Johnny goes down, the sooner the better."

"True," Christina said, "but he stood up pretty well to your pummeling on cross. To tell you the truth, Ben—I didn't get the impression he was lying."

"If he wasn't lying, then—"

"Yeah. I know."

A silence fell across the conference table. A grim sense of inevitability blanketed the room.

"The marshals are bringing Johnny by later tonight," Christina said. "We'll talk about it. How he explains his absence."

"And if he can't?"

No one answered that question. No one wanted to.

Vicki was at the door. "Mr. Kincaid? I mean—Ben."

"Yeah?"

"There's someone here to see you."

"Vicki, we're in the middle of—"

"It's Ellen Christensen."

Ben's neck twitched. "I'm working."

"She says it's important. It's about the case."

Ben stared down at the table, his eyes hooded.

Christina looked at him. "Please, Ben? We need all the help we can get."

After a long moment, Ben slowly pushed himself out of his chair. "This won't take long."

BEN STARTED SPEAKING before he entered the room.

"I thought I made it clear that I didn't want to have any—"

"I wanted to thank you," she said. She was a thin,

fragile woman, and she seemed particularly so now. "For helping with my son's case. I appreciate it."

"I did it for Christina," he said, his voice low and flat. "Because she asked me. That's the only reason."

"Whatever the reason, I appreciate it." Her face was red and a trifle puffy. She had obviously been crying, which Ben supposed should come as no surprise, given the circumstances. "Johnny is losing, isn't he?"

Ben had never been one to comfort people with false hope, and he was less inclined than ever now. "Yes."

"You think he will be convicted?"

"I think juries are utterly unpredictable. But at this moment—it doesn't look good. That last witness destroyed our defense. If Johnny left the bar at 11:10, and no one knows where he went, then—"

"I know where he went."

"You do?"

She nodded slightly. "I . . . I had hoped it wouldn't come up. But I can testify."

"We can't put the defendant's mother on the stand. The jury would think you were just trying to get your son off the hook. Who else knows?"

"No one. I'm the only one."

Ben grimaced. "If we put you up there, Drabble will tear you apart."

"I know that. But I still—"

"No. I'm totally against it. It's a bad idea."

"Is that because you don't care about him?" she said, her voice rising for the first time. "Or because you don't care about me?"

Ben turned, his hand pressed against his forehead. "Ellen—"

Tears sprang from her eyes. "I know how you must hate me. And I don't blame you."

"Ellen . . . I . . ."

"But I can't believe you don't care. Not even a little bit."

Ben remained quiet.

"And I can't believe you'd let my son suffer just to punish me. But that's how it looks. As if you're not even trying. As if you want Johnny to be convicted."

"That's ridiculous."

"*Is it?*" A short explosion, then once again her voice crumbled. She wiped away a stream of tears, which were immediately replaced by new ones. "I know I made a terrible mistake, Ben. Don't you think I would change things? If I could? If I could do it all over again?"

Ben couldn't bring himself to look at her.

"But I can't. I can't turn back the hands of time. All I can do is . . . move forward." She looked up at him, eyes pleading. "Can't you move forward, too?"

Ben stared at the desktop, trying to reason with himself, trying to force himself to take the next step. Without success. It was as if there was some sort of wall, some psychological barrier that prevented him from making even the tiniest movement in her direction, even when his brain—or perhaps his heart—told him that he should.

"I'll notify Christina that you want to testify," he said, moving rapidly toward the door. "It's her call. You should be ready to go tomorrow morning. In any case."

"You been here all night?"

Mike looked up from his temporary desk. "As a matter of fact. How'd you guess?"

"Easy," Baxter said. "You look like a piece of meat that's been left out too long in the sun. Been working? Or have you perhaps finally taken Special Agent Swift up on her many offers?"

"Swift just likes to kid around."

"Who's kidding who? She's been after your bones since she showed up in Tulsa. They sure make 'em horny down South."

"Don't be so crude."

"How else do you explain it? I mean, you're okay-looking, but honestly."

Mike tapped his pencil eraser on his desk. "I seem to recall a night when you didn't think I was all that unpleasant to be with."

"I must've been feverish. Or seriously bored. You working on the murders?"

"What else would I be working on?"

"How should I know?" She paced around his desk. "Your obsessions seem to come and go. I mean, a few days ago you were all wrapped up in that kidnapping case. Now another mystery comes along, and you're staying up all night working on that. It's as if you have no personal life. As if the normal cycles of life never—"

Mike sat upright. "Wait a minute. You're right."

"About what?"

He ran for his coat. "You should be proud of yourself."

"I'd be prouder if I knew what I'd done."

"What every muse does. 'Open thine eyes / That the blind might see.' " He cupped her face in his hands and kissed her. "You're brilliant."

Her response was a little slow in coming. "I thought we agreed—"

"Sorry. I was momentarily overcome. I'll be back soon."

"Morelli! I want to know what—"

But it was too late. He was gone.

CHAPTER
41

THE NEXT MORNING the courtroom atmosphere was even more agitated than it had been before. The throng outside had doubled, and three incidents of violence were reported before Ben and Christina even arrived. The corridors of the courtroom were jam-packed, and spectators jostled and thrust for a chance to get one of the treasured gallery seats. It seemed everyone was anxious to hear what the defense had to say.

Ben was amazed that the case still seemed to hold the media's interest; he couldn't think of a network that didn't have someone on the premises. Most of the familiar faces he'd noticed in the gallery were back again: Roger Hartnell, still hobbling along with his cane, Gary Scholes, the frat boy turncoat. Mario Roma was there, too; Ben made sure he never had a chance to get anywhere near Christina.

And Ellen was present, of course.

"You know I'm a reasonable man," Drabble said, running his fingers through his hair. "You know it. Tell me I'm a reasonable man."

"You've been a reasonable man," Ben answered. "Most of the time."

"I don't go in for dirty tricks."

"Right," Christina said. "That little prank you pulled on me my first day was a clean trick."

Drabble ignored her. "I've turned over the evidence

I'm supposed to turn over. I've given you access to the witnesses."

"You coached Gary Scholes to hold back the kicker."

"I did nothing of the sort. I play by the rules."

Ben was becoming impatient. "Fine, fine. You're a paragon among prosecutors. Of course, that's rather like being the Earl of Earwigs."

Drabble drew himself up. "But I absolutely draw the line at surprise witnesses plopped into my lap seconds before they testify."

"It's not as if Ellen Christensen dropped out of the heavens. You've known about her. You've talked to her on several occasions. She's on our list."

"Only in a pro forma way. You never suggested she was a material alibi witness."

"Look, if you want to talk fairness, I didn't know Scholes was going to say Johnny left the bar at exactly the coroner's estimated time of death, did I? I'm calling her to rebut your surprise assault on our defense. I need her."

"Well . . . that's just too diddly-doggone bad."

"Don't be vulgar. It detracts from your rugged good looks."

"You heard what I said." Drabble projected his voice so every reporter in the courtroom could hear. "I won't stand by quietly while you thwart justice. The answer is no."

But Judge Lacayo's answer, happily, was yes. He was wary of denying the defense anyone they called a critical alibi witness—especially, Ben suspected, when the case looked like a prosecution win, which would guarantee an appeal. He offered Drabble extra time to prepare his cross which, to Ben's surprise, he declined.

"That won't be necessary, your honor," Drabble grumbled. "I have a pretty good idea what I'm going to do."

What can he be thinking? Ben wondered. As always,

any time a prosecutor knew something he didn't, he was left with an unshakable foreboding.

CHRISTINA HANDLED THE direct examination of Ellen Christensen. It wasn't an easy task for her—especially knowing what she did about the woman's past with Ben—but she also knew it would be a mistake to ask Ben to do it.

After establishing who she was, where she lived, and her relationship to the defendant, Christina took her directly to the time in question.

"What were you doing on the night of March 22?"

"I was at home. Alone. I'm a widow—my husband died two and a half years ago."

"What were you doing?"

"After dinner, I read a novel. The new Anne Tyler."

"Would you please tell the jury where you live?"

"At the corner of Madison and 21st. Near campus."

"And near Remote Control?"

"Yes. Very near."

"Did you have any visitors that night?"

"One." She paused. "My son. John Christensen."

"And what time was it when he came by?"

"I can't say exactly, but I remember my grandfather clock striking 11:00, so it was a little later than that. About 11:10, 11:20, I'd guess."

There was a discernible rustling in the gallery. Now the crowd—and the jury—understood the importance of her testimony. While she had their attention, Christina thought it would be an advantageous time to establish a little essential background information.

"Have you been close to your son in recent years, Mrs. Christensen?"

Ellen's gaze went downward, not toward the jury, as Christina would've preferred. It was acceptable to seem a little nervous—jurors expected that. But Christina didn't want it to be too extreme—especially not with a witness whom they were likely to be skeptical of from the outset. "We were close for many years. After I married his father. I loved him—I love him—just as if he were my biological son. In my mind, he is. But after Larry died . . . he seemed to change. He became distant. It was almost as if he blamed me for Larry's premature heart attack. He started spending less time at home and more time with his friends—often friends I did not approve of. When he finished high school and wanted to go to college, it was a relief."

"Did you know about his involvement with the fraternity? And the Christian Minutemen?"

"Yes, even as little as I saw him, he made sure I knew about that."

"Did you approve?"

"Of course not. Larry and I were always very liberal in our thinking. In a way I think perhaps that was why he did it. It was the ultimate way of punishing me, of rebelling. By being a part of something I found truly appalling."

"How did he look when he came to see you that night?"

"Horrible. Strung out. His hair was a mess, he was drenched in sweat. His clothes were dirty and there were . . . splatters of blood on his shirt and hands. And he reeked of alcohol."

"Why did he come?"

"He said he needed to talk to someone—someone he could trust. I was pleased and flattered of course, but that died fast. When he told me what he'd done."

"What did he say?"

"He said he'd been with a friend. They'd both been drinking. Johnny is not a good drinker. It turns him into someone . . . someone entirely different from himself. He said they kidnapped a man in a parking lot and beat him. It wasn't his idea, he said, it was his friend's—but he felt as if he had to go along with it. He said they hurt this poor man—for a long time. Johnny said he had tried to stop his friend, but the friend wouldn't listen."

"Why would he tell you this?"

"Because he felt awful about it. The alcohol had worn off, his friend's influence had diminished—and he was riddled with guilt."

Out the corner of her eye, Christina checked the expression on the jurors' faces. They were skeptical—understandably so. This was directly contradictory to everything they'd heard so far, and the first hint of remorse they'd heard in the entire trial. It was coming too late to be readily convincing.

"How so?"

"He knew they'd done a horrible thing. He hadn't forgotten everything his father and I taught him. It had just been . . . buried somewhere. Somewhere deep. But now it all came pouring out of him."

"What did you do?"

"Not much. I just held him. Tried to comfort him. Told him . . ." She paused, drawing in her breath. Christina sensed she was struggling to retain her composure. "Told him I still loved him and always would. No matter what. And then he left."

"Did you notice what time he left?"

"I did. By then, I knew it might be important. It was 11:28, according to the clock in my kitchen. He'd only been there about ten minutes."

Christina closed her notebook. There were only two more questions left, and it was important that her witness get them both right. "Ellen, in the aftermath of the tragedy, you spoke to the police, didn't you?"

"Yes. Several times."

Rather than let the prosecution make a fuss about this on cross, Christina knew it was best to raise the issue on direct. "Did you tell them what you just told us?"

"No. I couldn't. I wouldn't have lied about it. But I

couldn't volunteer that he had come to my house and . . . basically confessed. I didn't know then that Johnny himself would admit what he had done. I didn't know then that the principal remaining question would be where he went when he left the bar a little after eleven. When that became an issue—I knew I had to come forward."

"And you're absolutely sure that Johnny was with you at the time of approximately 11:10 to 11:28?"

"Absolutely. And there wasn't time for him to go anywhere else."

Christina nodded. So far, so good. Only one more hurdle to jump. "Mrs. Christensen, as you know, the main question before this jury at present is not whether your son beat Tony Barovick, but whether he killed him. When he visited you that night, did he refer to that at all?"

"He did."

"What did he say?"

"He said that his friend Brett had wanted to kill him. As he described it, Brett had been consumed with something like a blood rage, had all but lost his mind. He wanted to murder the boy in some horrible fashion. But my Johnny stopped him."

"So you're certain Johnny didn't kill Tony Barovick?"

"More than that. As ironic as it might seem, Johnny saved that boy's life."

"Thank you. Pass the witness."

That had gone well, Christina thought, as she returned to her seat. Better than she'd expected, actually. She couldn't gauge whether the jury was buying it, but the points had been established. Whether they made an impact, ultimately, would depend on whether the jury believed Mrs. Christensen was telling the truth. At any rate, she hadn't left any openings for Drabble's cross, at least as far as she knew.

Drabble slowly approached the podium. Christina could only imagine what he had up his sleeve. She had cautioned Ellen not to become restless; this cross could easily go on for hours.

Drabble gazed at the witness for a long time. When he finally spoke, it was with a sort of sigh. "Mrs. Christensen, aren't you the defendant's mother?"

She hesitated a moment. "I'm his stepmother. I said that."

He continued to look at her for a long while. "Mrs. Christensen," he repeated. "Aren't you the defendant's mother?"

"Y-yes. Yes, I am."

Drabble smiled, nodded, closed his notebook. "Thank you, ma'am. I have no more questions."

CHAPTER
42

MIKE FINALLY FOUND Special Agent Swift in the basement firing range, protective earphones over her head. She was pouring long-range automatic ammunition into a man-shaped figure fifty feet away, and she looked as if she was enjoying herself. Which Mike didn't doubt.

She didn't hear him coming, no surprise, given the earphones and the thunderous clatter. He lifted the cushioned cones over her ears and said, "Boo!"

She started, but quickly recovered herself. "Mike! What's up, sugah? Come to take out your frustrations on a cardboard target?"

"No. Came looking for you."

"Really?" Her eyebrows danced. "You finally gonna take me up on my offer?"

"Yes, but possibly not the one you have in mind. Remember when you said you were going to come clean with me?"

"Ye-esss . . ."

"Well, now you really are." He guided her into a nearby room and closed the door. "I want to know why you came down to Tulsa and started messing around in my murder investigation. And this time don't give me any bull about drugs."

"But Mike—"

"Mind you, I'm not saying there aren't drugs running around that club or that Manny Nowosky wasn't peddling them as a sideline. But that's not enough to get a top Feeb wrapped up in an Oklahoma murder."

"I'm certain that your murder was connected to our Chicago murder."

"I am, too, but that still wouldn't bring it under federal purview. What's the real reason you thrust yourself into this case?"

She locked a finger around one of the buttons on his shirt. "With you involved, Mike, I didn't need much of an excuse. For thrusting myself into things."

He slapped her hand away. "Oh, give me some credit. I'm not so blind that a little flirting will turn me into an unquestioning idiot."

"But I—"

"You're not working any drugs case. You're working the same case you were always working. The Metzger kidnapping."

The humor drained from her face. "What makes you so sure?"

"Because I finally realized where I've seen that guy before. Charlie the Chicken. I knew I'd seen his face, but the image was slightly different, and I couldn't figure out why. Until I did." He paused. "It seemed different because the last time I saw him, I was way down looking up at him. Through the crosshairs of a sniperscope."

"Indeed."

"Yeah. That creep was one of the thugs who kidnapped the Metzger boy, and I'm willing to bet that Manny Nowosky was in on it, too. And Tony Barovick. My hunch was right about them being co-conspirators in some crime—I just had the wrong crime."

"What a theory."

"It explains a lot. Like why a two-bit punk like Manny had fifty grand lying around. And it helps me figure why Charlie was leaving town—given what had already happened to two of his partners."

"I'm not following you."

"We always thought the kidnapping was handled by a gang of four, and we were right. The fourth man—the only one who isn't dead—is still on the loose, having knocked off his former partners."

"But—why?"

"Maybe he doesn't want to share the ransom they got away with. Maybe he knows they're the only ones who can testify against him." Mike turned, pacing around the tiny room. "But why am I telling you this? You've known all along these murders were linked to the kidnapping. That's why you're on the case. Right?" He leaned in closer. "Am I right?"

She stared back at him. "You are so hot when you're mad."

It was all Mike could do to restrain himself. "Am I *right*?"

She released a long stream of air. "Yes, you're right."

"Then why the hell—"

"But don't start screaming at me. We had an anonymous tip linking the drill bit murder to the kidnapping, but I was under strict instructions from my superiors not to give you the lowdown. I didn't like it, but it wasn't my call."

"Did it ever occur to you . . . pompous . . . goddamn white-shirts . . . that local law enforcement might actually be able to help you? If you'd give us half a clue what's really going on!"

"I told you. It wasn't my decision!" She stomped around a few moments. "But now that you know, I don't see why I can't tell you the rest."

"Please do."

"We think the fourth man—the remaining living kidnapper—is based here in Chicago. Now that he's killed off his associates, assuming he has the ransom money, he should have no reason to remain. So we've got to catch him quick."

Mike folded his arms across his chest. He still wasn't

pleased about this, but he was happier inside the loop than out. "And how do we do that?"

"Remote Control seems to be the nerve center of this operation, even after Tony Barovick's death. Since we don't have any leads and don't know who Mr. Big is— we look for his shadow. Traces of his presence. Disruptions in the normal routine. People flashing a lot of cash who shouldn't be. Signs of people being roughed up or acting in a strange—"

"Wait a second," Mike interrupted. "Go back to the part about being roughed up."

"You would like that part." The corner of her lips turned up. "You know someone who's been roughed up?"

His eyes seemed intensely focused, but not on anything in the firing range. "I think just maybe I do. Come on."

She followed close behind. "Where are we going?"

"Out for a drink," he said, putting on his coat. "Back to Remote Control."

HARD TO KNOW what to think of that development, he thought, as he left the courtroom. Mother taking the witness stand. Pleading on her boy's behalf. Surely the jury would take that for being exactly what it was. A desperate attempt by a loved one to save her son—by lying. Not to be believed. More sad than evil.

I should've killed those damn lawyers when I had the chance, he thought, as he crushed the newspaper between his hands. I had them in my sights. And I let them get away.

He'd been beating himself up about it ever since, not that that made the two any more dead. He'd screwed up—and now he was paying the price. Sure, he'd been reluctant to tote up another murder or two when there had already been so many. How long could the cops remain so ignorant? But it seemed as if every time he rested a bit, every time he thought he might be secure, could relax, prop up his feet and watch this case go away permanently—something happened. Something that made him worry that the whole mess was going to crumble all around him. Again.

He'd gotten another revolver, to replace the one he had dropped before. He was ready to go. He would content himself to watch and wait, for the time being. But when the time to move arrived—and given the way he felt at the moment, it wouldn't be long—he wouldn't hesitate. He'd go after them. The chick and her partner. If he got half a chance, he'd take out Christensen, too. Save the state the trouble.

Your days are numbered, he thought, as he passed through the courthouse doors and stepped into the sunlight. He had a plan now. One that was certain to solve his difficulties, once and for all. And leave the world with two less lawyers.

So much the better.

CHAPTER
43

"PERSONALLY," CHRISTINA SAID, taking her seat at the head of the office conference table, "I thought Drabble's cross of Ellen was lame."

Ben's eyes fluttered closed. He hated these posttrial postmortems. "I thought it was brilliant. What did you think, Vicki?"

The petite intern couldn't seem to bring her eyes up off the table. "I . . . did think he made his point."

Christina frowned. "Well, whether the jury bought it or not, Johnny has to make a good impression."

"You're telling the wrong person," Ben said, pointing at the defendant sitting between them.

"Johnny," she said, looking intently into his eyes. "You understand how serious this is, don't you?"

"Hard to miss." He was wearing more casual clothes than the blue suit Christina dressed him in for court each day, but under the conference table, his feet were shackled. The marshals were posted in the corridor just outside their office. The court had allowed him to come back to the office to prep for his testimony, but they still weren't taking any chances. "This trial isn't exactly going my way."

"That's all right. Tomorrow is another day. Have you got that legal research I asked for, Vicki?"

"On restricting hearsay admitted against the defendant's interest? Some." Her voice became even less audible than usual. "Most of it isn't helpful."

"Then keep looking. If we could suppress some of the testimony Drabble is sure to use to impeach Johnny, it would be a big help."

She nodded. "I'll be at the computer terminal just across the hall." She left the room.

"The most important thing is that you seem sincere," Christina explained to Johnny. "Even when you admit to less-than-admirable things, as you're going to have to do. You must seem truthful. And remorseful. The prosecution has been painting you as a monster. You have to show them that you're not."

"I'm not anyone's monster," Johnny said indignantly.

"Don't act defensive. Best to speak in a calm, relaxed manner," Ben said. "Maybe a little slower than you normally would. Give yourself time to think."

"That's especially important on cross," Christina added. "Drabble will try to rev things up, get you talking fast, talking before thinking, leading you down the garden path, then catching you in some kind of trap. Before you answer any question, you have to ask yourself—what is he after?"

"You think he'll cross me more than he did my mother?"

"I can guarantee it. Your mother was a sympathetic figure, so he made his point delicately and sat down. With you, the gloves will be off."

"Is it so important that he trashes me?"

"To his case, yes," Christina answered. "But more to the point—it will be easy."

"What, because I'm so stupid?"

"No. Because what you did—what you've admitted you did—makes you such an easy target."

"Look at the jury from time to time," Ben advised, "but not all the time. They don't want someone playing to them, they want to observe you interacting with the prosecutor. But glance their way occasionally, especially when you're making important points. Just to show them you're not afraid to. Eye contact always suggests sincerity."

"Okay. I can do that."

"Most of all," Christina said, leaning in close, "you must not lose your temper. No matter what Drabble says. Losing your temper would be disastrous."

"Not a problem. I'm not a hothead."

"Johnny—"

"I'm not!"

"Johnny, almost every time I've talked to you, you've started shouting."

"That's because you ask me things just to cause trouble."

"And you think Drabble won't? His whole cross will be designed to get your goat. Because if he can make you blow up on the stand, the jury will be all that much more likely to believe you lost it the night of March 22 and beat a man to death. Intentionally. With malice."

"Okay, no temper flares. I promise."

"One more thing," Ben interjected. "You cannot rattle on about your personal beliefs regarding gay people or gay lifestyles. Not a word of it."

"I thought we had the First Amendment in this country."

Ben's teeth clenched. "If you want to die by lethal injection for your First Amendment rights, fine. Because I can guarantee that if you start rattling on about wreaking God's vengeance on sodomists, that's what's going to happen."

"This isn't San Francisco, you know. Some of those jurors might agree with me."

"Yeah, they might, but this isn't a political debate. It's not a referendum on lifestyle choices. This is your trial for your life."

"It goes to motive," Christina explained. "If you start some jeremiad about homosexuals, the jury will believe you could feel self-righteous enough to do what the prosecutor says you did for the reason he says you did it."

"Well, I'm not going to lie."

"I'm not asking you to lie."

"But," Ben jumped in, "I can guarantee Drabble will grill you on your beliefs regarding gay people. And if you launch into some hyperzealous screed, he'll crucify you. No—you'll crucify yourself."

Johnny's brow creased. "Then what the hell am I going to say?"

"I think it's okay to say that based on your Christian values, you disagree with the homosexual lifestyle," Christina said. "But there's no reason to go on and on about it. And you have to say it without the least trace of anger or malice." She paused. "I think that's the most important thing, don't you, Ben?"

"No. I think the most important thing is to seem re-morseful. That's what the forgiving, unconvinced jurors—if there are any—will be looking for."

"I don't get you."

"It's a lead-pipe cinch Drabble will ask you about the beating—the part to which you've already confessed. He'll probably take you through it blow by blow. You'll have to repeat what you've already admitted—but you can't seem proud of it. You can't try to justify what you did. To the contrary, you need to seem awash in regret. Tell the jury it was a mistake—you lost control, you were swayed by your friend, whatever. But don't say you were right to do what you did or that you enjoyed it or that you were doing God's work. You do that, you're blowfish."

"I can't pretend to be someone I'm not."

"I'm just asking you to be smart. I know for you that may be a tall order. But your life depends upon it."

*   *   *

AT TEN O'CLOCK sharp, the marshals knocked on the door and escorted Johnny back to the county jail.

"Think he can pull it off?" Christina asked.

"No," Ben said flatly. "But you have no choice. You have to put him on. And hope for the best."

"I still don't see where he came from. His mother is so different." She shook her head. "It must be particularly hard for you. Since you knew her, all those years ago. And cared for her."

"No discussion."

"I know, I know." She sighed. It was late, and they were the only two people left in the office . . .

"Thanks again," she said quietly. "For helping with this case. I know you didn't want to."

Ben shook his head. "I should've been on board from the start. I just—" He turned his eyes toward the window. "I can't explain it. Hearing from her again, after all this time. Because she needed something from me. Seeing her again. It just . . . I don't know. Threw me for a loop. I wasn't rational."

"You've got ample cause."

"No excuses. Just—I'm sorry."

They sat for a long while, not looking at each other. Ben stared out the window; Christina pretended to be intrigued by the stack of unopened transcripts on the table. Finally, when she couldn't stand it any longer, she reached out and squeezed his hand.

"Ben?"

"Yes?" he said, looking up.

"I—I—" She fumbled for a moment. "I'm sorry we haven't had time for Scrabble lately."

"I think there have been extenuating circumstances."

"I just wondered . . ." She pursed her lips, tried again. "I wondered if you would like to . . ."

Their faces drew closer together.

"Yes?" he said, when their noses were practically touching.

"I wondered if . . ."

They heard a clattering in the corridor outside. Perhaps it was Jones, locking up.

"We should probably get some sleep," Ben said.

"You're right, of course." She pushed away from the table, suddenly very embarrassed. "Big day, tomorrow. Make or break."

"Right," he agreed. "Best to get a good night's sleep."

And a moment later, she was gone.

You STUPID FOOL, he told himself, as he watched Christina leave the office.

But the timing wasn't right. It couldn't possibly be, not with the trial, and Ellen, and . . .

And the wounds all too present and deep and well remembered. Like that day at her apartment. The one that turned out to be the true last time he ever saw her. Until now.

WHEN SHE WOULDN'T answer the bell, he pounded on the apartment door. When she still didn't answer, he shouted, so loud that everyone in that Toronto apartment complex near campus could hear. It wasn't until he threatened to set fire to the place that she finally answered.

"Ben!" she said, standing in the doorway. "What are you doing here? I told you—"

"I couldn't stay away, Ellen. We're meant to be together."

Her eyes rolled up. "Did you hear anything I told you in the subway yesterday?"

"I heard it all. And I don't care."

Her neck stiffened. "I can't take this, Ben. I'm not well—"

He reached out desperately, grabbing her arm. "I know that, Ellen. That's why we should be together."

"That isn't possible. It wouldn't be fair."

"Splitting up isn't fair! I want to be with you. We'll fight this thing together. I'll be with you in the clinics, in the hospital. Wherever you need me to be."

"There's more to it than that."

"Fine! I don't care. Whatever there is, we'll deal with it."

"You're not being realistic, Ben. It's over."

"It can't be over! I won't let it be."

"You just don't have any idea—"

"I know what you mean to me. What we mean to each other."

"Ben, would you just listen to me for a minute?"

"I know I'm probably not being practical. But why should I be? We're in love, and—"

"Ben, you don't—"

"And I know that if we try we can—"

"Ben—"

"—do anything we want. We can make it work."

"Ben—"

"We can still get married, just like—"

"Ben, stop!"

"We can do it, Ellen, I know we can, if we—"

"Ben, I'm pregnant!"

Silence descended, like a sudden black curtain drawn across the sun. Like an immovable barrier that could not be crossed.

"You mean, we—"

"No, Ben. I don't mean *we* anything."

Ben heard a rustling in the apartment. "Who's in there?"

"No one."

"There is someone. You're not alone." He tried to push past her in the doorway, but she wouldn't let him through. "Who is it?"

Her eyes closed. "It's . . . Larry."

"Larry? Who the hell—"

"My boss. At the oil company."

Ben's face twisted up in anger and disgust. "You . . . and your boss?"

"It wasn't supposed to happen, Ben. It was an accident. Sort of. He'd been acting interested for months, and you and I were about to get married, and I—" She looked at him, her eyes wide and saddened. "I wasn't supposed to get pregnant. But I am."

"And—and it's Larry's—"

"Yes. Absolutely. But it's okay. He's agreed to marry me."

"He?" Ben reached out to her. "Marry *me,* Ellen—just as we planned. I don't care what happened. I'll take care of you. And the baby."

"Ben." She looked at him, and a soft smile trickled across her lips. "You know I love you—but you're just a kid. You can't even take care of yourself."

"And Larry—"

"Is older than we are. He's got a good executive seat with the oil company, a steady income. He's got one child already from a previous marriage. He wants to do the right thing by me." She paused, looking as though all the energy had drained out of her. "And I'm going to let him."

Ben grabbed her shoulders. "Ellen . . . please. I—I don't understand any of this. I don't know why you would—" He shook her helplessly back and forth. "My father's a doctor, and he knows lots of others. He's got lots of cash and—"

"No, Ben."

"Why would you marry some guy you don't love when you can still marry me? It's all arranged. We've got a church reservation, for God's sake. My parents and everyone will be here in two days."

"Ben! Haven't you told them it's off?"

"I—I couldn't do it until—I was sure—"

"Ben!" All at once, anger flared across her face. "This *is* sure. You and I are not getting married."

"But why not?"

Her eyes began to mist. "You just won't let this be easy, will you? Won't let me leave without—" She turned away, her lips trembling. "I want you to go away, Ben. I want you to leave me alone and never come back. I don't want to see you ever again. Ever!"

"But we could still—"

"Would you listen to me for once!" she screamed. *"Go away!"* She broke loose, then shoved him backward as hard as she could. Ben tumbled down the concrete steps onto the sidewalk.

Before he could pull himself off the pavement, he heard her door slam shut. All around, he saw neighbors peering out of their doors and windows, watching the show. He felt stupid and embarrassed and desperate. He felt as if a part of him had been torn away, like something had been ripped out of his body, more like he'd lost a limb than a lover.

He stood shakily, brushed himself off, and stared at the closed door. It really was over, he realized. After everything they'd shared, after feeling like he had never felt before. She wasn't his any longer.

She was gone. Forever.

CHAPTER
44

As a good Scotch-Irish-extraction Presbyterian, Christina didn't believe God intervened in the everyday minutiae of people's lives. Consequently, she didn't pray for positive outcomes from traffic lights, parking lots, Scrabble, basketball games, or criminal trials. Usually. This time, she was making an exception.

I can't promise to get me to a nunnery, she thought, eyes clenched shut. But I'll try to come up with something else good. Ministering to the poor. Caring for the sick. I'd offer to adopt a child, but I've already got Ben to take care of, and that's about the same thing.

"Ms. McCall," Judge Lacayo said, in clear, crisp tones that rang through the crowded courtroom. "Are you ready to proceed?"

"We are," she said, rising. "We call Johnny Christensen to the stand."

Ben had told her long ago that every trial had a pivotal moment, the one upon which everything depended. Usually that was the part of the trial that was most anticipated, the part the spectators—and the jury—had been waiting for. No question about what that was in this trial. They wanted to hear what Johnny Christensen had to say for himself. What he could possibly say for himself.

As before, Christina had put him in a good suit, but not too good. He was from a reasonably well-off family, and the jury knew it, but she didn't want them to feel as if he were trying to con them with the slick pantlines of Italian designers. Johnny looked as though he had made an effort—it would be disrespectful to do otherwise—but not as if he were trying to put anything over on them.

Johnny had been out in the corridor with the marshal when the judge called the case, and she did not envy Johnny his walk to the front of the courtroom. Must be like running the gauntlet. Just to his left was Mario Roma, growling and glaring and looking as if it was all he could do to keep from driving a stake through Johnny's heart. Gary Scholes and the other fraternity guys collectively turned their heads as he passed. Roger Hartnell looked as if he were about to cry. And in the very front row sat Johnny's mother, her head cradled in her hands, tears seeping through her fingers.

Must be the longest walk in the world.

Except for the one he'd be taking down death row, if this didn't go well.

"I DON'T HATE all homosexuals," Johnny said, his voice smooth and flat as a pane of glass. "I don't know why people keep calling this a hate crime. It wasn't."

"You are a member of the Christian Minutemen, correct?"

"Yes, and they don't hate homosexuals, either. It was like Gary said. We disapprove of the gay lifestyle. We think it's contrary to what God taught us through the Holy Scriptures. But that doesn't equal hate. I disapprove of people who cheat on their taxes, too. But I don't hate them."

Point made, and let's move on, Christina thought quietly. She wasn't going to give him a chance to get into any major philosophical exegesis. "But you don't deny that you participated in the beating of Tony Barovick."

"That's true. I admit it. It was wrong, but . . . I did it."

He even hung his head a bit, and Christina thought he looked genuinely sorry. Maybe he was remembering what Ben had told him about the importance of remorse. Or maybe he meant it—who could know?

"And you did it because he was gay?"

"No, we did it because he was a gay guy who came on to us. In public." He swiveled around in his chair, choosing this moment to make brief eye contact with the jurors. "I'm not saying I was right, or that I was justified, or anything like that. But you have to understand the situation. Here I was in this bar. It's a popular place. All my friends go there. All my fraternity brothers. And it's a singles bar—people go there to hook up. So I'm sitting there minding my own business, and this obviously, flamboyantly gay man comes up and starts propositioning me. More that that—starts making seriously crude suggestions and insinuations to me. And everyone can hear. Can you imagine what people thought?"

"So you were embarrassed?"

"More than that. I was humiliated. Thinking what it could do to me, if word got around. The stigma. The rumors. You can't fight that sort of thing, once it gets started. I had to make it clear that I didn't like it. And I had to make sure that it didn't happen again."

"So that's why you beat up Tony Barovick. To teach him a lesson?"

"That's how it started, yes." Johnny ran a hand along his smooth white cheek. He was a handsome boy, especially when he'd scrubbed up a bit. It wasn't hard to believe someone might single him out in a bar. "I admit—it got way out of control. We'd both been drinking. I don't do that much and I'm not used to it. Still, the really crazy, mean stuff—that was Brett's doing, and I'm not just saying that because he isn't here. And I'm not saying that means I'm not responsible. But I tried to get Brett to stop, I really did. I tried to get him to slow down, cool off. But he wouldn't listen to me. He just kept at that kid, and he acted like if I didn't participate—then maybe I was gay, too."

"So you're saying Brett Mathers was the principal actor during the beating?"

"He did the worst of it. I admit I was willing to punch the guy around a few times. But all that extreme stuff was Brett's idea. He was the one who brought the Taser. He was the one who brought the hammer. His finger-prints were found on the hammer—only his. It was his idea to break the kid's legs. I thought that was way too cruel—almost insane. And I tried to stop him—I really did. Tried hard. But Brett wouldn't listen."

"When did the beating finally stop?"

"After he broke both legs. After that, the anger seemed to wash out of Brett. Maybe he realized he'd gone too far. Plus, that poor man's screaming and wailing in pain was so loud—I think it kind of woke Brett up from whatever weird psycho state he was in. He grabbed all his stuff and said, 'Let's get out of here.' And we did."

"Where did you go?"

"Back to the house. We hung out for about an hour, then I went for a walk. To clear my head. Then Brett and I went back to Remote Control. A few minutes later, four more guys from our frat house arrived. They joined our table."

"And that was where you . . . bragged about what you had done?"

"Brett bragged. Mostly, I just sat still and kept my mouth closed. Nodded occasionally."

"Did you speak out against what had happened? Con-demn it. Express your regrets?"

"No." His eyes fell toward the floor. "I wish I had. I was feeling really guilty about what had happened. I knew we hadn't done right. I knew—we'd sinned. But I couldn't tell my brothers that. I had to play along."

"How long were you there?"

"Not all that long—I don't know exactly. But about

11:10 or so, the guilt I was feeling became so overpowering I couldn't stand it anymore. I had to get up—had to go somewhere. So I left the bar."

"And you went? . . ."

"I can't explain it, but—all at once, I knew what I had to do. I had to see my mother."

"Were the two of you close?"

"Not at the time. I'd been a real jerk to her lately. But—she was still my mother, you know? That's how I thought of her. So I went to her place. It's very near campus."

"And what happened there?"

"It was pretty much just as she described it. I wasn't looking to be forgiven—I knew I didn't deserve that. I just had to tell someone. And I suppose—" He looked up, his eyes misting. "I suppose deep down somewhere I knew that your mother always loves you. No matter what you've done. No matter how horrible it is."

Christina stared at the witness, wanting to be cynical about his testimony, but finding herself unable to do so. He seemed amazingly genuine—too good to be faked. And she considered herself a pretty good judge of character. Maybe this boy wasn't quite as heartless as he let on.

"How long were you at your mother's home?"

"Only about ten minutes. It was enough. Then I returned to the bar. It was—I don't know—another half hour or so before the group started to break up—and the cops stepped in."

"Did you resist arrest?"

"Not in the least. I knew what I'd done. I didn't clam up or demand a lawyer or any of that. I figured—I hurt someone. I'll do my time."

"Then what happened?"

"What happened was they didn't charge me with assault or battery—they charged me with murder! I tried to explain to them that we didn't kill him. We didn't beat him so badly he might die from it, either. I know we gave him a hard time, but there's no way the beating was fatal. Something else must've happened to him. After we left."

"Did you explain that to the police?"

"Of course. But they didn't listen. As far as they were concerned, they had two suspects who had confessed. They didn't want any complications."

Good enough, Christina thought. Maybe not quite a sow's ear into a silk purse, but the best she could hope for with this witness and these facts. "Johnny, how do feel now about what you did on that night?"

"Objection," Drabble said, breaking the spell they were casting for the first time. "The facts are relevant. His feelings are not."

"In this case, I disagree," Christina replied. "The prosecutor's motive is all about how my client supposedly felt. Most of his opening statement was a long rant about how my client supposedly feels. What he believes. How it motivated him. I think we're entitled to rebut."

Judge Lacayo pondered for a longer than average time before answering. "It is unusual, but I think Ms. McCall's point is not without merit. And I think this will be of interest—and perhaps of use—to the jury."

In sentencing, Christina thought. That's what he's thinking. The jury will want to know how he feels now when they decide later whether to give him the needle.

"The objection is overruled," Lacayo said. "The witness may answer."

"I'm very sorry about what I did," Johnny said, his voice raw and earnest. "Truly sorry. There's no excuse for it. Even though I didn't do the worst parts. But I watched them being done. And I didn't prevent them. I know it's not an excuse, but I really am not used to drinking like I had that night, and I think it somehow . . . sort of drained my will. I was just going along when I should've been resisting." He looked first at the jurors, then out into the gallery. "I truly regret what I did, and I believe I should be punished for it. I will accept any punishment for it. The only thing I ask is—don't punish me for a crime I didn't commit. I did not kill Tony Barovick. I did not cause his death. Brett did not cause his death. His death could not have resulted from the beating we gave him." He turned his eyes back to the jury. "And that's the God's honest truth."

AFTER THE DIRECT, Judge Lacayo called for a recess. Christina was glad for the chance to relax and tell Johnny how well he was doing—but she was not pleased to see Drabble get additional time to plan his cross. By the time the trial resumed, he was ready.

"You admit that you participated in a beating of the deceased, Tony Barovick, that lasted about thirty minutes, right?" It was interesting how Drabble's body language had changed, Christina noted. With his own witnesses, of course, he was friendly and open. Even with Ellen Christensen, he was gentle, respectful. But now his body was stiff and tense, his gestures were hard and direct, and his voice was cold, unyielding. Exactly what the jury would want him to be.

"I admit that, yes," Johnny said cautiously.

"And you say you did this not out of hatred for homosexuals, but because this particular homosexual made advances toward you."

"I'm not saying it was right, but . . . yes. That's what triggered it."

"And now we're supposed to believe you're sorry about what you did, and just say, well, no harm, no foul?"

"Objection," Christina said, rising. "Argumentative."

"Overruled," Lacayo responded. Judging from his manner, he had as little confidence in Johnny's contrition as Drabble.

"I am sorry," Johnny said. Somehow, even though his testimony hadn't changed, it played differently when Drabble stood behind the podium. Now Johnny's voice seemed thin, even strident. As if he were working to convince rather than simply explaining. "I mean that."

"And when did you have this sudden epiphany that you had done something wrong?"

Johnny tossed his shoulders. "I think I knew it all along. That's why I had to see my mother. Absolutely I knew it was wrong when Brett started . . . seriously hurting that man. When it was all over, I felt terrible."

"Mr. Christensen," Drabble said, one hand on his hip, "would you care to guess how many witnesses I have who will testify that you were bragging about what you did at Remote Control?"

He hesitated. "I . . . don't know."

"Come on, take a guess. I'll give you a hint—it's a two-digit number."

"Most of that was Brett."

"But not all of it."

"No," Johnny said quietly. "Not all of it."

"Why?" The sarcasm in Drabble's voice was unmistakable. "If you were so stricken with grief, so burdened with the horror of what you had done, why would you brag about it in that bar?"

"I was with my friends. Brett and Gary and the others. I suppose I was trying to impress them."

"Of course, we've heard Gary Scholes testify that he was anything but impressed by what he heard. He said he found your bragging heartless and grotesque."

"I wish he'd told me that."

"Maybe an hour later, when Officer Montgomery interrogated you, he said you were similarly lacking any remorse for what you had done."

"The cops aren't going to give me any breaks," Johnny answered. "They were and are determined to nail me to the wall."

"Imagine that." Drabble picked up a thick document bound between leather covers that Christina knew to be the transcript of the interrogation. "So did you or did you not express any of this sorrow when you were questioned?"

"I really don't remember."

"Well," Drabble said, turning the pages, "do you recall saying repeatedly, 'He asked for it! All he got was what he asked for!' "

"I . . . might've said that."

"I have to tell you, Johnny—that doesn't sound particularly contrite to me."

"I was just trying to explain—"

"Here's another one," Drabble said, flipping to another page. "Apologies to the court for the language, but I think the jury needs to hear it as it was spoken. You said, 'That goddamn queen touched me. He touched me! So I touched him back. Hard.' "

"I was still with Brett when I said that," Johnny said. "I suppose I was trying to impress him. I didn't want him to think I was weak."

"And here's my favorite," Drabble said, ignoring him. " 'God hates queers. That's why he sent AIDS. And that's why he sent me.' "

"Look, I was very upset that night. I'd been drinking, and it was late, and I wasn't thinking straight and—"

"And you just accidentally beat to death someone you hated and then acted self-righteous about it."

"No!" Johnny insisted. "It wasn't like that. I *was* sorry—"

"Why? After all, that flaming queen touched you."

"I don't know why I said that. I didn't mean—"

"I suppose you had to do something to speed things along, since AIDS wasn't doing it fast enough."

"That's not what I meant!" Johnny insisted, and each time he did Christina knew he sounded less persuasive. Drabble was ramming the kid's own words down his throat—probably the most effective cross-ex technique imaginable. "I've told you already what I felt, and what I believe. But I would never have done any serious harm to him."

"Right. Because all the serious harm was done by Brett."

"That's true!"

"All you did was rough him up a bit. Maybe cracked a few ribs, that's all."

"I did not—"

"Maybe cut him with your knife."

"That's not true, either."

"Isn't it?" Drabble glanced down at his notes. "It was your knife, wasn't it? You tried to push the hammer off on Brett, but the knife was yours. Right?"

Johnny's face began to sag. "Yes. It was mine. Just a Swiss Army knife that my—"

"According to the coroner's report," Drabble said, reading, " 'Tony Barovick was cut by knife in twelve different places.' Does that sound accurate?"

"I . . . don't remember."

"Twelve lacerations is not an accident, Mr. Christensen. That's the work of someone who is enjoying it."

"They weren't serious injuries! None of them. Just little cuts. They couldn't have killed him."

"No. They would've just hurt a lot. Possibly scarred him for life. And terrified him."

"I—suppose."

"So your defense is you weren't trying to kill him. You were only torturing him."

"Objection!" Christina shouted.

"I'll withdraw that," Drabble said, moving on before anyone could take a breath. "Now you've admitted you brought the knife to the party, but you claim the Taser was Brett's, correct?"

"Absolutely."

"But that isn't true, is it?" Christina felt a cold chill.

She didn't like the way Drabble said that at all. This was going to be bad; Drabble wouldn't accuse a witness of lying unless he had the goods.

"It is true. Brett was the one—"

"Mr. Christensen, take a look at this receipt from the P & J Pawn Shop." He passed it to the witness. "As you can see, it's for the purchase of a used Taser. Doesn't give a name, but we traced the credit card number." He looked up and smiled. "Guess who?"

Johnny looked like a fox surrounded by hounds. "We'd had a break-in at the fraternity house. We thought we needed some way to protect ourselves. Something that wouldn't be too dangerous to have around."

"Is that so."

"I was the floor chairman, so it was my job. I found the Taser."

"So it belonged to you."

"It belonged to the fraternity."

"You bought it."

"That's right."

"And you just happened to bring it along the night of March 22. Just in case you ran into any flaming queens."

"No! We kept it in the house. And Brett was the one who brought it that night. I didn't even know—"

"You were responsible for that Taser, weren't you?"

"Yes, but—"

"Thank you, Mr. Christensen. You've answered my question."

Christina looked across the table at Ben. She didn't need advanced body-reading skills to know what he was thinking.

"One last thing," Drabble said. "I know I was touched by your heartwarming reaffirmation of the importance of motherhood and how you turned to your mother when times were tough."

"It was because I felt so bad," Johnny said. "I was sorry for what—"

"Yes, yes, I'm sure. Here's my problem, though. If you went to see your mother, why didn't you mention it to the police?"

The silence that blanketed the courtroom was louder than any amount of shouting could be.

"I don't quite understand . . ."

"I read this transcript from start to finish last night, Mr. Christensen," Drabble continued. "I watched the interrogation video. And at no time do you mention being at your mother's. Not even after you're told when the estimated time of death was."

"I . . . was trying to leave her out of it."

"Why?"

"I just didn't want her involved."

"You thought you could be arrested for murder and your mother wouldn't be involved?"

"I didn't want to drag her into the—"

"So you had an alibi witness, but chose not to mention it? Very noble."

"I didn't know then how bad this would get."

"You're telling me—and the jury—that you knew you had a witness who could testify to being with you at the time of Tony Barovick's death, yet you chose not to tell anyone? Because you have such a strong sense of family loyalty?"

"I was trying to protect her!"

"Mr. Christensen, don't lie to us."

"I'm not."

"You didn't tell the police about going to your mother's house because you didn't go anywhere near your mother's house."

"That's not true!"

"You went back to the fraternity house and finished what you had started."

"I didn't!"

"It must've really bothered you, sitting there thinking that flaming queen was still alive. Your own fraternity brother heard you say you were going to finish what you started."

"It wasn't like that."

"And if you thought you could impress your friends by saying you beat that boy up, imagine how popular you'd be if you could say you killed him."

"That's not what happened!"

"Objection!" Christina shouted. "Badgering the witness."

"You had the motive and the opportunity," Drabble continued.

"The objection is sustained," Judge Lacayo said firmly.

Drabble pressed on. "You wanted Tony Barovick dead. Like you want all gay people dead. So you killed him."

"I did not!" Johnny screamed. He was sweating, his voice was strained, he seemed shaken and terrified and—

Christina couldn't pretend otherwise. And guilty.

"I said, the objection is sustained!" Lacayo barked, slamming his gavel.

"Sorry, your honor," Drabble said, suddenly quiet. He closed his notebook, then let his eyes wander toward the jury box. "No more questions."

CHAPTER
45

BEN HAD BEEN in Chicago only a week, but Garfield, the elderly gentleman working the courthouse snack bar, recognized him from the opposite end of the corridor. And the expression on Ben's face was apparently sufficient to tell him exactly what was called for.

"One chocolate milk, ice cold, coming up," he said.

"Make it a double," Ben groused.

"Bad?"

"Real bad. Lethal-injection bad."

Garfield winced. "Sorry to hear that." He passed the cup. "Here's your drink."

Ben took a long swallow. "Thanks. I needed that. Guess you must think this is pretty wimpy. A grown man, drinking chocolate milk."

Garfield laughed, rubbing a hand on his stubbled chin. "Hey, after the stuff I've seen some of the other attorneys drinking—or smelled on their breath—I'm relieved to see you sticking with the milk."

Before he could take another swallow, Ben felt a hand on his arm. Funny how he knew who it was, even before he looked. "Ben, we have to talk."

He looked at Ellen coldly. "That used to be my line."

"Johnny didn't do well, did he?"

Ben took another drink. "He did about as well as could be expected. It was an impossible situation. There's too much evidence against him. And too much of it came from his own mouth."

"You can't believe he killed that boy."

"It doesn't matter what I believe."

"He couldn't have. I know he couldn't have."

"Ellen . . ."

"There must be more you can do."

"After the break, Christina will redirect, but that's damage control at best."

"Aren't there any other witnesses? Someone who will speak on Johnny's behalf?"

"We have a doctor who will say that the beating, as described by Johnny and his late friend Brett, would not necessarily have been fatal."

"And that's it?"

"Two professors willing to appear as character witnesses."

"Nothing more?"

"Ellen, believe me when I say we've searched high and low. We've turned every stone. We haven't found any miracle witness. And frankly—I think that's because the miracle witness doesn't exist."

Long tapered fingers spread across her face.

"I'll give it all I can in closing," Ben continued. "I'll hammer away about reasonable doubt. The prosecution only has indirect evidence that Johnny caused Tony Barovick's death. It's possible that some juror might find that insufficient."

"But you don't think so."

Ben stared down into those black eyes, the dark pools that had once meant so much to him. There was still something there, no matter how hard he tried to pretend there wasn't, no matter how determined he was to deny that there had ever been any trace of affection.

"No, Ellen," he said quietly. "I don't think so. I think the jury will convict."

"Would you? If you were on the jury? Would you find him guilty?"

Ben didn't see how any good could come of answering that question. So he didn't.

"SHELLY!" MIKE BELLOWED.

Shelly Chimka froze in her tracks, just outside the front entrance to Remote Control. "Yes?"

Mike ran up to her, Swift and Baxter close behind. "Where have you been? I've been looking for you all over town!"

"I went to Springfield to visit a girlfriend. I told Mario I wouldn't—"

"You didn't tell him where you were going."

"Why would I?"

"Don't give us that innocent routine," Swift said. "You know you're a material witness. You were told not to leave town."

"I didn't, really. It was just Springfield." Her face scrunched up. "What's this all about, anyway?"

"This is about you," Mike said, gazing down at her right arm, still tucked into the blue sling. "And something that's bothered me since the first time I talked with you. You told me, not to mention an investigator named Loving, that you tried to commit suicide after Tony was killed. But something about that never seemed right to me. You may well have been close to Tony, but you don't seem the suicidal type, and your face gave off all the wrong signals when you said it. You're much too pragmatic. Too controlled."

"Excuse me?"

"It's a compliment, lady. But it left me with a major problem. If you didn't really try to off yourself, what happened to your arm?"

Shelly instinctively pulled the sling close to her. "I don't see why it matters to you."

"Oh, I think it matters a lot," Mike said. The three of them closed around her. "You told me you tried to kill yourself the night after Tony was killed, but Mario Roma says that the next time you came to work—the very next morning after the incident—your arm was already in a sling."

"He's misremembering."

"I don't think so. I've been reading Tony Barovick's journal. The last thing he records—the last thing he wrote before going off to his death—was that he had a phone call from you. Coincidence?" Mike shook his head. "I don't think so. Not anymore."

"You're way out of line."

"Are we?" Baxter asked. "Why did you call Tony?"

"I—I—hardly remember."

"Give me a break. Last time you talked to him before he's killed, and you don't remember what you called about?"

Shelly's eyes darted back and forth, searching for an avenue of escape. "It was just . . . just . . . some work thing."

"Cut the crap," Mike growled, pushing his nose into her face. "Someone else might go soft on you because you're cute and perky, but I don't give a damn about any of that. All I see is a liar. And now I want the truth!"

"Oh . . . God!" she gasped. She began to tremble, sobbing at a nearly hysterical pitch. "I didn't want to do it! They made me!"

"I'm sure they did," Swift said, wrapping an arm around her. "Now let's go inside and talk about it."

TWENTY MINUTES AND two cups of coffee later, Shelly had herself sufficiently under control that she could tell them her story without breaking down. And no one would dream of interrupting her. Because what she had to say was incredible.

"They came to my apartment, after my shift." She sat on a sofa in the break room behind the kitchen of the club. "I was getting ready for a date—all alone, totally vulnerable. Two men. They threw me down on the sofa." Her face turned ash white, just from the memory. "I thought they were going to kill me."

"What did they do?"

"They said things, called me ugly names, and they . . . touched me. Pawed me. One of them jerked up my shirt, and—and—he had a knife and—oh, God, I was so scared! I was afraid—"

"I can imagine," Baxter said, trying to calm her. "It sounds horrible."

"What did they want?" Mike asked.

"They wanted Tony. Poor Tony." Tears seeped from her eyes. "They wanted me to call him up, get him to come over to my place."

"Did they say why?"

"Not exactly. But they kept calling Tony their partner. Said they'd been working on something together."

"Did they say what?"

"No. But there was a lot of money involved. And a kid. Several times they referred to a kid."

Mike, Swift, and Baxter all exchanged looks.

"Why not just wait till Tony left the club after work?"

"Because then he would be with Roger, his boyfriend. They wanted him to leave alone."

"Was Manny Nowosky one of the men?" Mike asked.

She nodded. "With someone else. That chicken I'd seen in the bar."

"So what happened? Did you do it?"

"I didn't want to!" Her face was stricken, contorted by grief. "I refused, several times. Told them I wouldn't help them."

"And then?"

"One of them—Manny—knocked me across the face. Called me a dirty little bitch and told me I would do what he said or he'd hurt me. Hurt me bad."

"So you called."

"Not at first! I held out as long as I could. I told them I couldn't, wouldn't know what to say. Manny got really mad."

"Did he . . . hurt you?"

"Not just then. He and the other guy argued for a long time. Manny said he wanted to take me apart, limb by limb. Wanted to hurt me and hurt me till I would beg for the chance to do what they wanted. Then, suddenly, the argument ended. Manny grabbed my arm and jerked me into the kitchen. He pulled a butcher knife out of the drawer and—and—" She threw herself down, her face pressed against a sofa cushion. "He cut me! Don't you understand? He cut me!"

Mike motioned to Swift, encouraging her to try to comfort the woman. He was useless when it came to this kind of trauma.

Shelly continued. "He slashed my wrist. Not so bad I would die, but the pain was incredible. He wanted me to tell Tony I'd tried to kill myself, that I was losing blood fast. He knew that would get him out of the club and over here in a hurry." Another wave of tears followed. "And I did it. God help me, but I did it."

"You had no choice," Swift said softly, stroking her hair. "None at all."

"Manny listened in with the knife at my throat the whole time. I told Tony I'd been depressed and I'd slashed my wrist and I didn't know what to do. Of course, he said he'd come right over. He was always so good. He loved me, he really did. And I loved him." She buried her face again. "So he left the club in a hurry. Alone. Don't you see? I killed him! Just as much as anyone. It was my fault!"

"That's absurd," Swift said, cradling the distraught woman in her arms. "It was not your fault."

"This is all well and good," Baxter said, "but why didn't you say anything about it before now?"

"I think I can answer that question," Mike answered. "You didn't want to see those two men again."

"I was so scared," Shelly said. She was rocking back and forth, hugging her knees. "So terrified they would return. Even after I knew Manny and Charlie were dead. He killed Tony. And Manny, right?"

"Probably," Mike acknowledged. "And Charlie."

"And he would've killed me, if I'd told you what happened. I didn't like lying. But I had no choice. After I bandaged my wrist, I put my arm in a sling to try to conceal what had happened. I started telling people that I'd hurt myself, hysterical about what had happened to Tony. Any story. Just so no one would know what had really happened."

"Can't blame you for that," Mike said quietly. "A lot tougher types than you would've caved if something like that had happened to them."

"I'm still not getting this," Baxter said. "We know those two fraternity creeps beat up Tony after he left the club. Did Manny and his pals know they were after him? Were they all working together?"

"I don't think that's possible," Mike answered. "More likely the frat boys got to Tony before Manny had a chance."

"Lucky day for Tony Barovick," Swift said ruefully. "People waiting in line to hurt him."

"That's his reward for partnering with murderous thugs," Mike replied. He pulled his cell phone out of his coat pocket and started dialing. "That Christensen kid has been saying all along he and his friend didn't kill Tony, but no one believed him. Including me." He punched in a phone number. "Damn it. I hate it when Ben and Christina are right."

"Hello?" said Ben's voice on the other end of the phone.

"Good afternoon, counselor," Mike answered. "Court adjourned for the day?"

"Just a break."

"How's it looking?"

"Like our client is going down hard, barring a miracle."

"Well," Mike said, casting a look around the room, "I know I'm never going to convince you that I'm an angel. But I may have just the miracle you've been looking for."

CHAPTER
46

"DO YOU THINK this is going to work?" Christina whispered to Ben as she saw the bailiff emerging from the judge's chambers.

"I don't know," he said, lips tight. Christina knew the expression—it was a sign his brain was working, probably several steps ahead of hers. "Coming this late in the game, I'm afraid the jury won't believe it. It would be better if we could produce the fourth man, the remaining kidnapper."

"Well, yes, I'm sure the police would like that, too. But how do you plan to accomplish it?"

"I've got an idea, but it's risky."

"Ben, there will be no second chance. If we don't do something immediately, the case will end, it will go to the jury, Johnny will be on death row, and all the evidence on heaven and earth won't be enough to get him out."

"True." He hesitated. "I should probably run this by Mike first." He shook his head. "But he'd never permit it."

Judge Lacayo called the court back into session. "Ms. McCall, I understand you have an additional witness to call who is not on your list?"

"Yes, your honor." Christina rose to her feet. "We call Shelly Chimka to the stand."

Drabble was predictably outraged. He moaned about sleazy defense tricks and fair notice and the pointlessness of submitting witness lists if the parties weren't going to be bound by them. But in chambers, Christina produced Major Mike Morelli, who assured the judge that this witness had just been found, and furthermore that her testimony was not only critical to the case but that a gross miscarriage of justice might result if the witness was not heard. Under those circumstances, the judge had little choice.

All things considered, Shelly did an admirable job on the stand. Ben and Christina'd had little time to prepare her, and this was only the second time she'd told her story to anyone. But it was spellbinding, just the same. The jury hung on her every word. Christina couldn't be sure whether they believed her. But they were definitely listening.

"Did the two men who attacked you ever say what it was they were planning to do to Tony?"

Shelly took a deep breath, tried to steady herself. "Not in so many words. But it was clear they weren't planning to give him a big kiss and a hug. They kept saying that Tony had betrayed them. One time Manny said, 'I'll teach that little creep what happens when he holds out on his partners.' "

"What happened after you made the phone call?"

"That was all they wanted from me. Manny took the hilt of the butcher knife and hit me on the head—hard. I fell to the floor. I guess I passed out for a while—I'm not sure how long. I was already woozy from loss of blood. When I woke up, I bandaged myself. It was nasty, but not fatal. As soon as I could, I called Remote Control. But by that time it was one in the morning. Tony was already dead."

Christina nodded solemnly. "And you have no idea who the other man was?"

"I don't. I wish I did. But they were very careful never to call one another by name. I have no way of knowing."

"I understand," Christina said gently. "Thank you for testifying. I know how hard it must have been for you."

"It was the least I could do," she replied. "For Tony. I'll never be able to forgive myself for what I did to him. Even if he was involved with these kidnappers, the Tony I knew was kind, and gentle and . . . and he took care of me. Always. But when it came time for me to do something for him—I failed. Miserably." Tears filled her eyes. "And now he's gone. And he's never coming back."

NEEDLESS TO SAY, the reporters were riveted by this sudden, unforeseen development in the case. It had been juicy enough to attract major media attention when it was an antigay hate crime. Now that it had morphed and linked itself to a notorious kidnapping, the interest rate doubled. The media scrambled, trying to figure out how to spin the new developments. They'd been treating Tony Barovick as if he were a martyred angel; now it appeared he was considerably less angelic. Did that make his death less a tragedy?

In a rare acquiescence, Ben agreed to hold a press conference in the ground floor lobby of the courthouse. While the court clerk set up the conference platform, Ben conferred with Judge Lacayo's bailiff, Boxer Johnson.

"So you're available?"

"If you say so," the sturdy man replied. Ben only hoped he looked as good as Johnson when he was in his fifties. "Think I should bring my weapon?"

"Oh yeah. Bring several."

A few moments later, Ben stepped up to the platform. First, he read a prepared statement, then he took questions. The first few were softballs that he handled with no difficulty. But that didn't last long.

"This new development has taken us all by surprise—

and left some observers extremely dubious, if not down-right cynical," a CNN reporter said.

"Can't say that I'm surprised," Ben answered. "We live in a cynical world."

"When did you get the first indication that this murder was linked to the Metzger kidnapping?"

"We've had prior indications from an officer with the Tulsa PD that there might be a connection between this murder and two subsequent ones. We first believed there was a connection to an Ecstasy drug ring, but we had no evidence. It was only today that we learned about the connection to the Metzger kidnapping."

"Mr. Kincaid," the reporter from ABC chimed in, "the parents of Tony Barovick have released a statement saying that 'this is a typical trick of a desperate lawyer. We all know who killed Tony. Why are we putting up with this?' "

"With due respect to the Barovicks, who have suffered a horrible loss, they do not know who killed Tony. All they know is what the police have told them. And the police were wrong. I understand the need for the bereaved to seek closure, or at least retribution. But we can't convict the wrong man just to please his parents."

"I notice the prosecutor has not dropped the case," noted a reporter holding a Fox News mike. "What do you think it will take to convince him you're right?"

Ben took a moment before answering. "I think we're going to have to produce the fourth man. The other kidnapper. The one who's still at large."

"But you don't know who he is."

"That's where you're wrong," Ben said. "The kidnapper may think he's safe. He may think he's pulled off the perfect crime. But he hasn't. I know who he is. And tomorrow morning in court—I'll prove it."

* * *

HE SNAPPED OFF the television. Well, that didn't leave him much choice, did it? The time to act—finally and decisively—had arrived.

He wasn't sure whether Kincaid was telling the truth. It could be some kind of trick or trap. But he couldn't take the risk, could he? And he had been wanting to take the damn lawyers out, anyway. Toying with them obviously hadn't been enough. He had to deliver a more final solution. So why not now? He just had to make sure he avoided whatever little defenses Kincaid might've arranged. And the best way to do that was to strike fast—before he expected it.

They should never have left Oklahoma, he thought, chuckling as he loaded his gun. Come to the big city and rub shoulders with the big boys—and two hicks from the scrubs are bound to get hurt. Permanently.

Zero hour had arrived. They would be so sorry they came to Chicago—in those final nanoseconds before he blew their brains out.

CHAPTER
47

JOURNAL OF TONY BAROVICK

ONE NIGHT, CLAUDIA Brenner came into Remote Control. I was stunned. I recognized her immediately, of course. She's the woman who was hiking in Pennsylvania on the Appalachian Trail in 1988 with her girlfriend when a couple of backwoods freaks saw them making out and registered their displeasure—with a rifle. Her partner was killed; Claudia was seriously wounded. She wrote a book about it, *Eight Bullets,* probably the most moving testament I've read in my entire life. It was that book that inspired me to start keeping this journal. Not that anything that dramatic ever happened to me, or is even likely to. Sure, I know there are still people who don't like gays. But I can't imagine anything like that happening here. Not here.

Anyway, so I got a chance to talk to this woman, and she was incredible. I kept blathering on about how she was my hero and what an incredible role model she was. I probably made a gigantic jackass of myself, but she was nice about it. And when she left, I felt inspired.

I'd never been involved in gay politics. At first, because I didn't want anyone to know I was gay, and later, because I was busy with other things. And I suppose if I were honest about it, I'd have to admit that I'm not that political. It doesn't interest me much. But the thing is— gay rights doesn't seem political to me. Treating people

the same, not discriminating based upon sexual preference—is that political? Does that split down political
lines? That's not about Democrats and Republicans;
that's about human rights, about taking the freedoms
we claim are the philosophical basis of this nation and
making them real.

Ever since that night, I've been involved. I'm still not
what you'd call a big activist, but I try to do my part. I
joined the local Gay & Lesbian Alliance. I've marched in
their parades. I've even allowed them to hold some of
their meetings in the bar, in the back caverns.

The religious types still come to Remote Control,
which they perceive as a den of premarital lust and for-
nication, and they rattle on a lot about Judgment Day. I
don't know what Judgment Day is or will be, but I think
it's got to be more than just the celestial accountant tal-
lying up how many times you went to church. Surely,
at some point, what's more important is what you
felt. What you thought. What you held in your heart.
Whether you tried to make people happier, tried to
make their lives easier.

I firmly believe that most people are good at heart,
that they want to be good. It's hard sometimes, what
with ignorance and peer pressure and all our basest instincts constantly being hung out to dry. But I also know
that the world is changing. For the better. So many of
the evils that have plagued humanity since the dawn of
time have been eradicated. Slavery, racial discrimination,
gender discrimination, exploitation of children. With all
the good that is happening, how long can prejudice and
bigotry against gay and lesbian people survive? How
long can it be before we too shall be released? If being
part of the Alliance has made me realize anything, it is
that when all is said and done, people who hate gays
aren't prejudiced because of some obscure passage in the
Book of Leviticus. This prejudice, like every other prejudice, is based on the fact that we are different from

them. They don't care that mankind was made in God's image; they want the world to be made in *their* image. Bottom line, they get uptight because I'm not just like them. And that scares them. And scared bunnies do crazy things.

CHAPTER
48

"Is BEN HERE?" Loving said breathlessly as he ran through the front doors of their temporary offices.

"No," Jones said, looking down a long nose. "Could I possibly serve as a substitute?"

"I need Ben. When do you expect him back?"

"How should I know? He never tells me anything."

Loving's eyes widened. "Didn'tcha see the press conference? It was on television."

"As if I have time for television," Jones grunted. "Someone has to keep this office afloat." He paused, a puzzled expression on his face. "Ben gave a press conference? I thought he considered that the hallmark of sleaze."

"So you don't know nothin' 'bout what happened in the courtroom today?"

"As I said—"

"You're not gonna believe it. This case has had more twists and turns than the Million Dollar Highway." Loving continued recounting the day's events. It was only a matter of moments before Jones became so entranced he turned away from his computer monitor. After a minute, he dropped his pencil, hanging on every word. He was so wrapped up in Loving's account that he didn't even look up when the front door chime sounded.

The visitor crossed the front lobby and approached Jones's desk.

". . . and once Ben proves who the fourth partner is, my bookie's laying three-to-one odds that the judge—" He stopped abruptly as the visitor entered his field of vision. "Psst. Jones."

The visitor was a large man. His posture spoke of strength and power and a blustery sort of confidence. He was wearing a nondescript blue suit with a bland black tie. About the only noteworthy thing about him was his face—or lack thereof. He was wearing a mask, one of those cheap plastic Halloween masks that come from discount toy stores. Jones couldn't be certain, but he thought he was looking into the simulated face of Captain Kirk.

"May I help you?"

"Yes," said the deep voice behind the mask. "I'd like you both to come with me."

A deep furrow crossed Jones's brow. "Come where?"

"I can't tell you that."

Jones and Loving exchanged a look. "Then . . . why would we want to come?"

The man's hand emerged from his suit coat pocket holding a small revolver. "Because if you don't, I'll have to kill you."

BEN AND CHRISTINA trudged from the parking lot back to the building where Kevin Mahoney had his offices. Ben was carrying a large and heavy banker's box. Christina was hauling a catalog case in each hand.

"Have I mentioned that this is the worst part of any trial?" Ben said.

"Only every day," Christina grunted back.

"I don't know why they won't let us keep our stuff in the courtroom."

"Because it isn't safe. If something happened to it, they don't want you trying to blame the court because your case goes south. Besides, you never know what you'll need to prep for the next day."

Christina dropped one of the cases and opened the glass lobby door. "At least this time around we have Vicki—an extra set of hands and an extra car. That saves at least two or three trips a day." She gathered up the case with a grunt. "She's a bit on the timid side, of course, but she sure gets the job done. And her French is excellent."

Ben grinned. "And that's important when you're trying a brutal homicide case."

"Civility is always important," Christina replied airily.

They entered the elevator and rode up to the floor where they were borrowing space from Mahoney. When they entered the office, they found it deserted.

"I expected all of Kevin's people to be gone this late in the day. But where's Jones?" Christina asked.

"Or Loving? Dunno." Ben scratched his head. "Jones is usually right at the door waiting for us, so he can give me his complaints of the day."

Christina smiled. "He gives me doughnuts."

"I guess we know where his heart lies." Ben left his materials by the door—so they could be more easily carted back to court again tomorrow morning—then headed back to his office. He'd been there maybe ten minutes when he heard the front door chime.

Who would be coming in at this time of night? he wondered. It was way too late for business visitors. Probably just Jones returning from whatever errand he was on. Maybe a reporter. Or Ellen. Or . . . there was one other possibility. He clapped his side coat pocket. He was ready, in any case.

He pushed out of his chair and approached the door. He was almost through it when a man entered—wearing a Halloween mask.

Ben drew back. "Excuse me. What are you—"

The man did not wait for him to finish. He shoved Ben

back, hard. Ben fell against his desk, the edge slamming into him.

Ben didn't waste a second. He reached into his coat pocket and withdrew a small handheld radio. "Boxer? *Now!* Call the police and come!"

The man in the mask knocked the radio out of his hand. "Would you by chance be calling Boxer Johnson?"

Ben felt his mouth go dry.

The man reached into his coat and removed another radio, just like the one Ben had, then a black leather wallet. "Boxer Johnson, age fifty-five, blue eyes, one hundred and seventy-five pounds, eyesight restriction." He threw the wallet into Ben's face. "Bad news, Kincaid. He won't be coming."

Ben pressed back against the desk, trying to get as far as possible from the man. "Who are you? What do you want?"

"Oh, but you already know that, don't you? This is your party, after all."

"I don't know what—"

"Don't treat me like a jerk." He drew his hand back and slapped Ben hard across the face. "You set this up, with your little press conference. You knew I'd have no choice but to come after you. I wasn't going to let you screw everything up. Not after all the work, all the . . . killing. Maybe you thought I'd wait till you left the office, but I figured I better move quick, before it's too late. Before you were ready. First, I took out your two little friends. But I kept telling myself, this kid Kincaid can't be this stupid. He's practically inviting me to come after him. He must have backup. So after you went into the office, I sat back and waited. And sure enough, as predictable as clockwork, your rear guard showed up, chatting into his little radio, making his rounds."

"If you've hurt him—"

"Oh, I've hurt him all right. I hurt him good, like he

won't forget for a long time. If he can remember anything."

"Ben, have you got the ex—" Christina stepped through the doorway, then froze. A millisecond later, she turned to run. The man in the mask whirled around, grabbed her arm. As she tried to pull away, he jerked her backward. Ben knew that it hurt; he could see it in her eyes. She flew backward and careered into the desk beside him.

"And here's the pretty one," he said, contempt dripping from his voice. "I might have a little fun with you, before it's over. Or after."

"I don't know who you are or what—"

He slapped her, silencing her. "You may be an innocent victim of your boss's little prank. But you're going to suffer just as bad." He grabbed Ben by the collar, shaking him. "Did you think you could fuck with me? With *me*? You little punk." He threw Ben back with disgust. "This is going to be a pleasure." He pulled a revolver out of his coat pocket and pressed it against the side of Ben's skull. "Gonna take away all your troubles, lawyer-boy. You should thank me."

"No!" Christina screamed. "Please don't hurt him!"

"Don't waste your breath crying for this asswipe," the man said, pulling Ben up by the collar and pressing his head down with the gun. "Save it for yourself. You're next."

MIKE FOUND SERGEANT Baxter in the kitchen of the Chicago FBI office. She had a coffee cup in one hand and a half-eaten yogurt in the other.

"Care to join me for a little slash-and-burn operation?" he asked.

"Why would I?"

"Because you're my partner."

She pressed a hand against her chest. "He remembers!"

"Don't be so—"

"I thought you had totally forgotten. Or that Special Agent Swift had worked some kind of Deep South mojo on your brain."

"Hey, I didn't ask to have a Feeb babysitting me on this case."

"No, but you haven't exactly resisted, either. So what's a slash-and-burn, anyway?"

"Means I don't really have a clue. I'm going to thrust myself into the lion's den and see if I can stir something up. Hassle, threaten, intimidate. Take no prisoners."

"Sounds very sophisticated. Count me in. What is it we're trying to learn?"

"What else? The identity of the fourth kidnapper."

Baxter stared at him strangely. "But—I thought you already knew."

Mike returned an equally mystified expression. "Why in God's name would you think that?"

"Because I watched your pal Kincaid on television telling everyone he knew who the fourth man was."

"*What?*"

"And I figured he could only have gotten the scoop from you. Wrong?"

"Very." Mike thrust his hands into his pockets. "What the hell is he playing at?"

"Hard to tell with those defense shysters. Must be some kind of trick."

"Yeah. Must be. Maybe he—" All at once, Mike's face went white. "Oh, my God. That stupid idiot."

"What? What is it?"

"Change of plan." Mike began racing down the corridor. He pulled a cell phone out of his pocket and started dialing. "We've got to find him." He put the phone to his ear, got no answer, swore. "That incredible moron!" He punched the elevator button, then didn't have the patience to wait. He lurched toward the stairs. "Ben has pulled some stupid stunts in his time, take my word for it. But this one's going to get him killed."

CHRISTINA LOOKED ON in horror as the brutal man in the Halloween mask pressed a gun to Ben's temple. How had this plan gone so wrong so fast? Images flashed unbidden in her brain—Manny Nowosky with the drill bit through his skull; Charlie the Chicken with the gun in his mouth. And now Ben was poised to be the next victim.

"You brought this on yourself," the man growled. "You could've just let that son-of-a-bitch kid take the rap. But no, you had to go messin' around in my business. And now you're going to pay the price."

Christina's mind was racing. That voice, even hoarse and broken, sounded familiar, but with the mask concealing his face she couldn't be sure. She watched helplessly as his thumb pulled back the hammer of the pistol. He was really going to do it! She couldn't wait another second. Without warning, she lurched forward, head-butting the gun away from Ben.

The gun fired, but the bullet went off somewhere into the far wall. The man in the mask fell backward. Christina scrambled to her feet, but he was too quick for her. He caught her with the back of his gun hand and whipped her hard across the face. She felt her head explode, her neck bent by the force of the blow. Blood trickled down her cheek.

She began to topple, but the man in the mask grabbed her by the hair and jerked her head up. Ben scrambled to his feet and tried to rush him, but he shoved Ben back with ease.

"One more move like that and the girl dies!" he barked.

Ben froze in his tracks.

Christina tried to pull her head out of the daze and figure out what to do next. The man was still holding the gun in his spare hand, but it was pointing off to the side; during the struggle, it had pivoted around on his trigger finger. This would be a good time to do something. If she could only figure out what.

"You thought you could hurt me?" The man's former cool had evaporated. "I've been fighting all my life! I've taken out the biggest and the strongest. Never let anyone get in my way. And that includes you!"

He outweighed Christina by more than two-to-one, but she had been taking those self-defense classes at the Y for a reason, and no matter how tough the guy was, he had the same vulnerable points as everyone else. The eyes, which she couldn't get to. The temples, the ears, which she also couldn't get to. And the knees.

Now that was a different story.

She reared back with the heel of her shoe and smashed it into the small of his kneecap. He tumbled. Just like her instructor told her—no matter how big the man, a good swift kick to the knee will bring him down.

But he was still holding the gun. She brought her foot around, this time kicking his gun hand. He released it, then she kicked it to the other side of the room.

"Ben! Get it!"

Ben dove for that corner of the office, but the man grabbed his foot and fell right on top of him. They began to struggle. Christina tried to get around him, but he threw up his arm and tripped her. He pulled himself onto his knees, holding back Ben with one hand and Christina with the other.

The gun lay on the floor in the opposite corner.

Ben rammed his elbow into the man's nose. Christina came at his neck with her fingernails. He still did not release them. Christina could feel great power surging through his arms. He was stronger than Samson, and determined not to let them go.

With a mighty effort, he tossed the both of them back a few feet, then flung himself toward the gun. He grabbed the revolver, then rolled around on his shoulder. Christina raced forward—just in time to see a poised gun staring her down the throat.

"You goddamn punks!" the man shouted, almost hysterical. The gun was wavering, trembling, but not so much that there was any chance he would miss her if he pulled the trigger. "You goddamn smart-ass punks!"

"I thought so," Christina said quietly. "I know who you are."

In the midst of the struggle, the man's mask had been knocked to the side.

"You're Mario Roma," Christina continued. "You own Remote Control."

"Yeah," Roma said, his teeth clenched, both hands squeezing the shaking revolver. "And you're a corpse."

"HE'S NOT IN the courthouse!" Mike shouted back to Baxter, who was waiting in the unmarked Bureau car.

"I've been calling their office. No answer."

"Damn." He dove into the passenger seat. "You drive."

Given the urgency, she did as he instructed, but she was incredulous even as she slid across the seat.

"I want to keep working the phone," Mike explained. "And I need someone giving the road their full attention—and driving just as fast as possible."

Baxter pulled the car away from the curb, with a peel of rubber. "You must really be tight with this shyster."

Mike shrugged. "We go way back."

"Uh-huh."

"Besides, it's kind of like being a Good Samaritan. How many friends can a defense lawyer have?"

"Right."

"Just get to their office, Baxter," he said, punching the

tiny buttons on the phone. "I'm calling Swift. Maybe she can call in backup."

"BUT WHY?" BEN asked, genuinely curious and stalling for time. "Why would you go in for kidnapping? You have a successful restaurant."

"Are you kidding? No one makes money from restaurants. It's a money pit. And campus clubs are the worst. The kids are so damn fickle."

"But kidnapping?"

"Look, I grew up in Chicago. The mob rules, right? Everyone I ever knew was crooked. That was how we made money. It was expected."

"Mike told me he thought you were protesting too much when you said you had no mob connections."

"This job had nothing to do with the mob. Those jerks coulda never come up with something this smart." He wiped his brow with his free hand. "I left all that behind. Tried to start fresh. Clean. But I wasn't making money and the debts were piling up. If I didn't come up with some money—major money—I'd lose everything."

"So you went in for kidnapping. Then murder."

"I never wanted the murders. But Manny was making threats, saying he'd talk, and then Charlie—" He tightened his grip on Christina's hair. "Aw, what's the use? You wouldn't believe me. And you're both dead anyway." His lip curled as he pointed the gun at Christina's skull.

"You don't have to do this," Ben said, trying to keep his voice calm even though he was more terrified than he had ever been in his life. Not Christina. Please, God, not Christina. "You can stop the killing now."

"Too late," Roma said, sweat dripping from his chin. "Too goddamn late."

Outside Ben's office, in the front lobby, they all heard the sound of a door slamming shut.

"Who's that?" Roma hissed, lips tight.

"Probably Jones, my office manager," Ben answered. "Or my investigator, Loving."

"Like hell. I already took care of both of them."

"Ben? Christina? Where are you? I've got the stuff from the courthouse."

It was their new intern. Vicki.

"ANY LUCK?" BAXTER asked.

Mike shook his head. "No one's answering. Not in the office Ben's been using, not in any office in the building that I can find a number for."

"It's late," Baxter said, as she wove in and out of traffic, hitting speeds well beyond the limit. "Probably all gone home or not answering."

"That doesn't help me. I found a doorman at the Marriott across the street who thinks he saw Ben and Christina go in half an hour ago. Half an hour!" He wiped his brow. "And you know what that means."

"If they've been back that long, and they're not answering the phone . . ."

"Yeah." Mike bit his lower lip, trying to fight back the emotions that were flooding to the surface. "If that killer has been there for half an hour—"

Baxter swerved into the next lane, leaving a semi eating her dust. "I'm driving as fast as I can."

"It won't matter. We can't possibly get there in time. Neither will backup." He sat silent for a moment, hands gripping the console. "They're on their own."

"GODDAMN IT," ROMA muttered under his breath, still gripping Christina by the hair. "Goddamn it to hell."

"Don't drag Vicki into this," Ben whispered. "She's just a kid. She knows nothing."

"Goddamn it to hell!" He released Christina, then

waved them both away from the door. "Get back! In the corner."

Ben did as he was told, but he kept talking. "I haven't told her anything about the case. All she does is fetch coffee and hold paper clips. There's no need to hurt her."

"Shut up!" Roma hissed.

A moment later, Vicki's petite frame appeared in the doorway. She was carrying a large banker's box. "Ben?"

A second later, she saw the man, and a second after that, the gun. A small cry escaped from her.

"Get up against the wall," the man barked.

"What's happening?" she said, in a tiny trembling voice.

"Get up against the wall!" he shouted.

"Do as he says," Ben told her. "Please."

She scooted forward, her lips parted, her face ghost white. Her hands began to shake. Ben wondered how much longer she could hold that box.

"Hurry!"

She scooted forward—too fast. She stumbled, and the box tumbled out of her hands, taking Roma by surprise. Reams of paper spewed forth, knocking him backward. The gun spilled out of his hand. He stepped backward, hit the desk, then fell, as the floor was covered in paper.

"Oh!" Vicki screamed. "I'm so sorry. Don't hurt me! Please! I'll clean this up."

"Just get in the corner!" Roma bellowed, but Vicki knelt down and started rummaging through the paper—
—and came up holding a gun.

Ben and Christina gaped. Roma's hand was barely an inch away from his own weapon. "Don't do it," Vicki cautioned.

He didn't listen. He grabbed it. Vicki fired, but missed. Roma rolled away.

"Don't be a fool," Vicki said. "I will shoot."

Roma came up, gun in hand—

And Vicki fired. The bullet caught him in the neck, slamming him back against the wall. His eyes fluttered shut.

"Call 911," Vicki ordered. "Fast." She ran to Roma's side, looked at the wound, pressed two fingers against the side of his neck. "Damn," she muttered. "He's not going to make it."

While Christina made the call, Ben stared at his intern. And her pistol. "What the hell is going on?"

"I think a 'thank you' might be in order here," Vicki replied. There was a strength in her voice that he didn't recall being there before.

"What were you doing with a gun in your files?"

"A girl has to know how to protect herself. Especially if she's working for someone like you."

"My God," Ben said, slapping his forehead. "The press will be all over this. We'll have to get you a lawyer. Someone outside the firm. It was self-defense, of course, but we're going to have to convince the cops that—"

Vicki pushed herself back up to her feet. "Relax, Ben. You don't have to worry about the cops."

"How can you be sure?"

She smiled. "Because I am a cop."

CHAPTER
49

"IT WAS ALWAYS about the kidnapping," Ben explained. "From the very start. First an audacious plan to get money, then a desperate plan to keep it."

Ben sat in Judge Lacayo's chambers with Christina, Drabble, the judge's clerk, and most important, Mike, probably the only man in the room the judge really trusted. Although as far as that went, he was being pretty deferential to Ben today, especially compared to how the man had treated him since the trial began. Funny how a judge's attitude changed once a law enforcement officer came in and told him that the farfetched story the lawyer had been telling since the trial began was actually true.

"Mario Roma needed money," Mike said. "Actually, I don't know if he needed it so much as wanted it, but he was the one who concocted this plan. He had some contacts in Tulsa and he knew the Metzger family. And he'd seen Tommy. He knew the parents were loaded, attached to their child—but more than a bit negligent. He knew capturing the kid would not be that tricky. The hard part would be getting the money, keeping the money, and not getting caught."

"But he apparently managed it, right?" Drabble said.

"Right—because he enlisted help. He knew a small-time hood named Manny Nowosky because he hung out in Roma's club. Probably pushed drugs there, too, but Mario turned a blind eye to that. Call it a reciprocal

favor. Manny brought in a street chicken he knew
named Charlie. But Mario needed one more person to
make it all work, so he recruited Tony."

"Tony didn't write a word in his journal that suggests
that he was involved in anything criminal," Christina
protested.

"Well, it would be a pretty stupid move if he did,
given that someone might read his journal, which, come
to think of it, we all have."

"But he comes across as such a caring, gentle person.
Everyone who knew him says the same thing."

"I know," Mike said, "but there's no other explanation. Anyway, the kidnapping was a success. They made
off with the money. But that wasn't the end of the story.
I don't know exactly why Mario set out to get Tony.
Maybe he was afraid he would talk. Maybe he didn't
want to split the loot. At any rate, Manny and Charlie
lured Tony out so they could kill him. They couldn't
have known two frat hoods would make their job all the
easier. They probably followed Tony and the two frat
boys out of the club and watched while the beating took
place. By the time the frat boys left and they got to him,
strangling Tony was a cinch. Delivering his corpse to the
frat house was an obvious way to divert suspicion."

"But why was Manny killed?" Christina asked.

"Now there I can make a much more accurate guess.
We found fifty thousand bucks hidden in Manny's rental
home after he was killed. We checked the numbers. The
cash didn't come from the ransom money, at least not
directly. Roma must've laundered it somehow. The way
I see it, Manny was making demands, threatening to
talk unless he got paid immediately. Unless I miss my
guess, Charlie the Chicken joined in the ill-considered
extortion attempt."

"And then?"

"And then, after paying Manny a little something to
keep him quiet, Mario decided to tie up the loose ends.

With an electric drill. This was not only safer, it would allow him to keep all the money for himself. Once he took out Charlie, he must've thought he was safe." He paused. "Till he tuned in to Ben's idiotic press conference." He shook his head. "Roma must've left the club the second he heard that. Tied up Jones and Loving and shoved them in that closet where we found them. Took out your lame attempt at security, poor Boxer Johnson, who was lucky to get away with nothing worse than a concussion. And then Roma came after you."

Mike pursed his lips. "Let me tell you, Ben. Of all the stupid things you've done in a lifetime of stupid things, this one is the worst."

"It wasn't a bad idea," Ben said defensively. "I didn't think he'd move that quickly. I thought maybe he'd come that night, perhaps the next morning . . ."

"You were dead wrong."

"And in any case, I had a security guard watching. We were in radio contact and—"

"And it was a bad idea."

Ben sighed. "Well, it worked out in the end."

"It only worked out because I got undercover security assigned to your sorry little butt without telling you—since you refused it when I offered it. Not that easy to find a cop with a law background, either, let me tell you. Vicki Hecht is her real name. Graduated Northwestern Law School, 1992. Practiced law for five years, didn't care for it. Became a cop. And saved your miserable little life." Mike leaned in close. "But if you ever do anything like that again I will personally wring your neck."

"Why, Mike, I didn't know you cared."

Mike bristled. "About you, I don't. But I've gotten used to Christina." He gave her a wink. "She's cute."

"You should have told me what you were doing."

"Nah. If you'd known, you'd have blown it. Or kept Vicki out of the loop. Or sent her away."

"You don't know that."

"I do, Ben. I know how stupid you can be. It's staggering."

Christina gave Mike a stern look. "You told Vicki to put that stuff in her résumé about speaking French, didn't you? You knew that would reel me in."

Mike spread his hands. "What can I say?"

Christina feigned a hurt expression. "I feel so used."

"If I may, ladies and gentlemen," Judge Lacayo said, easing forward in his black leather chair. "I hate to interrupt a delightful conversation just because this is my chambers, but could we talk about the case at hand?"

Ben tucked in his chin. "Sorry, your honor."

"Major Morelli, are you absolutely certain about this?"

"With some regret," Mike answered. "Because I hate it when Ben and Christina are right and I'm wrong. But yes, I'm certain."

"Then Johnny Christensen—"

"Did not kill Tony Barovick. Hurt him badly, yes, and should be tried for aggravated assault. But not murder."

The judge glanced at the prosecutor. "Mr. Drabble?"

Drabble did not look happy, but Ben couldn't fault him for that. "Your honor, my people are saying the same thing. We want to drop the murder charge and refile for aggravated assault, if double jeopardy permits."

Lacayo nodded thoughtfully. "Very well. The clerk will so enter it into the court record. Ms. McCall, for the time being your client is free to go."

Christina closed her eyes, a smile spreading across her face. "Thank you, your honor."

"By the way—"

"Yes?"

"Am I right," the judge asked, "in thinking that this was your first trial as lead counsel?"

Christina nodded.

"You picked a hell of a case to start out with. Talk about trial by fire." Judge Lacayo fell back into his cushioned chair. "Well, ma'am, I hope Mr. Kincaid gives you a raise for this, because you handled it like a pro." He smiled. "You'll be welcome in my courtroom anytime."

MIKE WAS NOT surprised to find Special Agent Swift and Sergeant Baxter waiting for him outside the judge's chambers.

"Congratulations, tiger," Swift said. "You hit the jackpot."

He bowed his head with mock modesty. "Aw, shucks."

"You came through like a champ. You solved the case."

"Yes," Baxter said, inching forward. "We did."

"And I want to thank you for doing it," Swift added. "This kidnapping has been a burr in my side for far too long. You can't imagine how pleased I am to finally have it removed."

"Glad I could be of service."

"You know," Swift said, a smile dancing playfully on her lips, "I don't normally do this—well, never, actually—but I think I could get you in at the Bureau without any trouble. Especially now, after this case."

"That's nice, but—"

"Now think about it, sugah. You might get tired of chasing down trailer trash liquor store shooters someday. You might want to move up to the big time." She sidled closer to him, an eyebrow arched, a finger tugging at his belt. "And if you joined the Bureau, we'd see a whole lot more of each other."

"I appreciate the offer," Mike said. "Really. But I like it in Tulsa. With my friends." He paused a moment. "And my partner."

Baxter's face turned a bright crimson.

"Well, ain't that sweet?" Swift took a tiny step back. "But I'm not entirely surprised. You two be good, hear?"

"We'll do our best," Baxter said, the frost melting fast.

"You do that. And Mike?"

"Yes?"

She smiled. "Parting is such sweet sorrow / That I shall say good night till it be morrow."

PART FOUR

The Return of the Stranger

CHAPTER
50

JOURNAL OF TONY BAROVICK

TWO THINGS HAPPENED this week in the bar. Two bad things. And I'm not sure which of them disturbs me the most.

We had our first hate crime. It wasn't against me—but it could've been. It was against a friend of mine, Brian Meadows, the leader of the South Chicago Gay & Lesbian Alliance. He was here to conduct a meeting and three black street hoods got wind of it somehow. They drove into town in their pickups, hauled him outside to the back parking lot, threw a noose around his neck, tightened it, and dragged him around, humiliating him. They hit him a few times, cracked an egg over his head. One of them even peed on him. "We're gonna have us a lynching, boys!" That's what one of them said. The irony of the situation was, I'm sure, totally lost on him.

I eventually got a cop over to break it up. The punks were arrested; they spent two hours in lockup and then went free. Charges were never brought. Brian didn't want the bad press he knew would result. I was scared to death. I went to Mario and demanded that he hire security for the back parking lot. It's so big and dark and unfenced, anyone could get away with anything back there, especially in the wee hours of the morning. I didn't want what happened to Brian to happen to anyone else.

Mario told me to stop being a weak sister and to get back to work.

The second incident did not strike me as personally, but scared me just the same. I caught some kids in one of the back rooms using Ecstasy. We've never patrolled those back caverns very carefully. We figure some of the new hitches step in there to try a few sample smoochies before they commit to going home with each other. All well and good. But they weren't supposed to be party rooms—especially not for anything illegal. Turned out these were high school kids passing for college students. I don't know where they got the drugs; I just hope to God it wasn't in the bar. I confiscated what I could and told them to get the hell out and never come back. They gave me a little grief, but eventually they left.

I told Mario about it, and he responded with his typical indifference. What did he care what a bunch of punks did? If they want to ruin their lives with drugs, let 'em. After all, we serve alcohol, and that's a drug. It was no use. I don't think he gets it. If we develop a reputation for being a local rave house, our paying customers will be supplanted by crackheads and undercover cops. They'll look for an excuse to shut us down and eventually they'll succeed. I've put too much into this place to let that happen.

I told Shelly about it, but she didn't take it much more seriously than Mario had. She says being gay has made me paranoid, made me afraid of authority figures, afraid of everything. I know she loves me, and she probably can see some things about me I don't see myself. She thinks it was a fluke. She says our customers are way too smart and Ecstasy will never catch on here. And she's probably right. Maybe I'm just a worrywart.

Which is a hell of a lot better than being a weak sister. Maybe I'm crazy, but I do think of this place as my home. I created it, in a very real sense. I think of Mario as my grumpy dad, Shelly as my spunky little sister, our customers as my friends. I wouldn't want anything to happen to this little joint.

It's the one place in the world where I feel safe.

CHAPTER
51

MIKE MET BAXTER at Gate C-37 at O'Hare for their flight back to Tulsa, bearing a gift in a Starbucks cup.

"Heads up, Baxter."

"This is for me? What brings this on?"

"Just wanted to show you that I don't subscribe to any sexist old-world stereotypical notions. This time, I fetched the coffee."

She removed the lid and brought it close to her face, drawing in the rich aroma. "You mean there's coffee in there somewhere, beneath the whipped cream and chocolate sprinkles?"

Mike grinned. "That's the rumor."

She took a sip. "Any luck tracking down the source of Manny Nowosky's fifty grand?"

"Alas, no."

"And it didn't come from the kidnapping?"

"Not directly. We've checked the serial numbers. Common sense tells me the ransom money is the only big cash Manny ever came near. But how did he swap out the numbers?"

"What about the Ecstasy-pushing?"

"I don't think that would yield this kind of . . . of . . ."

Baxter leaned in. "Yes? Is something wrong?"

"Damn." Mike's eyes turned toward the sky, his brain racing. "Yes, something is very wrong. *Damn!*" He pushed out of his chair. "Call headquarters and tell them to cash in our tickets. We're taking a later flight."

"Why? Where are we going?"

Mike was already halfway across the terminal and accelerating with each step. "To correct a tragic error. Before it's too late."

THE PLACE WASN'T open yet, but that didn't stop Mike. She was there, and that was all he cared about.

"Shelly!"

The petite barmaid was dusting the back shelves, around and between the bottles of exotic liqueurs. She jumped when she heard his voice. "Wh—what?"

With one hand on the countertop, Mike vaulted over the bar and landed just before her. "Show me your arm."

Deep lines creased her face. "What? But it hasn't healed."

He reached forward and jerked her arm out of the sling.

"Ow!" Shelly cried.

On the other side of the bar, Baxter was gaping in amazement. "Mike, what the hell do you think—"

He wasn't listening. He grabbed the bandage on her wrist by one end.

"Ahhh!" Shelly cried out. "Please stop!"

Mike ripped off the bandage with one jerk.

And revealed . . . nothing. No wound, no scar.

Shelly fell silent. Her eyes scoured the bar, finally returning to the man standing just before her. "Look, I can ex—"

"Can it," Mike barked, pushing her toward a bar stool. "No more of your bull. You're going to sit down now and tell me what *really* happened. All of it."

"But I don't—"

"Quit the crap!" he bellowed. "You're already in so

deep you may be irredeemable. Perjury on top of everything else. Your only hope whatsoever at this point is to tell me the truth. And that's exactly what you're going to do."

ON A DAY like today no one should have to be inside, Mike groused as he rode the elevator to the fifth floor. This was a day for outdoor activity, rappelling and canoeing and playing touch football with the neighborhood children. And he wished that was what he was doing. Actually, he wished he was doing anything other than what he was doing.

FBI headquarters, of course, was open 24/7, and he'd kept his ID card, happily, and by luck he managed to catch her still in her office.

"Mike!" Special Agent Swift said, when she saw him coming her way. She was wearing another one of those turtleneck sweaters, and God but she looked good in it. "You decided to take me up on my offer." She put a mildly lascivious look on her face. "Which offer?"

"I'd like to talk to you for a moment."

"Sounds good to me, sugah."

"I don't mean the usual foreplay byplay. I mean really talk."

She frowned. "You're awfully serious today, tiger. What's up?"

He took a deep breath. "Shelly spilled. I mean everything. The truth." He gazed with a deep and penetrating expression into her eyes. "I know."

Her head craned back. "Know what?"

Mike stared at her, and as he did, that damned Billy Joel song, "The Stranger," started rattling through his head again. "Swift," he said quietly, "I know."

She seemed confused, trying to calculate what next to say, what next to do.

"I'd appreciate it if you'd play straight with me and

not try anything stupid. I haven't called for backup. Yet. And I've asked Baxter to remain outside."

"I don't suppose there's any point in trying to convince you that Shelly is lying."

Mike slowly shook his head.

"Stupid woman. It was a mistake to ever involve her." She fidgeted with her hands, her long red nails clicking together. "What tipped you off?"

"Tony Barovick," Mike replied succinctly. "I've read his journal. I've talked to his friends. Maybe it's just ego, but I came to feel as if . . . as if I knew the man. Even though I didn't. Felt like I knew what kind of person he was. He had flaws and problems and insecurities, just like the rest of us. But I think he was basically a good person. A decent person. That's why I had a hard time believing he was involved in some two-bit drug-running operation. And I had a particularly hard time believing he had any part in the abduction of a little boy, even when all the evidence pointed in that direction. I just couldn't believe he would ever want or need money that much."

"People aren't rational," Swift said. "Not all the time. They do strange and unpredictable things. You can never really know another person."

"Yeah," Mike continued. "I knew that fifty grand we found on Manny had to be the proceeds from the kidnapping, but the serial numbers didn't match. In other words, the loot had been laundered. But how? Manny didn't have any means or connections for laundering money. Charlie the Chicken certainly didn't. That would require someone with a legitimate business. Mario Roma."

"He has always maintained that he severed his mob ties."

"Not that that means much. But he didn't need mob ties. He had his own club. Money laundering would be a cinch, especially with Shelly helping. She hadn't been involved in the kidnapping, but she was more than happy to help out with the laundering once Mario promised her a small cut. All they had to do was replace the money that came into the cash register with money from the ransom, a little at a time. Not enough to create suspicion, or a trail. It would be a slow process. But it would work."

"Assuming no one found out."

"Yes, but someone did, didn't they? Tony Barovick, the poor chump. He says in his journal that he had responsibility for the cash register. He counted the daily receipts. He let Shelly do a lot of the accounting work because she was better at it, but he was ultimately responsible. And I also know from reading his journal that he took his responsibilities very seriously. He must've caught Shelly or Mario making the switch, or somehow figured out what they were doing. That's why he had to die."

"Shelly told you they used her to lure Tony out."

"Which was all a big con to bail herself out of trouble. She didn't have to be forced to do anything. She put on that fake sling and told people she'd tried to kill herself after Tony was killed to divert suspicion and give herself a story to tell in case anyone questioned her hard about her fatal phone call. After Mario realized Tony was onto the money-laundering scheme, I'm thinking he went ballistic. A hothead like him—I can see it happening. He thinks his little scheme is crumbling all around him. He panics. And he decides Tony has to die."

"Mario could never keep his head together under fire," Swift commented.

"So," Mike continued, "he needed to get Tony alone, fast, before he said anything to anyone, so Shelly lured him out. She knew he'd come. He loved her. He thought he knew her." He shoved his fists angrily into his pockets. "But you never really know anyone, do you, Swift? She betrayed him. Just like you did me."

"What?"

"Don't waste your breath," Mike grunted. "I was such an idiot. Tony Barovick, a kidnapper. In retrospect, it's so stupid." He swung his fist in the air, pummeling an imaginary punching bag. "Tony Barovick wasn't the fourth kidnapper. You were."

She took a step closer to the doorway. "That's a pretty serious accusation, sport."

"It's all too obvious. For months now I've been beating myself up over that botched rescue mission. I couldn't figure out what went wrong. How did the kidnappers know when the snipers had been pulled in tight, making it safe for them to flee through that underground passageway? How did they know you and I were coming up the rear fire escape? Easy. They had a man on the inside. You."

"Mike, I've been working with you to solve that case."

"No, you've been clinging to my side like a barnacle to make sure I didn't get too close to the truth. And I suppose if you ever thought I was too close, you would've taken care of me—just like you did the others."

Mike watched her eyes flit around the room—to her holstered weapon on the coat stand.

"Please don't," Mike said. "You wouldn't get past me. And even if you did, Baxter and three uniforms are waiting in the elevator lobby. There are dozens of people in this building. It's over."

"Guess this is the part where I ask to see my lawyer, huh?"

Mike felt a sadness so intense he could barely speak. "Before you go all Fifth Amendment, answer one question, okay? Why Manny and Charlie the Chicken? Why did they have to die? Just so you wouldn't have to share?"

She shrugged. "We could've handled Tony in a sensible, nonlethal way, but Mario didn't ask me. He just went off half-cocked and killed the poor kid. At least he had the sense to move the body to the frat house and crank up the air-conditioner—both to confuse the cops. Afterward, of course, the murder became this huge cause célèbre and got so much media attention, Manny and Charlie demanded more money, and fast. Manny was the instigator. We gave Manny all the loot we'd managed to launder so far, but I guess it wasn't enough. Manny threatened to talk if I didn't transfer all the money—even the unlaundered stuff—to him immediately. I tried to reason with him, but he wouldn't listen. He was hiding out in Tulsa, refusing to return to Chicago with the rest of us. He was panicking. With every reporter in the country working on the case, he thought we were doomed. He wanted every penny he could get so he could slip out of the country, and if he didn't get it, he and Charlie were threatening to make a deal with the DA, so . . ."

"A power drill?" Mike said incredulously.

"It wasn't planned. I went over just to reason with him. There was a fight and . . ." She sighed. "A good agent is trained to use whatever weapons are at hand. After Charlie learned what happened to Manny, he tried to hide. But I found him. I am a detective, after all."

"And you set up Mario."

She didn't deny it. "He was behind all the attempts on your lawyer buddies. The vandalism, the shooting incident. We made it look like that gay rights group was responsible. Basically, he wanted them to back off. He wanted Christensen convicted and the whole business put to rest. They were doing a lot of snooping around, too, you know. Mario was setting the stage to take them out—if they got too effective or too close to the truth." She paused. "Mario was always a hothead—to the bitter end. I eventually realized that keeping him around was . . . an unacceptable risk. After the lawyers gave that press conference, Mario had a meltdown. He tried to get me to kill them, but I told him I couldn't. Since I knew you all personally. So he went himself."

"You knew he'd end up getting himself killed."

"I had a strong suspicion, yeah. But of course, if he'd been successful, that would've worked for me, too. Mario's death left me with all the money, minus the fifty grand Manny had and whatever trivial sums went to Shelly. And all the known conspirators were eliminated." She sighed. "It seemed like the perfect crime."

Mike removed the cuffs from his belt. "There's no such thing." He was relieved when she allowed him to restrain her. All the combat scenarios that had run through his mind on the drive over—none of which ended well—were not going to materialize. "Care to tell me why?"

"Aw, who the hell knows?" Her voice seemed tired, drained of its usual effervescence. "I could use the money, sure. But—you know, I worked on all of those child kidnapping cases. For years. I saw all the mistakes crooks made, mostly just because they're so damn stupid. And I thought—I could do this. I could do this so well no one would ever catch me. And I did. Or so I thought." A soft echo of a laugh escaped her lips. "It was a lark."

"Not for Tony Barovick," Mike replied. "So that's it? You did it for the intellectual challenge? For kicks?"

She shrugged. "Would it be better if I told you the Metzger family betrayed me when I was a child? That I needed money desperately to save my ailing, sainted mother? Grow up, Morelli. A crime's a crime. We're all crooks, deep down. All we need is sufficient motivation."

"Some of us don't even need that, apparently," Mike muttered. He stopped at the threshold of the door. "I liked you, Swift. Did you know that? I'm not talking about all the teasing pseudosexual stuff. I mean I really liked you. I admired you. I thought you were a great cop." His head swayed from side to side. That damn Billy Joel song buzzed to the surface of his brain. "And then the stranger kicked me right between the eyes."

He turned her around and steered her out of the office.

AFTER MIKE MADE his report and put Swift in custody, he found Baxter waiting for him outside the downtown Cook County jail's rear entrance.

"Need any help?" she asked.

He shook his head slightly. "All done."

"Sorry it had to work out this way. I know you cared about her."

"Did I?" Mike walked slowly toward the car. "I think I just enjoyed working with someone who was so . . ." He thought for a moment. "So easy. In a good way, I mean."

"Yeah."

"And she liked poetry."

"Well, there's no accounting for taste." Baxter smiled, but it didn't take. "And she did all this . . . because she could?"

"Basically."

"Strange."

Mike nodded slowly. "Aren't we all."

They both slid into the car, Mike driving. Baxter waited until they were out on the highway and halfway back to the airport before she spoke.

"Mike . . . I think we should talk about it."

His chest deflated. "About what?"

"You know perfectly well. The kiss."

"I already apologized. I was buoyant."

"It wasn't the first time."

"Well, it was the last."

"I think we have to be realistic. These are our careers

we're talking about. We don't want to do something stupid and screw them up. I just don't think this is going to work."

"It's going to work," Mike said flatly.

"What?"

"I said, 'It's going to work.' "

"And how can you be so certain?"

He slowed to take the exit then, when it was safe, turned to face her. "It's going to work because I want it to work."

CHAPTER
52

IF IMMERSION IN a trial was like being submerged in a tank of water, then the end of a trial was like having your sub surface, like being released from prison, like being permitted to reenter the real world after a long absence. The firm of Kincaid & McCall celebrated the successful conclusion of this trial with a company picnic at Williams Park, named for the renowned Tulsa auctioneer, Tommy Williams. Jones reserved a pavilion, and it was a beautiful, warm but not too humid, mildly cloudy, all-in-all glorious day.

Jones and Paula were tossing a Frisbee out on the grassy stretch between the basketball court and the creek, Loving was climbing on the new playground equipment, and Christina was trying to teach Ben the fine art of barbecue.

Ben stared at the pink clump of raw hamburger meat. "So . . . you have to touch that?"

"Unless you've mastered the power of telekinesis, yes."

He extended one finger. "Kind of . . . slimy, isn't it?"

Christina's patience was wearing thin. "Come on, champ. Learn something here. You can't go on eating Cap'n Crunch all your life. Get your hands into it. Smoosh it into patties."

A pained expression crossed his face. "And then you put it on that hot grill?"

"That's the traditional method, yes," she said, drumming her fingers.

"When do you take it off?"

"When it's done."

"And how do you know when it's done?"

She made a tsking sound with her teeth as he pressed the meat into patties. "Didn't your parents ever have cookouts when you were growing up?"

"Sure."

"Who cooked the burgers?"

"Actually, we had people . . ."

FIFTEEN MINUTES LATER, Christina returned from the Frisbee field and peered at the smoking grill. "Burned?"

Ben tilted his head. "Well, it was my first time. And I was kind of worried about the *E. coli* thing."

Christina rolled her eyes. "Better stick with the cold cereal, Ben. I don't think cooking is your line."

"I'm not giving up that easily," Ben said, diving into the picnic basket. "I'll cook the hot dogs."

Christina snatched the package away from him. "I'll cook the hot dogs. You have a visitor."

"I—what?" On the other side of the pavilion, he spotted Ellen Christensen. "What is she doing in Tulsa? At our picnic?"

"I invited her."

He stared at Christina blankly. "You did what?"

"You two need to talk."

"I do not have the slightest need or—"

"You do. Don't leave things dangling, Ben. This may be your last chance." She pulled him to his feet. "Just—go." She gave him a little shove forward.

His face was a picture of unhappiness. "For the record, I'm only doing this for you."

"That works."

He crossed the pavilion till he reached the spot where

Ellen waited. He stood at least two feet away from her. She was dressed casually, shorts and a polo shirt, but she looked strong and much healthier than she had since this entire case had begun.

"I'm sorry to bother you," she said. She was obviously nervous. She fidgeted with the belt loops on her shorts. "I wanted to thank you. For what you did for Johnny. He's home now, for a little while. Till they file the assault charges, anyway. I can't tell you how wonderful it feels, having him back with me again." She looked up at Ben, eyes wide. "My boys are all I've got now."

Ben nodded.

"It was so wonderful, what you did for Johnny."

Ben craned his neck uncomfortably. "Christina did the hard work."

"But Christina didn't have to work through . . . what you had to work through. What you did . . ." She shook her head. "Was special. And I will always treasure it."

"You're making a big deal out of nothing. I didn't even want to take the case."

"That's my whole point. You didn't want to take the case, but you did. You didn't want to work on the case, but you did. You didn't want to help me, but you did." She closed her eyes, and a tiny smile illuminated her face. "I think maybe you haven't changed so much after all."

"Believe me, I have."

She looked at him, and when she did, it was with eyes that seemed to travel back farther than the events of the last few months. "You never like to let anything show. Withdrawn, cranky—that's what you want the world to see. But I know better."

Ben coughed, suddenly uncomfortable. "If you'll excuse me, I need to get back."

"To Christina?"

He stopped. "And Jones and everyone else."

"I like Christina a lot. She's wonderful."

"Well . . . yes."

"She thinks you're afraid to make a commitment. And I very much fear . . . that may be my fault."

"Don't be stupid. That was years ago."

"Yes, but . . . sometimes it's the old wounds that hurt the most."

Ben shifted awkwardly from one foot to the other.

"You know, Ben—what I did. All those years ago. It was a horrible mistake."

It was?

"You were so sweet and kind and I loved you so dearly. But when I knew the baby was coming, I just freaked. I lost faith. I thought I had to play it safe. Couldn't take a chance on a punk college kid. But look at you now!" She smiled. "I didn't know you as well as I thought I did."

"Who really knows anybody?" Ben wondered. "When all is said and done, we're all strangers."

"But there is one thing I do know—something I want you to know," Ellen continued. "Letting you go was the hardest thing I ever had to do. Ever. And my biggest mistake."

"No," he said quietly. "You did the right thing."

"I—but—"

"And I knew it. Even then. I just couldn't . . . *wouldn't* accept it."

Ellen's eyes widened. "In time, Larry and I made a life for ourselves. It was different with him. He didn't miss the girl I had been before the disease set in. He fell in love with the woman I became. And David is a wonderful boy. He reminds me of you in—" Her voice choked. "Truth is I never stopped missing you, Ben. You were the one who got away." She stood there another moment, then clasped her hands together. "Well . . . goodbye."

"Wait." He reached out, and a second later, he was

hugging her, her cheek to his, tight in his embrace. He couldn't know how long it lasted; it was ridiculously too long and impossibly too brief.

And then she was gone.

SHE WAS SO beautiful this morning—and every morning—Ben literally couldn't take his eyes off her. He had never felt anything like this in his entire twenty-three years of life. The warmth that gurgled up out of his chest every time he looked at her. The happiness he felt in the morning when he woke, just knowing she was somewhere near. The ache he felt whenever they were apart.

"How long have you been staring at me?" Ellen murmured, her eyes barely open.

"I don't know. An hour or so."

"Geez Louise. Turn on the television."

"I'd rather watch you."

She rolled over, tucking the sheet under her arms. "I bet my breath is atrocious."

"Like sweet lotus flowers," he said, leaning forward to give her a kiss. "Ambrosia. Nectar of the gods."

"You only think that because you have a vivid imagination."

"I only think that because I love you."

Her eyes sparkled. "And when did you decide that?"

Ben inched forward, throwing his leg over her hips. "The first moment I laid eyes on you."

"Oh, right."

"True."

"In that little coffee shop on Yonge?"

"Where you played guitar and wore that punk leather skirt. Fabulous."

"And you thought right then and there you were going to have me?"

"I thought right then and there that you would probably never let me anywhere near you. But I had to try."

"I'm glad you did."

He leaned forward again, and this time the kiss lasted for a long, mutually stimulating minute. After their lips parted, Ellen suddenly coughed, a deep throaty cough that grew in size till she was racked by the strain. It was at least a minute before she was able to stop.

"Are you all right?" Ben asked, his forehead creased with concern.

"Fine, fine," she assured him. "Just swallowed wrong or something. So what's our plan for the day? Shopping at Eaton? Movie at the Bloor? Maybe the Harbour-front?"

"I'd rather stay in bed with you."

"Even you might run out of steam after a while, lover boy."

"We can just cuddle. I don't care. Just so we're together."

Her forehead crinkled. "Man, you really are in love, aren't you? Is there anything I can do to help?"

He nodded. "Marry me."

She looked at him for a long time. "Peanut butter and jelly!"

"The traditional responses are *yes* or *no*."

She giggled. "Peanut butter and jelly."

"What the heck is that supposed to mean?"

Under the covers, she wrapped her arms around him and squeezed tight. "You and me, kid. Because we're so much better together than apart. And now that we've been stuck together, we can never be entirely separated."

BY SEVEN-THIRTY, the sun was setting. Everyone had eaten and returned to the playing fields. Loving and Jones had started with one-on-one basketball, but it had somehow degenerated into dodgeball. Loving was creaming Jones, which brought Paula no end of merriment.

Christina gazed across the stone picnic table at Ben. He seemed tired, but not unhappy. Most of the hostility she had seen these past few weeks was gone, and thank God for that. Perhaps it was finally time . . .

"Fun having a family, isn't it?" Christina said, as she and Ben watched from the shade of the pavilion.

"If they were my family," Ben groused, "I'd hang my-self."

"They are, you know."

"If they're our family, what does that make us?"

A question he almost immediately regretted verbaliz-ing. It hung in the air like a crystalline balloon, fragile, but refusing to go away.

"Thank you for talking to Ellen."

He shrugged. "No big."

"I'll bet." She paused a moment. "She has another son, right? Her own child."

"David. Thirteen."

"That'll be a comfort. Once Johnny starts doing his time."

"I would imagine."

"So . . . that means David was born just after—"

"I wouldn't know anything about it."

"Mmm." She looked at him for a long moment. "I liked Ellen. I can see why she meant so much to you."

Ben looked away, out at the horizon. "I thought I knew her. Stupid. Truth is that no matter what you do, how much time you spend, you can never know another person."

"I don't believe that."

"It's true. I thought I knew Ellen. Mike thought he knew Agent Swift. Tony Barovick thought he knew Shelly. You think you know someone and you put your trust in them and—pow! They betray you."

"Not always," Christina said firmly. "It doesn't have to be that way."

"Easy to say."

"Look at me," she said, gently turning his head until he faced her. "I would never betray you. And you would never do anything to hurt me. I know that. I *know* it."

A silence fell, one that threatened to become oppressive. Christina snapped her fingers, shattering the silence. "I almost forgot. I have something for you." She pulled a small tape player out of the picnic basket and turned it on.

"Is that Rachmaninoff?" Ben asked. " 'Rhapsody on a Theme of Paganini.' I love that piece." He peered at her strangely. "I didn't think anyone knew."

Foolish boy. Mothers know everything. But I'm taking credit. "I thought it seemed like something you'd enjoy."

"Heck of a good guess."

"Well, we have worked together for a good while now, Mr. Kincaid." She eyed him carefully. "I know you pretty darn well."

"I guess so." Christina wished she were telepathic; she'd give anything to know what was buzzing in that little brain of his.

"I've been a real horse's ass, haven't I?" he said.

"Not at all. Extenuating circumstances."

"I know I have. I was awful."

"You were just you."

"What's that supposed to mean?"

"Nothing."

"Like there's something wrong with just me?"

"Apparently not." She reached across the table and took his hand. "I'm still here, aren't I?"

He put his other hand on hers. "I think I'm ready. To take the next step."

She peered back at him. "You mean—beyond Scrabble?"

"If—it's okay with you."

"Ben Kincaid, it is so, so, *so* okay with me."

Their heads drew closer together . . .

And a basketball slammed into Ben's forehead.

"Hey, heads up!" Jones shouted. "What's with you two? Weren't you watching?"

Ben looked at Christina. Christina looked at Ben. They kissed.

CHAPTER
53

JOURNAL OF TONY BAROVICK

JUST CAME IN for a few minutes to jot down my thoughts. Wish I could be more upbeat about things, but there's no denying that this has been a tough week.

It started with Roger. After all we've shared, as long as we've been together, it looks as if our relationship may be coming to an end. I suppose in the cosmic scale of things it isn't that big a deal. More lovers fall apart than stay together. But I can't get over the feeling of loss, the sense that I'm giving up some part of me that I can never regain. It hurts in a way that nothing has ever hurt me before.

I'm very concerned about what's been going down at the bar. Remote Control has been my baby from the get-go, but I have the sense that it's slipping away from me, that outside forces are stealing my progeny. I don't know what to do about it. Word on the street is that an undercover cop is watching the place. Why? I'd like to think it was the hate crime those hoods perpetrated on Brian Meadows, but I know that incident isn't even a blip on the law enforcement radar. I adore Shelly and she knows it. I would never want her to be hurt. Why does life always have to be so hard?

There were two frat boys sitting at a table together tonight. They knew I was gay and were determined to give me grief about it. One of them seemed truly mean, almost psychotic mean. For a split second, I wondered if we were going to have a repeat of what happened to Brian. Fortunately, as soon as I backed away, they went back to swilling their overpriced Mexican beer.

The easiest thing would be to hate those two frat boys. Easiest thing in the world. But somehow I can't bring myself to do it. I don't know what made them the way they are, but I know in my heart that given half a chance, both of them would be capable of doing great things, wonderful things, of doing great good in the world. No one is born to be a villain. I believe that everyone—even those two—in their heart of hearts wants to be good. Wants to *do* good.

Oops—phone call from Shelly. Gotta wrap this up. I can't begin to know what the future holds for me. But I do know that the power of love is still out there, still waiting to be tapped. And I'm ready to play my part. I'm excited about it—looking forward to it, in fact. And why not?

I've got my whole life ahead of me.

AUTHOR'S NOTE

SINCE 1976, the year the U.S. Supreme Court reaffirmed the constitutionality of the death penalty, thirty-eight states have adopted death penalty statutes, and thirty-two of them have actually carried out executions. Polls show that most Americans favor the death penalty, at least in theory, even if they don't trust the system through which it is administered. In a May 2002 Gallop Poll, 69 percent of the respondents said they favored capital punishment, but 73 percent of the respondents said that they believed at least one innocent person had been put to death in the previous five years.

In January of 2003 (after this book was written), the Republican governor of Illinois, George Ryan, commuted the sentences of all 167 people on death row in his state. "Our capital system is haunted by the demon of error," he declared, "error in determining guilt and error in determining who among the guilty deserves to die." Among the problems he cited were racially motivated prosecutions, coerced confessions, district attorneys and judges subject to popular election, and unreliable witnesses—problems discussed in this novel; my previous work, *Death Row;* and other books in the Ben Kincaid series.

In the spring of 2000, a team of criminologists at Columbia University released the first phase of the most far-reaching study yet of the U.S. death penalty system. It showed that the system was riddled with unfairness and incompetence, with serious errors arising with alarming frequency at every stage of the process. The study also showed that of every three death sentences reviewed, two were overturned on appeal. No one knew what percentage of the remaining cases were tainted—until science provided us with a heretofore-unknown method for assessing guilt.

In recent years, DNA evidence has called many of those verdicts into question, but there is still no law in any state guaranteeing a defendant DNA testing or the right to an appeal based upon newly discovered DNA evidence. As of this writing, more than one hundred people on death row have had their convictions overturned because DNA or other scientific evidence provided irrefutable proof of their innocence. If these figures are typical of the national rate of wrongful conviction, that would mean that one in eight of the prisoners now on death row are not guilty of the crimes for which they were convicted.

In 1984, Jay Wesley Neill and Robert Johnson received separate trials in the State of Oklahoma for felony murders committed in the course of a bank robbery. In the prosecutor's closing argument in the Neill case, he referred repeatedly to the fact that Neill was openly gay. "I want you to think briefly about the man you're sitting in judgment on and determining what the appropriate punishment should be . . . I'd like to go through some things that to me depict the true person, what kind of person he is. He is a homosexual. The person you're sitting in judgment on—disregard Jay Neill. You're deciding life or death on a person that's a vowed [sic] homosexual . . . But these are areas you consider whenever you determine the type of person you're sitting in judgment on . . . The individual's homosexual."

The jury returned a death verdict. The Tenth Circuit upheld the conviction, 2-1, although the dissenting judge wrote that the prosecutor's comments were "susceptible of only one possible interpretation: among other factors, Neill should be put to death because he is gay." The Supreme Court declined to hear the case, so on December 12, 2002, Neill was executed by lethal injection. His partner, Robert Johnson, received a life sentence.

—William Bernhardt

Please read on for an exciting sneak preview
of William Bernhardt's new novel of
suspense

DARK EYE

"Showcasing William Bernhardt at the height of
his storytelling powers, *Dark Eye* is a *Silence of the
Lambs*–meets–*Rain Main* thriller that will chill you
while its two unique and endearing protagonists
steal your heart."
—LISA SCOTTOLINE

"Murder in Sin City, as investigated by a tough
woman cop and her incomparably gifted young
associate. Bernhardt and Vegas go together like
fire and gasoline."
—STEPHEN COONTS

Available in hardcover
from Ballantine Books

THREE TIMES I'VE fired my weapon. Three times. Twice because I had to. The third time was optional. But I never plugged
anyone for making a pass at me, no matter how tempting
it might be. It was a rule. Until that night in early October.
When the whole damn mess began.

I really don't know how it happened. For starters, I looked
like hell and I knew it, despite what the guy was saying. It was
all bullshit.

"Has anyone ever mentioned that you have a gorgeous pair of eyes?"

"Only my ophthalmologist," I told the kid in the Polo.

"No, seriously, you do. My mom says I've always been an eye man." He leaned closer. I could smell the whiskey on his breath. "Are they different?"

"Different from . . . your mom's?"

"From each other. It's like . . . your right eye is darker than the left."

I nodded. "Cat scratch. When I was five."

"Well, it works for you. Gives you an exotic aura."

If you like that, wait till you see my athlete's foot.

He smiled, which wasn't his best look. "You know what? You're funny."

"Not another reference to my appearance, I hope."

He scooted his chair closer to mine. "Look," he said, his voice suddenly low and tremulous. "I think it's obvious what's happening here. Why don't we cut through the baloney, go back to my place, and give each other what we both know we want?"

"At the moment, there's only two things I want."

"And they would be?"

"Another bourbon. Neat."

"I can arrange that. What else do you want?"

"You to leave."

THE BAR, GORDY'S, was a hellhole I'd discovered when I was working on a case. Mind you, Vegas has some beautiful neighborhoods. This just wasn't one of them. Cops get called to some of the seediest parts of the city—actually, I think I've been to all of them. My specialty is the psychological profiling of deviant personalities. They call me a detective, but what I really do is provide detailed descriptions of creeps they haven't been able to catch, which can be plenty challenging. I love it. Anyway, I tracked some low-life child molester here. Hated him but loved his bar. I bonded with it; I don't know why. It wasn't at all a Cheers thing. Barely anyone there knew my name, and I liked it that way.

The décor was deadly. Tacky like the worst small-town plywood watering hole, except this was buried in Vegas's old downtown. Noise thundered relentlessly, assaulting your eardrums, not just music but an endless stream of chatter—sports, politics, and lame come-on lines. The place stank, maybe because drunks kept leaving the men's room door open, maybe because a wino on one of the bar stools kept vomiting on himself. Even the tables reeked, moldering wood soaked in way too much spilled hooch. There was a staleness to the air that made your head throb the second you stepped inside, that made cigarette smoke seem like a welcome alternative. And Gordy's teemed with men of the worst sort—not the bikers, pimps, prostitutes, mobsters, gamblers, and bookies that gave Vegas its colorful reputation, although they were there in force, but preppy types from UNLV in starched golf shirts who knew they could treat anything with breasts like dirt and still get laid because they were so damned hot and hunky.

Be it ever so humble.

I wasn't even thinking about work, so it came as a surprise when I saw Hikuru Mikimoto enter this two-bit saloon. He was a big-time drug dealer. And I hate drug dealers. I'd been consulting with some of the boys in Narc, trying to draft a profile that might help them find him. I really wanted to help, to prove that I could still do the job, but we'd been looking for more than three weeks without results. And then I just look up and there he is.

I wasn't entirely sure I was up to an arrest, but I couldn't let a godsend like this slip through my fingers. I pushed to my feet, bumping the table over, and fumbled for my badge.

"LVPD. Freeze, Mikimoto!"

He was a middle-aged Asian man, his paunch masked by a black T-shirt and what looked to be an Armani sport coat. As soon as I spoke, he took a decisive step backward. And two men behind him surged forward.

Personal goons. This was going to be more complicated than I had realized.

They came on strong and quick. My only chance was to take them out before they could gang up on me. I pulled my gun and fired, but the shot went wide. It hit the mirror behind the bar and shattered it. The lounge lizards sitting at the bar scrambled. A second later, one of the goons knocked the gun out of my hand. I did a quick spin behind the table and a swing kick with my left leg, catching him full in the face. He dropped like a sandbag and didn't get up. The other one lunged from behind and grabbed me around the throat. I bit down on his arm, and when he released his grip, I gave him an elbow to the solar plexus. He doubled over. I grabbed him by the ears and propelled him into the hardwood bar.

Stupid fool didn't know when to quit. He pulled himself together and came at me again. I whirled around at the last moment and used a move they'd taught me at the academy, a little Judo 101, to flip him over my shoulder. He flew forward and crashed into that splintered mirror. Big chunks of glass sprayed the room. All the patrons ducked for cover.

Mikimoto tried to run away. Not likely. I dove for him, brought him down hard. By this time, the rest of the customers were racing for the doors, desperately trying to get out of my way. None of them offered to help.

I straddled Mikimoto, pinning him facedown against the filthy glass-strewn floor. He was raging, babbling incoherently in some language I didn't understand.

"You're under arrest," I said, wishing to God I had a pair of cuffs. "You have the right to remain silent. If you choose to waive that right—"

Mikimoto swung around with a speed that caught me by surprise. He had a small switchblade in his hand.

Now that pissed me off.

I twisted his arm at the socket, breaking it. The knife clattered to the floor. I wrenched his hand back, pinching it in the soft fleshy part between the thumb and forefinger. He screamed. With his slickedback hair in my fist, I pounded his head against the floor.

"Goddamn drug dealer," I muttered. "Preying on kids. Pulling a knife on me." I shoved his face down again, hard, and then repeated it, again and again and again.

I felt someone pulling on my shoulders, trying to interfere. Another accomplice?

No. It was Harry, the old guy who worked behind the bar.

"Susan!" He'd been shouting, but for some reason it hadn't registered until now. "Stop it! Stop it!"

"Keep cool," I said as I let Mikimoto's limp head flop to the floor. "This creep's the worst scum in Vegas. Pushes hard drugs to schoolchildren."

"Who the hell are you trying to kid?"

I didn't understand him, didn't get it at all. But as I stared at Mikimoto's face, it seemed to, I don't know, sort of shimmer. Like a shapeshifter in a science fiction movie.

"This is police work, Harry," I growled, still staring at the face on the floor. "I'm doing my job."

"You're drunk off your ass is what you are. Did you bloody that kid up just 'cause he was trying to make time with you?"

I kept watching as the face changed, the whole body changed, and instead of a slick black T there was a pink Polo. How had the drug scum pulled this off? I wondered. Disguising himself as some preppy creep!

I pushed up to my feet. All at once, I realized how wobbly I was. The room began to spin, so I sat down again. The problem with that was, my eyes went back to the face, that kid's face, and I saw all the splattered blood and swollen flesh surrounding it. That finely chiseled face was like a pound of ground round.

Strong hands rummaged under my coat, taking my gun and my flask, and I didn't resist. "I told you to lay off the sauce an hour ago," Harry said. "Didn't know you had a private stash, damn you. How the hell am I going to explain this?"

The room was still spinning, even though I was sitting. I felt like I might rip my stomach out with a dull knife if I could. Then I noticed that I was bleeding, too, that I was sitting in a pool of glass, and that there was an especially large shard right in front of me, and I recall thinking someone should do something about that because it could hurt someone, and then I grabbed it and jabbed it into my left wrist. Blood spewed everywhere.

I fell over onto the floor, head first, and the rest of the world went away. After that, I don't remember anything. I assumed I was dead.

* * *

"Am I dead?" the young girl asked.

He stared down at her, stretched out on the table before him, a luminescent tableau so full of innocence and youthful curiosity. Her lengthy stay in the basement, so far from the bright lights of the city, had caused her skin to etiolate, but rather than detracting from her natural splendor, it seemed to enhance it. The primordial was strong with her, he sensed. He had chosen well.

"Of course you're not dead, my darling. You can see, can't you? Hear, smell, taste, and touch?"

"I can't move. Not at all. Nothing below my neck."

"I know."

"I think I've wet myself, but I'm not sure."

"You have."

"Even talking is hard."

He brushed a hand gently across her forehead, straightening her bangs. "I'm so sorry."

"And I'm scared. Really scared. You're not going to hurt me, are you, mister?"

He was short of stature, but he liked to think he had a certain presence just the same. Did his accent thicken as he spoke to the offering? He suspected that it did. The genteel Southern gentleman rose to the surface.

He turned and gazed out the window, just above ground level. The sky was clear as glass; the air was pungently sweet. And oh, the stars—! The stars seemed to go on forever, traveling from his private aerie all the way to Dream-Land. Heaven was real here, far removed from the decay of the city, the fiberglass façades and organic stench. He did not look down but across, outward, into the desert, the vast untouched expanse, the low-lying Spring Mountains, feeling the arid warmth as it bathed and reassured him.

"Mister?" Her voice was slow and stuporous.

"Yes?"

"Am I—am I—" Her hair was caught in her mouth. She tried to blow it away, but it was sticky and wet and wouldn't go and there was nothing she could do. She was like a rag doll, unable to help herself.

He reached down and brushed the hair out of her mouth. "Is that better, my dear?"

"Yes. Thank you."

"And your question?"

Her eyes were swollen and red from the anger phase. Screaming, shouting, threatening. Testing the waters, learning the abject futility of it all. Now she was more subdued, acquiescent. "Am I naked?"

"Yes, love. You're just as God made you."

"W-why?"

"Because I wanted to see you as you truly are."

"Did you . . . do anything to me? While I was out?"

He pressed a hand against his black cotton vest. "What manner of monster do you take me for, madam?"

"Well . . . I didn't know."

"There has been no physical impropriety, I can assure you of that."

"Well . . . that's . . . good, I guess. So . . . could I have my clothes back?"

"I'm afraid not." He reached down and brushed another strand of hair out of her mouth. He held it for a moment, staring at the root. " 'The life upon her yellow hair but not within her eyes . . .' " He looked at her with opprobrium. "You're not a natural blonde."

"No."

"But your—your—" His face flushed.

"Dyed that, too."

"Oh, my. Oh, my." He assumed a stern expression. "My dear girl, this will never do. I mean, it simply isn't done."

"All the girls at my high school were doing it."

"Then I shall see that you never return to that pubescent whore-house." He cleared his throat, fanning himself. "I couldn't help but notice when I undressed you. You were wearing"—he bore a pained expression, as if the very words hurt him—"thong underwear. Do your parents know about this?"

"No. A girlfriend bought them for me. Amber."

"I thought as much. Well, I destroyed the offending article."
He leaned in close and whispered, "There's only one kind of
girl who needs thong underwear, Helen. And you aren't that
kind."

She spoke hesitantly, her words still slurring occasionally.
"You can't know what kind of girl I am. You don't know me."

"You're wrong, my lovely. I've been watching you. When
you slipped out."

"What?"

"I've even been to your website. I know you've been unhappy. I know your mother doesn't understand you. I know
you were contemplating leaving home for good. You want
something better than what you have been given, something
richer. A Dream-Land."

The fear in her eyes was so intense he felt it in his heart as if
it were his own. He had always been like that, sensitive to a
fault, so in tune with the feelings of others that it sometimes
became unbearable. He wished there were some way to turn it
off, to flick the switch, to distance himself. But he had learned
long ago that distance was not an option for him. He was a
part of this world, and so he would remain. And if he could
not escape the world, then his only recourse was to make it a
better world.

Staring down into her fearful eyes, golden locks encircling
her face, it was impossible not to think of another girl, another innocent, from that lost time so long ago. Following him
through the forest, splashing him at the beach, she was the
best of him, too pure to be tainted and forever young.

"Mister? Do you think if maybe I promised not to wear that
underwear anymore, you could, um, let me go?"

"But my sweet, we have so much work yet to do." He returned to the basin and placed a washcloth in damp water.
With great vigor, he began scrubbing her face.

"Mister? You're . . . you're hurting me."

"It's got to come off. All of it. A good girl doesn't need paint
to make herself attractive."

"But—you're tearing—"

"A little elbow grease. That's what's wanted here." He

made a small gasping noise. "Are those eyelashes false? Pity."
He ripped them off.

"Oww! Mister, please—"

"And the same goes for these earrings, I'm afraid. Imagine piercing your flesh so you can adorn yourself with colored glass. They've got to go." He yanked them off through the lobe.

The girl shrieked. "Please! Oh, my God, stop, please!"

"Don't fret. I'll get something to stanch the bleeding."

The girl began to tremble helplessly.

"And that leaves us with the problem of the hair. What to do about the hair?"

"Maybe—I could just wear a wig?"

He considered. "I fear that would only intensify the artificiality. No, there's only one thing to be done." In the cabinet beneath the basin, he found a battery-operated electric shear.

"Please, don't. Please." She breathed heavily, twisting her head back and forth.

"I don't want to. But I have no choice." He switched the clippers on. "Please don't move."

He applied the shear to the crown of her head and moved over the crest in a long straight line, like a Marine barber buzz-cutting a new inductee. The girl let loose hopeless streams of tears that she couldn't wipe away.

In a matter of minutes, the cutting was done and the hair was gone. He took a brush and dustpan and cleaned up the girl and the table she rested upon. He retrieved his damp warm cloth from the basin and used it to gently, tenderly rinse her face and scalp.

He ran the palm of his hand across the top of her head. "Smooth as a baby's bottom. There now. That wasn't so bad, was it?"

"You—you cut off my hair," she said, her voice loose and broken.

"It was a necessary unpleasantness, but there's an end to it. Now we can relax and wait until the moment of—" He stopped short. His mouth twitched. "You've painted your fingernails."

Her eyes were wide, pleading. "Everyone does it!"

"No, not everyone."

"Please don't hurt me anymore. I'm begging you."

He smiled reassuringly. "Fear not. You'll barely feel it."

It was a simple procedure; they were artificial, press-on aug
mentations that left little dots of glue on the true nails after he
tore them off. Then he pulled a chair to her side and rested
This process was more difficult than he had anticipated. He
gazed out the window into the crepuscular sky, contemplating
the outlines of the pretend palaces of the Strip, the headlights
rushing from one nowhere to the next, hustling people about
like the miserable ants they were. He was so fortunate to be
here—sanctified, removed, anointed. So lucky.

His eyes turned upward, tracing the rectilinear line where
the horizon melted into the sky. This was his favorite kind of
dusk, with no moon and just enough light to turn the sky a
rich roseate blush. Gazing at this masterpiece painting, he
thought: Who could doubt that there was a plan for us?

"Look at the stars," he said after he wiped the tears and
blood from her. "You can see the heavens so clearly. There
must be a million of them. They're beckoning to us, leading us
to the truth, telling us how we can live among them. But so
few listen. So few can."

"Mister," she said. Her voice was dry and coarse, a staccato
grating. "Are you going to kill me?"

"Why would you ask that?"

"Because you took me and you brought me here and I can't
move and, and—" Her voice broke down. "And I think
maybe you're going to kill me."

"Well, I'm not. Not precisely."

"Then why? Why have you kept me here so long? What are
you going to do to me?"

He pressed his head close against hers, and his eyes shone
with reflected starlight. "Something wonderful."